MW01378251

About the Author

Through his journey of challenges and triumphs, Sam Passer has come to the realization that he is not the typical individual one would think. He is a person living on the spectrum. Autism has given him the gift of a video-graphic memory, which allows him to replay moving images in crystal clear picture and sound. This includes the "cinema" that takes place on a screen, in real life and in his imagination. His colleagues and collaborators have encouraged him to use this gift as his contribution to the fields of creativity, including literature.

Anthromalia (Book 1: Memories)

Sam Passer

Anthromalia (Book 1: Memories)

Olympia Publishers
London

www.olympiapublishers.com
OLYMPIA PAPERBACK EDITION

A CIP catalogue record for this title is
available from the British Library.

ISBN: 978-1-80439-141-9

This is a work of fiction.
Names, characters, places and incidents originate from the writer's imagination. Any resemblance to actual persons, living or dead, is purely coincidental.

First Published in 2023

Olympia Publishers
Tallis House
2 Tallis Street
London
EC4Y 0AB

Printed in Great Britain

Dedication

I dedicate this book to my family and everyone else who has supported me on my journey.

Note to the Reader

For those of you, wondering whether this tale reflects my personal views of the world, or whether I'm trying to persuade people through these pages, I would like to express the following: This is not my attempt to spread a deep message, my vision of an ideal society, or my hope for humankind. I just want to make a good story. I made it because I wanted to create and share a world and characters, as my thoughts traveled to places unknown, ideas not spoken, and longings for peace and freedom.
Hope you enjoy.

Characters

Alan Whitestone: Human; Son of Mageck/Sam and Christine/Emily; Present time narrator; Works at the Population Control Center (PCC); Frequently visits his father at nursing home.

Ara: Red Squirrel; Aides Episko in sheltering humans; Has a fascination with human culture and advocates for their future survival.

Christine/Emily: Human; Escaped from Ghetto along with others; Refuge in woods; Marries Mageck; Alan Whitestone's mother.

Demeter: Dog; Labrador; Only survivor of his human/non-human infantry; Best friend of Photios; Rescued from POW camp; A leader in the Final Battle of the Amazon.

Episko (Epi/Uncle Epi): Yellow Parrot/Macaw; Works to secretly shelter humans from AVIACHT's forces; Kana's love interest.

Gaochek (General Gaochek): Scarlet Macaw; Highest ranking AVIACHT general; Kana's father; Leads AVIACHT military against humans.

Kana: Scarlet Macaw; AVIACHT Lieutenant; Episko's love interest; General Gaochek's daughter.

King Helios: Blue/Spix Macaw; Leader of AVIACHT; Aims to exterminate humans and make parrots the dominant species.

Mageck/Sam: Human; Escaped with his sister, Izobel, from one of AVIACHT's concentration camps to find refuge in woods; Later marries Christine; Alan Whitestone's father.

Photios: Dog; German Shepherd/Braque Francais mix; Co-leader of human rescue infantry along with Spartak; Best friends with Demeter; A leader in the final Battle of the Amazon.

Spartak: Cat (Black and Dark Grey); Co-leader of human rescue infantry along with Photios.

Trisco: Orphaned Macaw chick; Member of AVIACHT military Youth; General Gaochek's 'adopted' son and apprentice.

Prologue

The following is taken from the archives of the Elder Dept. Written five years prior to the Second Great War.

ANTHROMALIA: A co-habitual society composed of a symbiotic relationship between Homo sapiens and animals.

On our earth, in our time, domination is a fragment of pure memory. That time has long passed. The age of man has ceased to be nothing more than a passing relic, for nearly half a millennium to be exact. No species has been over the other, none has proclaimed itself as the dominant species. Most have now strived to keep in balance with the web life. Though, as history can tell us, it wasn't always this way. Man once was the superior race.

I still remember the origins; I still remember when we animals were inferior; I still remember the clouded times when our kind was all but lost, as if it were yesterday. Though so many years have come and gone, and as an aged tortoise, the visions of the past and the visions of the industrial age seem to play crystal clear in my eyes, just as they did then.

In the beginning, as science tells us, man was a strange folk to the land. A figure thrown out of place in the vast landscape soon to be called earth. Primal instinct was of disregard to all the Homo sapiens beings. Rather, the cleverness built in their minds was their way of navigating the terrain.

Thus, their kind did spread, like a cloud blanketing the sky.

With their creativity and ingenuity, man covered our home with artificial creations: some for living, others for riding, and many more for benefiting their brethren. Eventually, man was no longer merely a figure within the landscape; it had become the shape of the landscape.

Yet, as man was unaware of the consequences of its machinery, the balance of nature was in jeopardy. Habitats and oceans shrank in capacity, air and food dwindled in abundance, and creatures great and small were pushed further into obscurity and unknown terrain, many never to be seen again.

However, neither did man know we were capable of knowledge. Since the first books and tablets came into fruition, we secretly taught ourselves to read, unnoticed from the eyes of the upright creatures. We had begun to learn, to write, to think, and even to speak. The gift of gab was gradually bestowed on us. At first, we uttered simple words – phrases that any simple-minded being could understand. But eventually, our sentencing and grammar became more complex, evolving, progressing, generation after generation. We expanded our knowledge to fields of Science, Math and even the Arts. After a time, we even created philosophies and ideologies entirely of our own, just like our Homo sapiens predecessor. But unlike us, man was also stubborn, arrogant, and altogether, invalid.

At first, they saw our newfound gift as a mere novelty, a trick of trade useful to the advantage of an overbearing master.

So, they put us to work. Our earliest servitude was upon stages and platforms. They presented us to eager crowds, as we performed our gifts for the simple satisfaction and amusement of an upright spectator. Though we at first strived to explain ourselves in an orderly fashion, this was heard as a simple grunt and bark. Scoffed at by our superiors, we retreated to a point of obscurity. In their eyes, we had once again fallen to an inferior position. It was then that we knew. Our new voice would need to be heard by any means necessary.

It began with an uprising of unforeseen proportions. Yet, as stated before, for as long as we had placed our feet on the ground, we strived to expose our intellect and potential. We hid in libraries, listened to scholars, taught ourselves to read, write and calculate. We even conceived philosophies of our very own. By the 1900s, at the peak of the clouded times, we had finally reached the intelligence of man. Elocution had been rightfully earned on all creatures, and we had officially blossomed with our knowledge. Now was the time to have our voices sing to the heavens.

On the other hand, this discovery was not taken lightly by our dominant counterpart. They backed us in a corner and discriminated against us in the workforce. Thus, a war ensued: beast against creature, government against clan, industry against nature.

For several years, the seemingly endless war dragged on. Towns burned to rubble. Forests reduced to wasteland. Lives were lost in the battlefield. These dark ages saw many vanish and wither away. Yet, like all wars, there was an end.

When all was said and done, a truce was made. Though the former dominant ones would progress and achieve, we would keep an eye on what would be conceived. Thus, the clouded times had come to an end. The natural world fused itself with cities, towns and villages. For the first time in the history of this planet, we could truly communicate with one another.

In addition, man's new desire to respect and protect the web of life had collectively altered the human's conscience. The slavery and imprisonment of all Homo sapiens was soon abolished, for they could no longer concentrate on that which produces negative energy. A greater and more productive challenge would await them – the challenge to please and become one with the sacred land.

So, it was and so it went, the tolerance of all races, of all genders, of all creed, became the mindset of our once brutal adversary. Yet, this brutality will find its way to linger among those who long for dominance. This longing has not always found itself in the heart of man, but also in those of the most unexpected of species, as was shown in the years that followed. For none can fully bury a dark desire to rule, but strongly keep it at bay. Such is the way in the web of life.

Chapter 1

Where do I start? I wake up from my bed and open the blinds to my room. The sun gleams its welcoming yellow glow as its rays trickle across the apartnest floor. My pigeon mailman stops by my branch, wishing me a good morning as he does all other residents. I take my daily cleansing underneath the tree's waterfall, changing the flow to vibrate with the tap of a built-in heater. This is followed by another bundle of coffee beans, squashed and grounded, that I've harvested from my personal outdoor garden. Why should I find mine so special? I thought. Everyone has them. After breakfast, a change of apparel and one last minute check, I hop aboard my solar-fueled auto pod and hover over to work.

It is another dawn over the prosperous Foressity of New York. The year is 2014C. The air is clean, the water is fresh, and the food is pesticide-free. My family and I moved here about five years ago after traveling under the patience and watchful guard of the Human Resources Committee (or HRC for short). Personally, I don't think that group could have picked a better place. Here, every tree and building rubs against the clouds, whilst every trunk hugs around the artificial exterior of man; its roots and inner pipelines firmly rooted in the soil. The forest floor is a place most people need not visit, except for the occasional nourishment of the fallen salt mounds. It's actually quite a nutrient for those with arthritis and low bone marrow.

Vine streets stretch from building to tree hybrid, each one

averaging twelve to eighteen feet thick, twenty-five to forty-five feet wide, and an incalculable amount of feet long. She human and animal citizens make their daily commute by foot or by bike, but never by vehicle. It would most definitely tear a hole in the natural structure. The auto and passenger pods hum to and from their destinations, as their physical structures bother not the aviary residents. Well almost not all of them. (Cue the sneer of a passing parrot).

Regardless of how compact our town is, there have never been any air quality concerns within the past two or three generations. After all, the distribution of fossil fuel, oil, gas, and any other chemical containing a trace of carbon monoxide is considered an act of terrorism. In addition, littering so much as a candy wrapper would put you at one-hundred to two-hundred hours of community service. Also, the consumption of any animate species has been regulated for the past two human centuries. Although we can eat all the fish we desire, beef and pork is out of the question, and poultry can only be consumed at certain quantities.

But I'm getting a little sidetracked. My name is Alan Mayer Whitestone. I am ninety years old (5'8", 165 lbs, father, husband, and record keeper at the local Population Control Center (PCC)). It is here we make sure the population of the human race is kept at a steady three and a half billion. Each PCC compound on the planet consists of data, statistics, records, satellites, family planning classes, birth control centers, abortion clinics, education textbooks and other subjects in relation to human growth and reduction. Our sector is in charge of the state of New York. In recent years, it has undergone the risk of exceeding its population limit, probably relating to the Board's negligence in watching over the public-school system.

As for my age, well, since the abolishment of fossil fuel, thus leading to cleaner air and suitable resources in the last century, as well as advances in medication and supplements, the human age expectancy has tripled. Though I'm technically a "senior citizen," I have the physicality and stamina of a thirty-year-old man from the early to mid-nineteenth century.

My workstation is an adequate space: about seven to eight dozen fifty-foot-high shelves (give or take) of our state's history, four-hundred to five-hundred ladders that scoot over from one manuscript to the next, and of course, twenty to thirty coworkers with whom I share my shift. Whenever a section of our foressity exceeds its population limit, a red light signals in our cubicle, and we are ordered to investigate the reason. This situation has happened far too many times for me to count. So many people have just jumped into being parents without even considering family planning, but I can't really blame them. Human tradition sometimes becomes instinctive once you take a moment to observe it.

Well, I'd better return to my cubicle: calls to make, new incoming manuscripts, same old, same old and....hold the phone! What's this? A note on my cubicle? The letter says "Urgent!"

Dear Mr. Alan Whitestone,

It has come to our attention that at exactly 12:15 P.M this morning, your father underwent another panic attack over at the mental health clinic. It was believed he saw a shadow that triggered somewhat of a memory relapse. Please report to his presence at your soonest convenience.

Hope you are in well health
Head doctor and fellow Feline,
Chronosis III M.D.

I crumble up the paper and throw it in the recycle compactor nearby. My father, smart yet troubled, is at it again. Well, better pack my things and come to his rescue once more.

I march up to the front desk. The receptionist, a Labrador, is answering a few calls as usual. I tap on the bell nearby and ask where Samuel Whitestone is. He points to his left and I rush over to the elevator. A Tabby cat nurse and her human intern are right next to me on the way up. He'll need all the help he can get with his new hectic schedule. I walk out of the elevator, through the corridor, across the hallway, and towards a small door that leads to my father's room. I knock. It opens. It's a Dalmatian staring up at me. She has delivered my father's medications.

I take a sigh of relief as I enter my father's living quarters. The patient's room is more like a hotel suite than it is an emergency center. Complete with a bedroom, bathroom, living room and even a kitchen, it's almost hard to believe the place is in a psychiatric ward.

There he is; sitting on the couch, folded hands, a blank face, staring out of the window once more. I notice a pair of bandages on his wrists. He tried to slit them again. On his right arm is a title that reads 'Logger' forcibly etched on by a pair of claws. The idea is always painful to think about. But I admire him as a part of my life. I just can't seem to let go of him. The fact that he was able to go through all that, makes him an inspiration for me.

"Hey, Dad," I say as I close the blinds to get his attention. "What seems to be the trouble today?" I take a seat, and he begins to speak.

The way he talks now isn't the way it used to be. I remember when he used to talk miles upon miles of sentences a minute. But recently, his battle with a few strokes have triggered memory flash backs, causing frequent PTSD moments every now and then. One day he can be happy and carefree, and then all sad and broken the next. Such is the same for our mother, whom he met in the midst of the Holocaust.

Ever since we were children, we had been witness to their post-traumatic episodes. There had even come a time where the past finally overwhelmed them, to which they collapsed under the weight of their despair.

I suppose the only upside was how fluid mother and father would tell the tales of their past, almost worthy of becoming a bestselling novel. Every week, if father had the energy, we and our neighborhood children would gather around his easy chair and listen to him as he reminisced about his heroic saga. But on this particular morning, he is not willing to have an audience. All he asks is for this cycle of memories to go away for good.

My father opens his mouth, and with trembling lips, begins his recurring story.

Chapter 2

Excerpt from documentary: "The Holocaust Remembered"

How can I not remember a day that changes everything? So much happens, so much evolves, so much is destroyed in an instant. I am still amazed there are those like me who live tell it.

My name is Samuel L. Whitestone. That was established after we were transferred to America. My original name was Mageck Kiewpenski, I was 12 3/4 years old, just a few months shy of what could've been my Bar Mitzvah. My hometown was within walking distance of Lodz, Poland. We were a small but proud Jewish community, with all the necessary comforts a human could ask for: a bakery, a pharmacy, a library, a toyshop, a synagogue, and of course a vast farm for all to plant their seeds. Our harvest was plentiful, our home was adequate, and our fellow villagers were as trustworthy as anyone could wish. My home in Poland was more than just a community. We were like a family. Every man helped the other in his hour of need, and every woman guided another through life's joyous rituals.

My parents were of no exception. Papa was an exceptionally skilled carpenter. Every day, except on Shabbos, he could be seen in the backyard, gathering and collecting whatever material the nearby woods had to offer, dragging them to his makeshift toolshed, and sculpting the finest and most intricate of household luxuries and appliances. Mama was a farmer and bookkeeper. She was always sturdy with her hands, sprinkling seeds in our backyard and the community garden, and memorizing all volumes in the public library. Not a single book or sapling was out of place under her care.

Yes, we were fine, modest examples of what our town stood for. Giving back for the sake of others and placing the value of our community over our own was like a mantra to us, a code of how one could live in harmonious synchronization with the land and its people. But on this particular day, everything we knew, everything we had, everything we held dear, would change.

It was mid-afternoon, the sky was shrouded by thick, menacing clouds, typical among this time of year. We saw a few birds lurking over us on a nearby tree. Though as unusual as it sounds, they seemed a little odd. They were not from these parts, more exotic, somewhere along the lines of the Amazon that we had read about. There were parrots, macaws, parakeets, etc. Each one had what looked like a cap on their heads, somewhat military like, with a teal and white emblem in the center. They weren't doing anything, so my sister and I ignored them and continued with childish games. Throughout the hours the flock grew bigger and bigger until the trees were full. They were just perched there with menacing looks on their faces, if ready to strike.

Then, as soon as we went back inside, without warning, they began to swarm, and all hell broke loose. They crashed through our windows, smashed our belongings, ripped our upholstery to shreds, and even pecked at our skulls as if to crack them open. They took every belonging we had, flew them outside and burned them with a match between their beaks.

Next came the wolves, who appeared out of the darkness of the nearby woods. Attacked with snarled teeth and finely-sharpened claws, the men were thrashed with wounds and gashes while the women and we children got lashed with scrapes and cuts. A few of the macaws joined in as well, and started screeching at us with their high-pitched voices. I can still feel the movement of the nails against my skin. They stormed into our butcher shop, bakeries, tailor shops, toy stores and even the local hospital, ransacking us of all we had.

Finally, the wild boars emerged. They had risen from the depths of the soil. They too ransacked our houses, knocking them to the ground. All of our dreams, ambitions, goals and wishes had turned into a pile of rubble before our eyes. I just couldn't understand why they would do such a thing. What did we do to deserve this? What is this a punishment for?

With their large claws and behemoth wings, they dragged us outside and forced us to our knees. They all shouted, "Single file, single file," threatening to beat us again if we didn't obey. I could see a few parrot scouts checking the entire town for anyone they missed. Meanwhile, the wild boars made sure we were perfectly aligned by bumping at our backs. Finally, one of the scouts swiftly landed on the hard-cold pavement. "The perimeter is clear commander," he said amongst the avian crowd. Then, from out of the flock, a blue macaw approached us humans. He had eyes that were red and sunken, as if he had seen every ounce of hell. A scar was carved across his left cheek and over his eyelid, and a few feathers were popping out of him as if he hadn't groomed himself in a while. But most of all, he had a large hat like that of a commanding officer, and what looked like a switch in his talons. After a few moments of silence, he spoke.

"Arrogance of the earth! Your reign of waste is officially over! You have debilitated this land with your damned village and your greedy ways for far too long. For this, you will pay for these crimes!"

"What crimes?" spoke one of the villagers.

It was then one of the parrot soldiers barged into the nearby butcher shop and instantly flew out with a stuffed turkey in its beak. He plopped the cooked meal on the cement to which the head parrot slammed the villager's face into the meat.

"THAT! THAT! THAT!" He shouted as he pierced his talons into the skull "Do you see it? Do you see it?"

"Yes," The villager sobbed as he curled into fetal position. "Yes, I see it."

"Guards!"

Front and center approached three husky looking macaws.

Fetch this pathetic soul our last catch.

One of the guards gave a whistle to the wolves, to which they stepped forward. In one of their mouths was a strange sack carrying an unknown specimen. They placed a plate in front of the villager's knees and slowly unwrapped the meal from its burlap bondage. It was the liver of a human.

"Take them to the camps! Perhaps spending a lifetime in a cell would do them good!"

Before I could wrap my mind around what was going on, my whole town found itself crammed into small cages perched high up inside a small train. It was dark, damp, and smelled of sweat. We had no idea where we were going or what they had planned for us. My younger sister asked as she started crying, "Daddy, why are the birds being mean to us?" My father responded with, "Honestly, I don't know." I hugged her in my arms and despite my equal fear, I let her lay on my lap, and she drifted off to sleep. I wondered what she was dreaming: whether flights of fancy, or descents of damnation. I couldn't bear to think which.

Hours later, we arrived at the farms. They were dark, foul and unwholesome in appearance. Surrounding them were barbed wire fences, all prickly and sharp. They unloaded us one by one and lined us up into three lines: men, women and children. Each line was organized according to the rank of how many animals we affected, from a skilled hunter and/or butcher to an innocent passerby who stepped on a twig. Then approaching from left and right were two large African elephants wearing army-like caps and holding large switches in their trunks. “Heads up, eyes front, not a muscle be moved,” they shouted, threatening to whip us if we didn’t comply.

In front of us approached the head of the camp. Her name was Kana. She was a green and yellow macaw, with the same stature and personality of her male counterpart. Like him, she wore a military cap and a whip in her talons. Surrounding her were what appeared to be her guards – two wild boars with tusks that were slender and sharp. With one mighty thrust, she cracked the whip onto the ground. The deafening sound echoed across the ground and vibrated into our ears. Some of us crouched to the ground in pain while others moaned to the piercing might of noise. “SILENCE!” she squawked. The whole place was now completely quiet. She walked towards us with battered eyes and a snarl in her beak. I could hear my heart thumping against my chest and my legs wobble against the unforgiving cold.

“You’re all probably wondering why you are here,” she said as she flew over to us. “It’s no wonder you’re all so stupid. You should all know why at this point. You are here to pay for your inconceivable crimes against the animal kingdom. Because of you, I lost everything. My home, my family, and my sense of pride. For this, you shall undergo an eternity of torture and punishment. Here, you shall spend the remainder of your days separated from the rest of the world with only the natural elements being your savior. You shall be stripped of your clothing, your dignity, and above all things, your sanity, and we shall continue this until your pain equals ours and you breathe your very last breath. May Mother Earth have mercy on your soul. GUARDS, TAKE THEM INSIDE!”

And with that command, a group of rabid wolves shoved us

into the farms like a pile of rocks.

We were each placed into the different barns which would become the sleeping quarters for me and many others for the next two years. The place smelled of a foul combination of fecal matter and mold. The walls were completely bare; there were no beds, or bathrooms, not even windows to keep the cold air out. "What do you want us to do?" shouted a woman from behind. A red parrot went up to her ear and said, "We want to hear you scream."

First, they told us to take off our clothes. So, we did. I remember seeing the elderly as they stripped themselves to the flesh. Much like Adam and Eve, they felt so ashamed to be exposed in the cold, misty air. After the last garment was removed, the parrots immediately threw them into a furnace nearby, with which we were not allowed to warm ourselves. A few clothes were laid out at the edge of the gate, as a reminder of our "sin." Worst of it was, they had no concern for our bare bodies. No clothes, no uniform, no cloth at all. We were all naked. We were all ashamed.

Next, one by one they shoved us outside, strapped us to metal chairs, and shaved off our hair, eyebrows included. I'll never forget the weeping of my mother next to me as she gaped at her face in the mirror. "Look at me," she cried. "I'm hideous." "Shut up you miserable human," said the bird barber as he firmly slapped her in the face with his talon. On the other side of me, I could see a little toddler trying to squirm out of the chair. A group of hogs were pinning his fragile body to the ground as they gleefully tore at his hair. His father tried to come to his rescue as he unshackled himself free of the chains. "Don't you dare lay a claw on my daughter," he shouted. But soon as he ran toward them, an elephant stabbed him straight through the chest with his tusk. He lightly shook off the lifeless body as it plopped to the ground. I remember the toddler screaming and crying," Why did you do that?" Why did you do that? As she ran towards her now dead father, hugging the corpse against her naked chest. "Silence you spoiled crybaby," yelled a parrot guard, and soon they preceded to continue shaving off her hair. The cruelest part was they didn't even bother to bury her father. The image of his lifeless body has stayed in my head all these years.

Finally, the wolves forcibly pulled us onto the ground and told us to hold out our right arms. Bit by bit, the parrot soldiers started to etch into our skin, the names given us that would permanently be shown. We squealed in pain as the wolves pinned us to the ground and watched as the birds carved permanent names on the flesh. Some names spelled: Logger, Killer, Owner, Hunter. Others read: Polluter, Waster, Eater, and Drinker.

The degrading names went on and on.

We were then pulled back up and placed into our barns. My body was already shivering and weakened from the bitter cold. I didn't know how long I would be able to stand up or even stay conscious. From out of the back door approached a gray parrot with what looked like medals and badges attached to his feathers. "ATTENTION!" he shouted. Everyone in the room turned around immediately. He whistled with his beak as two other parrots flew in carrying a large burlap sack. They shook at it until a large corpse of an old woman fell to the floor. They had killed our beloved town librarian. They had pecked, tortured, and whipped her to death.

"You see this?" said the gray parrot to weeping eyes and quivering lips. "Doesn't feel good, does it? DOES IT?" All of us shook our heads in fear. "This is what we went through every day. Because of your arrogance, and personal selfish wants, we watched our brethren die off one by one. And now, you shall do the same. It is in these walls you shall sleep, walk, DEFECATE, and if you're lucky enough, eat a few crumbs. You are to wake up at precisely five o'clock sharp tomorrow morning where you will undergo your first, and definitely not last, day of torture and punishment. The rest is up to us. Au revoir vermin!" And with the click of his heel, he and two other birds flew outside and slammed the door on us.

Since there were no sheets or blankets for us, we all huddled up into a human bed, sleeping on each other's bodies. In the days to come, I could hear many crying out in hunger and anguish. As I climbed over the heap we made, I could barely make out what turned out to be my little sister. I never realized how delicate her body was. This made it more so with the subtraction of her hair and clothing. She was whimpering in a fetal position, like a newborn fresh out a mother's womb. I tumbled down the human mountain, trying my best not to hurt anyone, and slid towards her.

"Look at me," she whimpered as she felt her clean-shaven head. "Why did they do this to me? I didn't hurt any animal. Why are they doing this to me?" Her eyes watered up with tears as she buried her face into my chest. In spite of my uncertainty, I wrapped her in my arms and gave her a big hug. I didn't know what to say to her as she cried herself to sleep, and neither did I know how to comfort her, or how to assure her that everything would be all right. I remember she always looked up to me when she was afraid, and I always had the answer to keep her spirits up. Yet now, for the first time, I didn't know the correct words to come out of my mouth. All I knew, as I laid my head back against the living, breathing pile, was that things were going to change.

Chapter 3

Excerpt from "Holocaust Remembered" recorded 1998C

My name is Selina R. Whitestone. That name was established after our transfer to America. My original was Christine-Jean Bordeaux, and I was twelve and a half years old when the uprising began.

My family and I lived in a rather adequate flat in the middle of the market district of Paris. My father worked as a jewelry maker, specializing in engraved images of days gone by. Every month he would present our family with a small pocket, full of diamond-encrusted emblems, one for each of us. Such was a tradition on special days.

Mother, for her occupation, was an exquisite baker (the only female head of her own restaurant). Her confections of pastry and sweets were well known among the town, and well recommended among finest experts of such culinary delight. I do remember there were times when she and her team of chefs were even appointed by the city council to conjure up a few creations for stately meetings of visiting dignitaries.

In our flat we had a kitchen, a den, a dining hall, and five separate bedrooms, one for mother, father, and three siblings, me included. I was their only daughter, but frankly, I didn't mind. By this time, my elder brother, Andrzej, was just preparing for graduation while my younger brother, Wadja, was readying himself for the first day of sophomore year. Both had become fascinated with the art of toy making – a rather rare hobby for children in those times. Most boys between the ages of sixteen to nineteen would've wanted to partake in adventuring, sports, or at the very least, a seat in the city council.

Anderzej and Wadja never really dreamed so high, though their imagination would be encompassed in these miniature contraptions they created. With the permission of our mother, they would occasionally display for sale their latest mechanics in front of the restaurant, hoping to catch the glimpse of a random curious passerby. It wasn't much of a living, but enjoyable all the same. Funny: it's only when all is taken away from you that one stops taking the simple things for granted.

It was towards the end of one seemingly uneventful day. We were returning from our daily routine of education and toil, time well spent and rest well deserved. Mother and Father were easing their backs from their occupation of sustenance and accessory and washing their hands of any residue in the sink. My siblings had worked tirelessly honing their craftsmanship. It was the seventh commission they completed this week. I, the youngest, stepped outside for the milkman to pick up his nightly due. That's when I turned around and saw the notice, the large sign on our doorpost. It was composed of a thick large papyrus texture, worn out in color, yet fit for royalty, as if it came from another land. The rough inscription read *CONDEMNED* in blood red. At the bottom was a small inscription of a strange insignia. It was a faded teal circle with an emblem in its center. It took on the form of what seemed like the feet of a predatory bird, with its sharp talons caving inward, as if clutching onto an invisible force.

Then I turned around to the empty streets. It was dead silence that evening, as if the whole city had been abandoned. But more noticeable were the doors. Every house and business had the same posting attached to their entrance. Then I remember seeing in the windows, a few neighbors scurrying to turn out the light and close the blinds. Something serious must've happened, but I didn't know what.

"Christine," my father said as he sprinted out of the cellar. "I need you to come downstairs now."

Being the obedient daughter, I did as he said, without question.

My whole family had gathered itself in the cellar, huddled in front of a small ham radio. What important news was being broadcast? What earth-shattering event had occurred? And if so, what part of it would affect us?

As my father turned the dial, I opened my mouth, as if about to ask him something, to which he replied with his finger to his lips.

"Attention all Homo sapiens!" said a voice from the radio. "This is a message from the AVIACHT forces! We are spreading this transmission to inform you of our impending ascension as the dominant species."

We all looked at each other in confusion and fear.

"For far too long, your kind has spoiled our precious land: Logging down our homes; stealing our daily sustenance and massacring countless numbers of our feathered brethren. So, by the declaration of our glorious leader King Helios, the following cities receiving this transmission are to be barred from the rest of the world. As we speak, a wall is now being built around the perimeters of the city limit. Any human with the desire to escape shall be hunted down and shot on location. Never again are we to be pestered by a disease such as yourself. Never again are we to live in fear of the footsteps of you flat faces, trudging the soil and littering the ground. A new dawn has risen on Mother Earth, a dawn of Sacred Skies, a dawn of the Macaw. Now, it is with most distinct honor to present to you our international anthem: The Anthem of AVIACHT. HAIL HELIOS."

For a moment, all was silent, then we started to hear random chirps and squawks. These were unfamiliar to our country, as if they came from an exotic part of the world. At first, it sounded chaotic and out of tune, but soon, it started to harmonize itself into a collection of song and chant. It was then we heard their militaristic war cry:

Oh, Helios Mighty Leader
Praise this our holy sky
Feathers and talons together
And on the swift wind we fly
All Avian creatures far and wide

Father turned it off before they could finish. He stood up with his face staring blankly at the side wall, arms folded and legs shaking. A dap of sweat fell down his forehead as he walked towards a stool chair and sat on it with a thud. After a moment of looking at the ground, he stared at us, as we eagerly waited a response.

"You know," he started, "I remember, as a young boy, my father would take me on hunting trips every other weekend. I always hated him for that. Killing off any woodland creature that stood in our path. I mean, what was it to us to shoot them? Sometimes I thought about jumping in and protecting one of them, in hopes that my father would attain a soft spot for animals through me, but I never did. I can't even remember the last time I pondered on that memory. I suppose it was too much hurt to even have that guilt creep back in my head. Now, after all this, I can most likely guess this is the past coming back to haunt me."

Then he stood up once more, brushed his jacket, and silently headed back upstairs, with us following soon after.

The next morning, as the voice on the radio predicted, a large stone wall had been built blocking the exit to our town. Up in the sky, and perched on the wall, we saw large Amazonian birds swooping and circling all around the city, staring down at us like vultures awaiting our imminent death. Each one wore military regalia, which included a hat, a rifle, a satchel, and a patch on their right wing. On it was their insignia: a blue circle with a picture of a gray talon with sharp, black claws. Our police force had been disbanded, replaced by a Macaw security force that watched our every move with large, menacing eyes. Sometimes, they would stop you midway in the street, checking your records for any past experience with the woodlands. Even so much as the snapping of a twig or the eating of an egg, would land you in a dark and unsanitary cell room for at least a week.

All of us were to report to the chief parrot's headquarters, where we were given a set of patches to be sewn on our clothing. They came in the shape of yellow male bathroom signs with a large "SAPE" engraved in the center. We were to wear it wherever we went, indicating to all our shameful contribution to the planet.

Our telephone wires were cut off and our mailing cards were terminated, shading us from any news from the outside world. Our town had officially and forcefully become a hermit village. We had become a town lost in time, unaware of any atrocities or disasters our tyrannical ruler could be plotting.

Chapter 4

Excerpt from AVIACHT rally, circa 1937C

On a day…

On a day of no importance, I awoke to a morning welcomed by the trees. My family, spreading its wings, leaping up to the sky, sweeping through the canopy, both sacred, strong, and my home… our home.

My mother, the queen of the jungle, a beautiful spirit blazing atop the canopies, singing her sweet song to all of our fine feathered clan. She had wiped away pests of our land, from despicable primates, to disgusting rodents. These creatures, whom she and all of us knew, were threats to the world below and above, both holy to our clan. It was she who had been the other half of my world. It was she who ruled.

Now imagine all the beauty, all the splendid beauty that is the jungle. My friends, my loved ones, gone in an instant. I had always thought the trees were plentiful, teeming with life, never to run out...but I never thought, how fragile were all my winged brethren. This morning, a morning like no other, would be one I would never forget, nor forgive.

They had come in numbers, like a swarm of pestilent parasites, eating away the good of the earth. They walked on the homes of the root, whipped at the sapling before it could climb, and gnawed at the bark of our land. Their faces, flat and emotionless, and their ways, just as meaningless. When they first stepped foot in the world we knew they'd be of nuisance and could not be trusted. We knew their actions would only lead to disease and corruption. How blind was I, how blind were we, to allow them to thrive.

The fire, of which they breathed from their "artificial monsters" took hold of our trees, the flames engulfed lungs, discolored feathers, and left the elderly and chicks, trapped for death. Then, the sound of a thousand wasps came ringing from the forest floor. An artificial machine brought forth from the darkest of minds, tearing, billowing, and grinding through our fragile home.

What was once a promised land had been burned to ashes. My brothers, and I, orphaned by the slimy claws of the Homo sapiens race. This was not an act that could be forgotten. Our elders had always told of knowledge and wisdom. But one thing they got wrong was that not all species have a purpose. It was then I knew humans were mistakes in the evolutionary chain, bloodthirsty parasites scourging through every jungle, turning what is beautiful into filth. I could no longer accept this behavior; I could no longer approve of their existence. As long as they had breathed our air, I would always reject them.

Thankfully, we are not of the flesh, but of the feather. It is us who must fight back to survive. For all those who forsake our brethren, I bring this message to them. We were here long before they left the trees, and they will be gone soon, so long as we make it so. We must eliminate this pestilence from the earth if freedom is to become a reality. What is peace, if there is no freedom? For as long as man thrives, there will be no freedom, unless we fight for it.

It is we birds, descendants of the mighty dinosaurs, who are the true dominant species. We shall rule the earth, as our primal, reptilian ancestors did before us. Our time has come, our time to relinquish all of what humankind has created. We shall build jungles over cities. We shall cleanse the land of all indifference. We shall eliminate all humans until their blood is spilled on their landscape. We shall conquer, prosper, and rule what is rightfully ours: The EARTH.

The age of the simple-minded sape is over. Tomorrow, AVIACHT rules! I look onto You, and I see a world without the inconvenience of man. You shall make it so. And I shall lead you to that promise, for I am your leader, I am your savior, I am KING HELIOS.

Birds of all feather, annihilate together!

Chapter 5

Excerpt from "Holocaust Remembered," 1935C

The next morning came upon us faster than ever, and the valve of hell was soon to be opened and released upon us. We woke up to the sound of a horn blasted at high volume on a megaphone. All of us were in a complete daze, still disoriented, still naked, and still scared. At that moment, we were once again shoved outside of our barns and marched up a large hill within the camp. For the first time I could see the entire scope of the compound.

Surrounding its barbed wire perimeter was a vast forest of trees, vines, rocks and plants. It was as if we had all been transported to one of those South American countries we read about in school. Though as innocent as it may sound, it all looked threatening, and even menacing, as if this lush habitat forbid us to explore its sights and sounds. As we looked further, over the trees, I could see what was obviously the city of Lodz, yet, from that vantage point, it looked as if the city had been colored an emerald green, surrounded with a piece of the Amazon. As we turned our heads back towards the jungle, we noticed something frighteningly unbelievable. The forest was surrounding what appeared to be an abandoned town. As we observed how the moss, vines, leaves and other exotic plants coiled around the man-made structures, we came to a horrible realization. We had not traveled a thousand miles to another country. We were still home, still in our land, only the climate had changed rapidly. The birds had invaded our country of Poland and bleached it with their own natural vegetation.

"Front and center, Maggots!" shouted a red crested parrot.

We all clumsily shuffled into two lines. The red parrot placed his claws into his mouth and gave out a whistle that could be heard miles away. At that moment, several large wolves with militant emblems approached and started to sniff around our bodies. Attached to their backs and hanging against their fangs were what looked like sharp measuring objects. With the click of the parrot's talons, the wolves took out the instruments and started to examine our fragile bodies with their beaks.

They measured the roundness of our craniums, the length of our limbs, the thickness of our stomachs, the width of our hand and feet etc., while at the same time, chuckling at our recent misfortune. We never felt more uncomfortable in our lives, than during that very moment. But it was really the way they measured us that seemed the most unorthodox. For instance, some would grab at our private areas of soft flesh and rub us deviously while calculating our amount of sweat. Others would place their paws to our necks just so they could get our exact height number. I'm not sure to this day if whether they were planning which parts of us will be eaten, or if they were just trying to make us uncomfortable. Regardless, the memory has not left me, especially with what came next.

After they finished examining us, the red parrot walked up front and center and gave us a cold stare. One by one, he started to assign each of us to what they called our "punishments." If he pointed his wing to the left, you would force into hard, unforgiving labor. If he pointed to the right, you would be tortured to death. The left was for people, who either ate an animal, walked onto a plant, dislodged something from the forest or even so much as peeled a piece of bark from a tree. The right was reserved for woodcutters, miners, hunters, fishermen, drivers, or even those who simply littered a piece of trash somewhere.

Obviously, my sister and I were pointed to the left. Not much of a surprise there, since we never harmed a single living thing. It was at that moment we asked ourselves: "Where's Mama and Papa." Then, we turned, and to my and my sister's horror, our mother and father were escorted to the right. We screamed and cried, begging the red parrot to reconsider. But he just shoved us aside as we were assigned our first task. I can still remember my father, as he dug his nails into the wet, damp earth, trying to escape the clutches of two macaws that had him by the legs. With his loose flesh and bones, he looked like a worm dangling on a fishing line. The monsters had turned what was once a strong willed, confident man into a relic of himself, now at the mercy of birds. I did not want to remember him this way. Not like this. So, I shoved myself through the naked crowd of flesh and fur, lunged forward and grabbed my Papa's arms. As I gazed one last time at him, he gave me a strong, yet uncertain look. I knew he didn't want me to remember him as a man of fear and remorse.

"Be brave, my son," he said as he let go of me. "Don't let them break you." Then, just as fast as he spoke, they dragged him away. It was the last time I ever saw him. My influence, my guiding light, my inspiration for all things I wanted to be, cut down and stripped of his dignity by a simple group of birds. I had never felt so scared in all my life. If a man of such stamina and charisma could have it all taken away from him by a species not of his own, I couldn't even imagine what they would do to his children.

My sister and I, along with other human children, were given the daunting task of digging for pure soil and constructing a wall out of it. There were no safety gloves, no shovels, no shoes, not even goggles to keep the dirt from our eyes. We were simply forced to stick our bare legs in the mud and grab whatever our hands could carry. Then we were to run back to the camp, put it in a pile, and go back to our 'work' stations. Our reward was a small, pathetic slice of dried bread, and a tiny glass of water, which could not even fill the smallest of stomachs. The worst part of it, there was no point to the task. The wall in progress was placed in an open field at the edge of the compound. Why this task? Why a pointless duty? Then I realized it was just so they could drive us mad, to see what it felt like to do pointless tasks without reward.

The days rolled on into weeks. We had forgotten the taste of real food, the sound of laughter, and even the feeling of hope. We had even forgotten what day it was. It seemed as though these jungle dwellers had truly broken us. I kept asking myself if it was something we did that made us deserve this kind of torture. Did we do something long ago that triggered their hatred for us?

I remember, one hot afternoon, a female human, unrecognizable from torture and malnourishment, had stumbled upon the mud and slime. She had grown too weak to carry her share of work. I could see the guards massaging their whips with their sharp claws, ready to flog her to death. Fearing our own fate, the rest of us simply focused on our meaningless work, grabbing handfuls of mud and stacking it on a wall that would never be finished.

The elephant guards kicked her almost lifeless body, as one of them whistled with her trunk, calling forth Kana, the supreme commanding macaw of the camp. All was silent. The guards fluttered on top of the gates as they greeted the commander, flying from the watchtower with an ever-gazing eye. By now, Kana had been labeled "Winged Death" among us prisoners. Some so erased of hope would even beg to have her kill them, freeing them from the pain of this reality.

"What is this?" she asked with a switch in her claw.

"We found this sape passed out loafing on the job." One of the guards replied.

She picked up the almost lifeless human by her head and examined her tortured face.

"No," she said sharply. "This sape is just lazy."

She threw her face down in the mud, watching her sulk in her own filth. Kana then made a small, shrill, squawk, calling forth two pig guards.

"Please, Winged Death." The woman pitifully begged, "I'm just so hungry."

"Oh, so you're hungry?" Kana replied solemnly. "Why didn't you say so?"

With the snap of her right claw, the pig guards tossed a large, bloody, burlap sack to the woman's knees. Whatever was wrapped inside, it felt soft and slimy to the touch. The woman wrapped her arms around Kana's torso, as if mercifully thanking her, to which she was pushed back by her wings.

"Now, I've heard you have a son serving in the army." Kana said as she brushed off her feathered chest.

"Shimon Levi," the tired woman replied. "Seventh Battalion of the Polish army."

"I heard he was such a nice fellow, courageous, strong-willed, never backed out of a fight. If I didn't know better, I'd say he would've made a fine addition to our army, if he were one of us of course. Such a pity to see him die on a beautiful day. Our troops almost hesitated to kill him."

The female human broke down in a fit as Kana nonchalantly looked on.

"Shimon," she wept. "My Shimon."

She pitifully lunged forward as if to attack Kana, to which the winged death pushed her back with her talon. Then, her instinct kicked back in as she unwrapped the parcel of sustenance given to her. The structure of it became more and more visible with each removal of the parchment. Soon, it became clear to us what it was, a freshly plucked human heart.

"You've always had the delight of eating our young, eggs and all," Kana snickered. "Let's see how you feel when you eat your own."

The human fell down in disbelief. Presented at her knees was the heart of her own son, while the parrot guards laughed and scoffed at her unfortunate predicament. Kana then grabbed her chin with her left talon and smothered her face into her son's organ.

"You wanted food you got food, now eat it," Kana demanded.

"My son," the motherless woman whimpered, "my only son. Why would you ask me of this?"

The menacing macaw leaned closer to her.

"I'm not asking you," she snarled. "Eat it!"

She stared down at what remained of her child as Kana pointed her pistol at her skull. We all stood in horror as she grabbed the heart with her pruned fingers and started to nibble at the slimy exterior. As her teeth dug deeper and deeper into her son's organ, her humanity slowly deteriorated, exposing her inner animal. No longer did she care about her well-being, nor dignity. All she cared about now, was her survival.

She ate that heart all the way down to its creviced arteries.

When she finished, she looked at her clenched fists covered in blood. The smell was nauseating, even to us spectators. Some were fainting, others were crying, but most just covered their mouths in horror. The woman clumsily stood up and looked at us with blood dripping down her chin. In a split second, she threw up her unconventional meal, much to our horror.

"I'm not cleaning that up you know," Kana taunted.

The woman wept as she kneeled back down and forcibly started to slurp up her vomit.

"All right you sapes," said a wolf guard. "Show's over. Get back to work."

We all trudged back into the field of mud, packing up clumps with our bare palms and constructing the wall that would never be completed. I took a moment to glance at the poor woman, as she gobbled the fragments of what remained of her son. All I could do was watch, as she hopelessly lost what remained of her reason for living. Fearing the same would happen to me, I focused back on my pointless task.

The next day, that same human, now a shell of who we once were, walked blindly towards the electric fence and electrocuted herself. The elephant guards then picked up her body and threw it onto a pile. All felt lost. Hope seemed like a foreign soul, barred forever from our grasp.

Yet, like all totalitarian dictatorships, there was a flaw. You see, since pure soil could only be found in the thickness of the jungle, we children were the only humans allowed outside the camp barrier and into their artificially modified habitat. Of course, we were constantly under the watchful eye of the guards, which consisted of gray parrots perched on either the tree branches, or on the backs of their wolf, elephant, and pig droves. But like all species, they too have a weakness. As all-knowing they seemed of each one of us, they couldn't watch us forever. This was how my sister and I planned our escape.

It was midday. The sun was scorching over the tropical landscape. Sounds of exotic origin could be heard everywhere. The guards were taking a break from their daily patrolling as they sat down to a nice bowl of berries and nuts. I could see children my age looking up in the canopies with watering mouths, wishing one of those edibles would just fall to the forest floor. On that particular day, my sister and I were hiding under the shade of a tree, cooling off from the burden of the rays. It was at that moment I realized how dense and thick the jungle was. If not careful, you could lose someone in a few seconds flat. As the old saying goes, "You can never be too careful." For once, that saying was an advantage for the two of us.

By about that time, the guards would survey the northern end of the camps edge. For a moment, they were away from their vantage point. We dropped our chunks of mud, dashed around the camp perimeter, found some leaves to protect our skin and escaped. There was a small opening within a knot of tree vines where we could sneak out inconspicuously. As wet and damp as the ground was and thick and humid the air, the two of us had to leave those small worries in the back of our minds. We needed to find higher ground. We needed to find sanctuary.

Every night, my little sibling would wail in pain, begging for sustenance. But every edible fruit was high above the canopy. I still remember the sounds of my little sister crying, sounds I've not shaken out of my head since. She cried for her mother, she cried for her father, and she cried for a bed.

"Mageck, Mageck!" she howled those seven nights. "I don't want to be here anymore! Please get me out of here!Please!"

"Izobel! Izobel!" I would scream at her as I covered her

mouth. "Calm down! Now look, I know how hard all this looks, but you need to trust me on this. We can relax later, but for now, you need to stick with our plan! Understand?"

Then she would nod with a solemn, "Yes," and we would continue on our destination-less journey.

Here I was, in the middle of a jungle which once was a town, and I needed to be the best role model my sister could ask for. But what was I to do? How could I still make her look up to me?

About a week after we began our journey, the sky poured heavy rainfall on our heads, as was typical in such tropical weather. We were hiding underneath the least damp and shadiest of trees we could find. I looked around as I cradled my sister in my arms. I could vaguely see amongst the thick roots what was once a small bakery, now intwined with jungle vines and forest moss. The smell of fresh pastries and clean-cut bread slices could still be harkened by our nostrils. This made my sister whine in agony. I didn't know what to do. Should I let her starve or risk my life? After all, hundreds of AVIACHT's forces were hovering above us, and every second was precious.

"Just stay here," I told Izzy.

And in a split second, I closed my eyes and ran blindly across the muddy path, pattered by drizzling rain. Those brief seconds of exposure to moisture felt so good on my aching skin, turning the dry, cracked texture back to its soft, smooth self. Though only for a moment, the ordeals we had endured made this blessing an eternity. I wanted so badly to press my face against the rain, but before I knew it, I reached the other side.

The store was deteriorating fast, almost impounded by the weight of the surrounding vine growth. I smashed open the window with a nearby rock and headed inside. Strangely, its interior remained untouched. From the decor furniture to the used utensils, everything remained in it's exact place, abandoned long before the uprising. Supposedly, these humans didn't have time to pack. They must've been snatched away before they could even think of their valuables.

I sniffed around for any sustenance, like a dog left abandoned. My animal instinct kicked in as survival became my highest priority. I smelled through the cupboards, crawled onto the counter, and looked on the tables, but not a crumb could be found.

It was then I heard flapping sounds from the roof. I crawled back into a bottom drawer just beneath me and tightly covered my mouth. My eyes directed at the ceiling, as I heard sharp talons patter on the moss-covered wood. Now my sister's and my imminent capture was only barricaded by a few inches of plank and shingles.

As the stomps from the outside grew more and more distant, I cautiously resumed my search for a decent meal. Where else could I search? I examined every crack and crevice in the condemned store, except…

The pantry was only a few feet away as I stared at the door leading towards it. I crept over and looked inside. It was there I saw the largest array of pastries. Sweet bread, cupcakes, danishes, strudel, brownies, marble cake, all neatly stacked and perfectly aligned on a countertop, untouched since abandoned. Even more strange, not a single hint of decay or mold could be found on them. The aroma was so strong, I could taste it in my mouth.

As I started to forward, the flapping sounds approached again. And as I predicted, the sound of sharp claws landed with a thud right outside. Sweat came down my shaved head, across my cheek and off my chin. Knowing a single sound would blow my cover, I grabbed the drop of sweat, seconds before it could reach the ground.

All was quiet now. I thought perhaps this time would be my best chance. I slowly slithered my way through the pantry. A burlap sack was sitting nearby, seemingly ready to stuff away the displayed food. This seemed easy, but too easy. How could food left there for so long stay so fresh? It must've been a trap, so I had to go fast. I snatched the sack and quickly gathered every confection I could grab, hoping not to get caught.

I sped back to the door, at the same time checking for any signs of traps or alarms. The coast seemed clear. I hurled the heavy sack of food over my back. Now my sister and I would finally have something decent in our stomachs. But when I touched the handle, it signaled a loud screeching siren. A red light, attached by moss and sap, starting blinking on and off as a piercing sound echoed across the store. I had nowhere to run. The bird soldiers would find us for sure. Yet miraculously, they didn't.

As I sprinted out of the pantry, through the store and out the front door, I saw the birds had long flown away. There was an alarm on the outside wall. So, I grabbed a nearby stone and smashed it against the red lightbulb, thus silencing the ear-splitting noise.

I checked if all was accounted for. The sack hadn't broken open and my limbs were all intact. I took a sigh of relief as I trudged across the muddy path and into the hollow tree.

"MAGECK!" she cried as she wrapped her skinny arms around my now bony waist.

Her mouth watered for food as she dug into my sack. I told her to be patient as I reached in for any random piece of sustenance I could grab. We snarfed that treasure of edibles all night long. We didn't care if we resembled a sty of pigs. Our hunger was all we could think about at that moment. We couldn't remember the last time we tasted something so good.

That night, we slept better than we had in days. Our stomachs were full and our minds were momentarily still. My sister laid her bare skull on my bony lap as I pressed my back against the trunk. Though we did not know where the winding path would lead us, we felt more sure that our future would be much brighter over the horizon. If we could outsmart even the most cunning of creatures, maybe we could survive this atrocity. Maybe we could survive this holocaust.

I stared up at the stars, all gleaming in their galactic wonder, as they had for the last few billion years. My father and mother always told me if ever one got lost and was low on resources, the stars would always serve as a map to lead to where you were before. As doubtful as it sounded, I couldn't help but feel that maybe, just maybe, we could use the stars to guide us home, if it still existed. And even if it was flattened to a rubble by now, replaced by thick trees and tangled vines, I only wanted to hope that some of it would remain intact. My town was always strong, an example of pride, determination and teamwork. Perhaps not only me and my sister, but our whole community could prevail over this despairing nightmare.

And even if not, I felt if the two of us could journey just a little further, we would find a few more of our people, huddled somewhere in a crumbling structure, with the same mindset as we had at that moment. Thus, with that thought, I finally drifted into slumber, my head atop my sister's.

Chapter 6

Excerpt from "Holocaust Remembered," cont.

It had been six months since we were barred from the rest of the world. The prison we once called home seemed to be closing in on us. We were trapped like hamsters in a locked cage.

Our parents did the best they could to make ends meet and keep the sanity of our family intact. Father tried, in vain, to keep his business afloat, scraping up whatever metals or debris he could get a hold of. Somehow it seemed to pay off, as his craftsmanship combined with the little resources he had, ended up producing obscure yet beautiful creations of jewelry and accessories. Unfortunately, his ownership of the store was confiscated, and he was reduced to that of a peddler, walking door to door to friends' houses, just to put a little light in their lives and a few francs in his pocket.

Mother, on the other hand, struggled even more as wheat and flour was beginning to be rationed in our closed community. So, she grabbed whatever items were available (flowers, grass, oil bottles, wild berries, even a few scraps of dead fish dropped by the macaw guards). Sometimes, when lucky, she'd find a bag of unopened sugar, or barrel of untouched sweets left unchecked by the security checkpoint. With a careful eye, she'd sneak them behind the alleyway and store them in the cellar, looking towards the sky for anyone watching.

My brothers and I did our best to ease their burden. Andrzej would find any scrap of un-confiscated metal lying in the deserted yards, whittle them together and see what contraption would materialize. He would sell them at the corner of a deserted department store, hoping to bring a smile to a pessimistic passerby with one of his novelty items.

Meanwhile, Wadja and I would look for any jobs we could find. If we were lucky, our employment would be two weeks at the most. The majority of jobs ranged from window washing, to garbage handling, to pickpocketing if times were desperate. The one upside was we couldn't get caught for stealing, as the AVIACHT regime believed it was part of our decimation to extinction.

About once or twice a week, our neighbors would throw a little get-together for the townsfolk. So as not to cause the attention of any macaw guards, the little party would take place in a soundproof bunker just below a storage area. We would sing, play songs, compete in games and talk about days before the invasion, when we didn't need to live in fear, and freedom and peace was part of the human existence. Yet, as reality set back in and we returned to our houses, the hopes of our seemingly impossible dreams would begin to dwindle into obscurity.

As the weeks became months, the walls surrounding the city-turned-ghetto seemed to cave in deeper and deeper upon us. The barbed fences turned grimier with each passing day. It became a claustrophobic nightmare with only the unreachable clouds as a window to the outside world, and even that was guarded by the SS 'Sacred Skies' patrol, watching, waiting for the next human to lose his or her sanity. It was clear these walls and fences the birds built were a test to our resolve and faith in ourselves. I remember several instances where humans would just blindly run towards the barbed wire in the hopes they would catch the attention of the guards who would kill them. Even my father, who had lost almost all his personal processions, came to contemplate ending it all.

Soon after, the ideology of the AVIACHT regime painted itself across our walls and doors. First, any books and papers pertaining to the optimism or progression of the human race were confiscated and burned. I still remember the makeshift bonfire, set up in the middle of the town square. Libraries, schools, bookshops were completely ransacked of the rich literature we had known and loved. Shakespeare, Dickens, Bronte, Austen... all works to be forgotten in obscurity and burned away like leaves scattered on a tattered field.

The empty shelves were replaced by required readings given to us by the AVIACHT elite; works by Swift, Huxley, Lord Byron, Schopenhauer – all authors who had, in one way or another, a distaste for humanity. Words and sonnets to remind us how despicable of a species we were, how much of a mistake we were to god's eyes, all intended to lower our spirits and make us wish we had never evolved.

But the most required reading among our overlords was that of the autobiography of their leader, King Helios. We were each given a copy, all printed on sacred parchment made of the finest South American bark. To compliment it was a large poster with a portrait of the grand, self-supreme monarch. I can still remember his features to this day, as a portrait of him was laid on our walls. The avian ruler had a lean, sleek body, complimented by richly-cleansed blue feathers. Tied to the back was a robe made of flowers and vines, which covered one of his legs and half of his left wing. His face was a stern yet proud one, gazing into the viewer with valor, though to us, it always seemed threatening. Adorning his scalp was a flat crown of elongated feathers that stretched across his skull and hung over his forehead, dangling over his left eye. But one feature that stood out was the black burn on the tip of his beak, almost as if someone pasted on it a narrow strip of mustache. Under his eyes were deep, blue circles, as if he had gone through a lifetime of turmoil and grief.

According to his autobiography, his back story was heartbreaking indeed. These would be our words from now on, all we could ever read and pass on to our children. This literature wasn't meant to make us better ourselves; it was only meant to make us fall into despair, from the weight of our depression. These stories were told to make us feel deeply ashamed of our species. Not willing to change, but rather die out and wither away from memory.

Nine months had now gone by. Still no sign of any softening from our new dominant species flying above us, looking down in content. They watched as my father lost his business, and my mother lost her profession. They watched as my siblings were forbidden to showcase their craft. And they watched as they saw me, a small girl with the world changing before her, uncertain what would happen next in her now isolated life. It was a challenge at first to keep in contact with nearby friends, as they focused less on any remaining leisure and play, and more on how to survive and possibly escape this living nightmare.

It was not long before they created a secret resistance, a spy force of allies and countrymen ready to take back what was once theirs However, there were times, of course, when I'd be invited to these meetings. It was a place to reminisce about the good bygone days. To avoid the Macaw cadets from random suspicion, every meeting was held in a different cellar chosen locations around the ghetto. Though the macaws were keen of sight, they didn't have the best of luck guessing where we might meet next.

One night, I was told to put on a coat and boots brought out from under the stairs. As I dressed and looked in the mirror of my bedroom, I saw a frailer, gawky version of myself. My ribcage was clearly visible, and my face had the boniest of cheeks. "Had I really eaten so little during this ordeal?" I asked myself.

As I walked out the door and down the street (keeping my head to the sky for Red Crested patrols), I examined the coat I was wearing. This was only used for travel purposes, and my shoes were of the hiking sort. "Could tonight be the night?" I asked myself. "Could we really have our chance to escape? Could this be the day we rebel against AVIACHT's tyrannical rule?"

I approached that night's meeting place. It was in the basement of my friend Maya's florist shop, just a few blocks from the patrol border center. My father, Phillippe, was the first to answer as I tapped on the boarded door. He quickly shoved me into the space and covered my mouth as he escorted me down the stairs.

Everyone else but me had already settled in, as they took their seats and stared at what would become the speaker's platform. My mother was leaning against the wall, ear pressed against its texture, listening for the sound of any flapping wings or clicking talons. Wadja had binoculars tied to his head as he stared out the window for the occasional Wolfblitz guards, while my other brother Anderzej blocked the entrance. A man lit several candles and after a few minutes of murmuring and chattering, all was quiet. Andrzej approached the platform and cleared his throat.

"Fellow comrades of the liberation," he started. "We have with us tonight a special guest. He is a soldier of the one hundred and thirty-eighth American battalion."

We had heard of them before. They were a co-species

division that gained much attention and notoriety from word-of-mouth.

"He was able to sneak through the barbed vines and sneak past the guard last night, and he brought with us a plan to possibly escape the ghetto."

Everyone gasped and murmured.

"So, without further ado, let us all bring a warm welcome to Sgt. Demeter."

From out of the curtain behind him emerged a well-built black Labrador. I and the others glanced at him from head to paw and knew he was perfect for combat. His eyes were sharp, but sunken in from years of experience on the field. The tips of his ears and snout were slightly tattered in dried blood, probably from sneaking through the ghetto's barbed vines. Attached to his torso was a well-tightened vest, containing military medical supplies, so we knew he could treat himself when necessary.

Demeter quietly sat down on the wooden platform. He took a moment to look at all of us leeringly and cleared his throat.

"Thank you Andrzej," he started. "I am sure you are all anxious as to what I have to say. But be warned, the plan I embark upon is not easy, nor does it guarantee everyone's safety. As you can see from my face, it was already trouble enough for me to come here. I have been separated from my regiment to scout out Paris for the time being.

"Safety for you is enough for me to worry about. I cannot risk the lives of fellow human and canine brethren, which is why I need the best teamwork and cooperation if you intend to increase your chance of escape."

Demeter grabbed from his vest a small tube, containing what appeared to look like an old parchment. I stood on the tips of my feet for better inspection as everyone crowded in on him. With his paw, he rolled out the map, revealing an entire detailed diagram of the ghetto.

"I was able to draw this on my way to this location." Demeter explained. "The path from the gates to here gave an opportunity to adequately understand their security system. I have been scoping out your community for some time. The time when AVIACHT's forces are at their most vulnerable is every Wednesday. That's when the troops focus their attention on distributing supplies to and from their posts. It is then I have decided to plot your escape." With those words, Demeter took out a blue crayon with his snout and started to draw on the diagram.

"You will all meet here at the south side of the abandoned furniture store. It will be the least guarded area, so it will give you a better chance. From there you will split into three teams: Team A will travel via wagon cart, while Team B will escort itself using the abandoned tram car situated just off the dilapidated tracks. I found several usable tires in the garbage, so you'll be able to move more easily. Once both teams travel to their respected NE and SE ends, we'll give the 'all clear.'"

"Team C: As you situate yourselves in the store's cellar, you will wait for me to give out the signal, which you'll be able to see through the gap in the foundation. Once I give the 'all clear,' you will open the cellar's floorboard. There you will find the tunnel which I took the liberty of digging. One by one, you will trudge through the passageway, leading you all to the East end of the gates. This is where security is least aware of the resident's actions on Wednesdays."

"Now upon closer examination, I've come to realize the soil on the East side is of Amazonian descent. The terrain will be easy for you all to dig."

"Dig?" I asked.

"Yes." Demeter replied. "Once Team C reaches its location, they will give the rest of you the "all clear" via flashlight signals.

It is then that Team A and B will equip themselves with the cellar's shovels, digging until all three teams meet the wall.

"Finally, I will sneak behind the guards and meet you all at the concrete wall, onto which I will tap the ground to make sure you are all together. I will dig a supplementary hole which will escort you towards the other side of the wall and thus, to your freedom. It's risky and life-threatening, but it's the best chance we've got to escape."

We all looked at this plan in silent fascination. It was the quietest the room had been all night. For once, we had a plan. A true plan to escape, and what's more, with a chance of success. With all of us nodding in agreement, we quickly blew out the lights and headed back to our sleeping quarters. As my brothers and I settled into our beds, I could hear my mother in the kitchen. She had just been informed of the plan, and she started praying a hymn of gratitude and thanks. It was the first time in months she felt optimistic in her battered heart. I could hardly sleep that night, biting my sheet and tugging at the pillow. For once in a long time, something might work out.

Before we knew it, Wednesday had come. My siblings and I woke up at 4:00 AM, followed by my parents, and several other humans from whose houses they had been evicted. We had our meager bread, washed our faces, said a prayer and headed out the door. Since more people had been staying with us, we had selected ourselves in "Team B," thus giving us space in the tram to fit.

Just as any other Wednesday, and just as Demeter predicted, the streets were quieter and less guarded. With the exception of a carefree Scarlet Parakeet passing above our heads, the AVIACHT forces were nowhere to be seen. We could hear the thumping sounds of cargo being imported and exported, for whatever reason we may never know. The enemy had been distracted; it was time to make our move.

We approached the tram and hid underneath the discarded blankets on the seats. It took about three hours for us to realign the axles, which looked usable enough to make a smooth drive. Now all we needed were the tires. Surely, they were located in the next-door warehouse. But as Anderzej approached the door, he saw two half-awake Scarlet macaws, occupying the approach.

They were drunk off a fine bottle of blueberry nutmeg, hardly aware my brother was watching. With a laugh and a squawk, they flew over to the other side of the building. As he slowly opened the door, trying his best not to make a sound, my brother quickly got his hands on several tires, tucked them under his arms and scurried back, away from the visible perimeter of the guards. Andrzej took a moment to press his hand to his heart, then proceeded to assist Wadja in attaching the tires to the tram. He could have sworn his heart was going to lurch out of his chest.

As they finished their work, Team A appeared from behind the warehouse. As ordered, they pushed a large wagon, wide and long enough to fit thirty to forty people. Some of my closest friends were on this Team, some of whom I may never see again. They had all huddled around the center of the wooden post. Now all that was needed was something to pull the weight of the wagon. Certainly not people and the horses had long been freed into the wild, or at least we hoped. It was then we remembered how cables could pull immensely heavy objects with the right system, thickness and volume. My friends Michelle and Francois had given me the cable they had been saving for safekeeping, in case our telephone poles would ever reconnect with the outside world.

I rushed down the street, across the alleys and over the murky bridge as fast as I could until I reached our home. But just as I was about to touch the front door handle, there was a strange noise coming from a few blocks down. It was the combination of squawks and howls. As I dashed over and crouched against the wall. I tilted my head towards the alley, and saw Demeter being repeatedly kicked against the wall by AVIACHT guards.

Demeter had been caught. They had tortured him until he squealed. Our worst fear had come true. The plan had been foiled.

"I will tell you nothing," he sputtered. "You can all gnaw on my ass if you want me talk."

"Such a pity," a guard said. "You dogs still don't realize how brainwashed you are from those 'flat faces'. What proud species you once were, hunting for your own sake, now wasting yourselves for the petty affection of your owners."

Demeter spit onto the Parrot's beak, after which he was violently pinned down by four talons. Before I could bear what they would do next, I ran back to the direction of my Team. What was I to tell them? How would we escape now? I could hear from behind me the murmurs of "take him away," and "lock him up," echoing against the empty street.

Tears fell down as I turned around and looked at my house again. We had come so far with the plan. We were so close. I couldn't let it all end now. With shortness of breath, I crawled among the trash on the ground, doing my best not to make any noise. Within moments, I was lurking against the house's side window, still open, and still intact. As I climbed into the opening, I took a moment to gaze at our now-scattered abode. I never realized how dank and small it was. With all our items packed and stored in suitcases and waiting at our destination, the whole infrastructure seemed to lack any soul or purpose, as if the life we gave it had been drained out.

I settled my feet on the wooden floor, crouched on my hands and knees, headed for the stairs and entered the room where my friends and I had been staying. There, in the open closet facing the window, was a neatly stacked set of steeled wire, strong enough to pull both a wagon, and a tram. Without any time to think, I grabbed all the wires, slung them over my back, and jumped out of the window, gently onto a shrub. Before I knew it, I was back facing my designated Team.

"Christine? What happened?" my father asked, "Where were you?"

"No time to explain," I replied. "Demeter has been caught."

As expected, everyone looked at me in shock and dismay. I knew it did not, however, have to be the end of our escape plan.

"Well? What are you waiting for?" I responded. "Let's attach this cable."

Without questioning, my Team and Team B carefully tightened the end of each wire with the wagon and the tram. The tram was placed in the front and the wagon in the back. Team C was waiting for the signal, which we gave in Demeter's place. After a slight moment of confusion, they all nodded from their position and proceeded with their task. With one fell swoop, we got our makeshift contraption started. I never realized how easy it was to glide a hollowed bus and wagon with twelve people on each side. Now we were ready to proceed, Demeter or no Demeter.

Teams A and B met Team C at the East gate, who had signaled their presence with their flashlights. As we hoped, there were no guards. All was quiet. As Team C came out one by one, we touched the ground and felt the soft dirt against the wall. It was indeed easy to dig into, just like Demeter had predicted. Once every member of Team C had emerged, they handed out the shovels. With the greatest of ease, we dug at the walls edge, until we could see the bottom of the concrete structure. By now, it was so soft and so brittle, shovels were no longer needed. We all rolled up our sleeves, clawing our nails against the tunnels end, making it longer and longer until its length caused all to be pitch black.

For a few moments, we couldn't see a thing. Then, a sudden light burst in front of us. With the thrust of our bodies, we all climbed onto the other side. We had made it. We were free. Or at least we thought we were. A cluster of leaves started to fall sporadically on the jungle floor, as if something above us was shaking them off. We turned our heads up and saw a swarm of guards ready to pounce!

"Run," my father said quietly, to which we did.

As my feet sprinted across the rainforest terrain, I could hear the sounds of screams and squawks from behind me. But all I could see was the thick jungle in front of me, with no end in sight. My mind drifted to an end to this nightmare, a pause to this turmoil, a moment of rest to this fear.

We had reached the edge of the trek and hid behind a large, gnarled root. Some of our group was missing. Two, to be exact: My parents. I can still remember the last time I heard my mother's voice. I can't get it out of my head no matter how hard I try.

"Help me love! Help me!" she shouted to my father.

"Silence Flatface!" screeched a guard.

"Please! Please! Don't hurt her!" Father begged.

"Oh, don't worry," another guard scoffed. "She won't feel a thing."

My brothers turned my head away as I burst into tears. Then, I heard what sounded like the crunching of bones. My own mother had succumbed to the AVIACHT forces. Now, Papa would be next. But we had no time to wait. As painful as it was, we deserted him and ventured into the unknown that was once the European wilderness. "This biped will do nicely in our camp." was the last I heard from those guards, as they presumably carried Papa away to his fate. But we could not see what was going on. We couldn't. No time to see, no time to think, and no time to help.

We caught our breath beside the stony exteriors of what was once a neighborhood in Paris. My tears could not be held back as

I slunk in a heap of depression and exhaustion. All that I knew and grew up with (except my two brothers), was gone. Hope seemed lost at that moment, as well as our future. While scavenging for any sustenance in the abandoned structures, we came across a parchment nailed to a door. We could tell it was Demeter's handwriting. It read as follows:

Dear humans,

If you are reading this, it means you have all successfully escaped the Ghetto (or at the very least most of you). I'm sorry but I am not able join you on your quest to freedom. But it is a sacrifice for the many, as is the duty of all soldiers. Do not think my absence is the end of your journey

On the days preceding your escape, I was able to send a message to an enigmatic receiver. He's known by our allies as a formidable source for protecting humans in the war. I cannot tell you his name nor species out of fear of exposing us to the enemy. However, I can tell you his coordinates, located on the back of this parchment.

Darwin willing you make it alive.

Sgt. Demeter

We looked at each other and agreed to no questions, as my brothers led the way to our direction on the map.

Chapter 7

My name is Photios Metro II. I am a crossbreed between a German Shepherd and a Labrador. My occupation is a senior employee at the New York Sector of the Human Resources Committee (HRC). The workforce is made up mostly of dogs, cats, rodents and the occasional ape. Our mission is simple. Any human family who has been found with a history of hunting, clubbing, butchering, lumber cutting, oil drilling or any other occupation involving the interference of natural resources is put in our witness protection program, relocated to a safer location, given a recommended job, food benefits, a home, as well as any answers to legal issues that may turn up in their lives.

My father was a former first Lieutenant of the third infantry division of the Human Rescue Squad (HRS) during World War II. They were fighting against a group of four strong and dangerous axis powers: Tusken Reichstag, Hoggendragg, Wolfblitz, and their leading tyrannical empire, AVIACHT. Now AVIACHT, which was comprised mostly of macaws and parrots, was what you might call a bird supremacy group, whose one driving goal was to exterminate the human race and make birds the dominant species. That was where my father came in. He was an elite member of the human rescue squad.

Given the fact that us dogs, cats and rodents have lived alongside humans since the dawn of civilization, our canine and feline brethren found it appropriate to form a strong alliance with them in the battle against Homo sapiens extinction. The apes also joined in, although they were hesitant at first and didn't wish to take part in any war related activity. But that changed when AVIACHT started attacking their habitat.

I still have trouble recalling how many times my father told his stories to me. Every night, when my sisters and I were just pups, we would curl up on the rug floor and listen to dad's many heroic adventures. Though as fantastical as they sounded, they were all real to us. I suppose this was what made him the role model I know of today.

His infantry's assignment was a risky one, yet one where he felt the most pride. He and his troops were to scourge the war-torn areas for any human survivors, defend them against incoming attacks from the axis and escort them back into neutral society with an immigration passport. I remember him telling me as a pup all the proud memories of him saving a life and infiltrating a camp, and everything in between. But one that seemed to stick in his head the most is Duchau circa October 13, 1944B.

He and his canine/feline/rodent brethren were stationed at about sixty-three degrees longitude from a Wolfblitz headquarter station. As always, they were celebrating the recent rescue of human survivors that had escaped a Wolfblitz lab.

At that moment, one of their squirrel scouts received two incoming stress calls from an unknown source. Given our sense of keen smell, they were easily able to track down and pinpoint the stress signal. The life forms were approaching from about one-half of a kilometer north, and they appeared bruised and covered in rags. As they got closer, we saw what appeared to be two human girls, shaven to the flesh and covered with bruises and scars. From their appearance, they were cold, hungry and above all, shell-shocked. Being the loyal species we were, each one of us immediately escorted them to the safe tent, supplying all the basic needs and comforts a human could possibly need, including our trust. After a few hours in the emergency tent, they were able to gain enough strength to tell us from where they were escaping. They began with a heart-wrenching story of how their village was destroyed by AVIACHT as well as being forced to watch their parents mutilated to death via scalpel. The explanation of their miraculous escape to freedom was a tunnel they were secretly digging in their compound which led straight to the outside of the camp barrier.

My father gave them his deepest sympathies, assured them they will not be bothered by the axis powers again and printed them passports to neutral territory where they would be selected to a suitable family.

At that moment, one of the first-class privates, a hound dog, informed my father his troops had received word as to the direction of the death camp. Rather than expose the two girls to more crushed memories, he ordered the second in command to escort them away from the premises and onto higher ground. They traced the scent to the Dachau death camp, now abandoned and empty of any perpetrators. AVIACHT would later insist to the Human Resources Committee it was simply an innocently experimental facility for human specimens. But we knew better. As we searched for survivors around the deserted camp, we came across a whole mountain of dead bodies, cargos of human organs, brain dead prisoners and countless other unspeakable sights.

Just when they thought it was too late, they heard wailing human sounds within the confines of the structure. It was 2nd. Lt. Anakhaos Chronos, a female tabby cat with a special skill of opening locks with her claw. One by one, ten to twelve dozen skinny, malnourished humans spilled out onto the ground, gasping for air and screaming in pain. Their heads had been shaved bald and their body weight reduced to the bone, so thin they were too weak to stand up. As they laid on the soft, dry soil, they covered their eyes squinting from daylight, like bats when they first see day. Approaching with the greatest of care, they took portable fire hoses and cleansed the survivors of dirt and human excrement.

Some had their eyes cut from their sockets, others had their faces smashed in, and all had been battered and bruised from what looked like rocks, whips, talons, and beaks. Through closer examination, we saw how each of their right arms had certain words carved into their flesh. Words like: "Logger," "Polluter," "Waster," etc...

The morning had changed into midday. My father had personally cared for forty-seven survivors. Each one either shell shocked, muted in fear, or screaming in agony while being escorted to the medical tents. My father, Photios paired with Spartak as they sniffed for any discarded feathers or weaponry.

By the time we departed and the last human survivor was brought to safety, a hamster scout approached the two of them.

Their smell carried a putrid odor, like the carcass of a beast left out in the open. But as they came closer, it turned out it was coming from a torture chamber exclusively for humans. When we stepped inside, we found ourselves surrounded by a vast array of elaborate torture devices. We gaped in horror at the lying corpses of humans, each sight more painful than the other. The devices ranged from whips and dissection tables, to boiling pots and the Judas cradle.

At this time, the troops came across a poor soul who had the misfortune of being torn in half by two elephants. As one of the fellow feline companions took a little closer examination on the body, it, without warning, sprung back to agonizing life. My father pounced back in horror as the upper body squirmed and squealed in pain, begging for us to help him with a mouth full of blood. While we were calling out for paramedics, one of the human child survivors, who seemed to be hiding from all the destruction, sprinted over to the body.

"PAPA! PAPA! THAT'S MY PAPA!" he shouted as he hugged the torn torso against his body. Though disgusting as it was, it was good to have a heartwarming moment for my father to witness among the despairing landscape.

A few incoming scouts immediately transported the male body to the hospital tent, where he miraculously survived the operation. I still ponder as to how all those souls we saved were able to endure so much pain, yet not give up on life. Perhaps this is something I'll never understand, a human quality if you will. I mean, what do I know? I'm just a dog trying to help out the human race.

I've lost count how many times my dad told me these stories. I remember almost every word, down to the last inflection. In my puppy days, they always captured my imagination, giving me the inspiration to be a hero, just like him. However, as I grew older, these dreams started to diminish. The world just had no room for the likes of him. There were simply no adventures to conquer, no discoveries to grasp, nothing unknown to search, and even if there were, the animals residing there wouldn't permit it.

As is according to world law, one must go through a series of test screenings and file reports if they wish to excavate within non-human territory. Many of these places are strictly prohibited of any sort of industrialization. As a member of HRC, it is my duty to make sure my human clients accused of questionable acts, such as the one stated above, can be relocated to another habitat and to help them adjust to their new surroundings. Among them is the Whitestone family, who had a history of meddling with natural ecosystems.

Speaking of which, I gotta take this call. Apologies for cutting this interview short. Let's pick this up tomorrow.

Chapter 8

Dear Mr. Whitestone,

It is with our most unfortunate duty to inform you that your son Eric was just involved in a fight with one of his non-human classmates. The other participant, a female wolf named Chara, had challenged Eric in a race to the top of a nearby rock hill. After committing this illegal action, the confrontation turned ugly and escalated to a violent level. Both have been rushed to medical emergency services and we are awaiting their condition as well as deciding their punishment. We do not tolerate this behavior under any circumstances and strongly suggest your son be instructed by a guidance counselor.

Hope you, your wife and family are in good health.

Principal ANAKHAOS CHRONOS III

Breed: tabby cat

My son, in recent years has had trouble attempting to ace his grades. Plus, ever since his sister underwent that species change operation, he's been quite the rowdy individual among his peers. I mean I'm not saying he's an outcast, goodness no. He does have more than an adequate group of friends. That I am sure of. It's just, I'm not so convinced whether the crowd he's chosen is the best influence. But what do I know? I'm not the same generation as he. And besides, I haven't stayed in touch with today's culture since I was twenty-one. Eric belongs to a crowd of humans that have assimilated with animals of the carnivorous category.

Anyway, being the ever-good parent I am, I put everything

on hold once more and head on over to the nurse's office at my son's school, Gregor Mendel High. I find a human nurse checking for any ointment shortage. She catches my eye and escorts me to where they are. She leads me into a medium-sized room with two large beds serving as centerpieces. On one side is a large female wolf, lying down on her side with bandages covering her ribs and paws. On the other side is, of course, my son, sitting upright with the damage mostly around his neck and legs. I take a deep breath and sit down.

"Son," I say as I sit next to his cot. "You know you can't keep on doing this to us anymore."

But he just stays silent. Apparently, he has too much fun with whatever he does. He has become a very rambunctious student with a knack for getting scars as a badge of honor. If he keeps this up, one of these days, he's going to sacrifice more than a patch of skin.

"I'm aware how difficult it was for you to accept your sister's…decision," I continue. "But you must accept that there are limits with what you can do with your life."

"Well, why do you bother coming over to tell me about this?" replies my son in a tired voice. "You always said you wanted me to grow up and do something worthwhile. Why are you being different all of the sudden? What happened to shoot for the stars, Dad?"

"I just don't want my son to come back from school with a limb missing!"

"You've been spending too much time at your workspace, Dad. Plus, Mom is always out there doing whatever she's doing, while my sister is off with her furry friends and I'm stuck here with no one to talk to. Maybe if you took an hour or two to listen to me or at least acknowledge my stress, none of this, would be likely to happen."

I massage my brain, trying to think of what other anecdote

to say. Just something that would soothe my son's tension toward me. At least I would accomplish something today.

I admit, it has been hard being a role model for my son. There have been too many issues involving overpopulation. Plus, our rental agreement with the landlady hasn't really proved to be the fairest.

"Look," I say. "I know I've been a bit negligent these past few years. But I promise I'll make it up to you."

"That's what you always say," Eric replied under a breath of distrust.

"Excuse me. I need to sign a few release papers. You know the drill in case I'm not home by dinner."

"I know, grab the produce from the garden and set the oven to four-hundred."

"That's my boy."

I walk outside the nurse's office, leaving my son to his thoughts. There's a whole stack of forms waiting for me to sign. I massage my forehead and get to work. As I begin the paperwork, in comes Photios Metro from the HRC. He gives me the cute puppy dog stare and walks in the nurse's office to check on my son's acquaintance. Ever since he saved my dad, he's been our trustworthy lawyer and agent in times of crisis. I don't think we ever would've survived if it hadn't been for him. After a few minutes, he walks back out and looks at me again. Then he gives me a nod as we both leave the school.

"So?" I ask as we walk to the parking lot.

"Injuries are serious but not fatal," Photios replies. "I for one suggest the two get a little R&R while you find another hobby for your son."

"So…are they suspended?"

"They almost snapped each other's necks. What do you think? In a situation as repetitive as this, I'd say It might last the rest of their semester."

"Listen, I know it's probably unfair for me to say this, but maybe we should reconsider his punishment? I mean he's not flunking or anything, as far as I know. Maybe we…"

"Alan, every time you say those words that just means trouble for me, and the HRC as well. We've been bombarded with too much bad publicity recently. Blackmail from habitats, court hearings, eviction notices, lawsuit after lawsuit. Do you have any idea what our overtime was this month?"

"I can't imagine."

"Alan, there was a time not too long ago when a situation like this was much easier. Those days are over. We need to sart monitoring predicaments such as these and end them before they get out of control."

After scratching his ears with his back leg, he walks over to his auto pod.

"Wait." He pauses before he hops in. "What do you say I relocate you and your family to another town, for safety sake? I mean, your landlady's giving you enough trouble as it is."

"I'll think about it."

Then he shuts the door with his mouth, gives me the typical take care of yourself routine and rides off, leaving a small puff of hydrogen smoke behind. I take another deep breath and begin to search for my own pod. It is at this moment I think about my son. I wonder how he's going to handle all this. I wonder how my brother is doing. I wonder if my daughter's fitting in with her newfound pride. I wonder if my wife even got the promotion, she was talking about. Like the saying goes, "So much to do, so little time."

Chapter 9

Apologies for the delay. There was an important affair I had to attend to.

The makeshift ward my father supervised was a risk to construct. It was stationed in AVIACHT occupied France, deep in the thick vegetation of a former village. Every day, he and his troops would risk getting caught by the axis powers. They would always fly just above their heads, scouting for any escaped humans. To fool them, the durable tent was of a camouflage hue, blending in with its foreign, jungle surroundings.

Inside was a ready-made, yet adequate, station. Not glamorous, of course, but still unnoticeable from enemy eyes. The exterior building plan was textured to look like a large boulder, resting among the thick trunk of a tree. Even its durability would fool the most discerning of eyes, mistaking it for a hard, stone slab to rest his or her tiring wings.

Its interior was divided into two sections: Operation and Rehabilitation. As one would expect, the operation ward was filled with wounded humans: Hungry, traumatized, and barely able to stand. Surrounding these patients were some of the best canine and feline surgeons, doctors, and nurses the allied forces could afford. Each paw and snout diligently pacing around their patients scorched bodies, carefully attending to their wounds.

The rehab center was a less chaotic sector. Here, humans already stripped of their faculties were tested with what was left of their cognitive abilities. Some were asked simple tasks (how many claws am I holding up, can you count to three, look at my paw), others more complicated (tie your shoes, draw a picture, write a sentence).

Every day, my father would inspect these wards, assuring the comfort of the living, and accounting for the dead.

The cot beds were nicely attended to, while the patients were lovingly watched over by a trustworthy dog or cat and eased by a hug from our fur, or a lick from our tongues. They had cared for our species. Now the role had been reversed.

Yet, not all his comrades were satisfied with the positions they held. One of the first lieutenants, a black tabby cat named Spartak, stayed his distance from the bipedal patients. Though he stayed to administer flu shots and chloroform, he hardly tried to convene in a conversation. Usually, in his spare time, he would bathe himself, play canasta with his soldiers, climb up a tree or just calmly sit and stare at the expanse of the jungle.

In addition, he and others were pressured by the fact that a few of the dog soldiers had gone missing after a few days scouting for any macaw soldiers.

One morning, my father found him standing on a rock near the equipment sector. Spartak was bowing his head, as if hiding something. My father slowly walked towards him, fearing he may conceal a weapon. Indeed, a small pistol was found dangling from his left paw. Photios slowly yanked the weapon from him for a closer examination. It had belonged to a soldier in the AVIACHT forces, a small parakeet whom Spartak had broken its neck with his bare teeth.

“You know,” Spartak said. “I only signed up for this due to my strong craving for bird meat.”

My father quietly sat next to him.

“I know how hard all this is for you.” He said after a long pause. “But these humans have gone through so much turmoil—”

“Good,” Spartak replied bluntly, to which he journeyed further into the terra formic expanse, to which Dad blocked his path.

“What do you mean, ′good?’” he asked. “Don’t you even know what we’re fighting for?”

“Yes. A petty cause involving a species that enslaved my own.”

“I’m not going to stand idly by and let Helios destroy the human race.”

“And where does that leave us Photios? Huh? Dangling at the bottom of the food chain?”

The two stared at each other in awkward silence as my father tried to think of the right words. Spartak just shook his head in disappointment as he walked further into the woods.

“I know how everything seems Spartak.” He continued as he followed him. “But you must understand this is no longer just a fight to save only humans. We are being persecuted just as much. Now, you must come back inside. Helios’s forces are already…”

“LIEUTENANT!” shouted one of his dog comrades from afar. “We’ve picked up the 78th regiment’s scents. They carried them down south of Bordeaux.”

“Round up a search party,” Photios responded. “We’ll head them off at the nearest gorge.”

“Yes, sir.”

For days now, one of their highest regiments had left without a trace. They had been last seen escorting several human refugees down the Northern French border. Among them was one his dearest friends: SGT. Demeter, whom he had known since pup hood. My father would always tell of how they’d do just about anything together. Whether it was mischief on campus, partnership in the air forces, or even standing up for one another during grade reductions, they would always be side by side, like brothers in spirit.

From what my father last heard; Demeter had been promoted to 1st Lieutenant of the co-species 138th regiment (a title rarely given to non-human personnel). As one could imagine, tension was abundant in the first few weeks of his command. Sometimes a few of the cadets would threaten to kill one another, thus prompting the army to reconsider the promotion. But with determination and a few new and sometimes controversial tactics, things went smoothly for the regiment.

By late June, Demeter and his team had become somewhat small celebrities among the European crowd, some even begged to join them. Clearly their reputations had grown with each conquest. It was by then Photios started to lose touch with his former colleague, their letter exchanges diminishing as the war raged on. Demeter was taking pretty good care of himself, with no longer the need to depend on others…Or, so that's how it seemed.

My father hadn't thought about Demeter for so long, he had almost forgotten his transmission was lost. Regret fell on his face as he and Spartak entered the makeshift ward. 'What will he think of me?' He thought. '"What would I say to him once he's found?' "What would he say to me?"

To his left, in the rehab center, was a battered human, recovering from an excruciating surgery. As expected, his head was cleanly shaven with a bandage on the skull. His left leg was removed due to infection, replaced with a temporary stump to stop the bleeding. He was placed sideways on his cot, so he wouldn't suffocate from the stitches applied to his whipped and bruised back. Twitching in pain and curled in a fetal position, he mumbled several incoherent words as a red ooze trickled out of his mouth. My father walked towards him and placed a cotton ball at the corner of his lips. He then looked at his wristband bearing his name.

"Mr. Bordeau?" Photios asked, to which the patient opened his bloodshot eyes. "Phillippe Bordeau. Is that your name?"

Plillipe responded with forced nod as he breathed a wheezing cough.

"My name is Officer Photios Metro, the leader of the division in which you are currently stationed. I need to ask you several questions. Can you answer?"

"Chuugh." Phillippe gurgled, to which he made a sharp, sickly cough and turned towards the ceiling.

"Phillipe, listen to me! I know it hurts but we need to have your attention."

They readjusted Phillipe's back to his side as Spartak cupped the patient's face with his paws. Phillipe reopened his eyes and gave a rather deadpan look at my father. It was as if all the life had been taken out of him, like a fresh corpse from the grave. What horrors this human saw, the cadet may never know. Dad grabbed a stool and sat eye to eye with Phillipe.

"All right, good," Dad said. "Now listen. We need you to think carefully, have you seen this dog?"

He took out a tattered picture of Demeter from his satchel and held it close to his face. After a few moments of silence…

"D…Deme—" Phillipe mumbled. "Demeter!… Demeter!"

"Yes. Yes. His name is Demeter, we know that." Replied Spartak. "We need to know…"

"Have… you… seen… him?" asked Philipe.

"That's what we're asking you," Photios replied. "We need you to recall the last time you saw him. Can you do that?"

After a moment's pause, Phillippe propped up on his bed and grabbed my father by the collar, like a madman snatching a passerby off the streets.

"Don't…take me back there!" He shouted maniacally as he shook Photios back and forth. "Don't take me! Don't take me!"

"Emergency Aid! Emergency Aid!" Spartak shouted. "Restrain him."

With those words, several Great Danes rushed into the ward and grabbed the groping patient by the shoulders.

"They made me watch her die," Phillipe muttered, as he was strapped right into his cotton bed. "They made me watch her die!"

"Who died?" my panicked father asked, "who died?"

"My wife didn't deserve this!" Philippe replied under a pool of tears. "God! Help us all!"

"Photios, are you sure about this?" asked Spartak as he pushed his ally to the side. "At the very best, he could be delusional."

"Photios replied with a sigh, "We couldn't find any other members in Demeter's rescue squad. He's the best chance we have of finding him and the others."

"Sometimes I don't really know what you're trying to play here."

"Stay strong feline."

He turned back to Phillippe and rested his wet paw on his forehead. I couldn't bear to even think of the horrors this poor human witnessed. He'd be lucky if he would come out of this war with at least a lingering thread of sanity.

But now their sympathy was the least of importance. After a

tense hour or two of getting information out of Phillippe, Photios noticed what looked like a small follicle of hair hanging out of the patient's tattered pocket. Without even thinking, Phillippe yanked the hair pieces out and into my father's open paw. After a careful examination of its scent, he knew it was the fur of Demeter's.

"I wanted to give you this," Phillipe said. "To let…you know…he was thinking of you."

And with those words, he gave in to unconsciousness. My father and Spartak respectfully left the human to his slumber as they continued sniffing his friend's fur.

"Well?" Spartan asked. "What do you smell?"

"Grass sod, from the Ardennes, and it's still wet," Photios proclaimed.

"Can you trace anything else?" asked Spartak.

"Soot… concrete… blood… all the ingredients of a POW camp. Its location is most likely laying to the South. That's where we'll most likely find him, and his division."

"What? Are you insane!" yelled a Labrador cadet, who was overhearing the conversation. "That place is swarming with parrots of the African Gray sector."

"I know," my father responded, "but it's the best chance we've got if we ever want to see them again."

"But just going there would be suicide. I don't want to risk having my forelegs blown off by a land mine."

"Much as I disagree on many of our lieutenant's positions," Spartak intervened, "I'm going to have to side with him on this one."

"But, sir—"

"We have ourselves at the cusp of winning this war Private and I can't afford hesitancy."

The moans of several human patients could be heard in the background as he, Spartak, and the cadet looked to all sides. How long could this go on? They wondered. When would this war come to an end? How many more lives must be sacrificed for the sake of those with just as much value? Obviously, the answers were beyond their reach, but what good was standing there doing nothing?

The cadet noticed a piece of bandage hanging from one of the patients, so he licked it back in place. Then he took a deep breath and finally nodded in agreement.

"So," he said. "What's the plan?"

Chapter 10

"Listen, Eric. I know we might not be able to see each other for a while, but you took a good beating."

"Same goes for you, Chara. I don't think I ever saw anyone take that many blows to the stomach."

"Hey. I'm a wolf. I'm used to that kind of rough and tough stuff."

"Listen, Eric, I know my dad can be a bit of an asshole sometimes. I mean, there's nothing that excuses what he did to you last week. But he's sociable once you get to know him. Besides, he's really nothing compared to my brother."

"What are you talking about, Chara? Your dad's so aggressive he's next in line for pack leadership. If he finds out we're together, you are grounded for life. It's not like it would be the first time you were caught with a human."

"Oh please. my old man wouldn't stand a chance against you. "

"Hey! Hey! Easy where you're putting those claws."

"Come on man! You could totally whoop his ass?"

"Look, I might be a rebel, but that don't mean I pick fights for nothin."

"Right back at ya bro."

"So, what's your sentencing this time?"

"Probably not leaving the cave for seven days, and babysitting my nephew, again!"

"You got it easy. I'm suspended for two weeks."

"Well at least it isn't during prom season, which I'm STILL WAITING FOR A PROPOSAL."

"Patience, pal! You ever heard of building up suspense?"

"Yeah, that's what you said last year, and the year before that, and the year before that."

"Not everyone gets it right the second or third time. I'm pretty sure this time it will not be a disappointment."

"It better not be. Cause you might as well find another teammate in soccer if… Oh, hi, Dad. Gotta run."

"Thanks for not exposing me."

"Any-time."

ATTENTION!

All youth of the Avian Brotherhood

For years now, you have all struggled to survive against the incoming invasion of the spawn known as human.

No longer shall we cower in fear, for we are to crush the evil of sape from the root, before it chokes out every flower of our sacred jungles.

You have looked unto them for your protection; now do the same for yourselves. Take part in saving our home from the sapien cockroaches that threaten our peaceful existence. Your life just may depend on it.

Remember Helios. Remember your flock, and remember:

"BIRDS OF ALL FEATHER, ANNIHILATE TOGETHER!"

JOIN AVIACHT

approved by THE GRAND KING HELIOS

Chapter 11

Interview entry: May 19th, 2004A, 10:15 AM

Excerpt from book "The Unexpected Hero"

For those who know nothing of my accomplishments I am Kana Metuke, hyacinth macaw and former commander of the death camps of AVIACHT occupied Europe. For most individuals in this world, I am viewed as a murderer, a sociopath, and merciless torturer of countless lives. Indeed, in my years, I have scoured across the European landscape, turning decrepit towns and cities into lush jungles for my species to thrive. And indeed, a great many of my decisions had been irrational and unforgivable to those I affected. Yet, I had not thought of what consequences it would bring to the many citizens below us. In contrast, to this day, I do have a belief that a great quantity of King Helios's actions did have a large fraction of justice.

Now, if one were to ask an old macaw such as myself, "What was the right thing I did? Did all those poor souls get what was coming to them, so to speak? Or should I feel guilty in myself for leaving hundreds of human lives to die in the wild, or succumb to the majesty of the jungle?"

You see, when one utters terms such as "Wild" and "Jungle" (especially humans), he or she sees images of discord and unmannerly state. However, one must take the devoted time to stare in awe at these words, which have always been my personal favorites. To me, "Wild" and "Jungle" are words close to my heart. These are words that represent freedom and independence from approaching enemies who had rattled our soil floor since the day they left the trees. Yes, I am joyous to say that to this day, I am a "Wild" animal.

My memories of the day the loggers came are as visible as if they happened today. I was a chick, about eight to nine months old, a carefree, energetic, and graceful chick without a care in the world. My family was of typical size, consisting of five birds, including my siblings. Our home was a large and proud tribe who embraced every aspect of the Jungle, and took seriously our position as wild animals, so much that we saw ourselves as the most civilized of Amazon species. For you see, creatures like us are not savage simply because we are born into a feral existence. This was a mistakable correlation with which all humans had stupidly confused us.

We were a functioning tribe, adequate, punctual and generous to the green land Mother Earth had provided us. Though different in the pigment of our feathers, my brethren lived as one, with not a quarrel to be found. In spite of the bloodshed you heard, peace was always our priority. It's just the humans were in the way.

As chicks, our fragile innocence was as fruitful as a million saplings which grew on the forest floor, capturing the sunlight that peaked through the thick leaves and branches. Our curiosity was no different, laying our eyes on the inhabitants great and small, even though they weren't to be trusted. Besides, as possessors of the power of flight, we could easily escape them.

Our mothers were like protectors of our souls, bearing us the gift of tradition and heritage. For three good years, they were the center of our lives, showing us the ways of family. As such, they taught us to nurture and cherish all that nature brought from the ground.

Fathers were of equal importance. They humbly served as defenders of the jungle, patrolling each tree as a sacred home for our winged brethren. I remember their bright wings, swooping through the canopies, adding even more color to the shining leafed branches.

As for us chicks, we were encouraged to explore and discover. As dangerous as life was and would soon be, our elders taught us not to fear what hid among our home, for all was familiar to the eyes of the earth mother and the father that was the sky.

It was past the rainy season when all that was good, all that was pure came to a bitter, crashing end. The night had fallen on the peaceful jungle. My father was out gathering any last-minute berries and nuts for the next morning. The rest of us had huddled up in the nest, ready to unwind our wings and stretch out our talons on the soft, aloe leaves. My mother gently stroked us with her outstretched wing and sung to us an age-old lullaby. Then, we closed our eyes, fell on mother's teat, and drifted into slumber.

At this time, the alpha males, my father included, were gliding back to our nests, when suddenly; they saw a flickering orange glow coming from the North canopies. It grew larger and larger and crept closer and closer. From what survivors described, it assumed the form of a large flower, spreading its petals across the tips of the branches. Being the cautious flock, my father and other well-equipped macaws flew over to investigate.

A few hours later, we were suddenly awakened by the alarm of the alpha males, flying right toward us. I was confused. Was today an early safety drill? Were we to be called to a meeting?

Nothing was scheduled soon. My family and I rubbed our eyes as we looked out of our hole. The orange glow was not only bigger, it was close enough to see its true shape and form. Fire had come to our home.

Without a chance to think, everyone flew out of their nests. We glided over the rainforest and sounded the alarm. More birds flew to our level as we soared above our magnificent home. No one knew it would be the last time.

Where was this coming from? What would want to destroy us? As we looked below in examination, the force behind the fire caught up with our "seeing-eye" perimeter. We discovered it was not of mother earth's creation. Right below, we saw a large group of loggers, going about their usual routine of clearing the forest homeland.

We had always wondered why they hated us so? What did we do to deserve such punishment? How did our presence upset the balance of nature? But on that day, we knew the answer: It wasn't us; it was them.

Moments later, father was flying right behind us. We split in two, with dad carrying our smallest sibling under his wing, and my mother in charge of the rest of us. I started to cry as I hugged my brother for dear life. We were losing everything! All was disappearing.

There was a squawk from down below. It was another macaw family, succumbing to the smog and soot of man's wrathful fire. My father, being among the elite, swooped down with my brother, knowing he had no time for mother.

The smoke started to rise higher, consuming us in its dampness. Our eyes burned in anguish while the singe of red sparks tapped on our feathers. For a moment, we couldn't see.

We were literally as blind as bats. We had no idea where we were, or where we were going. Just anywhere but here.

At last, we had escaped the fumes, but not without loss. Over half our flock had now succumbed to the fires and fumes of man. So many lives, free and full of promise, destroyed by the waste exhumed upon the glorious jungle. It took seven hours for the orange glow to finally cease.

What it left was hell. A barren landscape. An empty shell of what was once home. It was hard to believe the gray and black lumps were once trees.

My mother, sister and I clung onto nests at the face of the North clay wall, along with other lucky survivors. But even we had a few deep bruises, both external and internal. As we settled into our new, refugee homes, the pain inside us began to evolve, churning itself into anger. It was not of spite, but of justice.

A few days later, we saw another bird fly in from the direction of the charred remains, landing on one of the unoccupied nests. He was not of our breed as he was blue, Spix, to be exact. But he was indeed large, and well built, at least for a parrot of his kind. His wingspan was large enough to fit two macaws, and his talons were nicely sharpened to claw at even the hardest of stone. The feathers on the top of his head were combed over, and his tail firm and adaptable to any wind pattern. But the part of him that stood out the most, were his eyes. Sunken, full of experience, battered with bruises and complemented by a mighty beak with a burnt end at its tip.

For a few moments, he stared into every nest. Each was hollow, inadequate, unfit for any decent sized family. What's more, the food he observed was rationed, only a few crumpled-up leaves and a dried berry per bird. The water wasn't satisfactory either, as he choked on a sip of it. Then he came towards us, with a sad look on his face. He took a deep breath and lifted his head up high.

"My friends, brothers and sisters alike," he began. "My name is Helios. I have traveled over our once prosperous land. I have seen the horrors and massacres of what is played in front of us. Humankind has come once more to shove away all that is good. But it is not only here. My land too was destroyed by the evil grip that is the Homo sapiens: trees destroyed, homes vanquished, and lives dead from the gun. As I fled away, I saw great patches of jungles from other lands gone in an instant. The devastation of the fire is large, but so are the fires of freedom."

"Comrades, I have come not to help you escape, nor find other land, but to say we are in this together, and encourage you all to fight back for this once, by any means necessary. We are a strong, proud, resourceful species, able to fly everywhere we want, and learn everything we need. We know the jungle. We've known it ever since we evolved from our reptilian selves. But now we know humans, and we know that no matter how far we go, they will find us, enslave us, and maybe even eat us...unless we stop them."

"It is time to rebel against the flat faces and bring new order to the planet. Now, more than ever, we must unite as one! If we are to survive this ordeal, if are to continue to prosper. If we are to go forth, and multiply, then now is the time, to show them who we really are! If you wish to see that promising future, a future where we no longer live in fear, then now is the time to join AVIACHT! Protectors of the sacred sky and land! Let us show these flatheads a message: THIS IS OUR LAND! WE CANNOT LET THEM TAKE OUR HOME! LET'S FIGHT FOR IT!

That's when the uprising started. That was when a call to freedom would soon be heard. The voice that was Helios would echo through every canopy and treetop, through every luscious, green piece of the land, through every corner of the Brazilian landscape. The time for call-to-action was now, and that call was AVIACHT.

Chapter 12

Interviewee: XENIA Species: Leopard

Former Species: Human

Excerpts from 60 Minutes special: Dealing with Changes

My former name was Tiffany Whitestone. I was born on September 15 1988C in the foressity of Pittsburgh, Pennsylvania. My childhood was what you might say a little abnormal compared to other young lives. The family, in which I was raised, traveled a lot from residence to residence, doing our best to blend in with the human crowd. This, unfortunately, didn't really give me a lot of time to become friends with anyone. Personally, I don't really blame my folks for this, given the fact we were under protection by the HRC. To make up for the lack of companions, I spent a great deal of my adolescent years playing with my little brother.

Yeah, we did about everything together. We went to parks, played in each other's rooms, made secret handshakes, took turns on each other's school projects, even gave one another a word of wisdom or two. I know, this seems kind of boring for a typical sibling relationship, but to him, I was the source of fun.

For as long as I can remember, I kind of always knew in my heart I was a cheetah. It's not that I didn't like humans. Goodness no.

I just felt…I felt it was best for me and my self-conscious to be in the form of a species not originally my own. I mean, I always ate raw meat, would try to walk all fours, even hang out with non-human friends.

When I told my family, I decided on Species Reassignment Surgery, they were both skeptical and overwhelmed about my choice, especially my brother. I can see why he freaked out. Before he turned double digits, we were inseparable, a special sibling relationship.

I'd expected his reaction to be typical. The decision and process of species change is a controversial one, something that hasn't been taken lightly. Many protests have occurred at the clinic where I first underwent the initial steps in my transformation. I can still remember a few protestors banging at my vehicle door, throwing fake blood at me on my way to the entrance. Also, a great number of fake statements have arisen over the years. One myth is if you decide to go through the transformation, you are making a vow to never talk to your loved ones, which is certainly not true. I have been in contact with my family ever since via Face Time.

Another circulating tale is that the procedure has the danger of decreasing one's lifespan. On the contrary, there have been individuals, many with whom I became personal acquaintances, who have undergone partial species change for cancer treatment, blood transfusions, cataract surgery, etc.

Anyway, the operation went as follows: First, the doctors engaged in executing organ transplants using artificial leopard organs. This resulted in two weeks of rehab at the clinic so as my body could adjust. But I knew it would be worthwhile in the end. I knew my reward would be justified and I knew being at peace would be right around the corner. So, I carried on with the procedure with little to no hesitation.

Next came the skin pigmentation, which is basically a tedious tattoo process where they surface your skin with the same color scheme and skin texture of the animal you've chosen. Side effects included occasional rashes and loss of all my hair. This was an uncomfortable experience since, during the process, I looked like a creature from another planet. I constantly covered my face and periodically took medicine to reduce the hive breakouts.

Luckily, the next step was taking a few injections that covered my skin with fur. There were two advantages to this: one, the hives stopped, and my skin texture smoothened out, and two, I no longer needed to wear clothing. By now I was able to move out of my apartment and they transferred me to the animal populated town of Etosha. At first, the residents were pretty skeptical as to whether I could assimilate into the wild or not. Not that they were against humans or anything. It's just that I was kind of the first former human to take residence there. Luckily, as my hands and feet turned into paws, my fangs and tail started to grow out and my hearing and eyesight improved. As a result, I was immediately welcomed in the community, where they assigned me to a position in the Alpha Female Starter's group and put me to work in the scouting department, where I exceeded through the ranks with ease.

Finally came the most painful part: The anatomical structure transfusion. I was in constant pain as the bones started to shift and my face expanded into a snout. It was a grueling three months of me getting used to walking on all fours and trying to control my tail. The thrice-daily supply of medications was the only way I could stand the pain. But eventually, as my arms feet turned into fore and hind legs, my claws began to show, my spine clicked into place, and my skull/face features aligned with that of a cheetah's, I knew it would be worth it in the end.

As my transformation was nearing an end, I met a rather very attractive male cheetah named VASILLIUS. He was adequately lean for his type: strong, well-built and highly skilled among the pack. Aggressive at times, yet reliable, nonetheless, he taught me many of the basic tricks and trades of being a big cat. He taught me skills such as how to climb a tree, how to plan a sneak attack, how to roar from the diaphragm etc. Most of the females in the pack thought I couldn't hunt properly due to my human background, but of course, I proved them wrong. With some practice and Vasillius on my side, I was able to make my first kill. We've been together ever since.

Impressed, they promoted me to the hunting division where I became one of their star members, even going so far as leading a few hunting patterns. I couldn't have been more satisfied. Now the thing about species change is, unlike sex change, the effects are more easily reversible, but I don't plan to change back anytime soon. I really do feel like I've found my place in the world and I am comfortable with the skin I'm in, though I'm not so sure all my family approves this decision.

In the events that followed the change, my brother has kept his distance from me. This is easily understandable. After-all, every time I've tried to reconnect, he always responds with: "I just don't see my sister underneath all that fur." So, though as heartbreaking as it sounds, I must move on with my life, striving to continue to fit in with my four-legged friends. I for one am grateful. I mean, at least we're not off the grid.

Chapter 13

'Incoming call. Incoming call'

"Hello? Oh, hey, Tiffy."

"Dad, I've told you, my name is XENIA now."

"Sorry. Sorry. Still getting used to the idea my kid's a leopard."

"Look. I'm still the same loving girl underneath all this. You know that."

"Well, I wish your brother was able to handle this transition more easily than me."

"How's he doing by the way?"

"Not as good as we hoped. He got suspended again the other day after a brawl with one of his classmates."

"Really? Isn't that the third time this month?"

"Fraid so."

"Well, I hope next week turns out better for him."

"Not to be critical or anything, but I'm not sure if your situation is helping. I just don't think he's ever going to fully accept this change in the family. I mean I'm not one for restraining my kid from her ambitions, but I'm starting to believe this wasn't the best for any of us."

"Listen Dad, I know it's still difficult for you all to process this change of events in your life, but I've never felt more like myself before. For the first time, I actually feel comfortable with the skin, or in this case, fur, that I'm in. Plus, I'm adapting really well to my new environment. I don't think that has ever happened in my old life before."

"Honey, you know our real concern was the idea that you wouldn't like your old species anymore."

"Dad! You know that's a myth. I don't hate humans. I never did. I just wasn't comfortable being one."

"Right. Right. You've told me that already."

"How about this, next time you come over to the savannah, I can teach Eric some of the ways of the pack."

"I don't know."

"C'mon, Daddy. Who's the best father in the world?"

"I…I am."

"That's right. I love you, Dad and in my eyes, you will always be the best father ever."

"Thanks. I suppose so. How's your boyfriend vasi…vaso…vasum."

"Vasillius."

"Yeah, him. How's he treating you?"

"Oh, he's treating me well."

"Good. Good."

"Um, Dad! This is kind of the reason why I've called you. I have some news."

"What is it?"

"I…think he's going to propose and ask me to get… married."

"Oh, that's ni… wait what?"

"Now I'm not sure about this, Dad, but I'm going to check again, and if he offers me another wild flower, as according to tradition, then I think we'll have another in the family."

"Well, that's…that's great. I get to be the father-in-law of a big cat."

"I'm pretty sure if this happens, he will be very grateful.

Besides he's really eager to meet you."

"Where is he now?"

"Oh, he's probably off with the boys parading his kill of the day."

"Well, tell him I said hi."

"Will do."

"Love you, sweetie."

"Love you too, Dad."

"Bye."

Call ended

Chapter 14

My father and his division had been tracing Demeter's scent for days now, while Trisco, and several other feline privates, kept their ears open for any incoming attacks. The patients of the ward were now being placed in mobile ambulances, blending seamlessly with the jungle background. Treating them had been a hectic ordeal, even though several of them were not going to make it.

The soldiers were feeling the heat already, even though we dogs are known to withstand the elements for longer than humans. Soldiers were split into pairs, taking turns carrying the other on his or her back. Even though panting had decreased, as it seemed to have stopped working.

It was at this time the cadets looked up and saw several birds, swooping in a mid-high V formation. Only an African Gray Parrot would be gliding with that distinct accuracy. My father gave the signal and they all ducked in the high stalks of the forest floor, they were getting close.

After a moments silence, Photios took a small whiff with his nose. The scent was faint but definitely recognizable. He knew he and his friend would be reunited soon. The flock went out of peripheral view, and his infantry marched on. Now the scent grew stronger and stronger as all the weary soldiers trudged deeper into the trackless jungle. Some were beginning to have doubt.

"Sergeant, are you sure of this?" Spartak asked my father as he hopped off the back of a private. "For all we know, this could be a trap."

"It can't be," the sergeant responded while taking in more whiffs. "I'd know this scent from anywhere."

Just as he predicted, the scent grew stronger and stronger with each step. At last, my father would again be with his friend. Days of agonizing search and rescue would finally pay off.

The division had reached the summit of the hill. It was empty.

My father collapsed in exhaustion and defeat, panting like I'd never seen. Once again, the allied forces had reached a dead end. 'How could this happen?' Photios asked himself. 'How could we be so wrong?' 'How could we be fooled this easily?'

"Search for survivors," A high-ranking dog ordered as all ran down the hill and into the seemingly deserted camp.

The place looked like something out of a dog's or cat's nightmare. To their left were rusty, rundown cabins, each with a flag belonging to a different breed. Inside was a germ-infested bunkhouse, with urine and vomit coated mattresses for sleeping. There was no running water, no urinals, not even a medicine cabinet.

To their right were shacks specifically designed for torturing prisoners, each one worse than the last. Among them was concreted textured room facing an old-timey soundboard. My father turned on the machine. It played a screeching sound over and over again that only a dog could hear, driving even the sanest of canines into savage madness.

My father took a sniff of the humid, jungle air. To his horror, it was his friend Demeter's scent. Demeter was definitely here.

"What have they done to you?" he whispered with a crack in his voice.

He kicked the audio torture machine with brutal force and

let out a long howl of despair.

"We have failed them," a cadet solemnly said nearby. "Our friends are gone."

Spartak said nothing and bowed his head in respect. It was then he noticed a freshly plucked feather beside his paw.

As my father was sitting down in shame, he heard a trudging sound coming from one of the entrances. It grew louder and louder with each second. Photios popped his head up and sniffed the air once more.

"What is that?" he whispered. "Cadets, scan the perimeter."

But the cadets were too busy watching leaves falling from the rush of wings and talons through the branches.

"AMBUSH!" shouted Spartak.

Pellets starting firing down on the ground as everyone jumped into a battle formation. It seemed clear this was a last-minute standoff by the gray parrot division, and they were not ready to give up easily.

My father and his infantry split off into two groups, one hid behind the shacks and the other under a heap of corpses. My father was, unfortunately, in the later. To this day he remembers that foul stench of decaying flesh rotting above him. Options were few, since pellets were now darting above them, and places to hide were limited.

The birds were fast, silent, and barely visible, as they swooped past them from all directions. Spartak and his group tore down the shack in front of them using the wooden planks as a pathetically equipped barricade. It almost proved useless, as several privates and cadets were shot down immediately, bleeding to death before Spartak's eyes.

Photios's team was in no better shape. The sapiens remaining were no match for incoming pellets, darting through organs and penetrating his comrades with one, fatal blow.

"Spartak! Status report!" Photios shouted into his radio.

"We've lost twelve of our comrades, Photios." Spartak replied. "Ammo is running thin! I don't know if we can hold much longer."

"Send in the second battalion now!" my father ordered.

"Sir, that option is out of the question unless authorized by…"

"There's no time for arguments! Do as I say!"

With a moment's hesitation, Spartak blew the whistle on his knapsack, calling forth a pack of Huskies who were waiting just over the hill for instructions. They were a group of mercenaries designed to shoot and kill the enemy. They were a group not to be trifled with, which made sense since half their lineage was of wolf descent.

In their accustomed act of brute force, they pounced and sunk their sharp fangs into the gray birds, without even giving them a moment to prepare. The mercenaries flung helpless avian bodies around, tearing out their feathers and and breaking their beaks with every chance they had. My father can still remember the painful squawks and screeches of those parrots, as they were torn to shreds by the mere slash of wolf claws. Looking back, he somehow felt sorry for their ordeal.

Before they knew it, all was quiet again. Just as quiet as they found it. My father's division looked up from their makeshift corpse mound, and saw the battalion picking up pieces of parrot bodies and heads. That was when they heard a small whimper coming from underneath one of the camp houses.

"Private!" Photios said to a scout. "Investigate."

The scout nodded and proceeded to dig beneath the planks. What he found was a familiar face. Demeter had been hiding under the camp house for nearly three weeks, crippled from unspeakable torture. He was the only prisoner still present in the camp.

My father rushed towards him and licked his bloodied face and neck. It was amazing he had survived this long. He was one lucky mutt. Three others carefully dragged him up to the surface, escorting him directly onto a stretcher and to medical aid.

"Still got it huh?" Photios joked with Demeter. "Like back at the academy."

"Just you wait," Demeter said under his wheezing breath. "You haven't seen nothin yet."

Well, at last my father was reunited with his friend. The biggest thing on his mind was over. Now the only question remaining was: Where were the humans? It was at that moment two feline scouts heard what sounded like a squawk coming from the mound of lifeless macaw bodies. One of the avian soldiers had survived the attack, shielding itself under his fallen comrades. As it tried to crawl away, a feline from the second battalion grabbed it with its paw and chained it to a rock.

"Where are the others?" a collie asked in a deep voice. "Where are you hiding them?"

"You can all suck my feathery ridges if you want an answer from me," the Macaw sneered under its breath.

"I don't think you have a choice in this matter," Spartak said as he approached.

"You don't scare me."

With those words, the battalion swiftly unchained it, and pinned the Macaw locked to the ground.

"Where are they?" Spartak asked cooly to its face.

"Around the corner of your ass." the Macaw mocked.

Spartak nodded and the battalion doused a bucket of freezing water over its beak.

"Where are the humans?" Spartak asked.

"AVIACHT…makes…my skull strong and firm. My brain is indestructible to the deception of the pet."

Spartak nodded again as the dogs emptied another bucket, kicking it repeatedly.

"Where did you hide them?"

"My mind is safely secure, like a Brazil nut."

The dogs smacked it again, kicking it harder with every blow.

At this point the Macaw was now coughing up blood. Even my father was questioning the tactics as he looked on. But what other choice did they have? It's not like the bird would just come clean at the first threat. And why not? Despite the interrogation, no matter how brutal it became, the bird kept his mouth shut, mocking them as they proceeded.

"I think you leave us no other choice." Spartak said coldly. "Bring out the de-clawer."

"But, sir that's—"

"Now!"

"Yes, sir." a dog of the battalion nodded.

He reached into his sack and took out what looked like a large mechanical claw like arm, capable of tearing out both beaks and talons.

"Wait," said the Macaw, "What are you doing?"

Spartak turned the de-clawer on, causing it to make a buzzing sound as it began to move.

"We have ways to make you talk," Spartak said as he approached him.

"Listen…I take back what I said…look…we can make a deal…I won't hurt a single one of you any more."

"And you won't ever be able to."

Spartak slowly started pulling at his talons with the mechanical claw. The Gray parrot howled in pain as his body was being torn apart. It took about three agonizing minutes for him to finally yell out the truth.

"MACAPA!" he shouted.

"What?" they all asked.

"They're taking…the humans…and dogs…to Macapa!" the Macaw replied in exhaustion. "It's a…a former city…turned death camp…in northern Brazil."

"I've heard of that place," said Demeter, who was still on his stretcher. "That's where they were going to take me. No one has ever come out alive."

"Then they got what they deserved." The bird snickered to which he was met with a slap across the cheek.

"How do we get there without being seen?" one of the privates asked. "It's one of the most safely-guarded strongholds of AVIACHT."

"We don't," my father replied. "We simply make them think we are one of them. That's when we take them by surprise."

"What in the Galapagos do you mean?" asked Spartak.

Dad started to draw in the ground what looked like a crude map of the Atlantic Ocean, with Europe and South America on their respected sides. He pointed his paw towards Europe.

"This is where we are right?" he started. "Now every week, the AVIACHT forces export tank supplies from their European convey in France via submarine. From there it's a four-day long trip from France to the Brazilian border, without any interruption of course. About two to three of the submarines are decommissioned at the end of every month, where they are crushed into scrap metal…"

"So how are we going to board those subs?" Spartak asked. "Put on parrot costumes."

Photios rolled his eyes.

"Mind you that Macaws don't know shit from hell about how to swim long distances. Look. It's obvious the subs are on auto pilot. Why do you think the Macaws only travel the ocean by air?

He then drew in the dirt what looked like one of them.

"From what I heard, a hollow sub is able to store one hundred to two-hundred individuals at any given time. If we can explore the interior, we just might be able to customize them into manual transportation."

"Which of you are technician experts?" he asked his squadron, to which four to five raised their paws.

"Do you believe it is possible to rewire the circuits of an auto-pilot so that one can manually direct it?"

"It does seem plausible," one of the rodent technicians replied. "Improbable, but still plausible."

Another technician looked back and forth between the crudely drawn map and the pack.

"Hmmm…" she pondered. "It does seem far-fetched. And yet…"

"What? What?" my father pleaded.

"And yet I wonder."

She started to draw from the side a picture of a makeshift grid, full of wires and nuts and bolts. She erased a few and added some with her claws tentatively staring at her little hypothesis. After a few moments…

"Yes, yes. I think I've got it," she muttered in confidence. "I think I know how to make this plan work."

"How?"

"It's hard to explain. I'll tell you when we arrive on the

coast."

"It's worth a shot," Demeter added as he slowly rose up from his stretcher. "Besides, I have a few human escapees who I'm responsible for. Hopefully, they've followed my order and stayed put in a friend's house. I can send a telegram to him while we're on our way."

"Boy, you really will go to any lengths to save these humans, won't you?" Spartak asked.

"It gives me a purpose," he replied with a sneer.

"It's a long trip from Europe to Brazil." My father thought. "Might as well have some human company for the ride. We can take them to Argentina till the war is over. It is South America's last stronghold."

"Second battalion. Take that prisoner to our station," he commanded them. "Something tells me he might know more."

The rest of the division was weary, it was the end of a long day and they needed sleep for the long journey they now faced. My father and his friend were reunited, but a bigger mission still needed completion: salvation.

Chapter 15

Intertitles: CNN logo

Cue drums

Zoom in to

Announcer: live from CNN news, this is…

Cue theme music, title

Announcer: "360 With Anderson Cooper"

Zoom title out/music fade out

WS of Studio

Pan In

Anderson Cooper: Good evening world. I'm Anderson Cooper, and welcome to "360." Our main topic for tonight: Planet of the Apes. Is it truly offensive to future generations?

Cue poster

Anderson Cooper (cont.): Over the years, since its first release this controversial yet landmark of a Sci-Fi film has garnered both praise and ridicule from film critics and scientists alike.

Cut to pics from film

Anderson Cooper (cont.): Recently, the film has once again suffered another wave of criticism from various ape groups around the globe. Our special guests tonight…

Dr. Dioran Insignias, Chimp, scientist, social critic and head of the European Human Behavior Clinic, or EHBC.

Professor Frontida Oxbury, Gorilla, Theorist, and one of five managers of Child development and adoption at Mothers and

Fathers of America,

And Professor Pavion Epsky, Orangutan, Analyst, and coordinator of Human-Ape relations in the Euro-African sector.

It is an honor to have you three here this evening.

Prof. Oxbury: Good to be here Anderson.

Prof. Epsky: The pleasure's all ours.

Prof. Insignias: I concur.

Cooper: Now before we start, I must congratulate Prof. Insignias on his recent Nobel Prize in Psychology, for his discovery of reducing Alzheimers.

Prof. Insignias: Well, as far as I'm concerned, the only true rewards are my wife and children.

Cooper: Heartfelt words indeed. Now, onto our subject, the Ape Rights Alliance, or A.R.A has issued a statement to boycott the Blu Ray release of The Planet of the Apes box set as well as ban it from film festivals and video retailers due to what they call the degrading imagery and inaccurate portrayal of a dominant species. Can anyone bring me up to speed with this?

Prof. Epsky: Well, as a card-carrying member of A.R.A., I think it is best to be the spokesperson for this cause. Though impressive as it may be in allegorical storyline and special effects, I don't think it would be best to not show this piece of work to future generations.

Prof. Oxbury: Absolutely. Besides, there have been numerous accounts where apes have sided with Homo sapiens and vice versa, spanning from de-industrialization to World War II.

Prof. Insignias: Though at first, we hesitated to assist, being a pacifist species and not wishing to partake in any warfare. But after AVIACHT's attack on our homeland, we agreed to join the fight.

Cooper: Prof. Oxbury, you claim to have belonged to a gorilla family known for raising human children, is that correct?

Prof. Oxbury: Yes. It is a very proud fact of which I hold much self-esteem.

Cooper: When did this family tradition of child adoption begin?

Oxbury: Well, as far as my roots go, it all started with my ancestor Khalia about 4-500 years ago. From what I've learned, she was simply minding her own business, taking care of two baby gorillas, giving them their daily bath in a nearby river, when she noticed an unfamiliar, um, "specimen" on the other side. Being the curious species we are, Khalia went over to investigate. Turned out it was a human toddler that apparently wandered off from a nearby village.

Now if there's one truth I've learned from my research in child behavior it's that when a youngling reaches a certain age, he or she will regard a species as their own, even if they don't technically share the same DNA. As is also a common myth, most people have portrayed the idea of a feral child to be an individual who is shunned by the community in which they were raised. This was not the case at all when it came to Khalia's adopted child, who grew to be a strong member of the community. Thus, began an ever-expanding tradition of the Simian family looking after the abandoned Homo sapiens. We have been close ever since.

Cooper: Well apparently, that is not the vision of the filmmakers of the topic at hand. Which bring us to our main point.

Insignias: Ah, yes. Of course. The impressive, yet inaccurate "Planet of the Apes."

Cooper: Yes, roll the tape please.

Cue Film Footage

Insert side card

Dialogue Courtesy of 20th Century Fox

Clip 1

Zira: Look, he's using his fingers.

Dr. Zaius: Only because he saw you move yours.

Zira: But perhaps he understood.

Dr. Zaius: Man has no understanding. He can be taught a few simple tricks, nothing more.

Zira: I'm afraid I must disagree, according to my experiments...

Dr. Zaius: Dr. Zira, I must caution you. Experimental brain surgery on these creatures is one thing, and I'm in favor of it. But your behavioral studies are quite something else again. To think that we can learn anything from the simian nature through the study of man is pure nonsense. Man is a nuisance. He eats up his food supply, then migrates to our green belt circle, ravaging our crops. The sooner he is exterminated the better. It is a question of simian survival!

Clip 2

Ape: Tell the court Bright Eyes. What is the Second Article of nature?

Taylor: I know nothing of your culture I admit that.

Ape: Of course, he cannot know about our culture because he cannot think! Tell us. Why are all apes created equal?

Taylor: Some apes it seems are more equal than others.

Ape: Ridiculous. Tell us bright eyes. Why do men have no souls? Why does a divine spark exist in the simian brain? Huh?

Clip 3

Taylor: Don't try to follow us. I'm pretty handy with this.

Dr. Zaius: Of that I am sure, all my life I've awaited your coming and dreaded it, like death itself.

Taylor: Why? You're afraid of me and you hate me. Why?

Dr. Zaius: Because you're a man, and you're right. I have always known about man. From the evidence I believe his wisdom must fall hand in hand with his idiocy. His emotions must rule his brain. He must be a warlike creature who gives battle to everything around him, even himself.

Taylor: What evidence? There were no weapons in that cave.

Dr. Zaius: The forbidden zone was once a paradise. Your breed made a desert of it, ages ago.

Taylor: That doesn't explain a planet where apes evolved from men? There's got to be an answer.

Dr. Zaius: Don't look for it Taylor. You may not like what you find.

End of film footage.

Epsky: Well, I for one should be first to say that vision of an ape dominated society is inexcusably inaccurate.

Insignius: I couldn't agree more. Despite its impressive special effects, I do believe if ever we did strive become the supreme species, we'd have much more important things to do than waste our energy exterminating your species.

Oxbury: Basically, we would have more valuable subjects to focus on such as the ever-increasing value of bettering ourselves.

Cooper: What exactly do you three mean by that statement?

Insignius: Well, from our years of studies on combat and human warfare, we have come to this conclusion: If one species decides to avenge their suffering through destruction of the race and/or species of the perpetrator, they will become what they're against.

Cooper: Thank you Doctor. When we come back, more history of this film, plus Epsky's plans to co-finance what he calls an "Accurate Apes" film. Stay tuned.

Pan out

Fade to Commercials

Chapter 16

Among the five million individuals who religiously watch Anderson Cooper in the ANTHROMALIA of New York, the ultimate record keeper in viewership is me. Ever since its first broadcast, I'm pretty sure I haven't missed a single moment of the news program. With guest speakers, hardcore topics and documented truth, it's no wonder I've been hooked on it for the past eight years. Nothing tonight could possibly disturb me, or cause an interruption from the programming I like best...

"Alan, honey!"

...except perhaps a phone call.

"What is it?" I ask out of irritation.

"The local retirement center called," my wife replies "They said it's urgent."

So, I hop off the couch, and slunk over to the phone and press reply.

"Hello?"

"Is this the home of Alan Whitestone?" asks a voice.

"Yeah."

"Then I suppose you are aware of our bird resident, Episko Doulus."

"Yes, he saved my father's life in the Holocaust."

"Well, we regret to tell you the heart-breaking news. He has passed on."

"What?"

"Yes, it's true. He had a stroke this afternoon. Sadly, he did not survive. We're sorry."

"Oh… I see."

I try desperately to compose myself over the phone. My legs tremble in shock. My lips quiver at the sound of the news. My mind goes completely black for a fleeting moment. But, as I must do, I snap back into reality, trying desperately to hold back the tears

"As requested in his will, you are to receive a few personal items. Please also go down to the morgue to fill out some final documents."

"Understood," I reply in a remorseful tone.

"Please report to the center at your soonest convenience, and once again we are sorry for your loss."

"Thank you…bye."

I hang up the phone and take a moment to compose what was just stated to me. Sure, I knew of his ailing health, but why so soon? Why not a year from now? Or maybe the next?

Episko (Or Epi, as my father called him) was not only a dear friend to my family, he was like one of our own, like he was related to us. And why not? He was a hero in my own realm, in spite of the irony that he was a parrot, the species from whom my father was running.

So, I walk over to my wife, break the news to her; she sheds a tear, takes out her handkerchief, and goes over to call her friends. Not that I really care or anything, but she doesn't seem to cry as much as I expected. Then again, she and Epi only became acquainted a few years ago. Now I must get my act together and head over and sign a few papers.

Gliding through the vines and streets of the urban forest in my autopod, my mind tinkering with a memory per second, I think back to Episko in his adolescence. Days when I would visit

Uncle Epi's apartnest. Days when he stared out from his nest into the abyss of the jungle, more spacious than homes of his neighbors no doubt. But more importantly, days when Episko told us tales of how he rescued dozens of lives, and how he united my mother and father.

Chapter 17

Interview entry: May 17th, 2004A 9:38 AM

Excerpt footage (deleted scenes included) from documentary "THE UNEXPECTED HERO."

My name is Episko Doulus-Bird, social worker, humanitarian. I belong to the species of Yellow Headed Amazon Parros. My mother was the roommate of a loving, and free-spirited human. This was the same for her father, and his mother, her grandpa, and all others before. My father, on the other wing, was more of a mystery to me. Mom never discussed much about him. His background and fate were enigmatic to our family bloodline.

The era of WWII, as most may know, lasted from 1939A to 1945B, where the continents of South America, Africa and Europe were the center of an epic warfare. In addition, it was also a year of big change for us birds. The main axis power known as AVIACHT was under the tyrannical rule of King Helios, a cunning, yet merciless dictator who wanted nothing more than to see the last of humankind crumble before his talon. Personally, I don't really blame him for how he became the Helios we know of today.

As the history textbooks go, before he started pillaging villages and massacring towns, he was simply an innocent Spix macaw chick, living a quiet life in the Amazon. His mother was a matriarch in her section of the jungle, a position Helios was undoubtedly proud of. Every bird lived amongst each other, without a care in the world.

Then, one morning, a group of protesting loggers charged into their territory, calling out against the limit barrier in Brazil. Now, because of their "unfair" treatment, a torch and picket sign didn't seem to be the best way to catch their attention. So, they brought axes and chainsaws and started to chop away. Helios was playing with his siblings in the canopy just above their nest when they heard the buzzing sound of loggers approaching nearer, and nearer. His father and mother swooped up the family and flew away from their doomed home.

There was fire, smoke and ashes wherever they glided by. Then, the unspeakable happened. His mother and father left him and his siblings abandoned under a nearby hole in a tree and flew off to battle the blaze. Then, all was quiet, all was still. After an hour or two of waiting, the three of them flew out to search for the fate of their parents. Within half an hour of frantic search, Helios saw on the forest floor, Mother and Father: beaten, scarred and…dead. It was at that moment something changed within him. Something just snapped. He had transformed from an innocent, young bird, into a fierce tyrant hungry for revenge.

In the years that followed, Helios was taken under the wing of his fierce, disciplinary uncle. Soon, he started to become aggressive towards those that disagreed with him; his attack and defense skills improved sharply, winning the heart of his new guardian. Helios' fascination with weaponry and power grew stronger by the day. His leadership quality was beyond exception, especially towards his brother and sister. But most of all, he now despised humans more than anything else, hoping one day they would be eradicated from the earth.

He was not alone in this hatred he carried. As he grew older, almost every Macaw and Parrot would flock to his large tree. He would tell them of the wickedness of the flat heads and how never to trust them. Soon, whenever he went, he established a cult-following. The words of genocide and destruction of which he preached chirped like a newborn chick in the ears of those with beaks and wings. Ultimately, he and his fine-feathered brethren named themselves "AVIACHT" and swiftly took control of nearly the entire Amazon jungle, blowing away any human related activity. Eventually they spread beyond South America. Flocks of hundreds of thousands flew east and north of the Atlantic and took hold of the perimeter of western Africa and much of Europe.

AVIACHT carried with them herpetological capsules, which they developed after successfully infiltrating South American labs and testing facilities. Inside these capsules were modified seeds into which they injected growth hormones that allowed them to grow and spawn at alarming rates. If you were to drop one of the seeds in the middle of, oh, let's say, Barcelona, it would first sprout into a giant Amazon tree. Next, its roots would take hold of every street and sidewalk in the city, evolving into moss-covered vines, enveloping almost every building and house within a seven-mile radius. The vines, themselves would sprout even more seeds, which would drop to the ground and quickly transform into random vegetations, covering the entire city until it was unrecognizable. Within three days flat, the city would be transformed into another Amazon jungle, with a few buildings still standing, as relics of what it once was.

So many homes and lives were destroyed during the uprising including…my human friends. I still have the painful memory of watching them get shot in the back of their heads by feathered mercenaries. Even the children couldn't win the hearts of the assassins.

"Go fellow brethren." One of them said to me as they carried the bodies to a nearby pile. "You are free!"

Free. But at what cost? Until then, I thought I knew what it meant. For so long, I thought it meant for all creatures great and small to live with one another, one sharing gifts and vice versa. Apparently, this was something on which Helios and his AVIACHT regime did not agree. After all, what is freedom for one species if the other is enslaved? How can you consider yourself an advocate of freedom if all you wish for is the elimination of those who had wronged you? That is why in the end, I decided not to partake in AVIACHT's actions.

It was a tough decision. For a while, I thought I was forsaking my own kind. After all, I was already aware of all the destruction humans were capable of doing. On the other hand, as descendant of a domesticated family, I knew I had seen an immense amount of goodness and compassion through a great many Homo sapiens. I knew this knowledge and experience would keep me going forward.

Now you're also probably wondering how I became aware of the capsules. Well, this was another reason why my secret would put a heavy burden on my conscience. See, I fell in love with a female Hyacinth, who would carry out the task of dropping them. Her name was Kaa-ell-aa, but most just called her Kana. She was a high-ranking commander who was appointed the grisly task of watching the imprisonment camps for any human escapees and killing them. I came across her a few days after the slaughtering of my human friends. I was hiding in an old, abandoned theater in Berlin when one of the most gorgeous looking birds came into my life. I mean, with her set of head and tail feathers, what avian gent couldn't resist? And those eyes of emerald and sapphire could hardly be ignored. Aside from her elegance and beauty, one thing that lured me to her was her quick wit and spunky behavior. She was a like a city girl with enough street smarts to fill a book. We did a lot together, I must admit. We went to parties, drank from Brazilian nuts, played games, even did a few naughty pranks to her superiors. It was only when we flew over the AVIACHT-occupied cities that I realized the scope of the damage she had wrought.

Wherever we went, the town was covered in rainforest flora. While it was all good for us parrots, the humans were sealed in a large, unkempt ghetto, barred from the rest of the world. There was at least one corpse every day, lying in the moss-covered streets. There were even a few occasions where I saw a human child get shot right before my eyes for no reason. I still remember always staring down with my beak agape, wishing I could do something to help that poor kid.

What I remember most was how every human had a yellow patch sewn onto their shirts, coats and jackets. These patches were shaped like the symbol you'd see in a public men's bathroom, with a large "SAPE" engraved in the middle. In addition, they all had a tattoo clawed onto their left forearms. Each one was a label: "LOGGER" "POLLUTER" "USER" "HUNTER" "CONSUMER" words that echoed the vices of the human race. Even the children had their arms tarnished, though the names were less harsh: "Brat" "Spoiler" "Whiner" "Eater," names most children would call each other in a circle of acquaintances.

Day in, day out, my girlfriend and I would spread our wings and fly over that forsaken hellhole. There I was able to see everything, from the children playing a game of stick and poke the corpse, to an elderly gentleman sitting on the ground, breathing his last breath. I could hear the sounds of dozens of lives crying out in hunger and anguish. Almost every day I was able to map out their situation, and almost every night I cried in secrecy for their fate. One human would be lucky enough to get two tiny sacks of crumbs to last the day. Their condition began to worsen so much, there would be those who would contemplate eating each other, even going so far as killing themselves to have their corpses eaten by their loved ones.

Kana, in contrast, just laughed at the prospect of human suffering. Every night she would go to one of the outposts, swoop down, and peck on the skulls of a chosen human passerby. She would then proceed in taunting them in the cruelest way calling them: “SAPES” “POLLUTERS” and “FLAT FACES!” She’d start nipping them with her talons and tossing them around like an old rag doll to her content. Even long after she shook them to death, she would still gnaw at their skin and continue to do so until way into the night.

Now that I was able to openly judge her actions. I could see why she enjoyed it. Personally, I don’t blame her for how she turned cynical against the Upright Beings. As a chick, she became witness to an entire flattening of her home. The process of their deforestation was slow and merciless. On nights clear and clean, she would tell me how she still had recurring dreams of her home canopy succumbing to the fire below. Every fruitful moment, every treasured memory, from sweet air on top, to rich root below, was gone in an instant. Though she and her mother flew away sans a scratch, her sister and father were not so lucky. The last time she saw them, they disappeared amongst the climbing smoke and ashes, along with other doomed, feathered lives. With a situation like that, it seems hard to forgive an entire species.

Now in a circumstance such as my own, I can understand her grief and sorrow. But as a member of a long chain of domesticated parrots, it's hard to shake off the love and care of which these humans were capable. Then again, I really loved Kana just as much. This is what made my decision harder.

Yes, against the principles of the ruling Axis power, I made a rather life-changing decision. I was to gather any human prisoners I could find, provide them with food, clothing and shelter and lead them to my cottage at the edge of town. From there, I would fly to a trader's exchange in the Netherlands, one of the last human strongholds in Europe, and speed back with a sack of Euros. As this monotonous cycle continued, the money would finally be saved, which I used to purchase passports and a boat rental back in Poland. Though pretending I would sail solo, I would store the humans in a rather spacious cargo hold, sailing them to America.

I was aware of the risk which lay in front of me. Not only was my livelihood at stake, but also my reputation among the avian community. In many ways, I would have to forsake my roots. Would I be setting an example by benefitting them? That is a question I could not answer.

Anyway, one parrot could not accomplish this feat alone. He needed backup. he needed reinforcements. So, I was able to acquaint myself with twenty squirrels, fifteen mice, ten rabbits, five raccoons and a few other woodland critters. You see, though humans and creatures of this area had their numerous grudges, they had begun to understand their plight. Their coniferous forest was being overrun by the artificial jungle. Though as good as it may sound, these northern woodland creatures could not adapt to this new environment. Thus, they joined the resistance right away.

There was Gios, a half husky, half wolf breed, Photon, a field mouse who made the most exquisite meals from the most ordinary of sources, Dadelus, a superb rabbit craftsman who could meld items into gadgets needed for survival, and of course, our well-committed and beloved Dr. Ankhia, a fox who would sit beside a wounded soul for days on end.

But I'm running off on a tangent. For a while, the trickiest part of this mission wasn't getting the humans to safety but gaining trust among these critters. They knew firsthand as to how prejudice and unforgiving AVIACHT was to them. Regardless of how well-meaning any visitation of my species would be, any exotic bird (or exotic animal) would pose as a threat to their livelihood. Thus, to ensure a more peaceful agreement, I transferred back and forth a few letters to their headquarters, hoping a meeting would be scheduled. To my luck, as well as surprise, an opening was found for me.

I arrived with the customary greeting of sharpened twigs and bladed stones. It was clear they were ready for anything. With calmness and ease, I reminded them of our meeting, to which they hesitantly lowered their weapons and escorted me to the meeting tree.

Coincidently, Ara, a red squirrel and admirer of human activity, was a part of the forest council, located at the center of their habitat. Due to her knowledge of humans, she was ranked the position of "foreign" relations. It was she I was to speak to, and she with whom I was to plan the rescue.

At first, she thought this was a joke. Why would she trust a parrot like me? But I explained my background, my association with humans and admiration for them, thus slowly winning her heart. But the real challenge was coaxing the rest of the forest council. After all, they were indeed witness to deforestation and pollution. But, after a few weeks of bickering and coaxing, I was able to convince them it was their fight as well. In addition, I was able to present them with a few human items, such as a painting, a music box, and a reel of one of Chaplin's films. The woodland creatures indulged in them right away. Thus, trust was established and we could begin our rescue.

Yet like all rescues, especially in these circumstances, there was a bond that had to be broken. My love, my beautiful Kana, had to be discarded, and on top of it, I was risking the act of disowning my own species. But what is an exodus from slavery without a form of sacrifice?

Chapter 18

The New York Retirement Center is situated on a small island surrounded by the Hudson River, located about three to five miles west of the center of town. It's an adequate complex, suitable for any American retiree. With its spacious comforts and roomy apartments, one would be satisfied to die there. The employees and volunteers are exceptional, always greeting the senior individuals with a welcoming smile and a heart of gold and attending to every basic need and want. In addition, complimented by its five-star cafe, game nights and its top-notch library, one could easily confuse it for a grand scale hotel. A great many of the incoming and outgoing individuals who have made their stay in these walls have been highly regarded in the intellectual community, among them being, Episko Doulus.

But the true feature which stands out among all others is its vast outdoor garden. Located in the back of the complex, its vegetation boasts a vast array flora and plant life, with greenery that would make Central Park envious. Every gravel path, every bed of flowers, every sight and sound seem like something out of a fairy tale, down to the last sapling. It was here Episko chose a perch that hung by a tree as his final resting place. Though I will never know, I do wonder what exactly Uncle Epi was thinking, in those last few moments? I hope it was a thought without regret.

I arrive at the entrance, where I am greeted by a mortician and escorted to the garden. The body of Episko was found last night in a pile of soft soil and fallen petals. Though it certainly wasn't an ideal death, at least he didn't go in agony. I give a nod, confirming it's him as the mortician picks up the body and carries it to the morgue.

The room is closely monitored at a nice eight degrees celsius, each body carefully preserved in a bag of mylar surrounded by a germ-free environment. Even the ones who expired a week ago look freshly dead.

By now, Epi's feathers are starting to fall off the wings as they are no longer connected to living tissue. That being the case, the procedure of preserving the body needs to be done quickly, but carefully. No one wants to see a rotting corpse in a casket.

After preserving the body, Alan is escorted to Epi's living quarters to attend to any final documents. The walls are filled with books and written papers. hobbies an elderly citizen would find amusing. On a coffee table there are a few picture frames, a cup of cold un-sipped tea, and a worn album, memories of a life well spent. As I walk over to open it, in comes Epi's former dog caretaker.

Here I receive a death certificate, indicating the date and time of Epi's expiration. Next, I'm told to cancel any bank statements and last-minute credit card charges. This follows discontinuation of any heating bills, utility statements, memberships, insurance claims, tax claims, etc. Next, any unaccounted-for mail would be delivered directly to his apartnest. The reason being that he'll be put in charge of breaking the news to Epi's friends. It will also be his duty to donate any unwanted items to charity, since throwing anything away would result in either a fine or community service.

As I forage through Epi's personal belongings, fumbling through knick knacks and memorabilia I come across a rather old parchment that looks like it hasn't been touched in years. I tediously unfold it, making sure not to cause any more tears or creases, and see it's a copy of an old passport. I look at the bottom right-hand corner to see whom it's for. The name says: Mageck Kiewpenski (Sam Whitestone).

I remember the times. The times when our parents were at their worst. When they would wake up screaming from memories of their anguish. As if Helios had truly scarred them for life. I prayed each day that I would find some way to break this cycle, so we could be a true family once more.

I sit down and further examine these objects, wondering how my mother and father could endure so much, yet raise two healthy children. Perhaps this lies in how they protected their siblings, from which must've sprouted their courage to move on.

Chapter 19

The jungle seemed like a most unforgiving terrain for the both of us. With its sharp rocks, dense atmosphere, and merciless predators, the two of us felt more vulnerable than ever. We were forced to crouch down every waking moment, so as not to be seen by Helios's forces. I still remember the groans and whines my sister would make.

"My legs hurt," Izobel would moan. "I'm tired. I need to rest."

But we couldn't rest. We had to be on constant move. We just couldn't let them find us. So, as hard it was, I was forced to ignore her cries for help, only stopping for the occasional fallen fruit and trickles of water.

Every day, I would look up through the dense canopy and see at least one soldier flying overhead, scourging for any escaped prisoners. When one flew near to us, we would hide under a large tree root, covering our mouths and sweating profusely. Even the tiniest sound could be heard above by the soldiers. The two of us would notice how the Amazon vegetation was slowly beginning to eat away the redwood trees. Once they left our perimeter, we continued on with our destination-less journey. Yet even then, a soldier could be lurking on top of a branch, waiting to strike any human trespasser. Those twelve tense days were perhaps the most frightening of my life.

It was now dusk over the ever-expanding jungle. The sun was shining its last glimmer of light for the day. The dirt coated path that once served as a road was becoming dimmer and dimmer to make out. We needed to find higher ground and fast. By now Izobel had become so weak that the body weight in her legs had vanished. It was at that moment, as I was carrying her fragile and malnourished body, that we heard the faint sound of wings flapping against the thick air. Whoever, or whatever it was, it was getting closer. We were able to make out the creature. It was perhaps another Macaw scouting for any escaped humans. We tiptoed under the nearest tree we could find, waiting for it to go away. But it was too late. We were spotted. We were caught.

As the sound of flapping died down, we slowly turned to our right as a large, ominous, feathered shadow overcast our bodies. My sister and I opened our jaws, ready to scream, but the action was interrupted by two large talons that swooped against our mouths and noses.

"Shhh. It's okay. It's okay. Please don't scream. Listen. Listen to me!" said the bird with his appendages still pressed to our faces. "My name is Episko. Yes, I'm a parrot. But I'm a good parrot. I'm not gonna hurt you. I'm gonna help you. But you have to stay quiet until I say so. Understood?"

We nodded our heads as tears ran down my sister's cheek. As the moonlight lit the forest floor, and his wings balanced midair against the wind, we saw how his color scheme was a bright, daisy-like yellow. The top of his head sprouted a few unkempt feathers as if he just got out of bed. On his back was a small sack of basic goods and needs, enough to satisfy a tired traveler.

"Now when I let go of your lips," Episko continued, "you're not going to scream. Understood?"

We nodded our heads again.

"Okay. One… Two… Three."

His talons came off our faces like tape-against-skin as he guided us out of the fungi filled trench.

"Follow me," he proclaimed. And with those words, he swooped into the sky, giving us the signal to trek his path. I took a nearby rock with sharp pointy edge and placed it in the pocket of my recently scavenged clothes. You never know whether you're being lured into a trap or not.

As we ran like wild dogs against the night air, the moonlight cast its first beam of visibility on the rocky path. For a while, the sound of our breath and feet crunching against the moss and vegetation below was all we could hear. Other than that, it was dead silent as if all but us had frozen in time. The silhouette of Episko against the full moon was mysterious yet reassuring as if he were a silent guardian, ready to protect any human running astray.

Off in the distance, we could see what looked like the shape of a well-sized cottage. Could this be our safe-haven? A place to finally rest our feet? As we got closer the smell of prepared food and herbal spices made our mouths water in anticipation. The material of brick and wood was easier to make out. A light could be seen flickering inside. Someone must've still been attending to this human made structure. Finally, with numb legs and clammy hands, we had reached the entrance.

Episko gently glided down from the sky and grabbed the door handle with his talons.

"You can talk when we get inside," he assured us.

The door slowly opened as we entered the main room. It was a simple living space complete with a table, chairs, a fire kettle with utensils, a couch, a fridge, and a king size bed. Certainly, wasn't our home, but we knew it would do.

"Thank you so much, Episko," I said to him as I took a seat.

"You can call me Uncle Epi," he replied.

It was at that moment he flew onto the wooden floorboard and pecked his beak against a hollow piece. Then, to our surprise, a trap door appeared beneath him. He gave us the signal to follow his lead, but not before looking outside to check if any AVIACHT patrollers were passing by. Then he gave us the "all clear" and we cautiously walked down the soft wooden steps. We could hear murmuring and chattering beneath our feet as we walked deeper down the secret passage. What place was this? Was it a refuge, or a torture chamber? What was going to happen to us?

Then, at the bottom of the steps, we heard a cry of joy from a familiar voice.

"Izzy? Izzy!" cried our mother as she sprinted towards us from the darkness of the cellar.

"Mama! Mama!" cried my sister as the two of us ran to her.

We met with an embrace we wished would last forever. It felt so good to see a familiar face. Then, the cellar lights turned on, revealing what appeared to be almost a hundred humans backed against the wall. They walked towards us, congratulating us on our survival while my sister clung to my mother's arm. Soon, out of the camouflage of the wooden interior, appeared what looked like a few woodland critters. Among them were deer, rabbits, mice, raccoons, squirrels, and other varieties of forest animals. Behind them were clearly cots occupied by malnourished and wounded human patients. One of them coughed in agony as a field mouse helped him swallow a tablet. Another was being sedated by a red squirrel so they could treat his broken leg. Surrounding the cots were blankets, carts of food, jugs of water, wrapped clothing and other basic needs.

Was this a hospital of some sort? Whatever it was, we were thankful for the charity given to us, especially when we could walk no further. Before I knew it, we were finally clothed, nourished, and given our own separate cots. Izzy had already fallen asleep the moment she laid down. I looked at her face and thought about all we went through these past few weeks. No child, so young and innocent should've gone through such turmoil and sadness.

After a few stitches and bandages, our non-human attendees ushered me to the center of the floor. We saw ourselves surrounded by other victims. Some had scratches dug across their face, others had an arm or ear removed. There were even those too traumatized to move, shaken and stricken by the horrors of what they saw. Strangely though, their expressions were in a relaxed state – frozen yet calm, stiff yet serene, as if relieved from an unspeakable torture. Some had their hands squeezed in the paws of rabbits and bobcats, easing the prick of a medicine shot. Others were supported by deer and goats, attempting to regain their balance.

I was not sure what lay ahead of us, or if this was an elaborate trap, or not. But I was too weak to ponder on that idea. I laid down and slightly turned my head, and saw my mother and sister, breathing soundlessly in their cot. For the first time, I could close my eyes peacefully. The last scurrying mouse blew out the lantern as we all fell into the best sleep we'd had in days.

Chapter 20

By 10 A.M, Alan makes it to the funeral home – the final resting place for a family friend. As he steps out of his autopod, the funeral director (a badger) greets him with a sympathetic gesture. Alan takes out his card and presents it to him in an orderly fashion. The badger gives a nod of approval and escorts him to a room filled with grieving friends and acquaintances, both human and animal alike. Even Kana, his old girlfriend, has built up the courage to show up. Upon noticing his presence, members of the crowd gather around him, patting him on the back, shaking his hand, and expressing their condolences. Kana, on the other hand, just stares at him silently, gives a nod of respect, and flies over to her chair in the corner.

To his right is a large collection of photos and memorabilia pertaining to Episko's life. Alan walks over and sheds a tear as he writes his name among the scrabble of other signatures. The crowd of mourners share a joke or two, reminiscing on Episko's achievements, memories of their experiences with him, a joke he once told, a tale he once wrote, laughing at the good times, and forgetting the bad times. Such is what Episko would've wanted for this moment.

The church where their fine-feathered friend will be buried is a rather welcoming place. But on this day, all seems mysterious and uncertain. The sky is painted a deep gray, with one dark cloud looming over the other. However, the interior appears to contrast its stony exterior. Among its ancient features are a display of marble pillars with tapestries of saints and patrons tied to each side above the pews. In addition, there are scented, half-melted candles standing upon every windowsill, fuming the atmosphere with burning wax.

But of all the features, one that truly stands out are the stained-glass windows themselves. Each one a jewel in its own craft. Though the day is dreary, a little reflection from a shard of light shines through the art, transforming the natural luminescence into a kaleidoscope of every hue imaginable.

It seems as though the whole human community of New York showed up for this solemn occasion. Each survivor a storyteller in their own right. The senior citizens have probably told their children and grandchildren a hundred times about how they were saved by a yellow Macaw and his band of woodland misfits. As solemn klezmer music plays up in the high registers, every human and non-human takes a turn to gaze into the coffin where Episko will sleep an eternal slumber. The wooden structure is of recycled mahogany, indicating his origins. And on the lid is a single yellow feather serving as the centerpiece.

Many of his closest friends and acquaintances come up to the podium to share their words of remembrance. But none of them seems to be more heart lifting than my father's, who can barely stand up due to his deteriorating health. To him, his friend's death is almost as heart wrenching as his wife's.

In his eulogy, he states how Uncle Epi (as he called him), was always the loyal type, a tough individual who'd never abandon his duty.

Now it is time to carry the coffin to its final resting place. With a heavy heart, seven members of the procession who were closest to him pick up the coffin and proceed to transport their dead friend to the graveyard. Among them are, my father, my brother, a wolf-dog named Dilis, an owl named Elch-mocht, a squirrel named Ara and me.

Diary Log: 1936B

I am currently in the act of observing a few Homo sapiens from my tree branch. This is quite a treat for me. I've never seen so many up this close before at the same time.

From this vantage point, it appears as though the two males on the wooden platform are engaged in a courtship ritual where one acts like an authoritarian figure, while the other takes part in what they call a "COM-IC RE-LEAF" position. Meanwhile, the other humans, who sit comfortably in their wooden chairs, have focused their attention on the act with great intensity.

Now with closer examination, as the duo continues their ritual, I can see that the audience laughs more whole heartedly at the misfortunes of the authoritarian rather than at the comic relief. I find this chemistry very foreign yet very fascinating at the same time.

I hope to share this newfound information with my wood-dwelling-friends, just as soon as they start to accept my research on human behavior. I doubt if that will truly happen, yet I can't help thinking how the forces of nature work in mysterious ways, even in the most unexpected of circumstances.

Of all species with which my eyes have crossed paths, humans are the most complex. I am not sure here whether they are putting up this show for personal gain or are attempting to spread their knowledge to other creatures. Either way, the performance is quite entertaining. I will be further monitoring this abnormal ritual of theirs in the hopes of importing it into our own customs.

Chapter 21

My name is Aur-yien (Are-yeen), (or Ara, as I prefer to be called). Now I know from first glance I'm just your average nut-chucking squirrel. But if you take time to get to know me, I am clearly not your typical tree dwelling resident. My colleagues would say I was at the top of the food chain for a squirrel, excelling in such basic skills as foraging, burrowing, climbing, jumping and even fighting. As surprising as it may sound, a squirrel, as in a European born animal such as myself, am able to master the ancient, imported art of Jiu-Jitsu, able to knock out an opponent without a break in concentration, even if they measure ten times larger than me. Yes, I am one female with whom you do not want to pick a fight. This quality of mine would become an extreme advantage for Episko's rescue project. In addition, I became one his closest friends and most trustworthy aides.

However, this does not make me a hard-shelled animal. As the old shrink says, never judge a book by its cover. On the contrary, ever since my first sighting, I have always developed a deep fascination with human behavior. Though I admit, I was no stranger to the cruelty of man, I still couldn't help but feel sorry for their plight. Every day, while collecting my daily sustenance of nuts and berries, I would stop to ponder at the sight of a young couple, who just happened to have made the decision that day to explore the woods. In my eyes, they were the most adorable, yet most fascinating of all creatures. One minute they can be cynical and unsympathetic, and then gentle and entertaining the next.

I was fascinated by the way they moved their bodies (how they ran on two legs, how they survived with little fur, how they showed emotion with their small faces). I kept track of every activity in a personal log of mine. Now that I mention it, for a time I thought I was a scientist, and the children were my specimens. Sometimes I wondered what it would be like to be one of them. But I knew back then it would be impossible.

Anyway, my relationship with the yellow macaw named Episko began just a few years after the war broke out. AVIACHT and the axis powers were already taking control of most of Europe's borders, including one too many evergreen forests. As we critters expected, our home was under threat as well. Our daily food supply was already running thin; thus, we began to ration our sustenance. One of my rodent brethren would've been lucky to find a single acorn per day. In addition, our relatives from other parts of the woods were driven out by the foreign jungles and forced to hide out in one of our burrows. Clearly, we realized by now this wasn't just a war against humans, but rather, it was something I began to take very personally.

So, being efficient, we prepared ourselves the best way we could. We took fallen branches and made them into spears, gathered nut shells and carved them into helmets, and found soft shallow ground and dug underground fortresses. Our falcon eagle, and owl friends watched the skies for any exotic soldiers, while the deer, rabbits, and field mice scourged for any elephant, wolf, or boar tracks. All of us were on high alert, wondering when or where the enemy forces would strike next.

One afternoon, after an intense morning of foraging what remained on the forest floor, a sparrow scout swooped down with a note tied to his foot from an unspecified source. As always, with any foreign note, I immediately scurried away and presented it to the council. The strange letter was wrapped in a parchment of bark and string with a message:

I Come in Peace.

At first, we were skeptical of its origin. The way we saw it, it was either another part of the woods sending in reinforcements, or a trick sent by Tusken-Reichstag or Hoggendragg to lure us into a deadly trap. Either way, we carefully unfolded the parchment and read away.

Fellow citizens of the Northern European Woods:

My name is Episko Doulus. I am a yellow macaw residing in solitude at about 75-100 KM East from your threatened forest. I do not desire to trick you, bribe you, nor persuade you in anyway. I am here to ask your assistance in a project that I can assure you will benefit your precious habitat.

To those of you unaware of the situation at hand, a genocide has been brought by the Axis powers. A plan, (or 'final solution' as AVIACHT calls it) is being executed as we speak. By the order of King Helios, every Homo sapien is to be tortured, imprisoned, and/or forced into hard labor for "crimes" committed. Everywhere I fly, these fragile creatures lives and homes will be threatened by the incoming forces. Towns have been destroyed, antiquities have been lost, and individuals, both human and pet, have been gunned to death.

That being the case, I have recently conceived a plan in which I will gather as many humans as possible and transport them first to Argentina and then to the United States. But unlike other rescue missions, I cannot succeed in this one alone.

I am in need of the assistance of any non-Axis members within a 200-300 KM radius in order to perfectly execute this rather dangerous plan. Now I know, understand and even sympathize with the grudge you all hold against the human race. But if we do not do something about this threatening force, I predict this will not only be a war against humans, but every non-ally of AVIACT as well.

For anyone wishing to support and contribute to the mission at hand, it is imperative you read the enclosed instructions tied to the back of this parchment. I pray you say, "Yes" and allow me to fly over for further details.

Best wishes,

Episko

We held a meeting in front of the large oak tree. Skepticism was obviously brewing among the head council.

"Is this some kind of joke?" asked a chipmunk

"What kind of game are they playing at?" asked a weasel.

"Why should we save humans if they attacked us first?" asked a badger.

"We are already in more than enough turmoil as it is," a quail commented.

'Order please order!" cried the head owl, to which everyone calmed down.

"We are wild animals – not savages! I know it is not in our nature to trust the Homo sapien species, but it might be our last chance to defend ourselves against Helios's forces. Now, among us is someone who has taken the liberty of studying this enigmatic species."

"Aur-Yien?" said a skunk guard. "Step forward."

Time after time, I had begged the council to publicly teach of humans, but it always ended in rejection. This was the first moment I was granted permission to discuss my findings.

Hopefully, they would take it with a grain of salt and listen. I walked to the front of the woodland crowd, not knowing what to expect or what would come out of it. I scrambled through my knapsack, carefully unfolded my parchments of studies and laid them out on an old, nearby tree stump. Every human-related moment I had scribbled and sketched out was now here for everyone to see.

"As you can plainly see," I started to say as I passed each image among the circle. "Humans are a rather mysterious group of specimens. One minute they appear hostile and barbaric, and next thing you know they turn gentle and vulnerable. Through these studies I believe we have an excellent opportunity in our midst."

The hours rolled on as the council examined my findings, some with raised eyebrows, others with snorting nostrils. After a while I was told to go home as a decision would be made tomorrow.

Night came and passed. I tossed and turned in my leaf bed, hoping they'd accept my findings. Though I was anxious, I felt guilty as well. I knew, the human race committed acts beyond forgiveness. They spoiled many parts of the world including our own. Somehow, I felt as though I was forsaking my natural roots. Yet, I couldn't shake off my love for this species. Yes, I must confess, I was obsessed with saving the very race that tried to exterminate our own. I arrived at the oak tree first thing in the early morning. The counsel was still staring at my findings and mumbling a subject or two. Then, they focused their attention on me. The fate of all my work and effort would be decided now. After whispers in each other's ears, they cleared their throats.

"Aur-Yien," said the head owl. "We have come to our decision."

My hind legs shook in anticipation.

"After a great many hours of talk and debate, we have come to a narrow vote that your findings are indeed of value to us."

"Though a large minority of us here will remain skeptical and indifferent on this subject," an elder rabbit added.

"Nevertheless, given the circumstances," an elder field mouse added, "it seems as though we have no choice but to help with the survival of these humans, but under one condition."

"So as to prevent any further threats or attempts at hostility." The head owl declared. "We're to keep a close eye on the actions committed by the human escapees. Shall any questionable action occur, they are to be banished from our terrain. And that includes the rouge parrot. We have seen far too many broken promises from them. Tomorrow, we will announce how we plan to proceed."

I bowed in respect, collected my drawings, and returned to my nest. Finally, I knew all my observations had not been done in vain. As I settled into my bed of leaves and flowers, I started to wonder what outcome this would bring. Soon I began to realize that I have never pondered the consequences. After all, by siding with these humans, we could become an easy target for the axis powers. This war was not only endangering the human race, but now, every aspect of our existence.

The next morning, I woke up and jumped out of bed like a popped cork, not even minding to brush my fur. I rushed to my study, grabbed all I could and scurried out of my nest. I ran with all my might to the high council tree, pushing through the bark and into the large hole where the heads stood. My heart was drumming a million beats a minute, and my paws fidgeted in anticipation. I knew today would be the moment of truth, a moment that would alter my entire life's work.

There, before me, stood the forest council, whispering words I will never know. Before I could compose myself, the chief owl, head of the woodland birds, stared at me with his wide golden eyes. Then he gave me a slight nod, allowing me to have a seat. He cleared his throat, and after a moment's hesitation, he spoke.

"State your name."

"Aur-Yien," I replied. "Red Squirrel, resident of the East sector of the high woodlands."

"It has come to our conclusion this predicament is no longer a threat to only humankind. We too, the creatures of the woodlands, are at risk of being overthrown by these foreign flyers. That being said, it is with great reluctance, yet with great need, that we must comply with these demands and save the human species, if that means saving ourselves. Aur-Yien, your friend's proposal is hereby approved."

A smile grew across my face, but a small one so as not to flaunt myself. The other elders muttered in disbelief and confusion at the sound of this proclamation.

"We shall discuss this in further detail tomorrow morning." The owl concluded. "Meeting adjourned."

And with the tap of his talon, the elders scurried away. At last, my counseling and advice was acknowledged. Some of the critters scavenged for clothing in nearby abandoned towns, others would scour the woodlands for edible food and water, and a few crafted themselves some tools to build a large cellar for the humans to live and hide. Perhaps now the Woodlands would learn more about the enigmatic creature of humankind.

I gathered my findings and ran back to my nest. I could

hardly contain myself as all the excitement tingled across my furry body. I would at long last get the chance to study these Homo sapien creatures up close, and maybe learn more of their customs and practices first paw. After all, it had always been my dream to help create an ANTHROMALIA.

Chapter 22

Of all my encounters, I never realized how heavy Episko had gotten for a bird. Even with the assistance of five other individuals, the task of bringing him from casket to grave feels like a challenge. Perhaps his assimilation into a domesticated lifestyle had its negative consequences. Indeed, during his final days, his feathers had grown thicker and bulkier to the touch, and his neck had almost disappeared under the weight of his head.

The sky is free of any showers and storms, as the casket is finally laid under the hot gleaming sun. The cemetery is unique among others, since every animal grave is a large plant of some sort, creating the illusion of large, mythical garden found in storybooks of old. In accordance with tropical avian tradition, Epi is placed on a sandstone bed of moss and flowers, tucked underneath the hollow of an Amazonian tree.

Then, among the crowd of mourners, a chorus of birds, who belong to the family of the deceased, soar up above the canopies of nearby organic structures, singing perhaps the most lyrical of hymns any living soul would be capable of hearing. Their voices ring across the trunks and roots of their surroundings, almost as if a chamber of organs had been conjured.

All is calm now. The voices die down. A human priest (approved by the Human-Animal relations committee for such an event), recites a few prayers and gives the signal to my aunt Izzy. She is a small human with a slightly rotund, yet motherly stature. Her apparel is the usual hue of funeral black, complete with a hat and shades. Though she tries to hide her grief, I can see her lip quivering in anguish. She takes out a piece of paper and begins her speech.

"Here, on this day, we have come to bid farewell to one of our greatest saviors. Episkos Doulos, or Epi as his friends called him, was, however, more than a hero. He was dear friend to all of those he rescued. Even more, he seemed very attached to humans. I remember, when a human would first encounter him, he would have a firm grip on them, literally and figuratively. Many say this is due to his human upbringing, or, perhaps, simply because of a fascination with us. But we knew differently.

There will be those among us who will question his very actions. Some will even wish to shun him from the textbooks of history, wishing to view him as a strange, uncanny figure within the memories of those of us who claim to have known him best. Yet we know better. We saw a gallant, brave and loyal individual, who against all possible odds, defied the expectations of humanity. Epi taught us that humanity does not lie only in the confines of one species. It's in all of us, a lesson that will not be forgotten.

So, however much his kind may have differed from his ideals and values, however much a few of his brethren had distanced themselves from him and however much he stood out among his species, let his departure be a beacon of hope for all, both parrot and human.

EPI, we will miss you."

The crowd gives a heartfelt applause as she leaves the podium. Now everyone gathers around the casket. Each is given a small piece of mahogany leaf, representing Episko's natural heritage. We all take turns to gently drop the pieces onto their friend, as a symbol of their need to let go of the dead.

Finally, Epi's relatives all fly once more and form a circle formation as they descend on the edges of the coffin. With one mighty pull, they lift their loved one out of the casket into air. Our deceased is given one last feel of the sky. They spread out his fragile wings as they blow against the wind. Then, they descend back down, where they gently place him back in the casket. They close the lid, place a row of petals around the exposed feather, and wrap the coffin in fine mahogany and tree sap.

One by one, the spectators pick up a shovel and gather bits of soil in each cusp. We all owe him our life and our future, and though not much of a returning favor, it still shows our deepest gratitude. We sing a few songs and recite several chants until the last participant sprinkles his share of dirt. Epi, our Epi, has laid his surface on the earth for the last time, before entering that eternal slumber.

Chapter 23

Excerpt from Episko Doulus's personal journal

Days had rolled on and turned into weeks with hardly an incident. The human refugees went by and by their daily routines. Below the cabin they had created their own society unscathed by any intruders. Storage rooms had become small houses, the pantry had turned into a mess hall, and the center had become their own town square. There was even a small shop in the right corner for whoever wanted free clothing. All had been re-furbished and re-decorated, like a village underneath the surface.

And yet, fear was looming among their souls. To simply ascend to the surface was a life-or-death situation. One day the sky could be clear of any creatures, and the next it could be swarming with Helios's forces. Whenever a human needed to get fresh air, I would assign our owl scout, Nuxian, to scourge the area. Once it was clear, the human was allowed to arise and move freely on the surface, but not without the close surveillance of a field mouse or a sparrow.

It was one evening, however, that truly lifted my spirits. It was the holiday season for the refugees – a time where rest and charity were intertwined. There, at such a time of year, the underground bunkers seemed warm and welcoming to any traveler. Everyone had huddled into crowds of different activities. Twelve rabbits were telling a story to the children, a bear was playing peek-a-boo with the infants, and about half a dozen teenage humans were playing a made-up game of sorts with several raccoons, mice and deer. It was not much, but it surely was a taste of heaven.

In appreciation for our hospitality, the refugees would occasionally present us with a token or two of their immense gratitude. This would usually be either a simple meal, a tattered clothing item, a carved piece of wood, or on a very rare occasion, a makeshift toy. In addition, the humans would do their best to entertain us with a song, a dance, a tale or game of unknown origin.

Yet, among all the presents we animals were given, one seemed to stand out among the rest. It was towards the end of the evening, as everyone was settling in to their sleeping quarters, when a young gentleman by the name of Andrzej called out to Ara, who was turning in after a long day of excursion. The gift was a small, yet elegant ballroom gown sewn by the most delicate hands. It was just small enough to fit on the red squirrel. She gazed in awe at its beauty and texture and quickly tried to put it on.

"This is...this is incredible," she spoke with awe.

"It was once a dress to place on a doll," Andrzej described. "I was going to save it for my brother and I to clothe one of dolls in our shop. But since that is impossible now, I think today would be the best time to give it to someone...like you."

Then he artfully fastened it on her until it fit just right. He carefully shattered an empty bottle and used a piece as a mirror. The red squirrel gasped in wonder as she twirled in her new, elegant outfit.

"I always heard about how you make clothes," she said. "But I never thought I would look so good in one. Your father and mother would've been proud."

She leaped onto Adrzej's chest and spread her furry arms across as far as she could, as if trying to give him a hug. For so long, she had waited to touch a human, feeling the embrace as she pressed her cheek on his shirt, making true, physical contact on the smooth surface of a Homo sapien.

'Was this true, inter-species love?' I thought to myself as I witnessed the scene. 'Can a feral animal truly love a civilized creature?'

It was then I began to worry even more about the fate of this complex species. After all, the destiny of any life form lies in the actions of their choosing. I felt, in a spiritual sense, as if I was emotionally connected to each of these humans living underground, as if it was my duty to protect them from any dissonance and make sure none would go astray. Perhaps, just as much as human naturalists once surrounded themselves with species foreign to them, my long period of time under the care of humans made me comprehend the emotions and needs of which they carry. Like us, they have feelings, weaknesses, doubts, and of course, desires. In short, "WE WERE NOT SO DIFFERENT, THEM AND US."

As the night settled in and the humans fell into a deep slumber, we animals went on our nightly routine of scourging the area. On this special evening, I was to attend a special reception to which I was invited by Kana. It was at this time that Helios was visiting this area of AVIACHT occupied Europe as part of a tour,as well as an attempt to gather more recruits.

I flew over to the special occasion, headquartered in the former ardennes of France, which, as one expected, had been transformed into a massive, mile long tree. The organic mansion, which served as a summer home for special overseas guests, was complemented by thick roots, smooth bark, and of course, branches, where large nests were constructed for top-ranking officials and their families. Among the occasional guests was Kana herself. As an elite commanding officer, she had been given the privilege to take temporary residence on the largest, and sturdiest of branches, and sleep in a rather grandiose nest, made from the finest of South American twigs.

It was there I made my landing on the nest's ledge, where Kana was spotted on a sub-branch prepping herself for that evening's reception. It would be the first time I had seen her in weeks, since we had established ourselves as a couple.

"Epi?" she asked as she caught a glance of me, and a tear of joy rolled down her feathered beak. "EPI! Bless the Sacred Skies! It's so good to see you!"

"HAIL HELIOS," she proclaimed as she saluted with her wing.

"HAIL HELIOS," I sighed as I made the same salute.

"I cannot wait to tell you what has happened since we last met," she continued. "By the way, how was your excursion in former Britain?"

"As a matter of fact," I replied with a lie, "it is going quite smoothly."

"Excellent. Our leader will be most honored to hear of your part. But enough about that. I have such wonderful news to tell you. I have just been promoted by my superior officer to fight in the next upcoming battle of the Amazon!"

"Oh," I replied surprisingly. "That sounds...splendid."

"Splendid?" she gasped. "That is an understatement. This battle, which will be occurring in exactly six months, is predicted to be the tipping point as to who will be the dominant species."

"What do you mean?"

"I mean, that those pesky humans have gathered up all the energy they could muster, and comparing the size of our forces, I'm most definitely sure we will return victorious."

I stared at her with surprise as I tried to comprehend what she said.

"You mean the humans are outnumbered?" I asked.

She nodded back with a girl like squeal.

"It's gonna be a battle the humans will never forget, and hopefully the last thing they'll ever remember."

I took a step backward in shock as she said this.

"Are you all right?" she asked.

"I'm fine," I lied again. "I was just flying all day and night and needed a place to lie down."

"There's a couch of leaves if you wish," she said as she pointed her retracting talon to the nearby lounge.

To my left, a frog servant had placed on the nearby root stump with two quaint glasses of nut milk stirred with the finest mineral bound sap the jungle had to offer. As we exchanged glasses and swiveled them in our talons, I couldn't help but gaze outside at the expanse AVIACHT had wrought upon the European land. What was once a flat plain of mountains and small villages, now had become a forest of lush green, filled with the sounds of birds, wolves, insects, and other exotic specimens.

By now, the stars had covered the night sky, like fireflies against a black screen. I remember times before my secret mission when Kana and I would make stories out of the shapes of the constellations. She would always interpret them as warriors and rebels while I saw tricksters and shamans.

"Beautiful isn't it," Kana sighed as she perched next to me.

"Uhhh…yes," I added under my breath. "It is a sight to behold."

"I will look forward to the day when all this will cover every piece of this planet. Mother Earth will be proud."

"I'm...pretty sure she will."

"Birds of feather annihilate together," she proclaimed as she raised her glass to mine.

"Goes without saying," I lied through my beak as we touched glasses and sipped the lush liquid compound. Personally, I was not disappointed with the drink they provided us. The aroma that crawled up my nostrils and into my taste buds was like honey and sugar mixed with a chocolate haze. For a moment, I had wished I could share it with the humans.

As we stared silently into the jungle, I rehearsed in my head what to say to her: This may be of shock to you, but I have a rather unshakable connection to humans. It wasn't much of an eloquent sentence, but it was a good start. I knew she wouldn't take it lightly, but I knew my secret truth needed to be out sooner or later.

"Oh, I almost forgot," Kana continued after a minute of silence, "I planned something very special to show you towards the end of the banquet, something I believe our special guest will find most pleasing."

"Who is this special thing you speak of?" I asked.

"Patience my sweet," she replied as she took another sip. "I feel much more comfortable in surprising you."

"Umm, Kana. Speaking of surprises, there's something I must tell you. I..."

"Captain Kana," said a green macaw officer who had just entered through the vine-coated doors. Kana swiftly turned around and flew to her loyal cadet.

"Hail Helios," she said as her wing made a salute.

"Hail Helios," the macaw replied.

“Is everything ready for our guests, Officer Sheef?”

“As far as we know, yes. And I see you have a visitor in your room. I shall make sure the banquet has room for him.”

“Excellent! We shall be down shortly. Hail Helios.”

Sheef responded with a salute as he made a swift turn and flew away.

“Come, Episko,” Kana said as she closed the door and flew towards me. “Let’s ruffle you up. You need to look presentable.”

Moments later, I found myself assisted by little yellow parakeets. They cleaned my crevices, waxed my beak, sharpened my talons, and decorated me with a uniform fit for a Prince. Soon we flew out the door, down the hollow corridors and into the large ball room, right where the tree trunk met the roots.

The place was incredibly spacious for the inside of a tree. Its inner bark melded with crafted balconies and foyers. Among them perched delegates all the way from Brazil to Africa. It seemed as though the entire hierarchy of the AVIACT Empire had gathered here.

Even their family members were able to come for the occasion. Up above us soared adolescent brothers, sisters, cousins and close friends. Their chirps and chuckles filled the decadent canopies, singing to themselves and each other a song or recitation with which I was not familiar. Below the canopy were members of the Wolfblitz Tusken Reichstag elite. On their faces were emblems of their status, added and awarded for every kill they made. On their backs and in their tusks were weapons of the highest South American quality. And why not? The evening’s special guests were high emissaries from the African chapter. Among them were: Ree-Nay, gray African parrot and captain of the continent’s extermination squad; Adonis, Lovebird and chief of communication, and Citi-nitte, a red fronted parrot and organizer of the Buchenwald camps in Tanzania.

But of all the visiting guests, one stood out from them all. His name was Gorchak – a highly decorated great Hyacinth, minister of AVIACHT propaganda, and one of King Helios's closest associates and advisors. He had just returned from a year's-long tour of the African territory, scourging the land of any escaped humans. Though not always successful, he had his share of kills.

Escorting him was a young Spix macaw. From first glance, he looked like an enthusiastic chick, a determined, confident, and esteemed member of the AVIACHT youth. And why not? He had been selected as its poster child, given the prestigious honor of training alongside Helios's top advisors.

His presence caught the eye of Kana as a surprised look fell on her face. Gorchak, upon noticing her presence, did the same.

The two flew towards each other, beaks hanging open and legs shaking in disbelief. They examined each other, assuring themselves it was not a dream.

"I don't believe this," said Kana. "How could you survive the logging? I held onto you tightly, but…you disappeared."

"It seems I have returned," Gorchak responded as his eyes filled with tears. "But I never thought I would encounter…my own…"

"Daddy!" shouted Kana as she embraced him with her wings. "I thought I'd never see you again!"

"Ah, my daughter." Gorchak responded in a prideful tone and a tear down his cheek. "I see you have sprouted very ripely. I trust you have been handling your camp with care?"

"I have disciplined those nasty prisoners with the greatest of ease," she responded as she wiped her tears. "I know it would make my mother proud.

"Ah, my little flower," Gorchak added. "I'm sure if she saw you today, she would glow with happiness at your achievements."

"Oh, Daddy!" She remembered upon noticing my observation. "I'd like you meet my boyfriend and future fiancé, Episko."

"So, my daughter has found a lovebird," he chuckled as he approached me. "Not too shabby."

I gulped at his presence. He was tall and lean for a bird his age, unaltered by the passage of time, filled with vigor. I could see more clearly the medals decorating his chest. One was shaped like a cross-bone, another like a set of talons. His claws were finely manicured and delicately sharpened, making them the perfect deadly weapons to tear into a soft skull.

"It…is…quite the honor to meet you general." I stuttered as I lunged my talon forward for a shake.

"Now, boy." Gorchak replied with ease. "There's no need for such formality. All birds of feather are brethren in my eyes."

"Oh," I replied as I lowered my claw with a gulp. "Good to know."

At that moment, I had noticed the young macaw from before approaching our vicinity.

"Ah," Gorchak said upon noticing his presence. "I see you have noticed our young protege. Episko this is Trisco. He is our lucky honor student from Helios youth."

"Nice to meet you, sir," said Trisco with a small lisp. "I've never met a yellow parrot before."

"Trisco, why don't you show our guest your little medal."

Trisco dug into his back satchel and took out a large pendant. It was a gold medallion, almost half his size and with a weight that caused him to stumble.

"I won it after acing a perfect score," he said.

"And what was that in?" I asked.

"Log dodging, branch climbing, nut opening and gun assembling."

"Is that so?"

"He's the top of his class," Gorchak added while rubbing his head with his wing. "Going to make a fine patrol soldier someday. Trisco, why don't you go over and play with some of your friends for a while."

"Thanks, uncle Gorchak." He replied as he started to fly away.

"Oh, and remember." Gorchak reminded him. "Tonight, you will experience your first patrol duty."

"All right!" Trisco replied as he flew in place. "I'm gonna kill a human tonight!"

"That may have to wait." Gorchak replied with a chuckle, to which I discreetly sighed in relief. "But I admire your readiness."

"Hail Helios!" Trisco proclaimed with a salute.

"Hail Helios," we replied.

As he flew away, I noticed a little crimp in his left wing.

"Poor child," said a sympathetic Gorchak. "Had that injury since he was an infant."

"I heard he lost his parents among loggers," Kana added.

"That has never been verified," Gorchak corrected. "But they're presumed dead."

"I don't mean to be rude," I intervened. "But shouldn't we be enjoying the festivities?"

"Oh, yes. Where are our manners?" Kana chuckled. "Come love, the night is still young."

As we flew away, I turned to see several cadets approach Gorchak.

“My lord,” said one of them. “We just spotted several escaped humans near the grove.”

“Find them and take them out.” Gorchak replied, to which they nodded and flew out of the canopy.

Meanwhile, Kana escorted me to a giant nest, large enough to fit several hundred macaws and parakeets. We fitted ourselves with a bouquet of leaves and flowers and painted our faces with the finest of tree sap, a typical costume for an avian ball. She grabbed me by the wing as we flew to the center of the floor. On the top balcony was a neatly arranged orchestra of elephants, boars and wolves, each assigned to a South American instrument. The song they played seemed like a mixture of a tribal chant and a symphonic melody as Kana and I danced into the air along with many other decorated birds.

For a moment, I lost track of my mission. For a moment, nothing mattered to me. For a moment it was just me and my love flying above the flock of feathered friends, not aware of what would become. I almost wished for time to stop, to simply be in an eternity of bliss and joy. Yet, like all joyous moments, it had to eventually come to an end. Only this time, it wouldn’t be taken away from me; I alone had to finish it.

Chapter 24

Trisco's log: Early Evening; 1944B

It was an exciting night for me. General Gorchak had personally asked me to aide him in one of his hunts for Sape escapees. Though strangely, my friends were less excited for me. I guess they're too jealous for a bird their age to be with the top ranks. But more importantly, I hope my training will catch Helios's eye and promote me to the elite youth. Not to mention the top delegates are at a banquet at our central tree.

My teacher and I, and a couple other guards, were stationed a few feet above a former Sapien village. From my books, it used to be called the Wicked City of Bordeaux, but now it's a place for target practice, which I think is why Gorchak flew me here.

The pistol I had in my satchel was given to me by my nest mate as a token of my loyalty. None of my nut bullets seemed rusty or dull, so I knew I had a good shot. I wish I could say the same for loading them.

At first, no Sapes could be found. Most of them had either run away, with any remaining, camouflaged from plain sight. We youth, however, have been trained to see even in the darkest of corners and hide in more discreet spots.

As we waited, my mentor told me about his last travel into the African Congo, where AVIACHT's best foreign stronghold was being constructed. However, they still had some problems to overcome.

"If there is one thing that's really becoming a nuisance, my pupil," Gorchak started as he paced on a sturdy branch. "It's the interference of those pesky apes."

"Apes?" I asked. "But I thought humans were the real problem."

"Correct," he replied, "but if we really want to nip this sapien problem in the bud, we must take down the source. And that source comes from their primate relatives, both chimp and ape alike."

"Haven't we found use for them?" I asked.

"Only for a few tricks and trades. Nothing more. All they're truly good at is gobbling up our food supply and leaving the rest to rot. Food is scarce in the African quarters these days.

Suddenly, we heard a rustle below the ruins. A talon covered my beak as we all crept down the edge of the branch. We coated our feathers in the finest mud and clay the tree had to offer and laid on our backs against its sturdy bark. Now we were perfectly camouflaged while we cocked our guns and pointed them in the direction of the sound.

It was a family of humans, five of them to be exact, trudging into the thick, moist bushes and twigs. Judging from their tattered clothing, they had escaped from a ghetto nearby. How they even left without a scratch is anyone's guess. Leading them was a brown Labrador with a sound radar tied to his back.

"I've never seen any this close to the main tree grove before," Gorchak whispered.

"Get down," his right-hand colonel whispered. "Don't let them see you."

I nodded as I dipped my talons in a muddy part of the branch and rubbed myself with more of it. I touched the trigger on the gun with my talon and held the harness tightly with my beak.

"That's right," my mentor whispered. "Keep your target directly in your sight."

My heartbeat quickly as the humans drew closer and closer. I could now see them in all their disgusting glory: pudgy skin, saggy arms, weak jaws. I'm surprised they made it this far up the evolution chain. They looked weak yet terrifying, fearful yet shifty, clever yet dumbfounded, like all their other primate cousins (excepting of course Amazonians).

"Do not lose your prey," one of the guards whispered.

"Keep your stance firm." whispered another.

"Ready?" my mentor asked, to which I mechanically nodded.

"Aim…"

And without a thought, I pulled the trigger. The bullet flew across the canopy, echoing across the vines and trunks, letting out a screech as high pitched as a howler monkey in pain. The noise only stopped by its puncture into human flesh. I had only managed to slightly graze one of the Sape's legs.

"Nothing to worry my star pupil," Gorchak reassured me. "You've got them on the run. There's no way they can escape now."

"So, I did good?" I asked.

"You did marvelous. After their escape, it was priority number one to locate their coordinates, and you found them for us."

"You will make an excellent Lieutenant someday, Trisco," a guard added. "When we return to base, there will be a set of nicely plucked berries with your name on them."

"All Hail Helios!" I shouted with the accustomed salute.

"All Hail Helios!" they responded back.

Then we all flew off the branch and glided back towards HQ. Yes, it truly was an excellent and productive day for me. My parents would have been very proud.

Chapter 25

At last the sun was setting on another day as the party began to die down. Kana and I retreated to our nest, where we fashioned ourselves a cool drink of iced guava stirred with fig and mango powder. As desirable of a drink as it was, the availability was given only to those of the highest fleet. To receive mixed guava and touch it with your own beak was a high honor, for it meant you were welcomed as an ally of the SS (Sacred Skies) patrol.

The two of us perched ourselves on the edge and watched the sky fill more and more with galaxy clusters of fireflies. We felt for a moment like one bird. It was too bad the bonding would be over.

"What an evening, love," Kana sighed as she rested her head on my shoulder. "I felt like I could soar all night."

"I couldn't agree more," I said nonchalantly as I took a sip of my drink. "Wish we could buy ourselves a nest here."

"You know, Dear, I've been thinking, as long as we're together now, we should start thinking of getting one.

"What?" I asked.

"I mean think about it, we've doing this separation thing for too long. It's time we thought of a day where we can settle down, lay down our wings, have a few chicks of our own…"

"Actually, that's why I need to talk to you about something."

"Yes."

Kana replied with a hint of excitement as she lifted her head. I knew she thought I was about to propose. So I stood up and ruffled my feathers as I made a dignified position. Might as well have her love towards me last for a few more seconds.

"Kana," I started. "I know that I'm not like other birds."

"Of course, you're not, honey." Kana replied. "In fact, you're better than…"

"No, I mean…" I tried to think of the right words. "I do things you may not find acceptable. You know how I like some human things, right?"

"Hey, every bird has their secret shame," Kana reassured me. I mean, just the other day I confessed to liking GOETHE. Now there was a self-hating book."

"It goes beyond that for me, Kana!" My voice grew sterner.

"What do you mean? What are you talking about?" she asked with a trace of worry.

"I mean to say…well…I mean to say that the…world that humans lived in is kind of…"

"Epi, you're not really making any sense here."

"Do you realize how many times I've watched old reels of film and listened to music from before the invasion? I even tried things our enemy would do?"

"Okay, this isn't funny anymore, Epi! You better tell me what you're hiding from me!"

Suddenly, the rooted doors behind us burst open.

"Captain Kana!" Officer Sheef cried. The two gave the Hailing salute.

"What is the situation officer?" Kana asked.

"We have captured several human escapees, as well as one Canine Sergeant."

"Hmmm," she thought. "They might be able to lead us to where the others are hiding. Sheef, tell your boys to double…no…triple the patrol guard over this section of the jungle. Make sure none of them rest until every sape is found. I will go down and have a word with our prisoners."

"What of the dog, Your Grace?"

"Oh, send him over to the nearby POW; his canine and human comrades may be waiting for him. You may leave now."

"As you wish, Captain. Hail Helios!"

"Hail Helios!"

And with that the officer left the room. Good thing, as the two were conversing I had to leave as well.

But now my entire operation was endangered. By doubling the guard, General Gorchak and his comrades were getting that much closer to finding the survivors. At least for now my heartbreaking news to Kana would have to wait.

I flapped my wings with all the strength I could muster, hoping to reach the lodge before any soldiers could. The wind draped beneath my stomach, while bits of rain droplets hit across my feathery exterior. Clouds grew thicker, damper in texture, almost to a point where I felt I was flying through an empty, gray void.

Then, I could faintly see what looked like a macaw silhouette through a thin strip of stratus. It was true. They were following me. Or were they? As the clouds began to clear, the macaw turned out to be just another South American Fruit Bat continuing its nightly hunt of bugs and berries. I took a sigh of relief with my head in the desired direction.

After what seemed like dozens of hours, the sky cleared, and I could finally see the chimney top where my human and woodland friends were hiding. I could smell the aroma of the stove's nightly specialty. But they would need to eat fast given the situation.

I could see the house was dimly lit as I toddled my talons back onto the ground. Perhaps the owl Nuian was telling a story to the human children. But at this hour? Perhaps the fire was flaming for a little too long. No, those woodland critters would make sure an unattended fire would be put out.

I climbed to the windowsill and squeezed through the

opening. Nothing unusual, with the exception of a small note tied to the wall by several fireflies. My talons gripped the note and turned it over: no address. As I opened it, I peered closely at the parchment. Only an American could get that kind of texture, and only a dog would be able to scribble that handwriting. I knew it had come from a canine Sergeant.

Dear Episko,

My name is Sgt. Demetrius. Do not fear me for I am a member of the allied forces. My division is one of many responsible for the rescuing and safeguarding humans. Sadly, I have been separated from my crew and have not seen them for three weeks. Now, I have received word that you have conceived a strategical plan of gathering and relocating a group of Homo sapiens.

If this is true, and my coordinates are correct, then I wish to partake in this mission. I have brought with me five humans from a nearby ghetto just north of here. They are willing to take the risk and are about to trudge through the jungle to these precise coordinates. I can only hope my judgement is not in vain.

They expect to arrive at this point tomorrow.

Darwin willing,

Sgt. Demeter.

I folded the letter and flew down to the cellar. Everyone was now fast asleep in their cots. I perched on top of one of the cellar pipes, where I could see the view in full scale. How much room was left I had no idea. I had nearly filled every nook and cranny in this cellar. How could I possibly have room for five more?

Chapter 26

The Hudson Bay has recently become a popular swimming spot. And why not? There hasn't been a single, drop of toxic or artificial waste, since the end of the Industrial Age, or as non-humans like to call it: The Clouded Times. Among the free tourists is that of Alan Whitestone a native of New York Foressity. His laps in the river are average for the typical resident (three to four every forty-five minutes). Of course, one must always take rests on the small islands within the bay, among the most popular is that of Liberty Island.

Alan swims toward its shore, and lands feet first on the soft, wet sand. With the last, small waves bobbing against his ankles, he takes a moment to smell the harbor air fuming against his nostrils. The bay is cold this time of year. Luckily, his black wetsuit keeps away any possible hypothermia.

With exhaustion, he collapses to his knees, his head gazing at the magnificent Statue of Liberty, its lower half covered in sand and moss, and leaning just slightly in a diagonal position. On most days, he looks in admiration at this symbol of freedom and opportunity. Yet, in the week following Episko's funeral, he's lost concentration of what is beautiful. It is at this moment, Alan receives a video call from his friend, Photios Metro III.

"How's your weekly tread pal?" Photios asks.

"This better be good Photios," Alan sighs.

"Oh, don't worry. I believe you'll thank me for what I'm about to propose."

"Couldn't you have caught me at a more suitable time? I have deadlines to meet and quotas to make."

"Well, you're in luck, Alan. I've noticed your lack of concentration in recent days. Not that it's any of my business, but you are in need of assistance."

"Oh, believe me," Alan replies as he straightens his wetsuit. "I need all the help I can get."

"Excellent," Photios comments. "That's why I've assigned you to therapy."

A moment's silence echoes between the wireless call, interrupted by the obvious, "You've got to be kidding me!"

"Trust me" Photios continues. "You will thank me when it's over. And speaking of which, I believe your appointment will be starting in the next five minutes. Enjoy."

With that, the video goes dark on his waterproof phone. Before Alan can ask for directions, the GPS automatically appears with a route to his new psychiatrist's office. It is underwater, located on a cliffside of the Brooklyn harbor. The name reads:

DR. TRUNCA PHD Doctorate: BEHAVIORAL SCIENCES Genus: TURSIOPS (dolphin)

As he looks toward the harbor, a small otter perches atop the shore.

"Mr. Whitestone," he states. "Dr. Trunca is waiting for you."

The otter guides Alan back into the harbor, taking a deep breath from his special inhaler before submersion.

The doctor's office is not that far away, just a few yards to the right of Liberty Island, and situated in the middle of the artificial and natural reefs that complement the cliffside. This is no longer a problem for humans, as they've learned to hold their breath for minutes at a time.

Alan reaches the entrance to the offices situated at the underside of a large coral. He and the otter swim to the edge, press a few buttons and are welcomed by a platform beneath their feet. They find themselves taking a breath of dry air in a tightly contained, waiting room, with a pool at the center of it all. The otter nods and submerges itself back in the water, but not without a tip from another satisfied customer.

Mr. Whitestone steps out of the pool and dries himself off with a kelp towel. The floor closes beneath him, followed by a tuft of wet, cool steam, just to keep the interior moist for some employees. The room is adequate for most places: chairs, sofas, coffee tables and magazines, decorated with mundane wooden tile. In front of Mr. Whitestone is a large, glass window, exposing patients to the wonders of the deep. Here, as they wait, they may gaze at the passing fish, or wave at any marine mammal friends on their daily commute.

"Good afternoon, Mr. Whitestone," says a voice. "We've been expecting you."

To his right, Alan sees the receptionist behind the transparent panel; A human female, dressed in a rather fashionable one-piece suit. Though she seems normal at first, there is a peculiarity to her features. She stands up, walks around her desk and comes out the left door.

"I take it this session is already paid?" she adds.

"I…suppose so," Alan replies. It is at this moment he realizes the frontal lobe of her face.

"I take it you are a partial trans-species. Seal?"

"Yes," She replies while rubbing her snout and whiskers. "Why do you ask?"

"I just…my family and all."

"Is one of your children partial too?"

"Full, actually. It's my daughter. She's a cheetah now."

"I take it that's one of the reasons you're here?"

"Absolutely."

The receptionist sighs in exhaustion and disappointment.

"I see." She rubs her two seal eyes together. "No matter, this way."

Alan is escorted to a large office. The decor is a mixture of colonial and victorian choices, one good enough to satisfy the most studious of professors. Complete with shelves of books, a neatly cluttered desk, knick knacks, awards, relics and victorian decor, the proprietor is clearly a respected individual. And yes, like the waiting room, a large glass window envelops the walls and exposes the wonders of the deep.

"About what I said earlier," says Alan while settling in. "I didn't..."

"There's no need to apologize Mr. Whitestone," the receptionist replies. "My family too had their doubts about it."

"So, should I keep myself busy?"

"No need to. The doctor will be with you shortly." And with that, she exits.

Before Alan can take time to admire more of the surroundings, Alan realizes that, "shortly" is merely a matter of seconds. For just a few meters in the watery abyss, a female Atlantic dolphin swims closer and closer into view.

Dr. Trunca nosedives underneath the building platform; emerging from a hole under her desk. Her presence signals a light shower of dew from the ceiling, as she cleanses her flippers of any algae residue. Then, with the greatest of ease, she props her belly on a mobile platform.

"Dr...Trunca?" the patient asks.

"Who else were you expecting?" the dolphin replies.

"Um…I suppose you know by now why I'm here."

"Your friend told me. No need for details."

With the command of her tail, her mechanism makes her move in any direction she chooses. It almost gives her the illusion of gliding in thin air. She comes toward Alan for closer inspection.

"You're new to this whole therapeutic business," she comments. "I'm surprised you waited this long. I mean, given your family's history."

"I am as well," Alan adds as he sits on a recliner. "But what am I to blame? My life's been too complicated to even consider my family history these days."

"Well you're here and that's what counts."

The doctor glides to the corner of the room, giving her the right perspective to see eye-to-eye with Alan. On the glass wall appears a digital notepad, ready to take anything down at the tap of her flipper.

"So, what seems to be the trouble today Mr. Whitsestone?" Trunca asks.

Alan takes a few moments to get comfortable and compose himself. Then he clears his throat.

"Well, I've had a rather strenuous week," he begins "The birth rate in five states has risen by twenty percent, so work at population control is relentless. I'm working about three hours more than usual – collecting data, storing catalogs, signing record statements, etc., etc. I don't know, I'm usually in a fog most of the time. Guess that's why I have a hard time concentrating on anything these days. Everyone wants to be parents for some reason, like that's all they care about."

"From what I'm sensing," Dr. Trunca replies as she writes down her notes, "that doesn't seem to be the only thing on your mind."

"How would you know?" Alan asks spitefully. "I'm telling you everything I know."

"I delve into people minds," she replies. "I know when you're hiding something."

Alan rubs his face and takes a deep sigh.

"A long-time family friend, was buried about ten days ago."

"Yes, I know," the Dr. replies solemnly. "His passing is a great loss to our community."

"And on top of that, my relationship with my kids has become more complex. Tiffany, or Xenia as she likes to be called, has recently completed her species reassignment. I have nothing against it and she's happy with the change; we're just getting used to it is all. Eric, on the other hand, is lagging behind what he's capable of. He's gotten into his share of trouble lately at school. Just a week or two before the funeral, he and a friend got suspended. I don't think whoever he's hanging out with has been a good influence."

To top that all off, my father has been drifting in and out of dementia, and his PTSD is not helping either. I've had to visit him twice this week just to make sure he doesn't harm himself. I don't know how I can keep that up any longer. I have the feeling that it may be time to pull the plug on my old man."

Alan pauses as Dr. Trunca taps on her notepad.

"Okay, so from what I hear from you," she comments. "That's a lot to handle then. Why don't we explore more of that personal avenue of yours, particularly about your parents?"

"How the hell is that going to help?" Alan asks, to which Trunca glides toward him.

"Well, I think the source of your imbalance starts with the relationship towards your dad," she comments. "He was a survivor, was he not?"

"Every year he talks about how he met his wife," Alan adds. "I know the whole story from beginning to end."

After a pause, the dolphin moves so she can face the back of his head.

"What I'm going to do Mr. Whitestone…" Trunca explains "…is implement a little technique I learned in my ocean travels. We submerge the patient's mind into a deep, almost unconscious state. However, at the same time, your sub-conscious is wide awake. So, while you can't move, you are still able to explain what you're seeing."

"Now I want you to close your eyes and try to think about what I'm about to say."

With a sigh, Alan does just that.

"Breathe in," she begins. "And breathe out. There is nothing but the rise and flow of your lungs. The air glides towards and away from your mouth. All around you is the empty abyss of the ocean. There is nothing to cling onto, nothing to distract, nothing to restrain. A few rays of light from the surface waves complement this peaceful image. You breathe in, and you breathe out, as your body succumbs to the weight of the water. It is not dangerous, nor is it painful. It is simply welcoming. You breathe in, and you breathe out."

With every command, Alan experiences a clearer visualization.

"Suddenly, there is a collection of objects off in the distance. They start to become more and more familiar with every inch. It is your childhood home, a place where your family resided and raised you. You breathe in, and you breathe out. And with each breath, you feel yourself regress younger and younger. Before you know it, you are a boy playing in your parent's den. Your whole life is ahead of you. The possibilities are endless."

"As you play with your toys and knick knacks, your father and mother appear in their easy chairs. You ask them how they met. It is the first time you've asked that question. With a sigh, your parents welcome you to sit between them, and they begin their story."

Chapter 27

Excerpt from "HOLOCAUST REMEMBERED" Continued

My nerves were shot. I thought we were lost. What would become of ourselves now?

We had been running through the jungle for nearly two weeks now, stopping over at one abandoned structure after another, and with hardly a moment's rest. The thick vines had blocked our sense of direction. We could not tell where was east or west, or even if there was an east or west anymore.

My brother Andrzej had been paying close attention to the map's coordinates. Sometimes, I curiously peered over his shoulder, just to see where we were, to which he gives me a snarl and pushed me from his perimeter. It wasn't really fair. Without any knowledge of our coordinates, how could I possibly know whether we'd reach sanctuary or not. Now the days had become weeks, which were becoming half a month. I could not take it anymore, and neither could most in my group.

"Please let us rest for a moment," one of my friends pleaded to my brother. "I'm not sure if I can take another step."

"I just know we're almost there," Andrzej reassured them. "Just one more mile and we will be at our beacon."

"Some of us are getting very weak, brother," I sternly proclaim to him. "Regardless of how close we are. I don't really think we should carry on for today. Let's just find a hollow stump and…"

Before I could finish, we felt the ground's friction slip from our feet. Before I could think, we had lost our balance. Before I could get up, we were all sliding on a muddy runway leading to who knows where. Before I could comprehend, we were falling down a slope, into a seemingly endless abyss. And before I could…

THUMP.

We awoke several minutes later in what at first seemed like a muddy ditch. Then, as we shook the brown residue from our clothes, turned around and realized more jungle was in front of us. Only this time, there was a light in the distance.

"Keep close everyone," Anderzej stated as we got back on our feet. "This is it!"

We all walked towards the light. As it got bigger and bigger, it started to take shape, somewhat in the form of a gas lamp by a windowsill. Could this be it? Could this be what the map had led us to? Could this mean our long trek would finally end?

Suddenly, we heard a swooping sound above us. My friend gasped and froze with fear, as did I. I knew they had found us. The older, more well-built members of our group made a fighting stance, ready to defend those of us faint of heart. Oddly, the AVIACHT troops had only sent one soldier, and it was flying at a much lower altitude. Regardless, we stood ready.

The bird exposed itself to the moonlight. It was a yellow macaw. Strangely it did not have any uniform or weapons on it, just a satchel with a few unrecognizable items. A friend and I took deep breaths, about to let out a scream. But before we could utter a sound, the bird covered our mouths with two big talons.

"Please do not scream," he said quietly. "I do not wish to harm you."

"But you're a…" Wadja began.

"Yes, I know, I am a parrot. But I'm a good parrot. I'm on your side."

"How would we know that?"

"Remember that so-called 'MYSTERIOUS SOURCE' Demeter talked to you about? That was me."

Everyone stood down, believing now this specimen could be trusted.

"Now I can help you get to safety, but you have to do exactly as I say. Understand?"

My friend and I, our mouths still sealed, nodded.

"Good. Now when I let go of your mouths, you are not… going… to scream. Is that clear?"

We nodded again.

"One… two… three."

His talons flew off of us, our mouths still shut. He turned around a few times, examining the perimeter. Then he nodded.

"My name is Episko, Episko Doulus." He proclaimed. But you can call me Epi. Follow me."

With that, he spread out his wings and hovered just a few feet above our height. We looked at one another and entered what we now knew was a back door to a shack.

The inside was dark and hallow. Only tunnels supported by beams could be seen. It felt like emptiness in its purest form. Something uncomfortable was forming in the pit of my stomach. Was this a trap with no hope of escape? Was Episko secretly working for the enemy? Had they pulled the information out of Demeter?

With my eyes wide, a lantern lit open. Our eyes followed. We gazed at a brown room filled with a treasure trove of supplies. Our faces of bewilderment then turned to relief, as we stared at many of faces of our kind. Some were reading, others were sleeping. A few of them were tending to daily tasks: sweeping floors, sewing clothing, storing food or looking out a top window for enemies.

But strangely, they had assistants. Not of our kind. No, Woodland critter assistants. They were tending to injured humans, collecting edible specimens, and even digging tunnels. Each one was giving their paw, wing, antler and webbed foot for the sake of protecting us.

We had learned in school and the library of these intellectually advanced, feral creatures. But we had only come in occasional contact with the domesticated type. For the first time, we had come face to face with these fascinating forest inhabitants.

"Please," said a red squirrel. "Come this way."

She walked us to a back room. The walls were covered with large holes, dug by the finest and most intricate of rabbit diggers. At the back wall was a set of stairs that led a hatch door. At each cot was a small mouse, standing on top of a first aid kit, on a small dresser. The squirrel gave us a number, which we then used to locate our new beds. The mice opened their kits and gently turned on several gas lamps. They examined our skin, our hair, our hygiene, and our fluids. When the mice were finished, they scurried off to their beds, leaving us alone with the squirrel.

With her climbing acrobatics, she hung to the ceiling and knocked on a beam three times. From the back of us, the hatch door opened. Down came two elderly looking animals, a great horned owl, and a brown rabbit. We looked at them, with stiff backs, hoping their next move was welcoming.

"First off," the owl spoke. "Let us make this clear. We do not wish to harm you. We are here to make sure your journey is not in vain and that you may return to human civilization safely."

"Who are you?" Wadja asked with skepticism.

"My name is Tah-Kain. leader of the ground inhabitants," the fox replied. "This is my co-leader, Elch-Mocht, leader of the tree dwellers. We know what you're going through."

"What do you mean?" I asked.

"AVIACHT does not just believe in extermination," Elch-Mocht replied. "They also believe in invasion. Our forest is being threatened by the jungle, just as much as you are."

"We have lost so much from Helios's grasp," Tah-Kain added. "Nearly half our home has succumbed to soil and flora we were not familiar with, and we don't know how long we can hold back."

"It is not only a battle for humans," said the red squirrel as she climbed back down. "It's a battle for all of us. But do not worry about it tonight."

"She's right," Ealch-Mocht acknowledged.

"Please sleep," Tah-Kain approved.

We all nodded agreement as we took to our complimentary water buckets and bathroom kits set out by the rabbits. It was such a relief to wash ourselves from the muck and grime from days and days of travel. The cooling feeling of water splashing down our aching backs and crusted soles was like heaven. Then, once we settled into our nightgowns and sheets, the red squirrel got our attention.

"Now remember," she stated. "If you need anything, I am the head of human affairs around here, so you can holler for me anytime."

"We never really got your name." Andrzej commented as he lied on his pillow.

"It's Aur-yen," she replied. "But you can call me Ara."

And with that, she blew out all the lights and scurried towards the stairs and through the hatch door. Now all was finally quiet – all cool, calm and collected. The only small sound was a breeze from the humid air, and a rabbit on night patrol, clawing itself a new tunnel. We had arrived at a cedar tinted cellar thriving with food and water and life. Little did I know it would also thrive with love.

Chapter 28

Excerpt from "Holocaust Remembered" Continued

Morning came to us with no excitement. The rising sun peered its rays through a slit in our cellar. Funny, it was like a small, artificial spotlight casting its emphasis on the wooden stage.

Izzy and I were the first to wake, followed by everyone else, and finally, our mother. She had been waning under the weather in recent days and her life clock was running low. Sure, medicine could easily extend it, but where were we to go? It's like we had to now choose between our matriarch's wellbeing and our own.

Izzy hopped over and nudged the side of the cot. After a few attempts, mother clumsily lifted towards the side, grabbed a beam, and slowly stood upright. After a few staggers, a mouse nurse quickly gave her a fresh mug of Lavender Willow tea, just to ease the pain.

"Good morning everyone!" shouted a pleasant voice from the front. "I trust your sleep served you well."

Ara scurried around us inspecting our bedsheets, rummaging through our cupboards examining our faces, searching for any serious infection (or "wire," in case of any traitors.) She stopped over at our mother, noticing her feeble stance. Ara whispered into a mouse's ear, giving it the clue to bring more pain relief from the woods.

"All right," Ara continued. "Our first item today is new guests. They have come all the way from France and are eager to begin their duties. They are waiting outside in the back, so please give them a warm welcome."

Ara guided us upstairs to the back lawn, an open field covered by tall stocks of grain and wildflower and surrounded by thick elmwood trees. Occupying the space were leaders of the forest: Elch-Moht and Tah-Kain, and of the course other newly arrived human survivors, guided by Uncle Epi. It was then I noticed the most beautiful face I had ever seen.

She was right in the middle of the crowd, dwarfed by a few able-bodied men. Her body, on the other hand, was fragile, bruised and somewhat malnourished, like mine. Her hair though, had sprouted. I hadn't seen so much hair in so long. Yet, her face seemed different. It looked pure, shy, untouched by the blemishes on her body. Everything from the line of her jawbone, to the curvature in her eyebrows, was of an innocent life, a life that now seemed so far away. She tilted her head up slightly in my direction. I swiftly looked away, prying my ears on what Uncle Epi had to say.

"Friends," he began as he perched on a treetop. "Our rescue effort has taken us far and wide. It has created bonds; it has created trusts; it has created friends. With that in mind, I pray you may do the same for these new recruits. They are lost souls, looking for sanctuary as you are. Treat them as your brethren, and all will be saved. That is all."

With that, Uncle Epi flew away to his other duties. I was curious as to why he would bring all that up for us. It's not like they would bring any harm to our well-being. That was when I saw a cross hanging from one of the newcomer's necklaces. They were, unlike us, gentile. We had known the tension and quarrel that had beseeched us, god's Chosen people, and those who follow Christ. Since those early days, we have kept a fair distance from they and their customs. But now, times were different. It was not the time and place to be judged on one's creed. We were all in this together.

It was two days later that I built up the courage to talk to this strange girl. The newcomers were already settling in to their daily tasks. The taller, more well-built humans ventured into the woods to assist any wild aide, fetch for sustenance, or stretch for exercise. Because of my mother's health, I stayed behind to assist with the less conditioned humans. Some were tending to the chores of the shack, others playing in the open field with critters, and a few more were guarding the perimeter of our hideout. That was where I was standing that day, with my rifle and helmet close to my chest.

I saw her. She was just standing on a small hill. Her head turned away from me, clothing blowing in the air, absolutely motionless.

Carefully, I took my rifle down and placed a red stone on the left beam, indicating my absence. I walked through the high-stalked knoll and trekked up the small mound where she stood, until I finally could get a good glimpse of her face.

Just like two days before, it was pale but pure. Yet her eyes read something different. They were wide open, staring out into the abyss that was the jungle. She looked like a life sized, porcelain doll, coated with human hair and trappings. With the greatest of ease, I moved my hand up towards her eyes. She let out a loud gasp, startling me in the process.

"I'm so sorry," I said as I pulled myself together. "What were you doing?"

"Uh, nothing," she replied, "just…staring at the trees."

"It didn't seem like it."

After a moment's hesitation, she took a deep breath and stared at me, with the most wanting of eyes.

"I have never been more scared in my entire life," she began to explain. "I was always told to prepare for the unprepared. It's kind of funny. When I was younger, more carefree than I am now, I thought I could conquer anything. No matter what opponent got in my way, or obstacle I had to overcome, I felt if I put my mind to it, I could easily succeed. I only wish I could have known what it would lead me to do."

A few seconds passed with nothing but silence.

"You don't need to feel down on yourself." I assured her. "I mean, we're still here."

"But at what cost?" she snapped. "My home has been all but destroyed. My mother and father are both probably dead. You've lost your father too, from what I heard at least. We are in the middle of a forest, slowly being consumed by a foreign jungle. There is no certainty as to what lies ahead. I am so unsure as to what my path has in store for me. And for that, I am frightened…I am so…so…frightened."

With the weight of her sorrow, I collapsed on her knees. There was strong wind followed by a soft breeze, inducing a hypnotic series of waves across the tall grass. This wind calmed her as she cried more quietly. I slowly lowered myself to her level to comfort her.

"If it is any consultation," I began as I wrapped my arm around her back. "I…understand what it's like to be afraid of the unknown."

"How would you know?" she asked bitterly.

"Because that's what my sister and I had to face in order to get here."

"You…you two came here on our own?" she asked in

bewilderment.

"As hard as it is to believe, yes. On a day like any other, we bore witness to the hell that would soon unfold. My whole town, men, women, sons and daughters, all taken by the mighty talon of AVIACHT's forces."

We were all placed in a camp in the most unsanitary of confinements, shaved, stripped naked, and split off to our slavery (or our death). I can still remember my father being carried to his fate. The lucky ones, like Izzy and me, were forced to toil in the mud for eternity, building a wall that would never be completed.

"On the sidelines we witnessed the worst atrocities; children were beaten soundly; elderly gave in to malnutrition; and mothers watched their infants die. Just like our feathered counterparts, we were animals in a barred cage, without future, and without promise."

"But Izzy and I got smart. We grew determined. We knew for every wall there was a crack, a weakness to the enemy. That's why on one hot day, we plotted our escape. When the enemy wasn't looking, we slid through that crack, leaping to our freedom. For days and days, we trudged through the unforgiving jungle. Our future was uncertain, but our determination was sealed."

"Finally, we came across this sanctuary. A place where we could rest our legs and live in ease among our own kind, including our mother."

"How did your mother arrive here?" she asked.

"From what she told us, she and several others from the camp discovered our mode of escape. If only more of our other village friends would have done the same."

"What are you trying to tell me?" she asked a second time.

"I suppose what I'm saying, or at least trying to say, is try to see the luck you had. You stayed together no matter what the cost. Even more so, you had a plan, a more intricate plan, a plan that could save dozens if not hundreds of lives. We, on the other hand, didn't have that option. At the best, only two at a time could escape. We hardly even had time to plan it."

For a moment, Christine stared at the ground, and then to my arm. The word "*Polluter,*" engraved on my skin, was exposed to the sunlight.

"I can only imagine how much that hurt," she commented.

I covered the tattoo with my sleeve as we walked together, back into the shack.

Chapter 29

Interview entry: June 9th, 2004A 11:15 AM

Excerpt footage (deleted scenes included) from documentary "THE UNEXPECTED HERO."

Three weeks had passed since the French humans arrived. So far, they had quickly settled in to their new environment, even so far as making friends. The friendship of particular interest to me was the fresh bond between the humans Mageck and Christine.

Ever since their first encounter on the hilltop, they have remained inseparable, doing almost everything together: chores, games, leisures, etc. Sometimes I would fly over and spot them holding and caressing each other in the backwoods.

Alas, while it brought joy and comfort to them, it only brought me worry and distress – distress of memories gone by. For you see, every time I saw Christine, and the smile Mageck gave her, it reminded me of the times I brought smiles to my sweet, lovely Kana. It had been so long since our last encounter. I was barely able to speak to her of my feelings. Not about my feelings for her, which she already knew. I'm talking of course about humans. She would never forgive me if I told her, that I was sure of.

I had only been able to catch rare glimpses and occasional chats with Kana while I flew into town for supplies. She also had her own problems, what with the overseeing of camps, ghettos and their prisoners. If only she could break for a little longer, put her duties on the shelf and spend real bird time with me, like in the old days. If I had it my own way, we would have married, built our nest, settled down in the jungle, and had our own quartet of chicks.

But those days were drawing further and further away. I had to face reality. It was almost time to tell her the truth. There was hardly a way to put it lightly. And at what cost? To save many to sacrifice one?

It was the middle of the day. The sun had placed itself in the center of the sky, drying up all the dew from the jungle leaves. Everyone was going about their usual tasks, whether it be tending to the house, garden or any ailing individuals. I was stationed at a branch of the north side of the shack, watching Christine and Mageck. They reclined and leaned their heads on an untouched oak tree, staring at each other with the dreamiest of eyes.

"I…I know it's been a short time since we first met," Christine began. "But it seems like a whole new life has started for me."

"For me as well," Mageck added. "You look and sound so much different now. Your face, emotions, voice, are all more…more."

"Full of life?"

"Yeah…that…and more…"

"Confident? Brave? Sure of herself?"

"Took the words out of me," he chuckled. "Anyway, that being said, you really have filled a gap in me, in more ways than one. I would really much like it if we could…"

Before he was able to finish, Christine kissed him right on the lips. She turned away, staring out in the open, as if it never happened.

A few moments passed without a word or noise. Then, they slowly moved their hands closer and closer, until their fingers met in the middle.

"Let's stop pretending, Mageck," said Christine. "You and I both know we can't do this by ourselves. Everything around us is changing. Our home, our friends, our circumstances, and especially ourselves. The course of events is unstoppable. But with you by my side, it seems we can conquer anything."

"I don't know for sure what comes next," Mageck added. "But I'm not gonna hold this in any longer I know it sounds like something out of a sappy, overused fairy tale, but we were destined for each other; whether we knew it or not, I…I LOVE YOU!"

"And I love you too, Mageck." And with that, they caressed in a loving embrace.

"And by the way," she giggled in between their lips. "Fairy tales can be pretty dark. Just like ours."

It was at that moment, when they touched their lips, a dozen wings could be heard above the canopy. At first it sounded like just a passing flock, so I pretended not to worry. Yet, as the flock drew closer and closer, there was no denying the enemy had found us.

Without a word of hesitation, the newfound lovers sprinted into the shack, me following behind. I looked up and instantly recognized the flock was of AVIACHT, no other group of birds could fly at that altitude or formation at the same time.

As we approached the door, Christine gave everyone the signal of the enemy's presence. The humans dropped their items and ran down the stairs into the cellar, with the animals quickly clearing the premises of any evidence. They all scattered into the jungle, camouflaging themselves among the flora.

Now it was only me, Ara, and the refugees, huddled together in the damp, musty space beneath the dwelling, staring at the ceiling for the next move. Yet, despite the crowded circumstances, all was quiet. All feet were silent against the floorboards. Men and women held their breath, and children covered their mouths. I was rather impressed at how skilled the humans had increased their stealthiness. Even the loudest of breaths only complimented the wisps of wind humming from outside.

"DOULIS!" A familiar voice uttered from above.

I collected myself, fixed my feathers and flapped to the edge of the door. I pressed my ear against it, making sure it was the right voice.

"Mr. Doulis are you in here?" asked the voice again as the tap of several claws could be heard from above.

As I looked down at the stair where my talons were perched, I gave a worried sigh. Then I looked at the humans; eyes all fixated on me.

"Everyone," I quietly warned. "Not...a...word."

I opened the door and hopped upstairs, locked it with my beak on the other side, turned my head and stared at General Gorchak in all his admirable glory. Surrounding him were two Scarlet Macaw Guards, tall for their species, as was to be expected for any dignitary. Without a moment's hesitation, I walked towards them.

"Hail Helios," I proclaimed with my winged salute.

"Hail Helios," the guards said and saluted in return.

"Apologies for our rather brash entrance, Mr. Doulis," General Gorchak began.

"Oh, not at all, not at all," I replied. "I was simply stacking more supplies for my noteworthy Guyanna tea laced with Corage

Orchid."

"Splendid! Why don't you serve me and the boys some, eh?"

With a nod, I rushed into the cupboards and quickly put together a fresh batch. Upon serving it I noticed the general as he picked up his cup. He was peculiarly pointing his beak around the house, like a cat scourging for food.

"Epi," he said with a smooth tone. "Would you mind pouring me extra milk."

"Something troubling you, sir?" I asked innocently.

"Oh no, no," Gorchak replied. "I am simply marveling at the structure you've chosen for your abode."

"You are?" I asked in confusion while skimming milk into his drink.

"You have truly outdone yourself, Epi. A perfect model with a safety zone in case the enemy attacks. We need more birds like you, especially in these times."

"Absolutely," Guard 1 stated.

"No questions asked," Guard 2 added.

They sipped their tea simultaneously.

"I really don't see myself as an efficient member of your battalion," I cautiously replied while holding two cups with my talons.

"Oh, don't be so modest," said the General. "We have a system to operate, and every wing and claw counts."

"But, sir," I protested. "You have already become the highest-ranking squadron in the fleet. There really is no need to worry about shortages…"

"And there won't be. Which is why we would like to see your skills very soon."

"Without doubt," Guard 1 added.

"Unquestionable," Guard 2 added.

"So, what do you say, Mr. Doulis? Are you ready to join the heights of AVIACHT's Empire?"

"Well…I…." I tried to think of something to say. Nothing came out. I felt embarrassed.

"Then again, no need to rush," said Gorchak. "I know this is a lot to take in. Give yourself as much time as you want."

"Thank you, sir," I replied. "Are you ready for your tea?"

"Within the moment Comrade. There is something else I wish to discuss, something much more private."

"The perimeter is clear, sir," Guard 1 proclaimed.

"No one is in sight," Guard 2 added.

"Good," the general said.

It was a moment of awkward silence, as we both stared at each other with a dead glare. He made a slight nod, signaling me to offer him his drink.

"Episko," he began. "Are you aware of what we evolved from?"

"Oh, yes of course," I replied. "We have evolved from dinosaurs?"

"Precisely, my boy. We are direct descendants of the Stegosaur, Triceratops and Tyrannosaurus Rex, all mighty beasts that once dominated the gracious earth. Looking at that, I say why stop at one little extinction? After all, in spite of such cataclysm, we managed to survive, reproduce, flourish among the planet and its good soil. But none of that was possible without a certain feature. One only birds can truly harness."

"And what is that sir?" I asked while holding my cup nervously.

He took a sip and sighed in relief. Then he started to pace around me, as if cornering me in a duel.

"The feature that made our species so perfect for survival, is that we can sense danger right before it strikes. Picture this world before we came into power. It was a hostile world no doubt. If a little hen were to simply perch on a patio, the sapien owner would try to shoot its head clear off its shoulders, just in time for a barbaric dinner. And yet, I have seen hens that would outpace even the fastest of humans. Oh, and speaking of which, this brings us to the topic at claw."

He clicked two claws together, to which his guards revealed a small, red burlap sack, tossing it on the table. As I swirled my drink, and took a sip, I noticed upon closer examination that the red was coming from the inside of the sack. Gorchak cleared his throat as he gazed down at the precarious item.

"You can't deny," he began. "Growing up in a lush jungle, constantly threatened by mining and milling puts you into contact with a whole lot of flat faces. I can still remember my chickhood days. We were always on the move, flying deeper and deeper into the jungle, hardly finding time to ease our wings. And yet, most of us surprisingly survived. Most of us were able to spot the danger before it started. Most of us prepared long in advance. And because of that, we are still here, still winning. But to win is to know your enemy; to know him like the worm in the claw."

It was at that moment I heard a sharp cough from below the floor, which I disguised as my own. Gorchak raised his eyebrow as I patted my stomach, gathered myself together and took another sip.

"I have spent my whole adult career in these parts," he continued. "Scourging above from one European wood to the next, occupied by towns, with many other flat faces. Since the uprising I now have only one question: Why don't they sense us coming?"

"What do you mean?" I asked.

"A while back," Gorchak exclaimed as he walked circles around me. "One of my infantries successfully took control of a town in Poland. While I can't quite remember its name, I do know the operation went smoothly. It took about five minutes for those sapes to realize our presence, giving us more than enough time to execute the invasion. I don't think there was a single human untouched or unaccounted for."

"Now if I was in their shoes, I would have run and headed for safety, and it wouldn't have taken me five minutes either. But not them, Mr. Doulis. They always blackout. They always hesitate. They always waste those five precious minutes staring stupidly at their destiny. Why?"

"And this brings me to the subject at claw."

The general walked back towards the wet sack where, after calmly lowering his drink, he flung it, revealing the wet object inside...

"This is the brain of a human," he said cooly.

I shuddered as I tried to suppress any gag reflex.

"I know, I know," he reassured me. "It's disgusting, isn't it?"

"It... is... a... sight," I added.

"It was extracted from a rather...devilish individual. The male was a carpenter, from what we learned. Strong, able-bodied for his age, just enough to make creations entirely on his own. If I hadn't known he was human, even I would have considered buying his furniture."

"But yet I'm getting sidetracked. I can still recall his unique ability to sing prayers to himself, so that he would not scream as we put him down. A witty gent for his type. He was able to understand his predictament. Never could really remember his full name, but we'll just call him Mr. Kiewpensky."

I heard a whimper from below us, luckily it wasn't loud enough for my guests to hear.

"Now it took about ten minutes for my daughter, Kana, and her flock to corner him at the edge of the camp's fence, longer than most birds when tracking down prey. And yet, with the slash of a talon and the speed of a beak, they knocked him dead like mackerel on a stone slab."

He gazed once more at the sack of brain tissue, examining it in attentive detail. Then, using his claw like a hook, he ripped off the organic, protective sack, exposing the tissue and canals of this freshly extracted organ.

"By the way," he continued. "I trust you and my daughter are still in contact. She hasn't told me about you for days."

"I have been…" I tried to think of the right words to say. "…contemplating how precisely to express my feelings towards her." Changing subjects quickly, I ask, "Now why exactly is it that she decided to keep the brain intact?"

"I wish I had a nut for every time someone asked me," Gorchak chuckled. "The science of neurology is crucial to understanding how to know the enemy. The brain can be a very complex and an unfathomed terrain, regardless of our species. But with careful examination, and the right tools, we at AVIACHT are able to truly grasp what makes a human "tick." I'm talking of course about why they never sense us coming. And I've realized, upon examining the brains we collected, that one grand, distinct trait is that there seems to be a gap in what unites the areas associated with intellect and instinct."

The general sharpened his claw like a meat cleaver, and with the smoothest ease, sliced the brain in two. Then, he grabbed the left half with his beak, tearing out the residue from the nerve stems and cleaning out the canals of blood.

"If we can examine this piece of brain tissue here," he continued, as he threw it on the table. "You will notice a rather abnormal blockage in the cerebral cortex, right about here."

He pointed towards what seemed like white cartilage melding in with the membrane tissue.

"As a result, it takes a few extra minutes for the cells to cross over this genetic mutation. This means, the area of the brain associated with survival does not receive these instinctive messages in time."

"If this blockage were removed by some miraculous chain of evolutionary events, the nerve cells would be able to send messages through the cavern of instinct and straight into the cerebral cortex, allowing our friend here to sense danger from much further away. For you see, the area of the brain associated with survival, is right behind this blockage."

"Now if we were to examine the brain of say, a macaw, such as myself, or a parakeet or a duck, this blockage would be absent, undeterred by any mutation in the genome system. And thus, the nerve stems carrying these vital messages are able to freely migrate from one area to the next. They send out important messages to our fine-feathered friends. If danger is not far away, our kind is supplied with the instinct to flee or fight back before the fire even starts. Alas, this is unlike the brain of man. Thus, burdened by his genetic ignorance…he got the message a little too late."

"I…uhhh…" I cleared my throat as I tried desperately to keep my composure. "Excuse my brashness, but what exactly is your point, General?"

"Mr. Episko Doulis," said Gorchak as he placed his piece of the brain on the table. "I take it you are a very bright bird. One of the finest we've seen. In fact, I wouldn't be surprised if you joined us very soon. But, if I found any unsuspecting human within your confines, tore his or her skull open, and examined their brain, they would have the same blockage, in the same passageway, as our friend here. They would be too inherently stupid to see us coming, they wouldn't even have time to pack up and run."

"Just...like...your...FRIENDS!"

With that last word, the guards broke through the door and ripped through a chunk of the floorboard. It was all over. I just knew it! They would find the humans, take them away, and commit unspeakable punishment, not to mention what they would do to me. Not only us, but the woodland critters were doomed as well. My cover, blown. The operation, a failure. All had fallen apart. I quietly closed my eyes awaiting my fate and theirs.

It was ten seconds before I opened them again, looking over the hole in the floor. The general and I peered down, only to see another empty layer of wood between the cellar and the kitchen which was a barrier between us and my refugee friends. The humans were safe, but only by an inch. My cover was not blown. It was not all in vain. I had never been so relieved than at that very moment.

The general just stood there, a little bewildered by his misjudgment, like a boy who got the wrong answer in class. Then he looked at me with his rather puzzled face, immediately switching back to a more professional one.

"Well then, uh," he said while composing himself. "I must apologize. It has been a long week and I suppose my suspicion got the best of me. After-all, paranoia really takes a toll on you."

"Not at all, General," I replied. "Common mistake. Many birds have developed unwarranted suspicions."

"Well," concluded the general. "We best be leaving now. I bid you good day, oh and take my earlier proposal into consideration."

"I certainly will," I replied. "Hail Helios"

"Hail Helios," my guests responded, and with that salute, they took one last sip and flew out into the sky.

I looked around my empty kitchen as I exhaled a few sighs of relief. Then, I scuttled onto the floor and examined that hole. Christine tossed the floorboard out of the way as she and the escapees crawled out of the opening, brushing off their dust-laiden clothes.

"Is everyone accounted for?" I asked.

Everyone nodded as the critters entered from outside to inspect them.

"Good. We're leaving tomorrow night."

The looks on their faces turned ghostly white. I could swear I heard one of the human's jaws dropping to the ground.

"We're…leaving?" asked a confused Andrzej.

"Yes. Check all your loved-ones and pack what you can."

"But the majority of Europe is crawling with the enemy. This is all we have. We must stay put until…"

"You can't be here!" I shouted. "Not anymore. The general knows where I live. In approximately five days this place will be swarming with AVIACHT guards. We'll be sitting ducks if we stay here another week."

"Now I'm sorry to bring this abrupt news to you, but time is of the essence. This is no longer a battle for humans. It's a battle for them too."

I pointed my talon at the forest residents, who all had expressions of uncertainty.

"Speaking of which, I'd like to apologize to the non-humans

in this room, especially, Ara. I got you all in this mess, and I can't let you suffer the same fate other humans have endured."

It was then Elch-Mocht swooped down to my level, with Tah-Kahn sneaking up from behind.

"You don't seem to understand, Mr. Doulus," Elch-Mocht commented.

"We were hesitant at first," Tah-Kahn added. "But we realized that this is the first time a force threatens both humans and the natural world."

"It would be foolish for us to back out now," said Elch-Mocht. "We need to finish this."

"Only when AVIACHT is truly defeated can we go back to our old ways," Tah-Kahn proclaimed.

"And it seems as though the macaws have lost their way too," Ara said while confronting a child. "I mean, how can these birds care so much about their forest when they clearly want to destroy ours?"

"You can't blame them, Ara," I replied. "The plight of mankind pushed them to the edge. From humans they learned hate and wrath. But nothing more."

I fluttered to the other side of the room as I perched myself on the windowsill. The sky was becoming shrouded with clouds, but not enough for a storm.

"There are a few things I need to check before we leave," I said. "I suggest you all start packing your things. By tomorrow, we will have found a place from where you can be transported to Argentina in secret."

With a deep breath, I unfolded my wings, adjusted my tail, and prepared myself for takeoff. It was then I saw Mageck bowing his head in both sadness and anger.

"I know this is tough for you, son," I said to him. "But I assure you, you will find your freedom."

"It's not that, Uncle Ep," Mageck replied weakly. "It's about that human brain your friend demonstrated to you. I'm pretty sure it was my father's."

My eyes dipped in shame as he collapsed on the floor in tears. Luckily, Christine was there to comfort him as he wailed with the unbearable loss. A few minutes later, the crying died down, and I began to speak again.

"I'll be gone for only a few days," I said with a sigh. "By the time I return I should know the coordinates to the next boat. Farewell."

And with that I flew out of the window and back to my love…Kana. I had to tell her now. If I waited any longer, the scars would only be greater between us. Now was the time to reveal my secret to her. My deepest…darkest…secret…I CARE FOR HUMANS, I PROTECT HUMANS…I LOVE HUMANS.

Chapter 30

Interview entry: May 19th, 2004A, 10:15 AM

Excerpt from book "The Unexpected Hero."

I…could not believe it.

I should not have believed it.

I refused to believe it. My own love had betrayed me, my third and fourth wing. My Episko had succumbed to the temptation of the transgression that was Humanity.

Within the knapsack he left behind I found traces of old writings, film and music, all of which praised or adored the so-called human race. I knew as I rummaged through his belongings and threw his knapsack against the tree wall, that his deep, poisonous obsession with the sapien species had overtaken him, making such waste more important to him than his own kind.

Meanwhile, my father, who could be heard squawking just a branch below me, was experiencing the opposite of feelings. The Alpha troops were set to leave within a week for Brazil. The final showdown would soon commence with our enemies. If we won, the dominant species would be our own. I should have been happy for my father. He and his friends had worked nearly their whole adult lives for this moment. Yet my grief and anger were overwhelming.

To celebrate this achievement, a guard was asked to present his pet. A human…shaved, stripped naked and reduced to a shell of a creature was kept as a plaything for him and his guards. This was not uncommon, as any feral biped would likely be kept in a cage, left to die slowly in the claws of the highest of avian authority. But this was a rare treat, as the pet was allowed, for a very brief moment, to be pushed out of its cage and given a dose of fresh air.

The precarious thing hopped on his hind legs towards the center of the room. Glass shards were scattered below him, piercing his feet. He didn't seem to mind the penetration, as his brain had been depleted of any psychological defense cells, thanks to months of extreme isolation.

"DANCE!" my father shouted in a drunken stupor. "DANCE YOU BEAST!"

He took out his pistol and shot near the human's foot. It preceded to commence in a pathetic, yet amusing jig.

"DANCE! DANCE! DANCE!" chanted everyone in the room. They too took out their pistols, aimed them at the creature's feet and fired bullets whenever it slowed down.

It danced around the entire floor space, not even aware of what it was, where it was, or how it got there. With every footstep, and every waving of the arms, blood could be seen dripping from its soles, coating the glassed floor with a ruby red hue.

While the happy party continued down below, I continued to immerse myself in both anger and confusion. They had begged me to join them, yet I declined, telling them I needed to finish some last-minute items of a personal nature.

But how could I, with the state I was in? Epi and I had planned so much of our lives. We were to rule a part of this world together. We were to get married, buy our own nest, have a half dozen chicks and live the life any macaw would dream of having.

I could still see that outcome in my head, as clear as any thought could be. But now I knew that would never happen, not on my former lover's terms.

It was at that moment, I flew with Episko's knapsack to a book burning at the jungle floor. I needed to distract myself from this sudden realization. As predicted, it was a celebration of the final preparations for battle. A few young parrots were gleefully throwing any remaining items from a damaged library into the flames. I stared at my former lover's belongings, dangling just below my talons. A tear of both rage and sorrow fell down my feathered cheek. Just when I was about to toss the knapsack into the fire, Episko himself came flying towards me.

At first, I ignored the sounds he made as he landed his talons on the fallen leaves. I grabbed a few more books and threw them in, like he wasn't even there.

"Kana," he said sheepishly. "I know you may be busy but…"

"Oh, let me guess," I replied sarcastically. "You want to gloat about how you figuratively stabbed me in the back?"

"Actually I…"

"Don't even bother. After all, you're not the cause of all birds' misfortunes. You're the just the symptom."

"Kana…"

"A brainwashed drone, constricted, tarnished, and broken by our enemy. Why do I even bother talking or listening to you? I wouldn't expect a…a…PET…to understand."

A flew back up to my nest and slouched in a bundle of twigs. As I buried my face in a mope of depression, I saw the shadow that was my former love hover over me.

"Kana…" he said. "I know all of this can seem overwhelming to you, but…"

"If you don't want to see me this way," I replied. "Then, by all means, leave. Besides, don't you have some marvelous outing with a pair of other fine-feathered chicks?"

"You know I don't think that way about you at all."

At first, I ignored his plea for attention as I curled into a feathery ball. But then…

"From the moment I laid eyes on you," he continued, "I knew you stood out from among the flock. Do you remember how we met? I have a some-what good memory of that time. I think it was in the early days of the invasion. It had been three months since I was liberated from my cage. I saw you gliding over what was to be a vast jungle. You claimed you were patrolling for any stray humans. Yet I knew you were just playing pranks on the ranking guard."

"If I recall correctly Epi," I added, "you were playing pranks along with me. You saw how foolish I was compared to my other peers and you just decided to pitch in. It was a chance meeting. A dare, if you will."

"Kana I know this seems…"

"Don't you think you would've thought this over before you told me the news? Before you told me about this?"

I grabbed with my beak a few of his human relics from behind me and slammed them right in front of his claws. I looked at Epi's face, his eyes with a defeated look in them. I knew we were both thinking the same thing. He knew I figured it all out. We knew some news was about to be broken.

"Sweetie," he tried to explain pathetically. "It…it had to be told sooner or later. You knew perfectly well, as I did, that I was obsessed with…"

"I consider myself a rather reasonable and rational bird, Mr. Doulus," I interrupted while approaching him. "I have quietly witnessed the magnitude of this war, and I have quietly observed the true nature of both sides, and from what I have seen, I will not stand quietly by and watch as all we worked for is tarnished.

"Kana, you know I would never think of trying to hurt you in any way."

"Well congratulations, sweetheart, because you just did!"

"We can still love, Kana. If you open your heart, maybe we can figure this out. I made a vow to be on your side…"

"And I can't just stand side by side with a bird who is led astray. If you are tarnishing the cause, then I don't know how this story of us could possibly end well."

Episko sighed. He was aggravated for no reason. He had brought this on himself. I knew that with every love there must come sacrifice, even if it meant giving up a big part of who you were. Episko did not understand such wisdom. He did not accept the sacrifice he needed to make. And even that was no measure of the sacrifice we were all about to make. He approached me suspiciously as he lifted his head.

"Kana…well…" he began clumsily. "Sometimes there are those of us who don't really see eye-to-eye with the majority… that is the flock."

"What are you talking about?" I asked puzzled.

"I have friends that are very dear to me, almost as much as you are dear to me. And these certain friends don't want to get killed."

"Okay, clearly you are making no sense at all. Why am I wasting my time listening to you. Either you make up your mind right now and tell me what is going on, or you just…"

I noticed a foreign object stuck to his chest. I grabbed it before he could hide it.

"Is that…nylon?" I asked.

There was much for him to explain. I would know that illegal substance anywhere. Only the hairless paws of a human could place that on him, whether it be with an embrace, or along with a pat on the head or during a bathing from spidery fingers.

“It was a simple stakeout, honey,” Epi tried to explain.

“Dammit, Epi!” I interrupted. “How in Helious’ holy scripture could you do something so treacherous as this?”

“I wasn’t doing anything treasonous to anyone, Kana. All I was doing was admiring a piece of forgotten time.”

“You know how I feel about this, Epi. I can’t go out there with everyone knowing that I spend time with you.”

“Why does everything have to be black and white with you, Kana?”

“We don’t have any time for more choices, Episko. This moment is what our entire history has led to. If we back out now, it will have been all for nothing, and I can’t allow myself to be led astray if you don’t meet your end of the bargain!”

“I CAN’T! Don’t you see by now, Kana. I can’t just walk out on my friends. They need me.”

I walked out of my nest and approached him, my body now shaking in anger.

“What friends?” I asked ferociously. “Since when did you start caring more about your so-called friends, more than the cause? More than your kind! More than me!”

“Why would you say that? After all, holding onto a few human memories may be needy, but at least it’s better than pretending they didn’t happen.”

“Yes, they happened. But it’s over now. This, the War, the Empire, the entire future of our planet is what’s happening now, Epi, and the only bird missing out on this golden opportunity is you. I can’t believe you would rather waste your whole life collecting relics of our enemies than see our next generation of chicks grow up and be leaders of the world."

"Kana, don't thi—"

"Just answer me this, sweetie. Is it true that you are actually trying to save, rather than destroy, the human culture?"

"Bu—"

"ANSWER THE QUESTION!"

My screech was so loud the whole canopy grew dim. Now it was only my former love and me making noises. Epi just stared at me with a guilt-ridden face, contrary to my own which was filled with rage. He bowed his head in shame once more and looked up at me at again, staring for the longest time. I thought he would never answer until…

"Yes," he replied. "I am. I'm…I'm sorry."

My face changed from fiery ire to neutral piousness. I closed my eyes and breathed through my larynx.

"Epi," I said coldly after a long silence. "We may have been irresponsible, even disloyal in the old days – pranking the guards, plastering signs on slogans, even causing a scene at certain induction ceremonies. But if I recall correctly, there was one thing we didn't lose sight of, and that is our teachings. We would always arrive to class on time and listen to everything our teachers needed to say. Among the most sacred of their knowledge being the strict boundaries between us and the human world. You knew those teachings couldn't be broken. I knew that and every bird knew that as well."

"Well, that's some smart words coming out of you," he replied harshly. "And what do you say about all the human children you killed in the past? Has that ever crossed your mind, all those boys, girls and babies wiped out by the command of your word?"

"They got what was coming to them."

"How could you say that? How can you judge living beings if you never got to know who they were, or at least talk to them?"

"I have no need to know what the flat faces are; they are all the same: ignorant, savage, greedy forest killers. They are incapable of even the slightest of empathy. "

"We killed thousands of them!"

"And they killed millions of us! Because of them, I nearly lost everything. You cannot trust them. The sooner they die out the better…"

"It's no one's one's fault that I love humanity!"

He covered his beak as if he were a chick who had uttered a cuss word. The statement just ran past his tongue, as if he weren't even thinking. Meanwhile, my tongue and beak jarred wide open. I could not believe what he had just said. And like the action I condemned him for before, I refused to believe it. Of all the species of birds that would betray our true heritage, I never thought it would be the one closest to me.

"You…" I stuttered with bewildered eyes. "You like humans?"

"I tried to tell you this sooner, but…"

"YOU…LIKE…HUMANS! Are you impeccably out of your mental capacity?"

My former love approached my side.

"Kana, I can explain…" he cried. "Please, hear me…"

"I DON'T WANT TO HEAR IT!"

"You know I love you…"

"Don't you think I knew what this was all about? Do you really, honestly believe I was that naive? All those times you ran out on me, on nights when we were supposed to be together, dragging that thing on your neck you call a "satchel." Yeah, don't think I didn't notice what was in there."

"I'm sorry I couldn't shake off a piece of me you didn't approve Kana," Epi replied. "If you dare open your eyes, can you see the world through my own? Can you admit that not all humans are bad? "

"I am not going to be led astray again," I said as I approached him like a fighter in a ring. "I will not be tempted by those sapes. You are just a pawn, a former shell of your heritage."

"Just answer my question."

"No! You answer mine! Are you afraid of your own kind? Are you really that broken by the sapes? Are you not willing to take on change? Can you really not just let it all burn away?"

At that moment, a relic fell from his satchel. It was a copper locket with a photo bearing a human family. I stared at this forbidden object with my talon against the photo's grain. My face grew colder and colder as a few more silent seconds passed.

"I knew it," I said as I picked it up. "Just when I thought I could really convert an outsider."

"Kana, you must lis—" Epi tried to say. But he was interrupted by the locket being thrown at this chest.

"You backstabbing liar!" I screamed as I slapped my talon across his face. "I should've never trusted you! I should've never gotten distracted!

"Kana," I said. "Let go of hate before it destroys what you hold dear. Think of Trisco!"

I turned my head back to him and fluffed my feathers. Now what I had seen in him was truly shattered.

"I do," I replied bitterly. "Those sapes were always nothing but trouble. King Helios has the right idea of how to deal with their kind. He and all of us are following in the glorious footsteps of the Black Plague. That virus was a blessing to us, an omen from above of what could be. Yet, the Plague only thinned them out. Now I think it's time we fulfil the prophecy, and this time there will be a great cry all across the planet from a pestilent species that we will never hear from again!"

With that word I flew to a nearby branch and tore away a large drape, revealing the final blueprint of our glorious plan. It displayed a dozen missiles from the finest nut and oak, each carrying strong strains of the Black Plague. They were ready to be dropped, scattered across the last remaining strongholds of the humans.

Episko looked in abject horror at the intricacies of the design. I could not believe how distant we were in our views of the world. I thought that maybe he would congratulate me for my hard work and effort. But instead, he just stood there, beak wide open and eyes flying around my masterpiece. All that come out of his mouth was, "Kana, you brought this on yourself."

And with that, he flew away. I collapsed to the floor, both exhausted, shocked and saddened from the ordeal. I never saw him again after that. No matter. I had more on my plate than most birds to attend to in the coming months.

"Captain!" said a cadet as it flew in and gave me a salute, to which I replied with a flimsy extension of my wing. "The captors. They have not responded or complied with our demands. I don't think they know anything. What sho—"

"Oh, they know plenty." I replied menacingly. "Show me to them."

"But, your grace," the cadet commented. "It is strictly prohibited for any officer to enter the interrogation chamber with…"

"AM I THE ONE IN CHARGE OR NOT?" I responded with a bellowing squawk.

"Yes. You are most definitely."

"Then take me to them."

"Yes, your Grace."

At the click of my talons we flew down into the chamber with me desperately trying to hold back my tears. The area was a hollow, caved-in section of the tree; it was an encasement big enough to hold one to two dozen specimens at a time. And there, in the center of the dirt coated floor, surrounded by some of the best mercenaries our regime had to offer, were the prisoners themselves, three meekly, pathetic sapes, pecked, clawed and beaten to a pulp.

I stared at these precarious species, grimacing as I circled around them. It was at that moment I saw what looked like the contents of an envelope dangling on the side of one of the humans' pockets. On the front was written, "From Nathan."

"You know," I said with a cooling voice. "I can't help but remember the time I saw two young chicks playing tag underneath a waterfall. Or was it three? I don't recall. Either way, it was just a few days before the destruction of my home. They were accompanied by a rather stern and stoic guardian named, Busu. Not that his name matters, but he was the strongest, busiest and most diligent in our flock. He seemed to be a bird that didn't have time or need for silly nonsense in his life. And yet, as he looked on at what was child's play, something happened. He began to join in on the fun. He started playing tag as if he were one of the children. How incredible it is for a child's innocence to melt even the roughest of hearts. It really is Family that strengthens that innocence and keeps it intact."

"Do you have any children, Mr…?"

"Richardson," one of the humans mumbled as he coughed

up blood. "And my wife is expecting."

"Oh, isn't that wonderful?" I reply. "Then I believe your wife and unborn child will be proud to know you died a brave man."

His head bowed in shame as he started to cry. The two other humans, both equally wounded, just knelt there, emotionlessly, staring at a blank wall without purpose.

"What have you done with our commander?" one of them asked.

"You mean your dog?" I replied. "He had a little accident while escaping the camp. The last we heard from him was a scream for help over the nearby cliffs. Oh, and I'm afraid your other friends didn't make it either. But don't worry. You'll be joining them soon. Cadet, hand me the gun."

"Ma'am," he replied. "This is an XP - 478. I'm not sure if you're authorized."

"Give me the FUCKING WEAPON!"

All was silent. No one moved. I'm not sure if my colleague was deaf or just too shocked to act, but either way, I grabbed the gun from his satchel and pointed it to my captives. I still noticed the envelope dangling precariously from the human's coat. It seemed to be a letter to his family, or friend, or some other importance I had no business with.

"Get up," I said soullessly to them, which they did.

"Miss Kana," one of the humans said meekly. "From what we heard, you know what it's like to lose a family. Perhaps we can negotiate if you jus—"

"Turn around you pathetic flat face." I spat back.

The humans spun to face the wall, hands and stomachs pressed against the hollow tree bark. I was thankful that they weren't looking at me, for tears started to stream down my eyes, my voice seeming to break under the weight of the day's events. Both the love of my life had left me for his own self-interests, and I had come face to face to witness the very species we were craving to exterminate.

"You don't have to do this, ma'am," said another one of the humans. "I…"

"You don't get it do you," I said under my moistened eyes. "I can't just let you live. My love is gone because of you! I can never speak to him again! This is ALL YOUR FAULT!"

"My wife…" said the soldier with the envelope. "My wife is expecting a child. We own a small farm. I promised her we'd build a family…"

"SHUT THE FUCK UP!" I squawked wailingly as I ruffled my wings and pointed my gun to his cranium. The tenseness of my body overwhelmed me. Tears began to fall as my squawks melded with a loud sob. For a moment, I wasn't sure whether I controlled the weapon, or it controlled me.

For a fleeting minute, Epi's face crossed my mind. I couldn't believe it. I promised not to lose another bird in my flock. Yet, it happened again. Only now, that bird had failed me.

"Why don't we bash these sape's skulls off right now," I hissed. "Then we can see if my father's analysis of their brain blockage is correct."

"Ma'am plea—" a human tried to say.

"SHUT UP!"

At that moment, under my scream I heard some rather strange, faint chatter – a chant coming from the mouth of one of these creatures. The verses quoted:

He makes me lie down in green pastures; He leads me beside quiet waters.

He restores my soul; He guides me in the paths of righteousness For His name's sake.

Even though I walk through the valley of the shadow of death, I fear no evil, for You are with me; Your rod and Your staff, they comfort me.

Whatever he meant, whomever he was rambling about, I suppose didn't matter anymore. I dried my tears and closed my eyes in anguish.

First a deaf-toned silence, and then three loud "bangs," and then silence again. I opened my eyes. In place of three living humans were three dead corpses. It was over.

For a while, we all just stood there in silence. I could hear a few breaths whistling through beaks. As the cadets regained their composure, I turned around and groomed my wing of any residue.

"Comrades," I said softly. "Status Report."

"The last row of tanks are on schedule," the private said. "We will be leaving for the shore in matter of days."

"Ready your regiments and sound the call," I replied. "Prepare all birds for Brazil."

"And what of these?" a guard asked as he pointed to the corpses. "Should we dispose of their belongings?"

"Don't bother. Put them on the tanks when they arrive. Send those flat faces a message, that there was and will be more where that came from."

They nodded as they dragged the bodies out of the hollow as I flew outside and onto a branch. The air smelled thin, yet sour, in contrast to the sky as it transformed from orange to magenta, to black. I jolted my head left and right and saw no one was there. Then I started to cry again.

Chapter 31

Excerpt from “Holocaust Remembered” Continued

The night I both revealed and sealed my feelings about my future wife to our families was one of mixed feelings. It was at the end of the day. The last glare of sunlight had vanished over the horizon. Everyone was filling up their last quota, both inside the shack and out in the garden. We packed everything and said our goodbyes to our fellow non-human brethren. I could remember Ara shedding a great many tears. She had established a close connection to us humans. All that was left was to wait for a signal from Uncle Epi.

At last, night fell. We had quickly gathered the last precious items we could find and scurried out to the front of the shack. The scenery had turned to pitch black, with only a few gas lamps and the night sky glimmering specks of starry light to break the darkness. As strange as it was, my little sister was not tired as she grabbed my hand. Her face didn’t seem to have any worry or concern. For someone so small, Izobel had experienced much, so it didn’t surprise me to know she had developed a brave soul.

We all focused our lamps into the grassy landscape, hoping for something to fly out of the darkness. Seconds became minutes, minutes became half an hour. Half an hour beca—

“Christine and I want to marry.”

The words just blurted out of my mouth, shattering the silence. Everyone just looked at me in the most awkward of ways.

Even my sister had a perplexed expression. Perhaps I should have planned this sooner. Perhaps I should have told them at an earlier time. But my love and I were still children. What did we know?

"My boychek," Mother said as she approached me. "This is no time for your games. Now…"

"I mean it!" I interrupted. "We're going to get married." Now I felt even more stupid. What was I thinking?

Christine walked up from behind me, holding my hand, tightly, her fingers digging into my palm. I could feel her pulse, beating in sync with mine. Meanwhile, everyone just stood there like mannequins. Here we were, risking life and death, and I was about to ask for her hand in marriage. Christine just looked at me, and I looked at her.

"I…is that true?" Christine asked clumsily. "You want me to marry you?"

"Ara," I called, to which she came scurrying onto my shoulder. "Do you know of any marital rites within your forrest community that can be done in a few minutes?"

"There is one," Ara replied. "But it will require a few items, and I'm not sure…"

"Then we have no time to lose," I interrupted. "Gather what you can and meet us on the side of the shed."

She nodded, climbed down my legs, and hurried into the house. Given the circumstances, no one asked any further questions. We situated ourselves to the left wall, while Christine's brothers stood guard, continuing to look for any intrusion. The forest residents propped up a few rocks and stumps for chairs. Mice placed a bouquet of lilies on Christine's head and a rose on my right collar button. Elch-Moht etched a rectangle on the wooden wall with his talon, while Tahrain drew a square in the sand with his paw, creating a makeshift altar for us to use.

Now all was quiet, except for the buzzing of a few insects. Everyone, man and beast, took their seats, as Christine and I were situated in front of everyone, standing face to face. Ara scurried out of the shed as she brushed her tail against our feet, symbolizing our connection with the precious ground. Next, several deer bowed their heads in respect at our arms and torso, representing the pureness our bodies will have against any adultery. Finally, Elch Mocht stood in between us on Tahrain's head. He pursed his beak together and recited a small prayer in a native tongue we could never understand.

"Mageck," Tahrain said suddenly. "Do you take this female as your spouse, partner, and guiding light, to hold as your responsibility till age take you back to the weed?"

"I do," I replied with no problem.

"And you, Christine." He continued as he tilted his head to my love. "Do you take this male as your spouse, partner, and guiding light, to hold as your responsibility till age take you back to weed?"

"I…" She could not think of what to say. I couldn't blame her; it was all too sudden. But I looked over her shoulder for any incoming trouble, and knowing it wasn't the time for any more questions, she knew what had to be done. But just as she was about to open her mouth again, in came Episko, sweeping down from the sky like a mad bombardier.

"What the hell are you all doing?" he asked with rage.

"Uncle Epi," I replied in defense. "We were just…"

"We are on the verge of utter annihilation. And here you are playing games. I thought I made it clear there would be no spectacles!"

"Episko," Ara said. "Maybe it would be best if you took a moment to calm down."

“Don’t you think I’m under enough stress that calming down is not an option!” Epi squawked “There is a great weapon beyond any comprehension heading for this perimeter in a matter of days!”

Everyone gasped. I had thought from what the animals said that this was a neutral zone. We couldn’t possibly think it would be penetrable.

“Didn’t expect that did you?” Epi said sarcastically. “Sorry to have bothered whatever sort of party you were having.”

“This wasn’t a party Episko.” Christine said bluntly as she took my hand. “We were…getting married.”

Before I could think, move, or say another word, she kissed me right on my lips. My body swayed forward a bit as she hung on my face like a frog on a leaf. A little, sweet smile grew on everyone’s faces. All except Epi, still angry and confused.

“Oh…a marriage…ah…that’s what was going on,” he said with a snickering chuckle. “Now, now everything is fine! I overreacted! Sorry everyone. That one’s on me.”

“Epi? What has gotten into you?” I asked.

“Not to mention the ordeal I had to endure just a few hours ago,” he continued to ramble. “I HAD TO BREAK UP WITH MY GIRLFRIEND! And lo and behold, here I see a love conspiring to mock me, and you want to know what has gotten into me”

“Wait, wait,” Andrzej interrupted. “You had a girlfriend.”

“Kana was her name!” Epi barked at him. “Maybe it’s about time you should have known. I personally risked my own feathers by developing a relationship with the enemy. Her name was Kana.”

My heart just stopped after he said that name. I could feel my legs becoming loose as noodles. Izobel held my sides tightly, so as not to let me fall. The very leader of the prison we had tried to escape, was in love with our only hope of survival.

"Do you know of this Macaw?" asked Christine.

"She made one of our villagers eat her son's heart." I replied solemnly.

"I knew it!" shouted one of Christine's outraged friends. "I knew we shouldn't have put our trust in that parrot!"

"If it wasn't for me…" Episko explained. "You would have been dead."

"I think we would've managed."

"I'd have loved to see you try."

"BOYS!" my mother shouted as she broke them apart. "We're not going to solve anything this way. We've lost too much precious time already. I vote that we leave now and save our arguments for later."

"Go on, see if I care," Epi spat. "I've already lost more in a day than most birds have lost in a lifetime. I just came here to tell you that your time here is numbered!"

Suddenly, he collapsed on the ground, exhausted wings stretching on the pavement. Tears started coming down his feathery cheeks, flicking them off with his talon. Ara scurried over in attempt to console him, but he just shoved her away with his beak. After a few moments, he gathered his senses and took a deep breath.

"The patrollers will be on their way soon," he said calmly as he stood back up." If you wish to continue this mission, you should leave now. They probably have found out about my relationship with you. So, if you want to go forward, it's best you do it without me."

And without another word from him, and before anyone could respond, he turned his back to us and flew away into the trees. I had never seen him this cross before. But we humans all looked at each other and gave a simultaneous nod.

As we said our goodbyes, we took one last glance at the shack. So many memories were stuffed into one, convenient, residential package. It was all we knew that was a sanctuary to us. Now we had to become vulnerable once more. Without a word, we all ran into the thick fields, the shack slowly disappearing among the tall stalks. I could hear the woodland critters shouting from behind us –

"Do not fear!" they shouted in their tongue. "We continue to fight for you!"

"But we humans are the real ones in danger!' Wadja shouted back. "You have no need to be concern."

"This is no longer a battle for humans!" Tahrain barked as his face grew fainter. "It is a battle…For all of us!"

I didn't know what that meant then, or why would it matter? Before we knew it, the critters had disappeared from our peripheral vision. In a few minutes, we would find ourselves in the harsh jungle that continued to spread across the European landscape. We were together, all of us, and yet, I still felt alone. It felt as everything was against us, the government, the world, and even our optimism. I thought this feeling would never go way. Then, as we reached the edge of the vines, Christine pressed her lips against my ear, and spoke the words that brought back the courage to carry on:

"I do."

Chapter 32

My father and his division had been trudging the Northwest soil for days now. The enemy was drawing nearer, and not an hour of rest could they waste. Infantry-cats were already feeling the heat, and the dogs were no better. Meanwhile, rodents needed to collect droplets from various parts of the jungle just to keep them all hydrated.

On top of that, they had the responsibility of looking after the human survivors, who were already lagging behind. My father, Photios, had assigned himself to look after the humans, while Spartak led the pack.

"Unnngh," grunted Phillipe, who was on a stretcher like the other humans.

"Stay in there," Photios said. "Were almost at the border."

"Are you sure of that?"

"Absolutely. Just a little while and you can treat yourself to all the scraps and dishes you can take."

The gray parrot from the POW was granted the privilege to fly a few feet around the canopy, as long as it didn't leave the infantry's sight.

"Are you sure it's all right for him to hover around us like that?" asked an infantry mouse. "I mean, the bird's our prisoner and yet he's having it good, compared to us."

"I thought he might need some fresh air," Spartak explained. "Besides, if he even tries to escape, I'll eat him like poultry on rye."

"Do you think he might crack soon?" asked an infantry cat.

"Beats me," Spartak replied as he vigilantly looked up at the captive. "Gray parrots are known to resist a lot of things. Might take a week before we get any information from him."

Yes, it was a long, grueling trudge across the jungle floor, but soon it would pay off, as within the next few miles they would reach Sweden, neutral territory. Finally, they would find time to rest their weary, battered paws and share a drink or two, perhaps in a well-furnished inn or dainty bar in the town. Even more so, a small package of humans would find a fragment of sanctuary in these neutral parts, despite some of AVIACHT'S lower ranks hovering around the town's rooftops. Yet, doubt was beginning to shadow over the cadets. I mean, who could blame them? It had been days since they saw a full meal in front of them, and it felt as though they had been walking around a full circumference. One could swear they saw the same moss-covered boulder twice.

The infantry smelled what could only be identified as fresh steak and eggs. They must have been close. A few dogs ran toward the scent, saliva gushing from their jaws, only to be stopped by Spartak.

"Fools," he whispered. "Don't you remember the first line of defense? Suppose those in lower ranks might be planning something."

"I'll be the judge of that," my father replied as ran to the front of the line.

He let out a big whiff with his snout, checking the area for any foreign smells: a wiretap, a cage, a snare, anything hiding within the vegetation. He turned and said,

"Boys, you can unwind your paws tonight. This is where we will rest."

Everyone rushed into town, ready to fill their empty bellies and drink to their content. Even the gray parrot tried to swoop down in their direction, but was stopped by my father.

"You are not to leave this spot!" he said threateningly. "Atah! Hotep!"

From behind him came two rather husky St. Bernards. Both looked as though they lifted weights at least six times a day.

"Guard this prisoner, and make sure he doesn't do anything stupid. And don't worry, we will send you what we can find at the inn. There's plenty for all." To which they nodded back. With that, my father turned the other way to catch up with his crew.

Just as he predicted, a quaint village was waiting for them just over the hill. The place remained untouched, unaffected by the jungles encroaching just over the border. The winding road was cobblestone, highlighted by a few streetlamps that glistened the sidewalk as well. The buildings were sturdy, yet nicely crammed together, as if out of a children's storybook. In the background were the Alps, majestic and unspoiled, with their snowcapped peaks on top, and rocky terrain below; it was one of the very few natural wonders of Europe unaffected by the invading forces.

Father's infantry could smell the aroma of pastries and pasta all around the town. The odor was so heavenly, even the human survivors tried to muscle their way out of the stretchers, much to the medics' annoyance. Eventually, they settled on a quaint pub, a rather modest establishment nestled in the middle of a square. As was obligated by decree of neutral zone law; the sign on its post was etched out, so travelers could only judge by its texture and aroma, rather than name of business.

As they entered through the front door, a small "welcome" was heard among a crowd of allied soldiers, each sharing a bone, biscuit or cup of complimentary catnip. My father and Spartak took a sigh of relief as they gave the infantry the "okay" and nestled into the crowd. Some propped up on stools and ordered a drink; others dug into the complimentary hors d'oeuvres, and even a few just headed upstairs to a room to tucker out.

At this moment, my father spotted several AVIACHT loyalists, among them bodyguards – elephants and wolves who belonged to the Tusken-Reichstag and Wolfblitz sub-divisions. They were squawking, drinking, barking, and celebrating a recent defeat of the allied forces. In front of them was a screen, showcasing another "Sacred Skies" propaganda film. My father couldn't figure out what the title was, but the plot was clear. another heroic epic about a small clan of parrots who band together, to stop and kill a group of greedy human loggers from cutting down their forest. A typical synopsis, but the film proved popular.

Knowing that being caught with humans could mean sudden death, Photios carefully escorted the human survivors and the medics to the back of the inn. From there, they'd cover the humans with long dark cloths, giving them the appearance of food supply for the axis forces. Finally, these humans could rest secretly in one of many vacant rooms.

"What do you bet we get out of this alive?" asked an exhausted Spartak as he ordered a bottle of the finest catnip.

"You can bet $10 or $100,000." Photios replied as he reached for a tender bone on the counter, "and my answer will still be the same."

The two looked to make sure no one was watching or listening in. You could never be too careful when you have fugitives in your care.

"Come on, Photios," Spartak insisted, as the two tried to act discreet. "We're already behind schedule. Do you really think every damaged human we find is worth saving? I can name a great many different reasons why we shoul—"

"I'm not abandoning those humans Spartak! And that's my final word!" With that, my father took a huge lick on the bone marrow.

"Does the concept of 'The enemy on our tails' mean anything to you?" Spartak hissed quietly. "You can't expect us to pick up the pace with fugitives to worry about. If we leave them here, the best-case scenario is they can hide from AVIACHT's forces a little while longer."

"It is my solemn mission to bring them back to safety, and Argentina is our best route."

"The humans?" Spartak asked. "What about us? Have you not realized our water and nourishment supply is running dangerously low? And if you think another day of stalling is what you have in mind, you've got another thing coming."

Knowing he'd get no answer from my father, Spartak took a swig of condensed catnip and stormed upstairs, defeated. Meanwhile, Photios took a moment to gaze at the AVIACHT soldiers, who were sharing a drink of Brazilian Nut with their wolf and elephant comrades. Photios thought for a moment…

"Private Chronos," my father said as a Labrador private approached him.

"Yes, Commander?" he asked.

"Tell our captive macaw he's free to go. We have no use for him now."

"Are you insane? He just might…"

"Do as I say. He's given us the information we need. Besides, we're in neutral territory now. I don't think his information will be of much use to them anyhow."

Without question, Chronos bowed his head and headed outside where their captive was flying just above the tavern. With a sigh, Photios sat at the bar and ordered a small drink from the bartender. Given that the bartender was a bird from the Amazon, it gave him a small, unfriendly sneer before slapping the bottle on the counter. It was there Photios noticed a rather peculiar-looking Yellow Macaw off in the corner.

For whatever the reason may be, something was different about this bird. His eyes seemed tired and sunken in, as if he hadn't slept in days. His beak had a slight discoloration with a few marks indicating a little sun bleach. His feathers were slightly shuffled and unkempt, unlike other macaws' whose feathery coatings were aligned and neatly polished. Caressed in his right talon was a small shot of gin, which he just filled with a bottle nearby.

He was the only bird who didn't have a smile on his face. Father knew something was different about him, and he felt the need to investigate. He dropped off his stool and slowly started to walk over, believing somehow, he could get answers. Maybe this rogue macaw had answers, a way out or a map to more survivors. But just before Father could turn in his direction, the piano started to play. It was the anthem of the AVIACHT nation:

Oh, Helios Mighty Leader
Praise this our holy sky
Feathers and talons together
And on the swift wind we fly

My father nudged a few feet away and propped back onto his stool. At that moment, a rather tired out doberman pincher whispered into the ear of his rodent friend. Who nodded back and began to play a song on his small harmonica. A tune father had not heard for a very long time.

Oh Say, Can You See
By The Dawn's Early Light?
Soon, a few cats and dogs began to join in.
What So Proudly We Hail,
At The Twilight's Last Gleaming

They were followed by other domesticated critters, who started to sing their own country's tune.

God Save Our Gracious Queen,
Long Live Our Noble Queen,
God Save The Queen!

Eventually, another pack of foreigners sprung into an anthem almost forgotten:

Juntos Con Ellos Cantemos De Pie La Vida
Nueva Y Fuerte De Trabajo Y Paz

This rousing collection of songs surely caught the attention of the macaws, as they began to sing louder:

All Avian creatures far and wide
We shall fight for what is home
Our trees and our skies shall...

But yet, they were drowned out once more as a Canadian Tabby Cat bellowed out along with his comrades:

O, Canada, Our Home and Native Land
True Patriot Love, In All Thy Sons Command

It was then that they were followed by another group of soldiers from France, singing their anthem:

Allons Enfants de la Patrie
Le Jour de Gloire Est Arrivé
Contre Nous de la Tyrannie

They were then succeeded by an infantry from China with their national song:

Arise, Ye Who Refuse to be Slaves!
With Our Flesh and Blood,

Soon, the Russians joined in.

Then the Japanese.
Followed by the Dutch:

Wilhelmus van Nassouwe
Ben ick van Duytschen Bloet

And a few more even sang in a language and from a nation newly-established and rarely heard of in the world. Soon, the whole tavern was thundering with harmonious noise and song. Even infantry members, who had turned in upstairs, leapt out of their rooms and joined the cacophonous chorus. The dismayed AVIACHT troops flew over to the manager, demanding a stop to what they called "Unruly Behavior," but it was no use, and the manager gave the allies the okay to carry on. With a smile and a shrug, my father joined in too.

The only pet not singing was Spartak, who sat quietly at the railing after having just awakened to the ruckus. Yet, Photios noticed a small, weak smile creep around his jawline, the first he had made in many moons.

Eventually, like all events, the music died down, and all went back to their independent businesses. Photios finished the marrow within his bone and proceeded to his sleeping quarters. Spartak joined him at the middle of the stairs when Photius noticed a hint on suspicion on his face.

"Are the human safe in their beds?" my father asked.

"Everyone is fit and accounted for," Spartak replied as he licked his paw. "But I suppose that is not why you have such a distinct look now is it?"

"No, no it is not," my father admitted. "I…I just couldn't help but notice the most peculiar yellow macaw at the edge of the bar?"

"What do you mean?"

"He seemed to be…singing along with us."

Chapter 33

It has been a month since my first encounter with Dr. Trunca. She has been, for the most part helpful, and surprisingly constructive in my relationship towards others.

Indeed, it does seem odd, as my time in her office mostly starts off as unproductive conversation, jumping across each other's common knowledge and opinions, rambling on about our day, and what hobbies we have discovered. Still, I find it fascinating, beginning a nice talk between human and dolphin.

But eventually, the session gains momentum as Trunca helps me engage in Tai chi, aerobics and a few other exercise recommendations. My body becomes clearer, and more aware of its surroundings. She puts me into a meditative trance, breathing softly against the cool, soft waves hovering from above. From there, I clear my thoughts, enter my memories, and try to peel back any secrets from my parents that I had forgotten. Until now I haven't thought of my childhood for several decades. Though painful at times, it gives me a moment to ponder on where I am and where I could still be.

I begin to express myself in ways I never thought possible. I recall remembrances from my childhood, from when I lost my first tooth, to when I received my pod licences, to when I earned my degree in Population Control. I start to tell the dolphin a few regrets, triumphs and lessons that carried me in life. The routine ends with a nice cup of Ginseng tea, plucked straight from Dr. Trunca's kelp garden outside.

Lately, I'd have to admit, my relationship with my son has remained strained. I hardly have time to really sit down and engage with him. I'm lucky to even have a conversation with him at the table. Yet, I know it really isn't his fault. His adjustment with this changing world has not been easy, a transpecies daughter, a flimsy school system and a neglectful mother. Eric has slumped into an unfathomable depression. Adding to that is his relationship to us as a species. He feels rather guilty being human, as if the fact he is one had somehow caused other animals to magically suffer. Of course, that could not be logically proven just by being human. Still, I understand where he is coming from. After all, our ancestors were specialized in woodcutting and meat packing, and that is why I decided to bring him to this particular session.

My son and I arrive at the vine-entangled station of Ellis Island, once only a stop for human immigrants, such as my father. Now it is a shrine, a welcoming beacon to all species wishing to make their mark in the United States and its habitats. We step outside at the edge of the shore. The day is ideal for underwater transportation: partly cloudy, temperatures in the mid-seventies, and only a few gusts of wind floating in the air. Thus, we strip of our garments, put on our one-piece swim gear, and check our special inhalers for any inconsistencies. Just then, the otter from my first meeting emerges from the shoreline. He gives us the nod as we descend into the depths of Hudson Bay once more.

We swim for about five to six minutes before finding the doctor's office perched on the edge of the reef. From there, we arrive on the platform, transporting us to the dry, self-contained, waiting room where we dry off, and sit comfortably in our seats. I try to converse with Eric, but he is unresponsive, and he blankly stares into the watery abyss. The receptionist calls and escorts us to Trunca's office. Moments later, the dolphin swims up from the hole below, and plops onto her chair.

"Hello there, you must be Eric," she says to my son, to which he nods back. "Your father has told me many things about you. From what I heard, you've been having a difficult time lately."

"What's it to you?" Eric barks back.

"Son, please be nice," I reply.

"It's no trouble, Mr. Whitestone," says Trunca. "After all, a child is a child."

"Truth is, doctor" I say back, "I think he's too much of a child. I had to pick him up from court earlier today following a misdemeanor."

"Explain."

"Well, he was in violation of law 15B, Littering. He's been doing the same deed for over a month, but authorities finally caught up with him and…"

"I would throw my things away more easily if they had more disposal units Dad!" My son replies with a whine.

"You know what you did, son," I reply sternly. "Who knows how many inhabitants could've choked on your disposable items."

"My wolf friends coaxed me into it. The whole thing was a dare."

"All right, all right!" Dr. Trunca interrupts, "I can sense a rather strong tension between the two of you. Let's all ease into our 'comfort places' and look back on where this all started."

Following my lead, my son and I both take a deep breath and take our positions in two easy chairs. Then with the smooth tranquil sounds of her slicing and squeaking, our doctor clears our minds, just like that. Eric opens his eyes first, followed by me, as I listen to my son:

"For many years," he begins. "I have felt ashamed of what I am, a Homo sapien. I look back on what my species did to this planet, what with deforestation and pollution and I felt like I personally had something to do with it. Somehow, I, Eric Whitestone, was indirectly responsible, at least partly, for your misery."

"I'm not really sure what you mean," a puzzled Trunca responds as she breathes through a hole in her head. "Indeed, the perpetrators of our plight were your species, but that does not explain why you, as an individual, should be guilty."

"I mean like small things," he replies. "You know, like my carbon footprint."

"Ah, I see."

"But strangely though, I decided not to be ashamed and just relish in these human shortcomings. I started combating with my non-human peers, getting into paw fights, taking perilous races, littering without any regard. Oddly, I still managed to make friends with some scavenger wolves. They're pretty used to leaving trash around, so it's not much of a problem for them. See, I like to surround myself with rebels, because I consider myself to be one."

After a moments silence…

"Mr. Whitestone," says Trunca. "Is there something you'd like to add?"

"What else is there?" I reply. "Do you have anything in mind?"

"Well, from what he said and what you told me," she explained. "I am sensing a rather strong rift between a father and son, and yet you two have something in common. You have a dynamic, if not unorthodox, relationship towards your species, which is not unusual among humans. Your son's love-hate relationship, though self-punishment, is not in the least rewardable. Given your family's past, it seems to reason you have the tendency to expose your vulnerability and erode your daily routine, and this creates a hostel mental environment towards yourselves."

"What the hell would you know!" my son blasts.

"Eric, please," I reply.

"You know nothing about us!" he continues. "We almost screwed up your ozone hole. We trashed your ecosystems; hell, I can even write a fifty-page list of how many species we made extinct!"

"Then, what is it that you really feel about yourself?" Trunca asks.

"I...feel...afraid," Eric replies. "I feel afraid that somehow I will be punished simply for what I am. That one day, I will be taken to the electric chair so I'll be one less human to worry about."

"Okay. and Alan, what is it you feel about yourself."

"I...feel." I try to think. "Frustrated that my son hasn't learned to respect private property, but also hopeful, because he is expressing his true emotions."

"I'd like to add another emotion," Eric adds. "I feel a bit of sadness. I'm sad that I haven't lived up to the expectations that I hoped I'd achieve. I feel like no matter what I try or do, I won't be able to give enough back to the non-human community. I mean, it's not like I can snap my fingers and bring back all the habitats my species destroyed. And talk doesn't physically solve anything either. I don't think any ocean, land or sky dweller would ever want to be friends with a polluter like me."

"Well, I want to be friends," Trunca replies sympathetically. "Hold on."

Our therapist dives into the waters and swims away. A few moments later, she is back and reveals what appears to be a moonstone pearl. She places the precarious object in Eric's hand as he looks at it with the deepest intrigue.

"This is a precious item among the Cetacean community," she explains. "We only give them to individuals we deem as friends. It's a millennia old tradition."

"Uh, thanks," Eric says puzzlingly. "What's your point?"

"My point is, the next time you feel doubtful about finding more friends in the animal community, just remember you can always count on me as a companion. There is nothing to fear or regret in my sessions."

Eric takes a sigh of relief. I've never seen him look this reassured in years.

"Now, Mr. Whitestone," Trunca continues. "Why don't you continue your story about your father? I've been hooked on it ever since our first meeting."

I clear my throat as I reminisce about my father's perilous journey, just after they left the shack. In a rare moment, my son listens as well.

Chapter 34

Excerpt from "Holocaust Remembered"

We arrived at the border of the tall stalks as instructed and what a relief it was. Our legs could no longer keep up with our bodies. My little sister was taking it especially hard. She had to be carried for the last few miles.

Exhausted from the running, we sat on a group of large, moss-coated boulders, the texture soft to the touch. It was peaceful in the night air, despite the jungle's humidity. A few tufts of breeze whistled through my hair as I took a whiff of the forest's aroma. I looked around and saw my frail Izobel nestle on my mother-in-law's lap, curling up like a caterpillar in a chrysalis. My brothers took the role of watchmen as they stood their ground and listened for any suspicious noises coming from the jungle. Others in the human kin laid on their organic rock beds, stretching their backs, cracking their wrists and massaging their palms. They were too weary to start up any further conversations.

Now, all was quiet; just the pure silence of night. All we could do was sleep and wait. Wait for some signal, some cue, some message of where to go next.

Several hours passed as we dozed into a deep slumber. Everyone was fast asleep, except for the three night guards: Andrzej, Wadja, and of course, Mageck. As I laid my head on the moss, I felt like I was once again in the shack. All safe, secure from any patrollers. And even more so, a group of different species, not of our own, opened their homes and hearts for us. Strange, despite what our species did to their homes, they still managed to forgive and become family. But now we were vulnerable again, unsure of what may happen next. Sure, we had a game plan, but the result was still to be written.

Then we heard a small sound like a paw rubbing against the dirt. I opened my eyes and the clean night sky was the first thing I saw. The sounds of people grumbling and worrying were around me. 'Did we get caught?' 'Did they find us?' The noise grew slightly louder.

I turned to see my brothers making a defensive stance with their makeshift weapons, ready for any creature looking to pounce upon us. They all had their backs to us as they faced the darkness. The digging sound grew even louder, chugging in our direction. Then we saw a strange, lump-like shape creeping closer towards us. Our hearts stopped as the object turned out to be coming from underneath the earth. Someone or something was digging a tunnel. Had the enemy found out how to adapt? Did they send a spy that lived in the earth?

Finally, a figure popped out of the dirt making a large hole in its path. We were overjoyed to be looking at a face we thought we'd never see again.

"DEMETER!" my brothers and I shouted as we ran to our canine friend and hugged him around his dirt-coated fur.

"Hello, friends," Demeter replied weakly. "It's wonderful to come across familiar faces."

"How did you find us?" asked Wadja.

"Let's just say a little bird told us your whereabouts."

"What do you mean us?" Mageck asked as he pointed his weapon towards Demeter. "How do we know we can still trust you?"

"Please forgive me. I am not here to hurt you," Demeter replied as he lowered Mageck's weapon and said, "I am a close friend of your associate Christine, and her family. Many moons ago I was able to infiltrate a ghetto where I found her and her family. They were desperate for freedom and I was able to devise an escape plan. At first it worked until her parents and several others were captured by the AVIACHT forces. I promised I would free the rest, but sadly I was captured with my infantry in a matter of days."

"What about my parents?" I asked.

"Your father is in good paws now," Demeter reassured me. "We found him after liberating a camp in the north. He is in the best care anyone could ask for."

"And our mother," Wadja asked. "What about her."

"I'm sorry," Demeter replied solemnly. "She didn't make it. She was killed on the spot after their capture."

My brothers and I collapsed on the ground. We couldn't believe the bread and milk of our life was gone. She was such a strong-willed woman, we couldn't imagine she'd be taken away so easily.

"How do you know of Uncle Epi?" Mageck's mother asked.

"Well, luckily, before my infantry and I were taken to the POW camp," Demeter explained. "I managed to send a message, via pigeon to a macaw I had heard that was smuggling human survivors out of Europe. I told him about my whereabouts and where to meet. Sadly, I wasn't able to make contact until my rescue.

"We met at one of the neutral zones in Switzerland, where the macaw was found in a pub after breaking up with a girlfriend. After introducing him to my friends Photios and Spartak, we managed to come up with a plan."

"See, this tunnel here? It leads right to the pub, which surprisingly is only a few hours away. And this is where our luck might be able to change. See, behind this pub, we managed to sniff out and discover a set of old submarines that were decommissioned following the invasion. However, King Helios ordered them to be repurposed and fashioned into weapons that will be transferred to Brazil – AVIACHT's biggest stronghold. Now, if we can manage to sneak into one of their storage compartments, we just might be able to get you there and take a scenic route to Buenos Aires, Argentina, the last South American nation untouched by the war.

"How do we know you're not lying?" Mageck's mother asked.

"Trust me or not," Demeter replied.

After a moment's thought, we all agreed to take a risk and follow his lead. One by one, we gathered our belongings and slowly muscled ourselves into the underground tunnel. I thought I would never again have to go down such a cramped place. But I was risking my sanity, and possibly life, for a chance of survival. As each one of us ventured in single file back into the ground, I could smell the aroma of fungi and rotting corpses. I could tell a few humans came this way and weren't as lucky as us, buried in secret by their feathered assassins.

About midway through the tunnel, I heard what sounded like murmurs and chirping from up above. Demeter, who was right in front of me, covered my mouth with his tail. We knew then we were right below the enemy again, and from the sound of their squawking laughter, it was the pub Demeter had told us about. They were just talking, scheming about something 'big' that would 'change the course of dominance' or something along those lines.

For what seemed like eternity, none of us made a sound. There was only the noise of claw steps, with a little drinking and tweeting in between. Eventually the noise dissipated. That signaled the room above was empty, as we trenched on through the muddy sarcophagus.

Hours had now passed. Our palms and knees were filthy with grime and our joints were aching in pain. I felt envious of Demeter, being a quadruped and all. Finally, I could make out over his shoulder a dim speck of light glowing in the distance. We trudged faster in anticipation, so much that Demeter, in the lead, needed to speed up. The light grew bigger and bigger until we reached the source – a wide opening big enough to fit two to three humans. Following Demeter's lead, we scrambled out of the hole and back to the surface, the smell of fresh oxygen filling our lungs.

As the last human squirmed out, Demeter quickly pawed some dirt and covered the hole, hiding the evidence. The atmosphere was a hazy fog heavily coating the landscape. The terrain was a flat field long abandoned from the invasion. He took a moment to stare around the place, sniffing for something, but we couldn't know what it was. His eyes and head were on full alert, like an owl on top a perch. Then his face looked up to the sky, jaw slightly ajar. At first, he panicked, but then sighed in relief, as another face came swooping down onto the empty field.

"Hello, Episko," said Demeter. "Thank you for coming."

Uncle Epi solemnly nodded back.

Chapter 35

The next morning, beings all over the woodlands were gathering at the meeting hole of the large tree. It was rare for the seating to be this packed, but who could blame them? This was now our darkest hour; every species was divided by class: Birds, Rodents, Reptiles, Amphibians, etc.

As I took my place among the Rodents; I realized I was still wearing the dress Andrzej had made for me. My left paw groped at the texture as a small tear fell down my cheek. I couldn't imagine what dangers our human friends were about to endure. But more importantly, now that we had defied the enemy, we wondered what dangers would await us. This is what this meeting was all about. The chirping and squeaking died down as Tah-Rain and Elch-Mocht called everyone to attention.

"Brothers, and Sisters," Tah-Rain began. "I know these are turbulent times, never before have we assisted the humans."

"AND WE NEVER SHOULD HAVE!" shouted a badger from afar, followed by barks of agreement. "Didn't we warn you those sapes were nothing but trouble? Look where they placed us?"

"We are now in the mouth of the enemies target!" shouted a deer.

"How can we assure our younglings safety now?" begged a mother rabbit.

"We're already below our winter food quota," a squirrel next to me acknowledged.

After the area erupted in protest for what seemed like awhile, Elch-Mocht let out a squawk. The place fell silent again, and all eyes and ears fell on our battered leader.

"Do you think we were not aware of these risks?" Elch-Mocht asked. "Our whole forest was already being consumed. Our homes obliterated. Our lives nearly shattered. Only this time, for the first time, it did not come from a human source."

"We have come too far in this mission," Tah-Rain added. "And if we can't continue to protect our natural home and those humans, from a force this large, then how are we better than them? How, I ask you?"

No one could find an answer to that. Yes, up until now, the human race served as our biggest threat, and even we were able to easily adapt. We were always prepared for such nuisances. We would gather our things, square our accounts and migrate further into the forest without a problem. But now, with our home not only being destroyed, but transforming into a landscape unrecognizable, how could we possibly run into hiding now? How could we stand idly by as our enemy inches closer and closer? After a few more minutes silence…

"I would like to continue my services," I said. "I want to help the humans."

Everyone gasped and whispered in gossip to my statement. The lines of "Are you crazy" and "That's basically suicide" reverberated off the holes' walls.

"Everyone just listen to me!" I continued. "I know that these are turbulent times, and we're risking more than we bargained for. But we've come too far to back out now. We face a threat far greater than any logging or polluting force combined. Trudging and hiding deeper into the forest may have worked before, but the enemy will find us. We need to fight back. We need to help those humans."

"Do you even realize this is the first time we were part of an ANTHROMALIA?" I added. "A real chance for peace with the humans. We might never even get this chance again if we stand idly by. Now is our time to protect what we created."

"Ara is right," Elch-Mocht replied solemnly, much to everyone's surprise. "I've scourged the landscape myself, and with every town, every house, every human life destroyed, AVIACHT comes one step closer to having us as their next target. And the more we stand our ground, the more susceptible we become. As I've stated before, this is no longer a battle for just the humans. It is a battle for all of us"

"I propose we mobilize a defense division," Tah-Rain added as he scratched his head with his paw. "BOC!"

A large, brawny elk came front and center, bowing at the presence of the elders.

"Yes, Your Grace," Boc replied.

"Are you capable of rounding up the strongest the forest has to offer?" Tah-Rain asked.

"I believe I can manage," Boc replied. "Though I must admit, it has been several generations since we have commenced in battle."

"But with the time we have, can you or can you not barricade what we have left of the woods?"

"I don't see why not."

"Then go and make haste."

Boc nodded back and left the meeting with several of the strongest critters following suit.

"Ara, you said earlier you were still willing to volunteer?" Elch-Mocht asked.

"Yes," I replied. "I would do anything to help my new

friends. Despite the countless shortcomings these humans have, I can't help but be fascinated with this species."

"Then do you have a plan to rescue them?"

"I certainly do. That is, if other critters would be willing to join me."

Surprisingly, nearly half of the rodents and tree dwellers raised their paws and talons. I never knew I'd get this much support.

"Then it is settled," Tah-Rain declared. "Ara, you will round up all the volunteers and hatch a plan to divert the enemy away from the humans. Boc and his companions will continue to gather the best the forest has to offer. This meeting is adjourned."

And with that, Elch-Mocht tapped the rock on the stone with his talon, and we all scurried away to our business.

Chapter 36

Now, I couldn't imagine how or why I would choose to continue saving humans. After all, they made me lose my one love. Yet, here I was, risking my feathers once more to aid these peculiar creatures.

The abandoned vehicles were all gently placed on a deserted open airfield, a typical spot for AVIACHT to round up any needed scrap. Demeter, a dog soldier I had only known through letters, led me and the humans to the back end. Before us was a large sea tank, capable of storing luggage five times its body weight, and just enough space to smuggle our friends to Argentina. Out of the fog and from behind the tank came a regiment of canines, felines and rodents tagging behind.

"Right on time," said Photios. "And not a moment too soon."

"Photios, Spartak!" commanded Demeter. "I'd like you to meet the humans I've been talking to you about."

After acquainting the crew with the humans and me, we stood and waited patiently for orders from his regiment, giving us the "all clear." All was quiet and calm as the humans took a moment to rest their backs against the tank, while Demeter and I stood behind the tank to keep watch and while Photios's group guarded the front to watch our cargo.

I clung my talons onto the topmost part of the cannon. Everything seemed peaceful and tranquil in the early morning air. The sky was just starting to turn a lighter blue, as the sun was beginning its ascent from the East. As a breeze trickled against my feathers I kept thinking of Kana and our last conversation. The memory felt like a knife piercing into my chest. I reached into my satchel and took out a picture of us in our early days standing in front of a liberated zoo. I placed the photo onto the ground, burying it and my memories, in the soil.

"Farewell, my love," I said quietly under tears.

Suddenly, we heard a small ruffle, coming from the thick jungle. A human started to stand up and panic but was immediately shoved down by a feline cadet. I flew over the mist and through the trees to investigate. There was nothing unusual, nothing but a large whiff of smoke, rising in the distance. Probably just another town AVIACHT had invaded. I swooped down and landed back on my perch.

"Mama?" said Izzy's voice from below. "What's an Anthromalia?"

"How did you learn that word?" her mother's voice asked.

"I heard Auntie Ara saying that to a few bunny rabbits a month ago."

A moment's silence, and then…

"Well, an Anthromalia is where we were," her mother replied. "It's a group, or town, of human and animals living side by side. We all shared the land, gave back what we could, and mixed together our work with theirs."

"Like a clubhouse?" Izzy asked.

"Yes, you might say that. Like a clubhouse."

"Mama, do you think we'll ever see an Anthromalia where we're going?"

"Oh, who knows child? We've been away from the world for so long. I have no idea what to expect on the other side of the ocean, 244ut I'm pretty sure there are others out there, just waiting to…"

Her voice was abruptly cut off.

"Izzy?" I said worryingly. "IZZY!"

Without delay, I swooped down onto one of the tank's wheels. Nobody was there. Just me and the thick fog.

"Mageck!" I shouted. "Christine! Demeter!"

But no one answered. Just dead silence. I scanned with my eyes, looking around to see if any life was creeping among the haze. Then, without warning, a blunt force knocked me off the wheel, pinning me to the ground. I tried to force myself back up, but to no avail. Looking down on me towered a familiar face from the AVIACHT youth.

"Kana was right!" shouted an anguished Trisco as he pointed his pistol at my beak. "Betrayal!"

"No! Trisco! This is not what it looks like!" I pleaded.

"Don't pretend like I don't know. You have been siding with the enemy all this time!"

"Well done, my I," said General Gorchak who was right behind him. "You helped lead us straight to the fugitives. I can tell you will be a very instrumental bird in the years to come."

I turned my head to the side and saw a few dozen AVIACHT guards dragging the humans onto the open field with their talons. The Infantry had been captured as well, with muzzles on their faces and chains tied to their necks.

The worst-case scenario had just happened! The plan had been exposed. My cover had been blown. And now there was no turning back. I watched helplessly as my human friends were lined up ready to be executed.

"I always expected you were a rather suspicious bird Episko," Gorchak commented as Trisco lowered his weapon. "Every time we met, you had secrets lurking in that brain of yours, smirking and laughing behind our back, always having somewhere to be. Well, now I know the reason. You…are…a TRAITOR!"

He smacked me hard across the face with his sharp talons, leaving a large, bloody gash across my cheek. After falling to the ground from the impact, he dragged me by my tail feathers to the captured humans. An angry Trisco flew over to them and stared at them menacingly in their eyes. I still could not understand how a being so young could be taught to hate so much.

"Trisco, please!" I begged him. "You don't have to get yourself involved in this…"

"We'll deal with you later…" Trisco squawked back, "and the dogs and cats!"

I could hear Izzy wailing in despair as she tugged her mother's coat. Then I looked at Trisco, who was almost the same age as she.

"You are still a chick," I continued. "You do not know all there is to know about the world, or humans. You…"

"I know all there is to know about Sapes," Trisco replied under heavy breath. "They lure you in with their false hopes. They trap you when you're at your weakest. Then, without any warning, they destroy your mind!"

As he said this, he jabbed Mageck in the stomach, causing him to cough up blood and fall to the ground. General Gorchak grabbed the pathetic human creature with his talon, examining his soft, facial structure.

"Please don't incinerate this human," I begged.

"Oh, don't worry," the general replied. "I think I have a much better use for this creature, and what makes him tick."

Without warning, Gorchak slammed Mageck to the ground, pinning his back down with his other talon. A few other humans and I lurched forward but were immediately restrained by guards.

"WHY DON'T WE BASH THIS SAPE'S HEAD OPEN RIGHT NOW, AND TEAR OPEN HIS BRAIN STEM!" Gorchak shouted maniacally. "THEN WE CAN EXAMINE THE BLOCKAGE IN HIS TISSUE THAT MAKES HIM AND ALL OTHERS LIKE HIM DAFT!"

"You don't have to do this!" I shouted.

"Shut the fuck up you pet!" A cadet spatted back.

"Is this going to make everything go away?" Andrzej screamed.

"You have no idea, human," the general replied. "An animal raised in a cage would never understand our…"

"I know," he admitted with a sob. "I know we devastated your species in ways I can't imagine and we will never know your pain general. I commend your efforts to free your kind but I need you to answer this question. If you kill us, will… it… go… away?"

"What?" Trisco asked.

"If you kill us humans, will it go away, that hurt that you carry? Will it bring back your parents? Will it bring back your trees? Will it bring back your world to the way it used to be? Just ask yourself that before you bash our heads open."

I saw the Gorchak's head tilt questionably. His eyes moved upward, looking at the gray, damp sky. He was clearly thinking about the question. This was the first time I had seen him stumped on finding a clear answer. Everyone just watched for the next move while Photios and his team dug their paws into the earth, as if ready to pounce in case of a fatality.

Then, something happened I thought would never occur. He

let go of his victim. Everyone gasped in disbelief, especially Trisco, who still had his weapon in his wings and a flaming ire in his eyes. The anger clearly enveloped him as his body shook and tears of rage fell down his beak. But Gorchak gave him a 'no' gesture, backing him away from the victims. For a moment, I thought the general had a change of heart. But then…

"Take them all back to the camps," he said coldly. "The dogs and cats can join them later."

"NO, NO PLEASE!" Mageck's mother shouted. "Don't send me back there!"

"Silence, you pathetic flat face," Gorchak replied with a slap to her face.

At that moment, we all heard a rustle in the treetops. Everyone fell silent again as we all looked towards the jungle, not knowing what was going to appear from the fog. Whatever it was, it was getting louder and louder. Had reinforcements from AVIACHT arrived? Did the Allied forces find us, or was it just another migration of an unrelated species? Either way, we honed in. Then, when the blare reached its climax, the sound stopped. A few moments later, a large, brawny elk trudged out of the bushes. He lowered his antlers and clopped his hoof into the dirt, as if ready to charge. The AVIACHT cadets fell on the floor laughing, shrugging off this minor inconvenience.

"Comrades," General Gorchak chuckled. "Take care of this beast. We can have cooked stag in celebration of our capture."

"With pleasure your grace," a cadet volunteered. "Hail Helios."

After a salute, the cadet with a hunting rifle gracefully flew towards the creature, but as he aimed his gun, dozens of deer, equally as strong, burst out of the thick fog and stampeded onto the field, trampling the cadet to death. They were followed by other creatures lesser in size, but nonetheless strong in the form of a mob: Squirrels, Rabbits, Owls, Robins, Muskrats, Bears, Foxes, Skunks, Mice, any forest creature one could think of running towards us in full force.

"FIRE AT WILL!" Gorchak shouted.

His cadets took out their weapons and started shooting at the charging herd. Trisco was front and center, firing his pistol like a maniac. But regardless of their firepower, they were no match for the herd of woodland creatures charging in their direction. And there, sitting atop the Elk's antlers was a familiar face I thought I'd never see again.

"ATAAAACK!" Shouted a paint-coated Ara with a stick strapped to her back. "TAKE NO PRISONERS!"

On her command, and with a stick in her paw for a weapon, a few of the critters shot a stream of arrows at their adversaries, taking a few down with just one blow. Eventually, the attack was too much, and several of Gorchak's infantry flew into the air and headed the other direction.

"COME BACK YOU FOOLS!" General Gorchak demanded. "THEY ARE JUST CONIFEROUS BEASTS! THEY'RE NO MATCH FOR…NNNNGH."

Before he could finish, he let out a painful squawk. All of us were stunned as he looked below his belly to find a spear shot straight through him.

"MASTER! NOOOOO!" Trisco shouted with tears down his cheeks.

He flew down to his beaten mentor and cradled him under his small wing. With his face buried underneath Gorchak's scuffled feathers, he burst into a scream of pain and remorse. Some of the humans covered their ears as they cried as well.

Though Trisco did belong to the enemy, they knew he was still just a child that fell into this mess. He looked up frantically to see where the source of the spear came from and found it quickly. It was Spartak, who had found a stray sharp branch on the ground and threw it into the chaos.

"Spartak, what the hell did you just do?" asked a bewildered Photios.

"I'm making amends to humans," Spartak replied. "That's what I'm doing."

"You...half-bred...betraying...PEEET!" Trisco screamed.

He fired his gun in Spartak's direction. Using his cat reflexes, Spartak was able to dodge a few bullets, but not all of them. He stared down at his left rib cage to see a deep, gouged hole with blood gushing from the inside out. Before he could think, the weight of the impact caused him to collapse on the dirt ridden field.

"SPARTAK!" Photios shouted as he ran towards his near-dead comrade.

The lieutenant dog cradled the fragile, feline body with his paws as he desperately searched for the bullet dodged in Spartak's intestines. All he could pick through were a few tattered bits of flesh and muscle tissue.

"Don't you die on me buddy!" he shouted through a stream of tears. "Not like this!"

From his left ear, he heard the clicking sound of Trisco's pistol ready to fire the last blow to finish them off. He knew he was finished, as he looked into the face of the anger-stricken chick, eyes filled with as many tears as his own. No way could he convince this poor feathered soul, nor could he find a way to, as he was stricken as well. So, he closed his eyes, and waited his fate, as I stared helplessly at the action.

Suddenly, Ara jumped from her antlered steed and pounced on top of Trisco's head. The two squirmed like a pair of angry dung beetles fighting over a piece of leftover droppings. Some fur was discarded, a few feathers were torn off, and a drop of spit and blood was cast on the ground. Soon, Ara put Trisco in a full headlock, while the other woodland critters followed suit, instigating a full-on battle between the forest critters and the loyal Axis soldiers.

"EPI!" Ara shouted as she struggled with her opponent. "Round up the humans and take them to the tank now!"

Without a moment's hesitation, I nodded and led the squadron and humans to an entrance behind a large, impenetrable submarine. The avian squadron tried to divert us but were held off by our woodland allies. Eventually they could not hold back and retreated to the skies.

The plan was in the final stages. As the last human hurried inside the hollow tank and closed the door behind him, we all settled in and pondered our surroundings. All was quiet, not a word or sound was made. We could only imagine what happened to Ara, Elch-Mocht, Tah-Rain or any of the others who bravely risked their own lives for us.

Suddenly, as Photios continued to cradle his seemingly lifeless friend, he began to hear the pattering footsteps of a few cargo pilots moving closer and closer to the aluminum edge. They were ready to ship us to Argentina – the last stronghold of the human race. It was time to complete the last phase of our rescue. Now all we could do was lie in silence and rest, as the cargo was lifted from the ground and onto a supposedly nearby shore.

"Ph…Photios…" grumbled Spartak as the rest of us went to sleep.

“S… Spartak?” Photios whispered.

“Photios. Did we win?”

“Yes, friend,” he said under a shower of tears. “We won.”

“Then…” Spartak continued with a weak smile. “I have finally repaid my debt. I can finally be at peace.”

“Don’t say that, Spartak. We are going to help you. We are going to get you aid.”

“I have done my part, Photios. It is now time to sleep, and so should you. Mine is only a little longer. Tell my kittens that…they were the greatest adventure…in my life.”

Then, Spartak closed his eyes one last time, and breathed a sigh of relief. For the remainder of the night, Photios pitifully cooed in his slumber.

Chapter 37

The dust settled after what seemed like an eternity. My body had felt so weak from all the clashing, stabbing and defending. I could see through the haze Elch-Mocht gliding overhead, examining the damage done to the field. To my left, Tah-rain gazed over the lifeless body of my horned steed. But there would be time to grieve later.

"Elch-Mocht," said Tah-Rain. "Round up the survivors."

Elch-Mocht nodded back and flew to a higher altitude.

We couldn't believe that we won against all odds. In spite of our lack in weaponry and knowledge of warfare, we still managed to fend off the enemy. Not bad for a band of woodland critters. In a way, it was a victory for our own status as creatures. It was something that maybe lifted us up on the food chain. Despite our sacrifices, the outcome was not all in vain.

"Where are the humans?" I asked.

"They appear to have already left," another squirrel replied.

"Our mission has been a success, I presume?" asked a field mouse.

"I suppose so," Elch-Mocht replied as he swooped down with survivors behind him.

It was then we took a moment to stare at the bodies of the fallen. So many lives were taken from us in a single day. Some with experienced pasts, others with promising futures. And yet, they had left a contribution far greater than they could imagine. They had left their mark.

After a traditional funeral for our brethren, we stared up at the sky and saw a few more AVIACHT forces heading for the sea. The war was not over yet for the humans, but it was over for us. We had done our part. We had fought a grand fight, and now the survival of humans would be easier, as well as for ourselves.

"Let us celebrate what we have now," Tah-Rain said with pride. "And never forget those that fought for it. Our terrain is free, a blessing from our fight. Let us now hope our human friends will someday meet the same fate."

And with that we all retreated back into the forest to live out our lives the way we saw fit. We knew that we had done our job, knowing we were that much closer to winning the war. All was quiet, all was peaceful, all was serene. For once we could rest easy. Our human friends were on their way to what was hopefully a peaceful outcome. Where their journey would lead next, only fate could tell. But now, the time had come for us forest animals to rejoice in our victory. Our forest was safe now. The enemy would retreat and things could finally return to the state we knew and loved.

Chapter 38

There is always something I wanted to ask my father: How exactly did he obtain that letter from that slain human soldier? So today, I stop over at his living quarters once more. Surprisingly, he has not had any fits or tantrum:. no glass smashed on the floor, no carpets or pillows torn up, not even a bruise or a cut on his body. He is just lying on his bed, staring at the ceiling, eyes fixated into the abyss.

I drop my coat on the easy chair, taking a moment to look around the room. It is an abnormally usual state a welcoming sign that things might be getting better for Dad. Perhaps the new medication is working out after all.

"Dad?" I ask as I sit next to his bedside. "Dad? Can you hear me?"

He does not respond. His face just looks lifeless, almost as if not attached to his body. I worriedly extend my hand and check his neck for a pulse. Then I take a sigh of relief, as my fingers feel the thump of blood vessels.

"Dad, I know you're still conscious," I continue. "But if you want me to let you be for a few minutes, that's fine too."

Suddenly, he slowly turns his head and stares at me. His eyes begin to wallow in tears. I wonder what he's crying about.

"Oh, son," he says wearily. "You don't know how much I wish to get rid of these memories. How I miss being happy all the time, to see you there as my son, playing and enjoying life. What I would give to see that life happen all over again. It's only now that I wanted to give you something."

He plops himself out of bed and slowly grabs his cane. After taking a moment to adjust his joints, he walks to a nearby cupboard and takes out a small, dusty box. With his fragile hands, he opens it to reveal an old, opened letter, the "From Nathan" on the front tainted with a few marks of blood.

"I haven't read this letter for who knows how long, but I think you should have it now."

For a moment, I don't know what to say, I just stare at the stained parchment, knowing that this is what I wanted to ask him about.

"Dad," I ask him solemnly. "How did, well…how exactly…"

"I never told you about that did I? How I got that letter."

"I'm afraid not."

"Well, you know that following our escape I served in the Army. Though briefly, it was life-altering."

"I know that those memories are too hard for you to re-live, so if you don't want to talk…"

"I need to, Son. I need to tell you how I got that letter. I've been holding this in for far too long. I've been setting a bad example for you. Now is the time to tell, before it's too late. Then we shall make peace with my old enemy: Kana."

Chapter 39

The wind rocked against the steel bars of the sub, as we tried to get some sleep. Uncle Epi had told us we would reach the coastline within a matter of days. But for now, our minds were not on that subject. All of us stared at the lifeless body of Spartak. He looked so peaceful and calm, as if in a state of serenity, a much different look, compared to how we encountered him: rough, sharp, and filled with a need to fight. But now his time was up; he had done his job, and he had fought all his battles.

Photios was still whimpering quietly as we all held hand and paw in sympathy, wondering what to do for a proper burial.

"We will have our funeral as soon as we reach land," Uncle Epi promised us. "But now we must get some rest. I will check the mast of the sub and see where we are."

Uncle Epi then flew to the top shaft and crawled through a small hole. What he saw and observed was anyone's guess. Then, a few minutes later, he crawled back inside. His feathers were slightly ruffled, probably from the gusts of wind that were howling in the night.

"We're heading to our destination," Uncle Epi reassured us. "And right on time, to be frankly honest."

"How do you know for sure?" I asked as I sat with my fiancé Christine.

"From how the direction of the wind is blowing from above, only the shores of Argentina or Brazil could bring that kind of gust. We should reach shore soon."

"At the way things are going," Andrzej commented. "That news is good for us."

"I don't know how long I can withstand this rocking and swaying," Christine added. "Land would be a welcoming sight."

We all slept the remainder of the time in that sub. Nothing eventful happened. We were all crammed in the confines of a machine with hardly any light. I could hear the echoes of our breathing and snoring reverberating against the steel hides of the sub. And yet, I slept very easily knowing that there was no way our plan could go wrong.

After what seemed like days, we heard a small thump on the bottom of the sub. We had presumably reached our destination. As we awakened from our slumber, stretched out our limbs and waited for the "all clear" from Uncle Epi, we heard a murmur from up above. It sounded like two birds having a conversation. Had the enemy found us? Were we in trouble again? Or were things going according to plan? All we could hear was muffled squawking. In a moment of relief, all went silent. Then, in a moment of more relief, Uncle Epi tapped his talons on the steel walls, signaling the all-clear. One by one we climbed out of the sub, and took a deep breath of the sweet, sweet air, almost like babies being pulled out of the womb and into the world for the first time. The scenery was a flat plain covered with discarded subs scattered all over. It would be a long time before the enemy wound find us along with their supplies.

"Photios," said Uncle Epi. "I think now is the time to bury our friend."

Photios nodded solemnly and grabbed his friend's carcass from the sub with his teeth. We all gathered in a circle as

Demetrius dug a hole in the middle of the grass. After we all quickly said our prayers and respects, it was Photios's turn to make the eulogy.

"Spartak," he began wearily, "was one of, if not The, greatest of comrades I had ever fought alongside. He always followed our commands, aided our allies in times of dire need, and never flinched when the battle was at its peak. Though we had disagreements on many fronts, he was always there to encourage what our greatest needs were, even in times of hardship and inner conflict."

"I shall never forget the times we spent in training camp or on the front lines. Even when he didn't show it, I knew he always had that soft side in him. He will always be a fighter; he will always be a soldier and he will always be…my friend."

Then, Photios nuzzled his nose on the feline's fur, as if giving him a kiss goodbye. He whispered…

"Your kits will know who you truly were."

We all bowed our heads in respect for the fallen, as the rest of the infantry buried Spartak's body into the earth. Knowing we didn't have time for our own speeches, my mother, sister, wife and I just stood there and stared at the feline, canine, and rodent crew. Strangely, it was as if we were staring at ourselves as a species. After all, we were the ones who bred the wolf and the wildcat back when we were the dominant species. After a few howled and mewed in respect for their fallen friend, they dried their tears and went back to the task at hand.

"Photios," Uncle Epi said. "The enemies will be arriving anytime soon. Round up our friends and lead them on the path to Argentina. I will fly into the Amazon to observe the scope of the battle. But before I do, I must tell you something."

"What is it?" Photios asked as he wiped away his tears.

"The AVIACHT forces are planning an attack far deadlier than we could've imagined," Epi said with a sigh.

"What?" Photios asked in alarm. "How can it possibly be deadlier?"

"Upon one of my final meetings with my…former girlfriend," he continued. "She showed me the plans for a set of specially-made bombs that will shipped here in a matter of days. Each one will contain a sample of the deadliest diseases humans have ever endured, from the Bubonic Plague, to the Spanish Flu to everything in between. Not even the AVIACHT forces may be able to fully recover from this outbreak. If we don't stop them now and try to negotiate with their leader, it will be a battle where both sides will lose."

"But what of that Macaw we captured?" asked Photios. "He said Demeter's friends were being carried to another concentration camp in Brazil."

"Well," Uncle Epi replied solemnly. "Apparently that was just a decoy to keep you from knowing the truth. I have seen the blueprints with my own eyes."

At that moment, we all just stood there in a moment of silence, shock and horror. As if we had already gone through so much, now our whole species was on the brink of possible extinction.

"We should've never let that Macaw go," said a cat cadet. "He would've given into us by now."

"Photios," I begged as I kneeled before him. "I know we have just met and you have already endured so much, but you must help us now more than ever. This is no longer a battle for the humans, but for the rest of your lives as well."

After a few moments of hesitation, Photios solemnly nodded back.

"Comrades," he said as he tried to hold himself together. "We shall split into two teams. Team A will escort the humans to their destination. Team B will be led by me, as we trudge into the final battle ground."

"Photios, please don't leave us," my little sister begged. "You're the best dog we ever had."

"Little one," he replied solemnly. "I've already lost one too many friends in this mission. I can't afford to lose another."

"But you might get killed in the Amazon," Wadja warned.

"Then I will be joining with my friend very soon."

After a few moments we decided there was no more time to waste.

"Godspeed," we all said in unison as we went our separate ways.

Epi flew up north to examine what would surely be the battle of the century, while Photios traveled with his crew into the harsh dampness of the Amazon jungle. So, with the rest of Photios's regiment leading the way, we found a road that led straight to Buenos Aires – the last thriving metropolis, safeguard and refuge in South America.

Chapter 40

I flew over the Pampas lowlands of Argentina, through the counties of Santa Fe, Entre Rios and Cordoba, and straight into the border that was the AVIACHT stronghold. I could feel the air becoming thicker and denser against my wings and tail. Through my nostrils, I smelled the morning dew of the Amazon that was fumigating amongst the trees, as the flat terrain was disappearing into the jungle.

After a few dozen miles of nothing but greenery and hillsides I saw, off in the distance, a plume of dark gray smoke growing over the horizon. From my presumption, it must have been another human infantry clearing a portion of the forest for the battle that would determine the winner in this war. So I flapped my wings towards the imminent danger, seeing if I could stop them before things got worse for both sides.

However, my presumption was very misleading. I swooped below to see that it was not a forest clearing at all, but rather an abandoned station of King Helios's forces. The tents were still perched up, the radio transmitters were unharmed, etc. I landed on one of the tables to see if anyone was still here, but there was not a bird to be found. Most likely, they all left for the Great Battle. All I needed figure out now was where the smoke was coming from.

So, I flew back to the canopy to find the source, and what I saw was beyond belief to describe. I landed on a firm tree branch to witness piles upon piles of dead, human bodies. There were bodies of families who trespassed into their territory, residents killed in a nearby camp, and even bodies of certain soldiers who perished overseas in Europe, each pile higher than the last. I wondered why they brought those bodies all the way across the ocean. Perhaps it was to send their adversaries a message of what was to come. There were a few piles in the background burning in a fiery blaze, as if the last macaws tried to hide the evidence from oncoming forces. My face bowed in sadness, as a sense of despair and hopelessness crept back in.

Then, after that moment of silence, I decided to glide over the devastation to (foolishly) see if there were any survivors. But alas, as I expected, not a living soul could be found. I landed on top of one of the human heaps and noticed at the bottom a soldier with what appeared to be a letter hanging from his coat pocket. With the carefullest of ease, I waddled down the pile and wiggled the paper out my beak. The envelope was still intact, with the exception of a few blood stains that smeared the "From Nathan" written across the parchment. I wondered who this man was, who killed him and what the letter was for. But I had no time to find out. I had to hide and look at the address later.

As I stuffed the letter into my satchel, and flew back up into the canopy, I saw another plume of smoke rising in the other direction. Now this was definitely where the battle would commence. There was no way of knowing what kind of destruction I would bear witness.

Once I reached the source, I was struck in horror by something equally, if not more frightening, than the mass human piles. A large patch of the thriving Amazon jungle had indeed been cleared away by large machines of steel and aluminum. The cranes, wheels, shovels and claws, all operated by several human handlers, looked like dinosaurs and creatures from a bygone era.

As they carelessly chomped, grabbed and shoveled their way through the lush vegetation, I could only wonder about the poor, defenseless inhabitants that were in the way of the battlefield.

Indeed, I had the right to be worried, for to my right I saw several capybara families huddling below on the forest floor, whilst high above were a few dozen bird species chirping in panic over how to save their precious eggs. On the vines were a troop of monkeys scattering away as fast as they could from the danger that was looming ahead, while a river, cutting through the soil and teeming with life, was slowly getting eaten away by the oncoming machines. The leftover fish and marine mammals flapped in wet mud, gasping for air.

There was nothing I could do for these poor creatures – nothing at all. Even though I had only recently saved certain creatures from the brink of death, I still felt like a failure, since this was where my ancestors thrived and left their mark. For the moment, I felt like a traitor, an outcast from my own kind. 'Why should my species have to suffer?' I asked myself as I helplessly watched. 'Why should they have to burn? Why are we even in this fight?'

Then I flew up even higher, turning my head once more as I watched another group of capybaras being run over by one of the machines. Now I could see both the destroyed jungle, and the piles of bodies from before. It was as if my eyes were looking in two directions at once, seeing both sides of the battle in all its detail. For the first time, I felt so torn between two forces: the plight of the Amazon jungle, and my commitment to saving humans. At that moment, I didn't even know which one was the enemy. Perhaps that was the grim cost of war. There are no real heroes or enemies, there are only fools that made shallow decisions, and poor souls that fell in the mess. Shapes of the landscape reduced to figures in the expanse, including myself.

Now was the time to hide away in the war that was already dotting the land. I would give that letter to that girl, somehow, when all of this was over.

Chapter 41

My father and his team trudged through the Amazon jungle. It was almost like running around the world and back to the same terrain from Europe: same trees, same shrubs, same soil.

Strangely, the only difference was in the air and the water. It seemed less dense, less damp, making it easier for the infantry to glide across the forest floor without making a sound. As they lapped their tongues for frequent drinking breaks, they noticed how the water tasted cleaner and fresher, like a cup of spring water plucked from the mountains. My father could only wonder why. Perhaps it was due to the different hemisphere or maybe that the water current was channeling itself away from the ocean, or maybe, just maybe, they were only at the right place at the right time.

"Why are we here, sir?" Demetris muttered during one of their drink breaks.

"What's that again?" asked Photios.

"I asked why are we even bothering to be here? We should be back on the front lines, saving our peers."

"I can see your point very clearly, Demetris," my father responded. "But we just need to find a way to make sure the enemy forces have less of an upper claw on the battlefield. If we can just get across the border into the AVIACHT territory, we can maybe, just maybe, reason and negotiate with their leader. All we need to do, is find King Helios, now..."

Suddenly, my father spread his legs apart, as if something

was coming. He sniffed the air, and tilted his head upward.

"What is…" an infantry cat tried to ask.

"Shhh." my father silenced them.

From the look on my father's face, they knew they had been caught. A top ranking AVIACHT commander swooped down from the canopy and straight into Photios's face. The very force of the macaw caused him to fly back at least twenty feet from where he stood. Before he knew it, the infantry was engaged in a battle with a single feathered opponent, who somehow managed to outsmart even the most skilled of the group.

This went on for about two to three minutes (at least from what my father told me) until a couple of canine cadets pinned the bird down by his wings. As he helplessly thrashed his talons against the air, the team heard a rather soothing voice off in the distance. They knew it was from another macaw, but it sounded more gentle, soothing, as if trying to put a young child to sleep. And that's exactly what it was.

My father and his team did their best to keep their breathing as quiet as they could, as they turned their heads up to see an elegantly tidied nest up in the canopy. A small, fiery light was glowing from inside the walls; a mother and three sleeping chicks silhouetted against the aligned bark and twig. They were just getting ready to tuck themselves in, as the mother was singing a lullaby to her children.

"Please… don't… wake up my family…" the struggling macaw begged.

Then, a moments silence.

"Stand down," my father whispered.

Everyone held their ground and breathed as quietly as possible. All that cut through the dead silence was the sweet lullaby of the mother from the nest above. Now that the infantry was once again at a crossroads, either they fail the mission and don't negotiate with the enemy leader, or they risk harming the macaw and devastating his family perched above. The soothing vocals pulled them into a hypnotic trance. As dire as the moment was, everything seemed so tranquil and peaceful, unlike the bitterness and harshness of the artificial jungles of Europe. Demetris intervened as he tiptoed towards the captured macaw and whispered into his ear.

"We need…to speak…to Helios," he said gently.

"That's…not…possible," the macaw sneered in spite. "I have not seen his presence in years, not since the uprising. Besides, you expect me to betray my kind and help you, 'Pets?'"

"Unless you give us answers," warned one of the harsher cats that had pinned him to the ground. "Then you are about ten seconds away from your clan having one less surviving member."

"That's enough, comrade!" my father barked as he pushed the cat aside. "We can't afford any more casualties."

My father looked at the helpless creature, The hate steaming from its eyes and the tiny squeaks lisping from its beak filled my father's mind with doubt. Our only chance now would have to rely on a little luck. But somehow, Photios often had luck on his side even when it came to conversations with the enemy.

"Listen," he said sternly. "We just need a word from your leader. There is something we wish to discuss."

"You…will never pick up his scent," the macaw replied. "None of us in AVIACHT have smelled it in months. His is the most unique among all birds in the sacred sky. It is an aroma that would make a Bird of Paradise leap in pride. Words cannot even describe his smell. It is the smell of the future…"

"When did you last catch his scent?" my father insisted, whilst carefully trying not to awake the family above.

The bird thought for a moment, and knowing there was no other option, he spoke.

"I last sniffed his whereabouts in the eastern basin of Rio De Janeiro. He was said to be planning final preparations for the Battle of the Amazon. I know by the time you reach him it will be too late for your kind. Our superior species will strike the last strongholds of those logging sapes, and our supremacy over all this lush green planet will finally be complete. There is nothing you can do. ALL HAIL KING HELIOS! MAY HIS REIGN FOREVER BE! I COMMEND MY SPIRIT TO THE SAC—"

He was interrupted by a call from his nest above.

"I request you release me," the macaw said quietly. "My family is my priority for now. But within seven days it will be my entire kind. Forget about your mission, 'pets.' You should surrender and join our side. Think about that, why don't you."

After a moment's thought…

"Release him," my father ordered.

The macaw flew back to his nest and turned to his family, but not before giving one last look of suggestion at the troops. My father shrugged it off as he and his battalion trudged further east.

Chapter 42

Excerpt from, "Holocaust Remembered"

We arrived at the checkpoint of Buenos Aires. It had been exactly seven days since we parted with Uncle Epi. Our memories and concerns for him were still burning in our minds. What if he would get caught? What if he led himself astray? What if he was killed, or worse, sided with the enemy? We would never know for a long time.

Our first greeting was by two human patrol soldiers; they were tall, yet at the same time average in height for their species. In both their hands were sterilization kits. At this point, we could tell what would happen next. The soldiers escorted us to a station located on our right. They swiftly stripped us naked and placed us against a wall where a long hose washed our bodies of any germ and contaminants that might be lurking in our systems. From there, they gave us a set of scrubs to wear, and a room in which to wait. Each one of us was given a doctor to inspect every crevice and possible wound in and around our bodies. Then they gave us a few pills, food, clothing and sent us on our way to our temporary housing arrangements.

Upon entering our living quarters, a private officer stopped us. He told us that we had to change our names for the sake of our safety. A clipboard with a list of names was given for each of us so that we could choose a name to our liking. Rather than risk having our lives desecrated all over again, we started to pick our new identities without delay. I chose "Samuel Whitestone," and Christine chose "Emily." He gave us an ID, a passport, a satchel of other false information, and a final salute as he unlocked the door.

Though we were in a different setting, and surrounded by more of our kind, the place was all together similar in our hearts. The wooden floors, the pale walls and the makeshift ceiling all reminded us of the shack in Europe. In a way, it made us feel homesick. As we slept, memories collected into our brains of a place more secure and familiar to our eyes.

The next morning, we woke to the sound of a bugle horn over a loudspeaker. We bathed ourselves got dressed, ate as much as we needed and went outside.

"MANDATORY MEETING! EVERYONE TO THE CIVIC CENTER!" said a voice over the loudspeaker. "MANDATORY MEETING!"

All of us hurried out onto the streets and towards a large civic center in the middle of town. With its Roman pillars and large clock on top, I could've sworn the building once served as a city hall. But as its original name was scratched out and unreadable on a stone block, who knows what was its original purpose?. The interior was built like a cleared dining hall with large, slanted windows to the side and wooden beams for a ceiling. At the far end was a large, empty stage, probably for any guest speaker. The place was large enough to house an entire town – much less a party for an unspecified event.

As everyone gathered inside and grabbed a chair or a place on the floor, I frantically looked for Mageck. I went everywhere, across the enormous hall, but he was nowhere to be found in the sea of people. Neither could I find my two brothers. After fifteen frantic minutes of looking and asking, I finally found them on the stage, lined in single formation, dressed in military uniform along with fifty to sixty other men and women. With a lump in my heart, I could only guess what this sight meant. My love and brothers were preparing for battle.

The noise and commotion died down as a border collie, dressed in Lieutenant attire, entered the stage. After a few moments to let everyone take their seats, the collie took a moment to inspect each of the new recruits.

"Is there anyone here in this room who is willing to volunteer?" she asked. "If so, please approach the stage and reserve your number."

Several dozen members of the audience raised their hands and were given the signal to come forward. They were each given a tag and joined my husband and brothers. The collie lifted her paw, thus signaling them to take their seats. Then she attached a small megaphone to her mouth and began her speech.

"I would like all of you to take a good look at these brave humans behind me," she stated. "They are only a fraction, very small percentage of the soldiers that will be joining us in the battle of the Amazon. Within the next week, they will find themselves staring on the barrel of war, ready to defend the last stronghold of the human and cat, dog, and rodent race."

"Now, from what has been reported from sources on the Brazilian border, King Helios's forces have taken hold of large portions of Mexico and Central America via flight patterns and air raids. So, the AVIACHT forces have officially blocked entry into the United States."

Everyone in the room gasped in terror. Some grabbed their loved ones, others buried their faces in tears, and a few just sat there in sheer shock.

"But as grim as these reports may seem," the collie

continued as she calmed the audience, "we still have a fighting chance. Refugees from all across the area and Europe have volunteered to fight in our squadron. Combined with our cat and dog infantry we may be able to create the most advance defense force ever."

"What? Do you think we stand a chance against AVIACHT?" yelled a panicked spectator.

"Our weapons are primitive compared to theirs!" yelled another. "We will be sitting ducks!"

"The best chance we have is to negotiate with them." Someone next to me suggested. "Maybe if we go easy on them, they might spare the last of human civilization! In a few years' time we'll have grown back to a reasonable size."

Soon everyone in the audience was yelling other options of surrender. As I looked around, I could see the hopelessness and despair on everyone's faces. They had endured and lost so much; they would do anything to end this madness.

"WE SURVIVED!" I shouted through the crowd, to which I caught everyone's attention. "One of those soldiers up there is my husband. The two of us, as well as several other human survivors, endured the worst of this war. We lost our homes, our health, and even loved ones, which I'm pretty sure you all have as well."

"Don't you think we know that already?" A member of the audience shouted. "I lost my home too. I lost my family, my work, my savings; I have nothing left."

"But we still prevailed!" I continued. "Despite everything, we managed to pull through all that hell. And now we are so close to the finish line. I know that because a little bird told me…literally!"

Everyone in the meeting hall gasped in shock, followed by

whispers and murmurs.

"In fact, that little macaw saved us," Mageck added.

"It saved you?" asked a volunteer soldier standing next him. "No way."

"A macaw would never soften his cold heart to rescue a human being," another soldier said. "Especially now."

My brother Anderzej added. "Even I had my doubts, but clearly my doubts needed to catch up with reality."

"When all hope seemed lost," my brother Wadja added. "Episko was able to rescue us from despair. We hid in a hut in the middle of the jungle, along with other woodland critters that fell victim to AVIACHT."

Now even more of the audience members were talking to themselves in disbelief over what they were hearing. It had become now a large cacophony of mutterings and conversations.

"This is obviously a set-up," someone in the audience jeered. "A practical joke."

"Will you just let us finish?" I shouted. "He was like family to us. And in a way, we all became family. We became: an ANTHROMALIA!"

"An Anthromalia!" Mageck's little sister shouted in glee, to which her mother tightened on her arm to ease her down.

"An Anthromalia?" a human spectator asked. "That's only been talked about in tales handed down from generations. I thought those were impossible! (or at least improbable.)"

"Oh, it is real my friend," my father said. "It is very much real, and we were part of it. The feeling of different species all under one community was something that goes beyond explanation. It was man and beast living side by side in the fullest tranquility."

"I never thought it was possible myself," Mageck concluded.

"But an Anthromalia can still be achievable. If we can avert this disaster and win just one for all that is sane. For all that is trustworthy. For all…that is hope."

It was then, we could start to hear a few claps in the audience. They grew louder and louder until the whole center joined in an uproarious applause. People were cheering, whistling, and even jumping with joy. A few of the soldiers on the podium even gave Mageck a firm, but friendly, pat on the back.

"I think we all owe a little kudos to these human friends of ours." The border collie acknowledged as she approached us. "I can truly see a glimmer of hope in the audience this afternoon. So, who will join us?"

Nearly a third of the entire room rose from their seats and muscled their way to the stage, willing to risk their lives for a greater cause. Everyone else raised their hands to volunteer in other areas, and consensually signed their names on pads of tattered paper. Some took on the roles of chefs, others medical assistants, even those who had significant wounds signed up with the shipping and transportation units. Before we knew it, everyone (except the children and elderly), had picked a seat at the table of battle.

As the morning turned into afternoon, and the center began to empty out, I approached my husband from the left side of the stage, greeting him with great embrace. It was then I could truly take a good look at him. With his firmly-pressed uniform, and his crew cut hair, I could've sworn I was looking at a different person. Needless to say, his warm smile and gentle eyes remained the same.

"Well," Mageck said nervously. "Within a week, I will be risking my life and neck. I don't even know if I'm ready for this, or anything like this for that matter."

"None of us were ready when AVIACHT began its invasion." I assured him with my hand towards his cheek, "and look where we are now. Our species is so close to freedom."

"Still," he added. "I do believe we owe a bit of fault to the motives behind Helios. I mean, after all, we were responsible for nearly obliterating his home. Not to mention countless others. Ever since we arrived here, and learned about AVIACHT, I sometimes wonder which one of us was the bad guy."

"Don't talk like that Mageck," I assured him. "I know we humans have made countless mistakes, and yes we are half to blame for this war, but we're going to fix and finish it. It will be over soon. I can feel it."

As I said this, we kissed and embraced once more. I knew deep in my heart that this week might be the last time I'd ever see him. Somehow, I wished we were all back home, in our houses, long before all this madness began, long before the trouble swept in from the skies, long before we were destitute, long before we were reduced to a sub-existing species.

"You know," Mageck suggested. "We still haven't had our honeymoon yet. Perhaps I can ask the guards to let us explore the town of Buenos Aires."

"I think that's a wonderful idea, Love," I replied. "After-all, it has been some time since we took a decent break from the running and hiding."

So, the two of us walked towards the tabby cat guard at the front gate. He showed us to a small room where we signed several release forms, ran a few disease tests and checked ourselves for any hidden spy ware. Once we were given the "all-clear," the gates opened, and we went on our way to the big city.

The sun glistened over the magnificent city. Surprisingly, the area remained unscathed. With its historic buildings, cobblestone roads, quaint shops and slightly worn-out signs, it felt as though we were back in civilization. The only part out of place were the frequent tanks, run by cat and dog infantries, rolling towards and away from our direction. Human couples like ourselves could be seen strolling among the sidewalks and passageways, talking, eating, drinking, singing and dancing with not a care in the world. For once we did not see fear in the eyes of our species. Rather, it was replaced by joy and laughter. Fair enough, as people needed to take a much-deserved break from the troubles of recent events.

Our first stop was at a record store. It had been a while since both of us listened to true music. So, we requested of the shopkeeper the first singer we could think of, Edith Piaf, a newcomer I had heard of prior to the invasion. As the shopkeeper turned on the jukebox and swayed to the orchestra, our arms held each other tightly, caressing like two monkeys on a vine. The music was soft yet powerful, gentle yet enlightening – a true achievement of the human spirit.

The next stop was dinner at the town square. We ordered the specialty of the night, as our tastebuds were in need of something succulent. After a few moments, our table was presented with a feast for the eyes and mouth: It was two veggie Asado supreme sandwiches, topped with the finest vegetables, spices and sauces the country had to offer, sliced between two, thick, roasted buns. Without a moment's hesitation we ate them and savored every moment.

Next, we entered Plaza Mayo and took a moment to gaze at its glorious obelisk. What ingenuity it must've taken to carve this city from the ground up. How these people and their ancestors must've felt when they first arrived in this foreign land. Our heads turned to see several couples dancing around the plaza garden. Soon we joined in the crowd of revelers and jubilees, spinning and twirling around the flowers and shrubs, all neatly trimmed and assorted.

Before we realized it, the sun was already dipping below the skyline. We wondered if we should get back to the post, as humans were most vulnerable at night. Then again, we were in safe territory. Plus, the lights in Buenos Aires were the brightest I'd seen. So, we decided to stroll around the shopping spots of town. Quaint and lovely, each store was complemented by the sepia toned cobblestone signs. Some sold jewelry, others sold toys, a few sold a knick knack or two. It was almost like being back in France, just before the invasion.

At that moment, I stared at the window of a rather peculiar shop. On display was a dress of familiar color and style. It was almost exactly like the dress one of my brothers had made for ARA back at the shack. I wasn't sure which of them it was that made it, but then again, it didn't really matter. I stared at my husband with dreamy eyes, giving him the signal to use the few bits of money the army had provided us to buy the dress. As we went outside with the package, I held it by the coat hanger against my chest and did a little twirl in the street. Now, I knew that this would be a perfect reminder of our woodland brethren, whom I hoped would win back their home.

Finally, as the day came to an end, we strolled over to the highest floor of the tallest building and took a moment to gaze at the magnificent skyline that was Buenos Aires. The lights were dim and sparse in size, which was fine, as we did not want to give ourselves away to the enemy. Still, the result was magnificent. I felt secure to be back in civilization, and more importantly, with my spouse. So, for a few minutes, Mageck and I clasped against each other's chests and gazed aimlessly at the last remaining human stronghold in South America. It was then I noticed the edge of the city off in the distance. The strip of darkness that enveloped the horizon was both frightening and at the same time mysterious.

"I wonder what those forest dwellers are planning?" I asked Mageck.

"We will soon find out," he replied. "I know you're frightened for me, Christine. But rest assured, I'm just as frightened as you. I don't have any idea what to expect on the field, nor if I'll come back in one piece, or any piece for that matter."

"Mageck," I replied as I looked down on the city. "I've been thinking about what you said earlier today, about whether we are the good side or not. It made me think about Uncle Epi. I mean, he does belong to their species. And he did have a commanding officer as a love partner. Since then, it's made me wonder about the true cost of this war. On one hand, we were oppressed and enslaved by AVIACHT, with hardly a sign of mercy. On the other, we were the ones who struck first, what with our logging, pillaging and destruction of their land. Is there really a hero or villain in all of this?"

"There are no heroes or villains in war," he replied solemnly. "Only privileged types who made poor choices, and victims who just fell in the mess."

It was getting late. Our families would soon be wondering where we were. So, we rushed back down and out of the building, through the street corridors, and towards the compound. It had been a short but rather pleasant honeymoon. At that moment, we heard what could only be the sound of wailing sirens. As the deafening noise echoed against the windows and people began to panically run to their underground shelters, it was clear the enemy was approaching. We only had a good five minutes to get back to temporary homes. So, with whatever muscle we could muster, we ran as fast as we could in that direction. Luckily, I was not wearing high heels that day, nor did either of us wear the most restrictive of clothing.

The road from where we were to where we needed to be was pitch black. As we blindly ran faster and faster, we could hear the faint sound of squawking coming from behind us. At this point, my breath needed catching up with my feet. As the sounds of AVIACHT guards grew louder and louder, we desperately searched for some source of light, but all we could see was the moonlit sky, and the cavernous darkness of the city. Then, just when we thought we would get caught, we saw a faint searchlight from what must've been the compound. Yet behind us, the shadows of macaws and parrots drew nearer and nearer. For a few moments, we closed our eyes, hoping that in some way, they wouldn't catch up with us. When we opened them, we were staring right at the border gates. A service dog, who was among those in charge of the searchlight, saw us as we waved our hands, thus immediately opening the entrance and allowing us in. We had barely missed becoming prisoners once again.

Yet, despite our close call, as we caught our breaths, we said our goodnights and headed back towards our housing arrangements. We knew that in two weeks' time, a real battle for our lives would commence.

That night, in my cot bed, I stared at both my weapon and the outside moon, wondering if it were the last time I would see such a beautiful night.

Chapter 43

My father's infantry had been wandering the East basin for five days now, and despite very few incidents, (a broken paw and some wounded ears), things had not gotten easier. This particular day was moist and humid, thus making the forest floor uneasy to walk on with the soil turning to mud and slime. On top of that, they all had to walk slower and with the carefullest of ease, so as not to bring any attention to possible soldiers from above. By now, the grittiness of the plateau had become so thick and slimy, that the rodents, (as well as smaller and skinnier felines), were forced to cling onto the backs of St. Bernards and Bloodhounds.

"Lieutenant!" shouted a rodent, whose canine friend was sinking into the weight of the mud, "I don't think we can go on like this any further. I motion we call off today's trek, find higher ground, and continue the next morning when it's less damp."

"We can't stop now!" my father asserted, with his eyes focused on what was ahead. "We must negotiate with Helios. It might be our one chance to end a catastrophe of irreversible proportions."

"We're on the verge of a catastrophe already!" Insisted a tabby cat clinging to the back of a St. Bernard. "We'll lose half the infantry if we continue at this rate."

"Then we will save the other half." Photios demanded. "It will be a sacrifice worth taking."

The tabby was shocked by this. Then his face turned to anger.

"You son of a bitch!" he snapped back. "Have you lost your mind? Don't tell me you care more about the humans than your own kind! Or more importantly my own kind!"

"I'm perfectly aware of what I'm doing," my father replied. He was starting to lose his temper. "But I can assure you, I don't care more about one species over my own. We just…"

"What? Have to sacrifice just so we can get an extra legging? If you had taken that left turn a few miles back, we might not even be in this situation now."

"If we had gone in that direction, we would've been further behind schedule. Time is running out by the minute."

"I don't think another day behind schedule would push us that further back. Beware your actions don't prompt a mutiny."

"DON'T YOU THINK I KNOW THAT ALREADY?" Photios snapped, as he barked and turned his head towards his private officer. "It's not like we hadn't had it any worse back in Europe! Spartak is dead! Do you hear me! He may have been a hothead on the outside but at least he kept us together and in line! When we were to return, he was going to teach how to do the things he knew! Now what do you think I should do? HUH!"

Everyone just stared at my father with shocked and confused faces. They had never seen him lose his cool like that. But I couldn't blame him. He had only recently lost one of his dearest and closest friends, making him feel more lost than ever before. As my father stopped to pant and catch his breath, Demeter trudged over and tilted his head onto his, comforting him in the process.

"I know this is still so much for you my friend." Demeter reassured him. "Spartak would've been proud of you and how far you've led us."

Photios just looked up towards him, as tears fell from his eyes. He felt like a puppy again, afraid and unsure.

"What am I going to do Demeter?" Photios asked weakly. "What am I going to do?"

He turned away in disgrace, but Demeter lifted his paw to his chin, and made him look back at him.

"We will make it," Demeter stated. "I know we will. It's what he would've wanted."

Photios weakly smiled back and licked away his tears, feeling guilty as he gulped a little, as if to apologize. At that moment, they noticed their legs were slowly sinking into the mud. So, without further talk, Demeter gave the infantry the signal and they all marched onward.

Eight more hours passed, and the sun was starting to set once more. This gave the infantry a slight breeze of comfort, as the air grew drier, and the ground became stiffer. So, my father decided they should take a few hours rest. The St. Bernards and Bloodhounds collapsed onto the dirt pavement, and the rodents slid off towards several tree roots, with the carefullest of ease. Everyone else lay down with panting mouths and failing legs, too exhausted to even know where to sleep. After a few more moment's hesitation, my father closed his eyes and took a long-deserved rest.

As he succumbed to his sleep, Photios dreamed of the place the humans described in the submarine – the place that Episko had kept them for all the months prior. He had always wondered what it was like for the domesticated man and the wild animal to truly live side by side. And yet, in his dreams he could only imagine.

A fantastical paradise set before his eyes. The fields of multicolored fauna had stretched far off into the forest ahead, an expanse only rivaled by the magnificent sky above him. To his right were a few dozen human children, frolicking and playing with the young deer, squirrels, raccoons, owls, foxes and rabbits, who were just as innocent as they. On the left, several human couples were tending to a crop and garden. Beside them were all the adult critters of the forest. They shared jokes, told stories, and lent each other a paw with their daily tasks. It was indeed a peaceful sight to observe.

Suddenly, my father's pleasant dream was disturbed by the waking nightmare. AVIACHT soldiers had surrounded him and his infantry. Somehow, in spite of their precautions, they had been captured. Without even a readiness to defend themselves, they were all held at gunpoint, stripped of their weapons, and pushed to the soil floor.

"What do you filthy pets think you're doing here?" one of the macaws squawked. "Do you realize your kind is forbidden on these sites, under penalty of death?"

"Please," Demeter pleaded. "We've come here for important matters. We demand…" At that instant, he was whacked to the ground by a pair of sharp talons.

"Silence, you filthy mutt!" scoffed the Macaw.

Photios tried to rush over but was stopped by a rifle aiming for his skull. He closed his eyes, trying to think of what to say. As he heard the squeaks and whimpers of his friends in the background, he blurted out his first thought.

"WE NEED…TO SPEAK…TO HELIOS!" he shouted to the treetops.

A few moments of echoes and deafening silence were interrupted by uproarious laughter from the AVIACHT soldiers.

"No one has seen him in months," one of them replied.

"Besides, do you actually think our glorious leader would

waste his time listening to you?" asked another.

"Please," a rodent tried to explain. "This is an urgency of life and death.

"The battle of the Amazon is far too catastrophic for any side to claim victory," a cat added.

"If you allow us to negotiate peacefully with your leader, we can end this madness now," said a St. Bernard, who was far too weak to even stand up.

"Don't you and inhabitants of this jungle want to live in peace once more? Do you really want to risk everything you hold dear and possibly let your kind be wiped out from the face of the earth?"

"Your kind may be wiped out," an AVIACHT soldier commented. "But we won't."

"We were destined to survive the greatest of catastrophes. We were descended from the mighty dinosaur, risen from the ashes of a cataclysmic asteroid. Despite everything they said about us, we…have…prevailed."

"And when we are through with this battle," another added, "Once we have defended our land, it will stretch all over the world. Our glorious leader will be there to lead us on and bring a new order to the planet."

"What you say may not matter in the next few days!" my father pleaded. "One of your associates gave word of a new bomb that your empire authorized. It would kill all of you and bring even more decimation to the jungle!"

"Are you talking about that wretched Episko, traitor to the cause and forsaker of his own kind? Why would we ever take notice of a blundering fool like that? You and he can die along with all the other sapes, for all we care."

"You must take this seriously!" Demeter demanded with a

rifle to his head. "If you don't allow us to talk with Helios now you will all die within a matter of weeks! Please, we must speak to your leader!"

"You sound desperate. But it could still be a trap," a rather younger-looking macaw commented.

"Are you mad Private?" an older macaw scolded. "Our law strictly forbids…"

"They can take care of these pets after their futile meeting. After all, it's not like Helios will bother to listen."

After a few moments of deafening silence, my father's infantry felt they would now be killed for sure.

"Take these prisoners to our leader," ordered the head sergeant. "He'll know what to do with them."

The forces lowered their weapons as Photios and his infantry breathed a sigh of relief. The next thing they knew, the cats and dogs were paw-cuffed together, like a chain gang in a prison work detail. The rodents were tied to the talons of the AVIACHT infantry, their skin lightly scraping against the sharp claws.

"If you lay so much as a claw on my friend…" shouted a feline private, words for which she was struck down by a beak.

"You're lucky we're not considering you for our feast before the fight," the macaw snickered. "Take them to the HQ. Our leader just might be there."

"Hail Helios!" the others replied with a salute, and with that, my father and friends were dragged further into the muddy jungle.

Chapter 44

Triscos Log: Early Afternoon, 1945B.

Today is perhaps the most important day of my life. I had just been given my first assignment on the front lines. Though I am young of age for a macaw, my grand tutor General Gorchak, had always wanted me to make him proud.

My assigned infantry had just departed from the sky and landed at the grand jungle that was once Rio De Janeiro. I am still reeling from the recent loss those sapes had inflicted upon us. There is no question as to why they should be extinguished, but now was not the time to grieve. Now was the time to leave first impressions on our glorious leader who was visiting our base for inspection.

Kana, who swore to look after me upon her father's death was fueled with anger, not just from Gorchak's death, but from the passing of her true love. Not in a physical way per se, but in a spiritual way. Of all the macaws to betray her and the glorious regime, it had to be Episko. Even as I am writing, shudder from just the thought. How could our own kind, who had suffered so much and who lost too many, still side with those…those…those flat-faced loggers!

As we landed in front of our military base, I saw Kana's soulless sneer of rage spread. Being the kind chick I am, I reach my wing out in an attempt to console her. But she swiftly tugs away from me and gives me a sneer.

"Straight back, my Trisco," Kana says under her breath. "This is our chance to show father's teachings were not in vain."

As everyone was accounted for, we stared in breathtaking awe at Helios's grand military bases. An immensely-sized tree, with the largest and thickest trunk of them all. It was large enough to fill nine to ten acres of land. Thousands of macaw troops walked and flew across its diameter, as they patrolled the jungle, resting on top of the palace's lushly-leafed branches above. Attached to the trunk were flags of various sectors and regions we conquered and renamed, the largest of them being the official AVIACHT symbol, a large talon within a circle against an aqua-marine background. Yes, it was a grand memento, a crowning achievement of all that we birds had done to get this far.

Suddenly, a set of roots, which were as large and thick as most trees I've seen, opened up in front of us. This was the entrance to the grand hall of our quarters. Without hesitation, we flew into the opening. Once inside, all was dark. For a moment, we could not tell where to go and where to stop. Then, the lights of a million fireflies lit up the ceiling, pouring a luminescence throughout the entire war room.

It was a grand hall, with wooden walls decorated with portraits of our leader and his generals. The floor was a moss-coated carpet covering the entire surface. It brought ease to our talons from the long flight here. In front of us was a large map stretched across each side of the room, with a table below to compliment the style. Surrounding it was some of the highest officials of the AVIACHT regime, planning their next strategy for the big battle ahead. And there, hiding in the shadow between the minister of war and propaganda, was the black silhouette of our dear leader himself, KING HELIOS.

Upon noticing our arrival, he and the others lifted their heads towards our direction, as if we had come uninvited. To be within Helios's presence was like coming to our destiny, and yet, we were only able to see his glistening eyes amongst the shadow that covered his body. After a few lengthy moments of silence…

"Proceed," said our leader to our relief.

"Hail Helios," we replied with a salute, to which they saluted back.

"Your great excellency," Kana began, as the rest of us followed behind her. "The plan you have sent for us is nearly complete. A submarine with infinite gallons worth of black plague venom has reached the coastline. And with the last of the Sapien stronghold on its way, it will be an offering of restless hearts that will be told for ages to come."

"Excellent," King Helios replied humbly. "General Gorchak had always expected great things from his daughter. I see you have brought guests to our palace."

Kana turned around to see we were still standing there.

"Of course, where are my manners?" she said. "I have brought before you an army of newly-bred soldiers, strong and equipped for battle."

We all gave our salutes to our leader once more, to which he nodded in gratitude. I could still hear in Kana's voice a small shard of pain, as if she were trying desperately to compose herself.

"This one in particular," she continued as she pointed her sharp talon at me, "is of exceptional promise."

"I will be the judge of that," Helios replied.

He hopped onto the map as his ministers cleared the way.

Though still hidden in the shadow, I gazed in both fear and respect at how immense and erect he was compared to his inferiors. He was just as they had described him: tall, brawny and full of vigor.

"Step forward, soldier," he commanded me, to which I started to do without hesitation.

I trembled slightly at the presence of our beloved ruler. It had been my dream to meet King Helios. I had always pictured the day would come when I would be able to present myself at the macaw that would rule us all. I had practiced in my head how it would play out: what words I'd say, what actions I would make, what plans I had for him to consider. And yet, at that moment, with no clue of his expression, my mind had drawn a blank.

"Do not be frightened." Helios reassured me. "You are among feathered brethren. State your name."

"I am Trisco," I spoke calmly. "Member of the AVIACHT youth, highest among my class and commander in training. My comrades and I are honored to be in your presence."

We saluted with our wings as high in the air as possible, to which our King nodded in humility once more. I felt shame in myself, as he began to notice that my body was still trembling. So, he marched forward for closer examination. Yet, he was still careful to hide himself in the shadows. I was able to see his eyes up close through the darkness. They were burning, with a hint of orange and brown, as if he had gone through the deepest pain imaginable.

"I can see you shaking," he commented with disappointment. "Weakness is for the land-dwelling Flat Faces. Never for us. Do you know why?"

I shook my head.

"Because we are descendants of the Mighty Dinosaurs. They were once the dominant species of this planet. But everything began small. First, they started off as tiny sauropods living off the shorelines of the river and the ocean. Then, as they diversified in where they lived, so did their appearance. Some grew long necks, others spawned spikes on their backs, and even a few bloomed gorgeous feathers on their skin. Within a few hundred million years, they had truly spawned into a fully-functioning, dominant species, free to roam the world as they pleased. Not only that, but they ruled the skies, seas and land all at once. And do you realize why they ruled?"

I shook my head again.

"They were not afraid to have this world for the taking. They did not give in to fear. They abolished their weaknesses long after they first merged on land. And what is more, their strength kept other species in their places. No other creatures would dare even try to overthrow them, not even the puny mammals."

At that moment, he turned his back on me and walked towards the large map. With the click of his talon, the other generals swiftly made room and turned on a glow-worm-powered light directed onto the atlas, giving us a clear view of its details. Several continents were covered with what looked like a bright paint, representing where we took over and where we planned to invade next.

"The flat-faced sapiens say that dinosaurs were obliterated long ago," he continued as he examined the map. "But we are living proof that they still not only exist but are thriving in great numbers. Now the time has come for us to send those pestilent humans back to their place and take what is rightfully ours. We are so inevitably close to our goal, I can taste it in the air."

"We will not fail you, your highness!" Kana replied nobly.

"Our troops are coming from all corners of the earth. It will be a battle that will go down in history."

"I am sure it will Kana," Helios replied as he turned towards us. "Your father would've been proud. Speaking of which, I am most sorry about your loss."

We saw a tear fall down one of Kana's eyes. It was the first time we saw her break down. But needless to say, Helios kindly walked over and lifted his talon to her beak.

"He was a brave, brave macaw," he said solemnly. "One of the finest in our fleet, his death will not be in vain. I can guarantee that."

"Thank you, dear leader," she replied as she dried her tears. "ALL HAIL HELIOS."

"All hail Helios," we replied with a salute.

"Our generals will show you to your sleeping quarters," Helios concluded. "I suspect you are tired from the long flight here."

Several of his elite marched towards us and we were escorted to the sleeping chambers, where I am currently writing as I speak. The space is adequate; it's not as tidy as my previous bedroom, but livable all the same. Besides, I get to be right next to my friends. Even now, a few of them are playing ball with a brazil nut just outside the window, while the others are giving last-minute inspections of their weapons.

As I look towards the future, I can only wonder what my parents would think of me now. How proud they would be to have had their egg hatch into the next generation of leaders for our glorious sky. I pray now they are looking down at me from the clouds, smiling at what they've seen, with hardly a cast of doubt about what I am to do next week.

Chapter 45

The following is an audio recording from the Brazilian archives; it's one of the last surviving, authentic audios from the Aviacht Forces.

Source: Unknown
Location: Northern tip of Brazil
Date: 1945B
Event: Battle of the Amazon
Camera: AVIACHT youth
Voice: HELIOS

Comrades…

We have reached the tipping point of our fate. As the war has raged on, many of you see the world we promised ourselves drift further and further into the expanse. Well, I say unto you, and I assure you, do not fall in despair. For as long as we stand, and as long as we fly, that future is nowhere near impossible. From what I have seen in my travels, this future is as clear as the jungle in which we dwell, and the sky we breathe.

Now as I stand before you, upon the threshold of our destiny, let me tell you this simple truth. The sky, the sacred sky, shall rule the earth! It shall command the clouds! It shall penetrate the very disease that is the human race!

(Cheers and chants from the crowd)

Many moons ago, my family was viciously attacked by the arrogant paw of Man. With his monstrosities that were axes and torches, Mother and Father disappeared into the flames, defending our jungle. I know nothing of where they are, nor if they are alive, but I know that justice and honor run strong in my family's veins. And this honor, and this justice, will always lean towards the blood spilt by my mother and father. With our crafted rifles, our precious talons and our stoic beaks, I know that justice will prevail!

(Cheers from crowd as Helios flips back his head feathers with his talon)

To all our enemies, I say unto them, "Prepare for the coming end of your pestilent days. Make way for the True rulers of this world! Your hours are numbered! Your fate is sealed and your Judgement Day has arrived! The age of the simple-minded flat face is over! A new dawn will shine over the clouds, over the mountains and over the trees! The DAWN OF AVIACHT!

(The macaw crowd makes a salute with their wings chanting, "Hail Helios! Hail Helios!" After which it dies down with the whip of a wing)

I may not be the wisest of birds, nor the most cunning among my finest-feathered generals and commandants. Hell, there are even those whom I envy and praise for their talents, that reach higher than my own. But I know what they stand for. Oh, yes. I know what you all stand for. We all stand for the same thing, brotherhood, family, honor, and our freedom!

(Cheers from crowd, Helios flips back feathers again and composes himself.)

You know the jungle – I know humans. I have watched their wicked ways, their careless deeds, and their corrupted minds. But within every wickedness, there is a crack. We have exposed and widened it for all to see. And I know, that together, on this righteous day, we have the chance, the privilege to stop them, grind their machines to a halt and take what is rightfully ours – the earth!

For too long we have suffered under the naked hand of the Sapien race! We have suppressed our hand for now, but if we wait any longer, Sapiens will spring back with great, unstoppable vengeance! And if they figure us out, there goes everything we have fought for up to this moment.

We cannot let them take away this Mother Earth that is home! This planet is our bones; these trees are our hearts; the soil is our skin and the clouds our fine feathers. Now the time has come to show them just who Earth was meant for…the Amazon! The Avian species!

(Tree erupts into a clutter of chirps and squawks, melting into "ALL HAIL HELIOS!" "All hail Helios!" "All hail Helios!").

Let us not forget who we are! We are bird! We are descended from the mighty dinosaur! Our reptilian ancestors ruled this earth for millions of years! Now the time has come to honor them with gratitude, to rule once more as they did! THIS land IS OURS! Let us ride the wind like never before, let us command the wind, let us create the thunder; let us penetrate the lightning and protect the future that is the Amazon jungle! Let's FIGHT FOR IT! FIGHT NOW! For we are AVIACHT! Who is with me?

(The cheer overwhelms the audio. The sounds and chants of "All hail Helios!" "All hail Helios!" grows louder and louder; almost to a point where the recording breaks the barrier).

"Then Let us fly! Fly now! Fly now! Birds of all feathers annihilate together!"

(The sound of flapping and squawking and gun-clicking can be heard as the anthem of AVIACHT is sung by several macaws) – end of audio.

Chapter 46

After hours, and maybe even days of grueling travel, my father and his infantry, who were now prisoners of the enemy, had reached the edge of the headquarters to King Helios. It was a sight more than anyone could describe, before or since. The town that was once Rio De Janeiro had succumbed to the invasive vegetation festered by enhancements AVIACHT scientists had perfected over the years. Buildings melded with vines and moss, houses had crumbled into mounded nests, and even the neighborhoods that were the Favelas had turned into unrecognizable hillsides for breeding and mating. Even the streetcars that once traveled in and out of the metro area had succumbed to shrubs and bushes.

As the infantry of prisoners walked into the now-abandoned dirt ridden streets and corridors, Photios and Demeter took a few moments to gaze at the hollow structures that once bore civilization and the like. The whistling sounds of wind drifted in and out of the cracked windows and doorways. A few misplaced objects that were not burned already, were scattered upon the sidewalk, littering their route. One of Photios's dogs stopped to sniff a tattered doll but was yanked away with the chain by his macaw captivator.

A few loud chirps could be heard up in the newly-built canopies, which had replaced the Brazilian skyline. Unlike the floor below, it was bustling with noises and lights. Some birds were tending to their tree nests. Others were teaching their young to fly, while a few were prepping their weapons and others were singing a patriotic song of Helios. Some were just kissing their loved ones on the beak and heading to the battlegrounds that would surely determine this war's conclusion. Some birds were scared, others were excited, and a few were even a little dazed, surely from the magnitude of what they were risking.

On closer inspection, some of the macaws were aligned in V and W formations, carrying below them a series of rather strange looking missiles by tightly woven ropes. Each of these missiles had a deep green serum encased in a large jar. This must've been the weapon, the weapon that all the Allied Forces were fearing that would exterminate not only the human race, but all other Eco-systems once and for all. But this was nothing compared to the next horror Photios and his infantry would witness.

Lo and behold, on a steep, ascending hillside, overlooking the abandoned city, my father and his team dropped their jaws in sheer shock and tears, as rows upon rows of human corpses decorated the steep, moss coated rocks. Humans were stripped of their clothing, shaved of their hair, flayed of their skin and impaled on large wooden spikes pointed upward to the sky. The scene intended to serve as a reminder for any human who dared so much as to cross into this land again. Men, women and children of all sizes had become monuments to the massacre AVIACHT had ravaged in the world. Some of them were still barely alive, instinctively twitching by their nerves, in pain and agony. As blood trickled down the spikes and meshed into the soil below, my father and Demeter just looked at them in utter horror, wishing they could just stab the still suffering in the heart, putting them out of their misery. Engraved on their muscle tissue were written words: Logger, Digger, Seller, Killer. Whatever they meant, these poor souls must've committed a misdemeanor beyond forgiveness, in the eyes of an Amazonian bird.

The team then heard a few howls and whines below their paws. The soil had disappeared and was replaced by thick glass cages of other dogs, cats and rodents. Once trying to overthrow the AVIACHT empire, they had been driven mad by sounds only they could hear. Their eyes turned bloodshot red and their mouths were foaming, devoid of their sanity. A rodent in Father's infantry foolishly tried to sneak through the thick glass, hoping to save a comrade or two, but was quickly squashed in the head by a pair of talons. It went so fast, no one had time to grieve.

These torturous sightings were but decorations for AVIACHT HQ, for at last Photios and his team had reached the living quarters of King Helios. The iconic Christ the Redeemer statue, which once stood there had been toppled and demolished. It was now replaced by a large, proud chested macaw with its wings outstretched from both sides, creating a shadow that trickled down the hill. Its concrete texture had been slightly coated with algae, vines and roots. No doubt this was a monument to Helios himself. Surrounding the large entrance were large, brawny guards consisting of two elephants, wolves and hogs.

"Who goes there?" asked an elephant with a bellowing voice and a spear-headed tusk.

"We have a group of prisoners who wish a rather peculiar request," the macaw soldier replied as they approached the entrance.

"And what is this request these 'Pets' wish to receive?" asked a snarling wolf who was sniffing my father.

Demeter growled back at the wolf, to which he was violently yanked back by a pair of talons and thrown to the ground. A few mice tried to intervene and help, but my father silenced them, reminding them of their mission.

"We wish to speak to King Helios," Photios replied.

The entire AVIACHT battalion burst into uproarious laughter upon hearing these words.

"You wish to speak to our dear leader?" asked an elephant with a patched eye. "You simple minded pets?"

"Please," Demeter begged as he staggered to his feet, "It is an urgent manner of life and death. We can't…"

"SILENCE YOU!" A boar officer with a set of razor-sharp fangs shouted "You are only to speak when spoken to by the Elite."

"YOU? ELITE?" A macaw soldier squawked back at the boar. "Remember, it is us to whom you pledge your allegiance. We only spared you because we sympathize with the plight humans have placed on your flesh."

To the surprise of my father's infantry, the pig whimpered away and stepped back into his post. On the order of the macaw, the rest of the infantry was stacked into a line and inspected by the noses of elephants and wolves. It felt as if they were getting their flea and tick shots from training camp all over again. This gave my father a moment to inspect these so-called 'loyalists' to the AVIACHT regime.

"Do you really think Helios will give you anything?" Photios asked a wolf guard. "You really think he's going to keep his word to an animal without feathers?"

"Deceiver," the wolf snarled back. "Liar!"

"You should know perfectly well by now what his empire intends to do."

"I'm not going to listen to this."

"After he takes control of the Americas, what then? Will there be anything left for you and your kind? Will there be any patch of land he will leave for wolves to roam free? Have you ever thought of that?"

"I don't have to hear this gab from a pet like yourself."

"Why? Why do I make you uncomfortable? After all, we are…relatives."

"You…are…traitors! Blind servants to those sapes. You should have abandoned your owners when you had the chance! But now, you're only as good as fresh meat."

A seeping level of drool fell down the wolf's jaw as he let out a menacing grin.

"You know nothing about us," said a cat who stepped out of line, and was quickly pinned to the ground by an elephant's trunk.

"How about we see how similar you are to those flat faces?" the elephant roared.

"I'd love to inspect that brain of yours!" barked another wolf with its fangs at the cat's skull. "Let's see if your blockage is in any way like a human's."

Suddenly, a flickering light came from the two eyes of the enormous bird statue. The guards and macaws dropped what they were doing and looked in awe.

"Proceed," said one of the pig guards.

And with that, the AVIACHT soldiers escorted their prisoners onto the drawbridge and through the large, gnarled gates. My father had no idea of what was going on. But for some reason, they were allowed into the presence of King Helios. Was it something they said? Did they offer something unknowingly valuable or was it something more instinctive? Either way, Father couldn't help but feel that Helios was looking down at them from one of those bird statue eyes.

Chapter 47

The gates opened like a pair of moss-covered knuckles being torn apart. The afternoon dew and steam trickled down the structure, giving way to a dark and humid hall. There was no way of telling what to expect in the next few hours; only the smell of algae and soil that fumigated the indoor air could provide any clue.

"Move," an elephant grunted as he poked Demeter in the side.

Photios and his infantry walked in as the gates closed behind them. For a moment they were in complete darkness. Only the sounds of incoming draft broke the silence. It felt warm and humid inside. The ground was even more moist and soft, making it more difficult for a land dweller to pace through. But regardless, they trudged blindly down the hallway carved into the cavern of this plant and sculpture hybrid.

Suddenly, blinding fluorescent lights were turned on above them. The ceiling was no different from the exterior, as it was made up of vines, branches and old, outdated moss. Yet the pattern they made was something out of a grand Versailles palace. The bright lanterns that adorned the center line also substituted as nests, where high-ranking privates and commanding lieutenants looked below, grimacing at the site of their new furry arrivals.

Surprisingly, the walls were smooth and gray. How they were able to do that inside a statue tree hybrid is anyone's guess.

Adorning these walls were pictures and portraits of various kinds. Some showed commanders and leaders from years past, others showed flocks and migrations of birds living in a jungle utopia, and of course, there were the sporadic images of the AVIACHT fleet conquering and slaughtering various human towns and cities. One that truly caught the infantry's eye was that of a large canvas of various dinosaurs bowing in respect and allegiance to parrots and macaws, who were perched on top of a large golden tree. Below was a plaque that read:

'Let us honor our once-dominant ancestors and take what is rightfully ours. For they, in spirit, honor us with our vow.'

"Quite a commitment, isn't it?" said a gravelly voice from above, followed by a snickering cackle.

My father, Demeter, and the others looked around to find the source of the voice, but it was nowhere to be found. They tried to use their sense of smell and lunged a little forward but were yanked back violently by the guards.

"Now, now comrades," the voice responded. "We don't wish to be rude with our guests. They may have possibly just wandered onto our turf by accident."

"WE ARE NOT HERE BY ACCIDENT!" yelled a defiant cat pvt. "WE ARE HERE TO WARN YOU…"

The cat was silenced with a slash to the eye by a pair of talons. As blood gushed from her socket and she let out a scream of pain, everyone just stood there, fearing they would be next.

"You are a strong, exceptional group of animals," the voice continued. "Reckless, but strong and exceptional. Even when you fell into our trap, you still managed to carry on, just like your saber-toothed ancestors."

After a few moments, Photios spoke.

"We do not wish to cause any harm here," he said as he tried to console his feline friend. “We only desire to speak with King Helios about a dire circumstance.”

“You’re talking to him now,” A wolf snarled.

“Bring our guests to the throne room,” ordered Helios’ voice. “I’ve prepared a special banquet just for them.”

“You mean to tell us you knew we were coming?” asked Demeter.

“Not you in particular,” Helios replied. “We just knew sooner or later an enemy infantry would come knocking at our bark, especially with how things are going now. Comrades, bring them to me.”

The guards looked at each other for a moment in confusion but knew not to question their dear leader’s command. My father and friends were escorted to a large cylinder-shaped rotunda at the edge of the hallway. This served as the main stairwell for all levels in Helios’ palace. Clearly, this was only meant for birds as there were no stairs to climb. There were however, a set of thick vines made just for non-avian guests, laid out in the center of the cylinder. The vines were slippery though, so they required a strong set of claws to hang on and keep a secure grip.

“We will accept your invitation,” Photios replied, “if, and only if, you aid our friend.”

Father pointed his nose to the wounded cat. At first the guards scoffed at the thought.

“Do as he says,” Helios spoke calmly. “We all want to show them our hospitality.”

With no help from the guards, Photios and his allies drew out their claws and stabbed into the vine’s material, while the feline private was escorted by her forelegs to an undisclosed location. What they would do to her was anyone’s guess, but now was not the time for such matters as the infantry began their ascension.

As the infantry pushed and scooted their way up like furry caterpillars, their faces looked in awe at the majesty of the column. The vertical pathway from the soil ground to the destination above looked like a vine into the heavens from their perspective. But knowing what was at stake, there was no time to gape. Yet, with every scrape and scratch of their vulnerable stomachs against the bark coated vine; a few squawking laughs could be heard in the background. The macaw soldiers mocked and threw blunt objects at my father's squadron, reveling in their misery.

"Comrades!" shouted Helios's voice from above. "Let us not provoke our guests!"

The soldiers reluctantly stopped as Photios and his team continued the long journey upwards. For a few minutes everything seemed fine. Suddenly, as they were about three-fourths of the way up, a sharp humming noise could be heard off in the distance, a noise only dogs could hear. For some reason, and without warning, Demeter snapped. He howled and barked and started clawing at the vine like a savage animal.

"What is it? What's the matter?" my father yelled as he leaped over to console his friend.

"The walls!" Demeter shouted with tears of pain. "The walls! They're coming to get me again!"

"What? What are you talking abou—"

But there was no need to explain. Photios looked into Demeter's eyes and saw what his cries of sorrow meant. The echoes of pain from the POW soundboard room had come back to haunt him again.

"Where's that humming sound coming from?" my father shouted. "Turn it off! Please! My friend is in pain! Turn it off!"

The humming died down until it could no longer be heard. My father was surprised they actually listened to him. Soon, Demeter calmed down and took a few deep sighs of relief. Why now? Why would the enemy show so much mercy? And if so, why on us?

Before they knew it, the infantry reached the top of the cylinder canopy. Before them stood another dark, empty void, with no clue of what would await them.

"Remove their shackles," Helios's voice commands.

Without hesitation, a few Hyacinth macaws flew up from below and followed his command. A few of Photios's infantry took deep whimpers of relief, as they stretched their paws from the burden of the metal.

Suddenly, a pair of fluorescent lights lit up from the front, revealing what was clearly the throne room of the AVIACHT leader. The roots, vines and bark perfectly and symmetrically aligned against the organic walls and ceiling, giving them a sort of Victorian Renaissance vibe. In the center were two large windows that must've doubled for the eyes of the statue palace's exterior.

Between them was the throne itself. The shape was almost indescribable. It seemed to be shaped from gnarled roots and broken branches that spread out onto the wall and across the floor, fusing the three together in near-perfect symbiosis. It was a decadent seating arrangement, complimented by flowers, leaves, nuts, and algae. And there, in the center of it all, amidst a carefully-caressed shadow, was assuredly King Helios himself, waiting for his guests to arrive. The only physical qualities my father saw of him, were a pair of ancient yellow eyes.

"Welcome, fellow travelers," his silhouette said humbly. "You must be tired from your journey. Come in. Take your shoes off, stay awhile."

"We don't wear shoes," Demeter growled in disgust. "And what about our feline friend?"

"All in due time, warrior. All in due time."

Between the throne and the guests stood a large, banquet styled table with various exotic food and refreshments. A few dogs' and mice mouths began to water. They hadn't seen such abundant food in months.

"Ah, yes," Helios continued. "I thought you would all be hungry. So, I asked my chefs to batch up some of the finest edible offerings our regime has to offer."

"What does this prove to us?" Photios asked as he approached further.

"If anything," Helios continued, "it proves our species is a culture of class and eloquence. Behold some of our succulent items we brought to the table – fried worm on sautéed carrots, softened Brazil nuts served in pineapple broth, palm fruit subs scattered with crisped flies, scalloped potatoes swimming in rich, and unspoiled palm oil, just to name a few. Please, feel free to dig in."

"We appreciate your seemingly generous hospitality Helios," Demeter replied sternly. "But we're not—"

Before he could finish, a handful of the infantry ran towards the table and began to gobble up what they could find. With a sigh of defeat, he and Photios took their seats at the table as well as their share of sustenance.

An hour passed, with everyone feasting and drinking without a word or murmur. Photios and Demeter grew impatient with the chewing and the silence, as Helios just looked on at his guests. What was this all about? Why was Helios treating them so well? Suddenly…

"That was quite a show you and your woodland critters made back in Europe," Helios commented. "I'm impressed."

"What are you talking about?" Demeter asked.

"I'm of course talking about your misadventure with the tanks How you were able to get pass one of my top-ranking generals is beyond me. You would've made great soldiers if you were among our species."

"You already have a great many wolves to fit your army."

"But not enough to go around. Despite our victorious outcomes, we seem to be running low on our WolfBlitz comrades. Some have been mistaken for the enemy forces, which sort of brings us to the subject at claw."

"What do you mean? Are you trying to lure us into a trap?" Photios asked. "Is there some chemical substance in this feast?"

"Far from it," Helios chuckled. "I've brought you here to offer a... proposal of sorts."

"What kind of proposal?" a rodent asked.

"I know much about all your species."

A large, sharp set of talons stepped out of shadows and into the light. And before they knew it, all of the so-called majesty and vigor that was King Helios came into full physical perspective. He revealed an old, yet strong-looking Blue Macaw. His feathers were slightly ruffled but sleek in texture. His beak had a black burn at its tip, probably from a past traumatic experience of sorts. On top of his head was a set of feathers made to look like a certain hairstyle. They were streaked across the skull cap with the ends hiding the left side of his face. For every seven to eight steps, he lifted his metal armored talon to pull it back, revealing a faint yet noticeable scar etched on his left cheek. Adorning his torso was a golden sash made to represent his status as king. Of course, like every other bird surrounding them, he wore a patch on his wing with the AVIACHT symbol shining against the light.

"Your Majesty," my father started after a moment's hesitation. "We have come to offer you a warning. This war has gone on for far too long. Both sides have suffered immeasurable casualties. If we go on any further, neither side will get what they want or need."

"You are absolutely right Lieutenant." Helios woefully sighed. "I for one have grown weary of this myself. But such is the price for victory."

"Do you really think this battle is all just another medal of honor for you birds? Do you?" Demeter asked. "And why are you treating us like honored guests?"

"Oh no," Helios replied. "I don't see this as an act of honor. On the contrary, I see this as an act…of…JUSTICE!"

The echo of Helios's mighty voice bounced across the natural structure, as if several other birds were answering his call.

"But that is beyond the subject of this conversation." He continued. "You have fought well, now is the time to surrender and face the facts. I want this war to end just as badly as you do. And I can offer you something you wouldn't ask your sapiens friends for – Freedom."

"Freedom?" A mouse replied as he ate a freshly plucked eucalyptus leaf. "But we already have freedom."

"Do you my rodent friend? Do you?" asked Helios. "Behind all those victories and celebrations, what are you really being rewarded with? What do those flat faces give you in return, a few more carbon footprints and a loss of more of your kin? You have fallen into their trap so many times. Ever since you first came into contact with them two hundred thousand years ago, you fell prey to their false promises, their wishes, their hatred, their warfare, and their deepest, darkest desires.

"Oh, yes they threw you a few of their scraps, a bowl of water, a mat to sleep on, a lousy piece of T-bone Steak! But other than that, you earned nothing. They took away your freedom, gave you a collar and a leash, a cage, and a set of guidelines on how to live and obey. The life you once had, no longer your own. I'm still amazed you continue to fall into their trap…"

"We didn't fall into any trap!" Demeter shouted. "No one forced us to serve our human friend. We chose this life."

"Precisely, which is what makes you stupid."

"You so much as try to dictate who's smarter than the other…" an angry cat cadet snarled.

"Quiet," my father said bluntly as he tried to keep the peace. "Helios, what kind of proposal are you trying to give us? Is it a treaty? Are you trying to make a compromise of some sort?"

"Not exactly," Helios replied. "My proposal is…one of unity, cooperation, understanding, and brotherhood."

"What are you talking about?"

"I'm talking about man's problem with both of us. You, pets, and we are target practice to them."

Helios flew to the opening eye of his throne and gazed out in the distance. A small, yet chilling, wind blew in as if some sense of uncertainty had befallen the chamber.

"Why couldn't they just let us be?" he said solemnly. "What did we ever do to them? What justifies their treatment? I was asking myself those same questions for a long time. But rather than find answers, I came to realize that I was only harming myself in pursuit of our flaws. I was naive, just like you. We had done nothing. And by doing nothing, my family's jungle was obliterated from the face of the earth. Nothing can forgive what those blasted sapes did. I can still hear the sounds of squeals and squawks and searing bouts of pain and horror from that day echoing all around me. But what was I to do? I was only an innocent chick at the time."

He grabbed a small, loose vine from the sill with his beak. As he continued to speak, he massaged the material with his talons, like he was about to sketch something with the tip.

"I was ready to have a joyous boyhood filled with beauty, vigor and promise. Yet, I was naive with myself as a species. Then that day came – that unholy day. It and was a disaster. None of us were ready. All that what was good, all that was pure, all that was earth was obliterated in an instant. It was the last time I ever saw my wonderful family. Luckily, I was raised by a strong and intelligent teacher. He never gave up on me. He knew I was destined for greatness. But I was still scarred, physically and emotionally. I still blindly thought it was our fault in some way. But as I grew and expanded my knowledge, I realized something – it wasn't partially our fault, nor was it partially theirs...IT WAS ALL THEIR FAULT! IT WAS ALL THE FAULT OF MAN!"

Helios snapped the vine like a whip on the floor, silencing any shrewd noise that dared echo.

"We can comprehend your pain your majesty." Father tried to reason with him. "It is true we have seen the evil in humans. We have seen despicable things beyond forgiveness. But we have been with them longer than you. And I know maybe you can learn a little more about them through our eyes."

"Unbelievable," Helios chuckled. "You still don't get it do you? You have been duped by your masters and brainwashed into slaves for their own self interests. But you're too stupid to see that. Figures. You have been coerced into submissiveness and unawareness, just like them. I wouldn't be surprised if I found a blockage in your brain, same as theirs."

"Then again, you were forced into their world. They just take and take and never mind who they hurt along the way physically or physiologically. I know there's a part of you pets that yearns to be free and wild like us. That is why I brought you here as our guests. The time has come to make a truce between the two us. To join forces and enforce justice on the flat faces and bring new order to the planet!"

Helios flew over to a dog cadet and several mice who were still focusing on their blessed meal. With the delicateness that was his talon, he lifted up their heads and gazed at them like a loving father.

"You know you are not allies. You are but slaves. If you seek into your hearts, you will know it to be true. No human ever showed you real kindness and love. It was all a con, a game for their own selfish amusement. From the second you were taken in, they tricked you, they bred you, devolved you, and deconstructed your inner, free, feral selves. Yet, blindly and foolishly, you continued to serve your slave masters, expecting some kind of reward in the process. But look what happened. Your pack was split up, sold away and worked to death. They broke your bones, fed you hormones, and put you on display like some sort of treasured and tortured relic."

"Decades turned to centuries, and centuries into millennia; yet, you still held your ground. Not one of you had the nerve to rebel against your oppressors. You continued to be tortured by them, and yourselves. And to this day you still do. While you place your necks on the line the humans sit by comfortably, enjoying the fruits of the earth and getting fat! Well, I'm here to tell you that now is the time to break yourselves of your denial. I can free your captive canine, feline and rodentia friends from down below us with the flick of my talon and give them an even greater freedom. Join us, and together we can overthrow the very thing that held you back! What do you say?"

For a few moments, silence fell across the room as father and Demeter began to ponder and think of what he said. This was a proposition that would mean a golden opportunity for most species. To reclaim the natural world as it was ages ago. What more could a species ask for.

But then, the two of them looked around and noticed several trophy cabinets hanging on the vine coated walls. Adorning them were samples and pieces of body parts. Legs, arms, bones, brains and even skin stripped to looked like a rug. All various parts of specimens – human specimens. Tortured, mutilated, likely to have suffered a slow, agonizing death. These relics brought them back to Europe, back to the harsh jungles, back to the ghettos, back to the death camps, back to all the horrors and despicable actions wrought upon by AVIACHT. And yet it felt ironic, despite all their suffering, it felt somewhat justified. The destruction upon the macaw's land had hardened them, transforming their consciousness into the very thing they tried to get rid of.

"Why would we ever want to join something that is precisely what we both hate?" Photios asked bitterly. "Don't you see what you're doing here? By trying to obliterate your oppressors, you transform into their image."

"Are you trying to mock us?" asked a macaw soldier from nearby who was about to charge.

"Patience Comrade," Helios calmed. "Our guests are clearly confused with their prospect."

"Prospect of what?" shouted Demeter as he walked to the eye window. "THAT?"

Demeter pointed his paw outside to the sight of impaled

humans and screams of caged pets from down below.

"You are NOT saviors of this planet," Demeter continued to bark. "You are scum! All of you!"

"Demeter! Get ahold of yourself!" my father pleaded as he ran towards him.

"You don't know half of what they're capable of doing!" Demeter spat back. "I have seen and endured tortures you dare wouldn't even think about. I've seen friends flayed, tortured and killed right before my eyes! I can never get the wailing sounds out of my head! I have gone all but mad because of them! And you still wish to make a deal with them!"

"This may be our only chance to end this once and for all," my father replied. "To prevent a bloodbath of epic proportions, you're planning to throw it all away?"

"What else is there to throw away? What else is there to lose? I lost my entire battalion, and I'm not going to let their deaths be in vain."

"I am just as weary as you, Demeter. But we've got to offer something reasonable. And…"

"There's no need for more reasonableness PETS!" said Helios, whose voice suddenly turned more sinister. "I think we have reasoned you enough. You are just like the others – weak, brainwashed, and committed to killing us all."

"Your justification for genocide was pitiful," Demeter mocked.

"Demeter!" Father shouted.

"I have seen good in the human race. I have seen women and children barred from the rest of world, yet they still hold on to their innocence. They are a brave species despite their flaws…"

"Demeter, Stop it!" Photios shouted. "You're only provoking them."

“I am not going to stoop to a kind that is blinded by hatred and fear! That pleasures itself in slowly watching a decent creature descend into madness! If you wish to have us join you, you can take us over my dead carcass!”

For a moment, dead silence once again fell across the room. Helios bobbed his head up and down, as if he were examining Demeter. Then, his face turned chalk white, like he had seen a ghost.

“Now I remember you,” he spoke more sinisterly. “You were the leader of that pesky battalion General Gorchak told me about. You were all too stubborn to talk. Oh, how they tried to break you with the tactics they used. But you just refused to give in. Now, how fortunate you’re here. I can finally fulfill the General’s wishes and extract his information. STRAP HIM UP!”

Suddenly, a flock of brute macaws swooped down from all sides. Several canine privates threw dishes at them as most hurried for the only exit, the eyed windows. Meanwhile, father and Demeter used their best martial arts skills to fend off their feathered friends. As they fought, swarms cluttered the throne room like a rave of multicolored arrows. The cries and squawks grew louder and louder, re-triggering PTSD in Demeter causing him to curl up and whimper for help.

“DEMETER!” Photios shouted desperately. “Come back to me my friend.”

“There are too many of them,” Demeter mumbled profusely. “Too many of them.”

“Don’t do this to me buddy!” Photios pleaded. “I’m not going to lose another friend!”

“They’re gonna take all of us. Just like they took my men. We can’t win.”

“SHUT UP!”

"We can't win!"

"I suggest you should heed your friend's words," Helios said, as the other macaws backed away behind him. "After all, that's what friends do."

Photios growled a nasty snarl as he guarded Demeter for dear life.

"Why don't you join us now?" Helios continued. "Support our cause. Think of the all the good it will do, for you and all pets like yourself."

"I will not subjugate myself to a group that tortured and killed my friends," Photios barked back. "We were offering you peace! We were wanting to promise you an end to all of this! We wanted to save your life, just as much as theirs! This can't go on for any of us! We are doomed if we persist this way!"

For a moment everything paused again. Helios's face began to change expression, from mockery to sympathy.

"Then…" Helios said through his beak as if he were ready to think about it, "…prepare to meet your DOOOM!"

He pointed his claw at the two, and the flock aimed straight towards them. Without thinking, father grabbed his friend and lunged out the right window, falling to the brown earth below. The birds flew over to the edge, but all they could see was a small crater below.

"The adversaries have been terminated, Your Majesty," said one of the soldiers as they turned to their leader.

"What a pity," Helios said solemnly. "They would have made excellent comrades. No matter. Round up the last ammunition and take it to the battlegrounds."

"Are you sure this is it, Your Majesty?" asked another macaw.

"It won't be long now," He replied as he looked out the

window. "We were destined to rule this earth. We will not be denied our prize! It's just a matter of time. I wish you a good fight my brothers."

"ALL HAIL HELIOS!" They said in unison as they left the room.

Meanwhile, Father was hiding below their peripheral vision. At the same time, he was clawing at a chipped part of the HQ exterior, while trying to balance his friend on his lap. He saw the piece of statue that had fallen off and had made a crater in the forest floor below. After a few frantic moments, Father saw a soft patch of moss nearby that trickled down far enough to land them to safety. So, he carefully grabbed his friend in his jaws, jumped onto the moss and slid down its texture and reached the floor.

"They're too powerful..." Demeter mumbled as he muscled out of those jaws. "They're just too powerful!"

"Snap out of it, Demeter!" Photios shouted.

"You know what they did to my infantry!" Demeter replied. "You saw what they did to those other infantries! They are just too strong! We are at the brink of extinction against them!"

Photios slapped Demeter across the face, snapping him back to reality.

"Nothing is hopeless as long as we're still here," my father stated as he held his friend by his head with his paws. "There's got to be a way to free those captives down below."

The two walked towards the rest of the infantry who were right nearby, awaiting his orders.

"Is anyone here a skilled digger and tunneler?" My father asked, to which several raised their paws. "All right, Demeter, I know you've been through more than all of us have, but we've got this one chance to bring in more troops. It's what your infantry would've wanted. Now, are you able to find shallow dirt to dig to the underground prisons below?"

Demeter, still a little shaken, thought for a moment, then nodded lightly.

"Everyone, Follow Me!" he said as his team began to dig into the earth.

"What if this doesn't...?" A cadet private began to ask to which she was silenced by Photios' paw.

"We can't think of that." Photios said calmly. "This has got to work. It just has to. For both sides. For all of us!"

My father looked on. as his allies continued to dredge into the forest soil. As his plan progressed, he began to wonder what each was doing at this point, where Episko was residing, and what those humans were planning next.

Chapter 48

The following is an excerpt from the archives of the Human Resources Committee aka HRC. This is one of the few remaining audios recorded just before D-Day.

Source: Unknown
Location: Northern tip of Brazil
Date: 1945B
Event: Battle of the Amazon
Camera: Volunteer
Speaker: Andrzej

"Friends and allies, we stand before a life-altering course. Today marks a Judgement Day for all of us, one that will be remembered for years to come. Today cements the fate of not only humans, but of all creatures big and small. Colleagues from all over the world will be coming together to initiate the Greatest Battle in the history of all species! That being said, we have a choice now. We can surrender and fall into the obscurity that is extinction, or we may hold onto our courage and have each of our species live to see another day. We may choose to clamor the threat to its knees – to blast AVIACHT sky high, and to cancel our extinction!"

(Cheers are heard in the background)

"But with all victories, comes sacrifice. I see in all your eyes: human, dog, cat and rodent, the fear that would make even the most stern of species tremble to their knees. But I say unto you, Remember that through the course of evolution, every creature faced an obstacle they had not endured before. And like us, they had a choice; either overcome or be overcome. Those that survived choose the former. To this day they still thrive. Yes, a great many perished, perhaps to the tipping point of extinction, but there were several who survived. And with those few they flourished and prospered in numbers, knowing they triumphed over the impossible – just like our ancestors did millions of years ago!"

(Cheers are heard once more)

"Now, once again, we face the same challenge. I'm not promising that we will win this battle. I'm not even promising that we will survive. But with every sacrifice, our courage is toughened, and our skill sharpened. So, let us hold on to our courage; let us hold on to our skill; let us hold on to what we strive for. Even with what lies in front of us, let us not only hold onto these precious gifts – let us fight for them! Let us fight for ourselves! Because this, this is our time!"

(The crowd cheers as the sounds of barks and squeaks can be heard in the background)

"I know many of you are full of doubt and full of uncertainty – unsure of what lies ahead, not only of who wins, but of who prospers for the centuries and millennia to come. We are so accustomed to planning for our future, to set the dominoes in place and charge them forward, knowing what comes next. But it is not the case for this day. So, for most, this is the first time you have experienced that feeling. And believe me, it is scary to not know where the story ends, or how things will turn out. You feel powerless against the obstacle, to not be mentally and physically ready for the battle such as the one we will soon endure. I know that feeling, because I, and my group experienced it before."

"But then, when it was least expected, there came hope. We were saved by the most unlikely of sources. A parrot, of all creatures, saved us all from total obliteration. He, along with his woodland friends in Europe, sheltered us from the impending swarm that threatened our lives. We were cared for, looked after, and given another chance to live. What's more, we made the improbable happen. We created an 'ANTHROMALIA,' a society where man and beast lived together in harmony. But that dream did come without sacrifice, as you all have been told by now. One of our dearest comrades, gave his life as we escaped en route to this destination. He was not afraid to die for what is now a greater cause, and for that, we will always hold him dear in our hearts."

"Now, believe me when I say, we have the chance to expand this hope. We have the chance to break this enemy army here and win just one for our story. We have the chance to have an ANTHROMALIA once more. Not one small clan, not one isolated patch of land, but all humans and beasts, across the world, all who fight for what truly is in our hearts: Love, Peace, Freedom and Unity!"

(The crowd cheers again)

"But if we truly wish to fulfill that promise, then you've got to take your fear, your doubt, and use it in your fight to fulfill the struggles our ancestors endured since the dawn of civilization. Let us charge forward. Let us scream to the heavens who we are! Let us charge through the enemy, one soldier after another, so they will know what we can do!"

(Crowd bangs on their weapons and clashes their armor)

"Let none of us forget how strong we are together! Together each of our species: Dog, Cat, Rodent, and Human creates a symbiotic organism that is all but impenetrable, an organism that exists without us and within us with the will to carry on, to seize the day, and to not concede to defeat! This is its time! This is its moment! This is it's chance for victory!"

"And now, at the threshold of hope, at the edge of infinity, let us now unite to become this specimen! Let us celebrate our chance for freedom – not as a race, not as a species, but as one co-existing ecosystem. An ecosystem that will say, 'We will not go quietly into the night! We will strive to carry on for what is true, what is kindness and what is love! Today is our chance to show who we truly are! Today is our time to shine among the ruins! Today is our time to fight so others may live!'"

"Today we are ready to protect our ANTHROMALIA!"

(An uproarious applause is heard as anthems and themes from every country around the globe can be heard in the background; the sound of them charging forward gets louder and louder.)

End of recording.

CHAPTER 49

It's the end of another workday at the PCC. I'm filling out a few last documents before I head home. Nothing seems to be out of the ordinary on this particular day. My co-workers and I are under the watchful eye of our supervisor: An uptight, no nonsense Orangutang named Prof. Zaiul. Though hardheaded in most situations, he always has good intentions and means well among the employees.

Surprisingly, things have been going smoothly in recent days. The trips to Dr. Trunca have proven very beneficial for me and my family dynamic. My father has had less and less PTSD attacks, giving us a few moments of quality time during my visits. On top of that, my son is becoming a more law-abiding citizen. Just recently, he focused his community service time towards watching over a new herd of Roe Deer up in the Appalachians. In the meantime, my wife and I have been able to find free time on virtual chats with our trans-species daughter. I think her cheetah husband is starting to grow on me. We are planning for a surprise visit to the African Grasslands in the near future.

As I pack up my briefcase and start to head for the door, I notice a rather peculiar set of rather old, dusty records hanging out of one of the file cabinets from above. Being the curious individual I am, I grab a mobile ladder and climb to the top shelf. A huge 'CLASSIFIED' is stamped on the folder containing the records. Since I'm a top-ranking employee, I have the fortune of gaining access to such a file. With the assistance of gloves and a set of tweezers, I carefully open the cover to reveal a stunning find. It is a collection of accounts from various individuals during the Holocaust and the Second World War, right down to the day the infamous BATTLE OF THE AMAZON occurred. But it's not just any individual's accounts, it's those of my family and their associates.

I tentatively read the papers inside where I get a first-hand experience of who was where on that day, just hours before carnage ensued. These were obtained based on written testimonies. My father and mother share one last intimate kiss in the barracks before he leaps into battle; Uncle Epi flying over the canopies, trying to pinpoint the location of his human friends, and Photios Metro, along with his infantry, secretly freeing captive prisoners for one final showdown among the AVIACHT powers. There are even a few documents from Epi's former lover, Kana as well as her adopted chick, Trisco. As I probe further into detail and thumb through the old, tattered pages, I feel as though a story is being told to me. Those are stories about fear and despair and about resistance and courage. These are stories about love and triumph against all odds.

"Mr. Whitestone?" says a voice from yonder. "MR. WHITESTONE!"

I look up to notice Prof. Zaiul hovering over me from a vine. I guess I spent too much time with my head somewhere else again.

"Must you always daydream during your work hours?" Zaiul asks impatiently.

"My apologies, sir," I respond back, carefully putting the records away. "It's just the end of the day is all. I couldn't help but notice this stack of unchecked documents and I saw a bit of my family's history. You see my father and mother…"

"In Darwin's name I pray thee," Zaiul interrupts. "I've heard this story seven times already from you. The least you can do is keep that to yourself while at work."

"I know, boss," I reply solemnly. "It's just father is better, and he's finally getting a few things off his chest. He finally revealed to me the other day how he got a mysterious letter from the war. On top of that, my son is finishing up his community service sentence and beginning to open up about a few feelings as well."

The Orangutang makes a sympathetic sigh.

"Mr. Whitestone," Prof. Zaiul says as he climbs down the shelves to console me. "I can understand your family hasn't had the most fortunate of luck over the years. It is 'challenging' to confront those things, yet leave them aside to focus on more important things. That is why I believe it is time to make amends with any demons you and your loved ones still have. Perhaps it's time your father meets with that old macaw you've been talking about recently."

"I see," I reply solemnly.

It is then I remember the stories my father told me. Of the horrors they experienced in the concentration camp, of the grueling conditions in the jungle led by Kana, of the countless human and allied lives he saw killed by the order of her wing. Would my father be able to forgive her after all these years? Did she now have the will to change her attitude towards humans? Had she lost the desire to kill off an entire species? I remember seeing her at Epi's funeral – solemn, flightless, her head bowed down in grief. She did not even bother to notice I was there, or anyone for that matter. It was as if she were all alone in this world. The only time she picked her head up was the moment she saw the corpse that was Episko. Would she ever be able to step out of her despair and make amends with my father?

"The thing is," I say as I snap back into reality. "A lot has already changed in my family for the better in recent weeks. Like I said, my father has had fewer and fewer panic attacks, and my son is getting into less trouble. He's even learned to accept his sister's transformation."

"That is excellent to hear," Zaiul replies. "But is all that really enough to lay your problems to rest. Think about that."

With those words, my boss climbs over the shelves and towards his studies. As I head for the door, I take a moment to think of what Zaiul said. Have I really squared away my problems for good? Is my family really at peace with themselves? Is everything all right with the world?

It is then I see few human children, several parrot chicks, and a few more canine pups, playing together on the terrace outside. I'm not sure what they're playing, but nonetheless, they all seem to get along smoothly like old friends. It is the textbook example of an Anthromalia, human and animal creatures joined together in inseparable harmony. Just as my father and mother had described when hiding in that shack, all lived peacefully among the other woodland creatures, along with the other human refugees. The moment of watching these youth though brief, warms my heart, giving me a feeling I haven't experienced in ages. Now I knew what I had to do. As I head for my autopod, I call my father on the phone. It is time to make amends with his foe.

Chapter 50

The following is based on firsthand accounts from "The Battle of the Amazon"

All was quiet on the bare, deforested tundra. Humans, dogs, cats, rodents and apes, all of us, stood in dead silence. We traveled by sea, plane and foot to fight for the sake of protecting what had remained of the Latin (and possibly human) culture. Only the breaths of soldiers and the clicks of rifles could now be heard around the perimeter. We were all that stood in the way of the last South American stronghold of the human race. Stationed behind us was the border that separated the country of Argentina and the Amazon rainforest.

The other night, we all said our prayers huddled underneath the barricades of our ships and carriers. That was where humans from every walk of life, whether European, American, Asian or African, prepared for the inevitable. For so long we viewed ourselves as an impenetrable species, unaltered by the tide of events and able to triumph over even the steepest of challenges. And yet this night, would determine who should inherit the rich brown earth. We were not even sure we could last until the next morning.

Yes, my sister and I escaped certain death. Yes, we risked our limbs and sanity through a harsh jungle. Yes, we almost got caught by AVIACHT under an inch of floorboard. And yes, we had nearly drowned after sailing across the Atlantic towards

Argentina. We had somehow survived all of it. A miracle, perhaps. Smart thinking, maybe. The right connections, who knows? I was not prepared to experience anything like what would happen in a few hours.

We were split into different battalions. Andrew and I were fortunately placed in the same one, while William was assigned to a battalion in the far back in the event that ours would fail defending our base. Each regiment was buried underneath the good soil of the Argentinian border. This underground tunnel in which we soldiers were placed was a giant catacomb of brown corridors and creviced dwellings. I could feel my heart beat against my ribcage as the hours counted down to the almost-certain moment of mortality and bloodshed.

My wife had been one of those put in charge of helping the humans who couldn't fight: mothers, fathers, children, the elderly, sick, and disabled; you name it. They were stationed at the boat stop nearby, ready to track into the port of Buenos Aires and sail their way to freedom. I could only imagine what was going on in each one of their heads. There was a chance this would be the last time they would see the world. For if we failed, the AVIACHT forces would surely kill them.

Meanwhile, outside, our battalion stood in the trenches, waiting for the signal to defend. Our commander, a great dane-shepherd mix, was standing at the ready. We coated ourselves in special soot and dirt to camouflage ourselves in the barren earth. All was quiet, just dead, undeterred silence. It was damp and wet as we hid behind the trenches, our weapons clutching to the armor of our uniforms. The smell in the air was foul with a slight tint of mold. I felt I was back in the camp, building that senseless wall for the sake of torture and misery. The silence was only slightly broken with a few personal prayers and massaging of weapons.

Yet, despite the majority of my comrades feeling dread and hopelessness, there were some who were surprisingly upbeat. In fact, they were looking forward to the sting of battle. These soldiers, human, dog and cat alike, had no armor covering their coats, no etchings and slogans on their knuckles and paws, and no war-paint dabbed all over their faces. I could see in their bloodshot eyes they no longer cared if they died on the battlefield, or even if they won. I do not know what they previously endured, or what they lost, but I knew this war had completely drained many poor souls of their sanity and humanity.

The clouds above us grew thick enough to make several sounds of thunder and scattered drops of rain. Our dirt-laded pathways quickly turned into mud, so we climbed slightly onto higher ground, hoping not enough for them to see us. Just as the thunder and lightning pounded all over the sky, I could feel my veins pounding throughout my body. It felt as though we were all standing at the edge of oblivion.

We could not see the enemy at first, as the sky grew darker and more menacing. Our infantry felt so alone, hanging on the edge of our breath, waiting for our adversary to strike at any minute. Some were praying, others were crying in fear. A few were even telling a joke or two to calm their nerves.

A few more long minutes passed and there was still no sign of the enemy. A handful of us were beginning to wonder if there would even be a battle. Maybe they had actually called off the fight, thinking maybe this battle really wasn't worth it. That would've been a relief now, wouldn't it?

Suddenly, a bright bolt of lightning flashed into the background, bright enough to see all the detail in the canopies above us. And there, in front and right above us, was a cacophony of AVIACHT forces. Parrots and macaws of magnificent colors and hues covered the thick, moss-coated branches and trunks. Their feathers, though coated for the most part in patches of mud, glistened amongst the lightning-filled sky, giving the trees a resemblance of the autumn day in my home country, the day our town was taken over.

"So, it begins." I shuddered to myself as the others and I fastened our armor tightly.

"That's the signal!" our commander shouted. "The enemy will strike any second! Everyone take your places now in the trenches!"

We all scurried to our fighting positions, readying our weapons with care and ease. Only a portion of our battalion was supplied with rifles and machine guns, while the others harnessed shanty bows and arrows to their forearms and legs. We had run low on military equipment as AVIACHT had scourged nearly all necessary resources. Now with arms at the ready, and the first shooters stationed at the front, the rest of us barricaded ourselves in the trenches and cocked our weapons to defend our stronghold. I held my breath and closed my eyes, as dead silence kicked in for one more fleeting moment.

"BIRDS OF ALL FEATHERS!" shouted a young macaw from above.

"ANNIHILATE TOGETHER!" the rest of flock shouted in unison.

I opened my eyes again and saw the swarm of forces flying straight toward us in exquisite unison. Together they looked like a multicolored cloud ready to drop rain comprised of different pellets and shells.

"FIRE THE WEAPONS!" shouted a human comrade.

The first fourth of the squadron released their arrows and

bullets into the air and headed straight into the flock. Though they managed to land a few, most were dodged by strategic formations and heavy armor. However, before we knew it, a handful of macaw soldiers plummeted straight into our crowd, killing both themselves and their targets.

"FIRE THE SECOND ROUND!" A cat comrade shouted.

"FIRE THE SECOND ROUND!" A human comrade replied.

And with that, a second battalion of amateur archers commenced shooting. As done previously, the enemy mostly dodged the attack again, flying over and under the shots of arrows and pellets. It seemed as though they were a sophisticated set of flying war machines.

For a moment, as the parrots and macaws started shooting their Brazilian nut bullets onto our helmets, I thought we were done for. Thankfully, a set of cats with exceptional jumping skills lunged into the air and snapped the necks of their foes, killing them instantly. A few other rodent comrades jumped onto sets of talons and beaks and bit on them off with their sharp sets of fine teeth. They were maniacally having the time of their lives, showing off their kills, flaunting bird parts in their mouths, and counting the number of fatalities.

"It's gonna be fresh, raw poultry tonight boys!" I heard one cat say. "Keep track of my kill Fur Balls! Haha!" laughed another. As menacing as this was, we had a little advantage now. The canine brethren joined in; they showed off their fangs and dug into the skin and muscle tissue of whatever avian attack they could. But it was not just for themselves, it was for the sake of us humans. Just like Episko and the woodland critters, they were giving their own lives for the benefit of our species.

"This is for my friend, Jane!" shouted a beagle who snapped

the neck of a red and blue macaw.

"This is for my soul brother, Lance!" cried a Greyhound who wrestled a green parrot to its death.

"And this is for Ortega's village, and the lives you took!" barked a Labrador who slashed open a blue macaw with his paws.

We human soldiers, who were still hunkered down in the trenches, looked on in amazement at their commitment and loyalty. Despite all we did to them, the pups we tortured, the kittens we drowned, the rats we wished to exterminate, they were still on our side.

Our amazement was short-lived though, as the AVIACHT forces pulled out more weapons, loaded them with silencers and started shooting down pellets of Brazil nuts right onto our heads and helmets, killing a handful in the process. In addition, a few cats and rodents were lifted from their stations and torn apart by talons and beaks. They fought back, as they plummeted to the ground in grimacing splats. A patch of the sky and ground had become a bloodbath. We knew our time had come.

"ATTACK!" shouted a human soldier.

And with that signal, we all climbed out of the ground and ran towards our adversaries. I closed my eyes and pulled the trigger. I had never before tried to kill any living being before, even if it was trying to attack me. But I knew too much was at stake. I opened my eyes and focused on my target. Our squadron had received only minimal training, from the time of our arrival in Argentina until today's imminent battle, was barely a month. So, we clumsily pointed our guns and shot at all that was not on our side. Only the dogs and cats seemed to have somewhat of a set sharpshooter skills.

As we ran further and further, we noticed something peculiar. There seemed to be far fewer macaws in the distance than when the battle started. That couldn't be possible. We had only managed to bring a handful of them down. How could the count go so low? It was then we heard a large blast to our left and felt a shock wave below us, a few feet off the ground.

When the dust settled, we saw a piece of our barricade blown to smithereens. Our question was answered. The AVIACHT forces used this attack as a decoy to distract us from protecting our precious barricade. In place of the targeted section of the wall was a large, smoldered hole with enough entryway for the enemy to barge through. A large pair of armored wolves with finely-sharped fangs stampeded through the opening, leading the way for a large army of birds and flying animals toward us.

I could see off on the other side of the damaged wall, Andrew and several other unfortunate soldiers who had been wounded and blown away some twenty to thirty feet, falling splat into the grimy mud that was their trenches. We could not simply leave them to suffer. We turned our focus on the inward barrier battle that was exploding behind us. We changed course and ran to our left towards our human and animal comrades, but not before we caught the AVIACHT force's attention. They aimed straight at our formation.

For a moment, all was complete silence – I mean complete, utter, shallow, dead silence. I couldn't hear the sounds of feet sloshing in the mud, or squawks coming nearer and nearer to us, nor even soldiers breathing in the thick wind, not even my own. It felt like we were being thrust into Infinity, no direction, no time, no anything. It felt like nothing existed, only me and the white, blank, oblivion. My feet felt so numb and frail like I was walking on air, my helmet protecting me from nothing, and my rifle, pointing and directing me to nowhere. The silence ended when the first fierce human and the first swift bird, clashed into each other like a pair of organic bricks.

Then, all chaos broke loose. It was now every man, every woman, every creature and every beast, clashing against each other, both in the rain-soaked sky above, and the dank, muddy, terrain below. I couldn't tell whether I was in the middle of a battle or an infused nightmare. Whatever my mind could comprehend, I did my obligations. I took out my clumsy rifle and shot at anything that wasn't on our side.

To make the defense more effective we split into two teams, one to defend the unscathed portion of the barricades and the other to assist the wounded soldiers. I was assigned to the latter by my commander. Our team huddled together like a flock of flamingoes watching for any sneak attack. But it seemed our vigilance was compromised by AVIACHT's cunning. For before we could comprehend what was happening, our team was hit by bombs made of tortoise shells. A few of us were obliterated into oblivion, while the rest, including me, were somersaulted into the air by sheer shell shock waves.

As I fell to the ground, and lifted my face up from the mud, I realized I was deaf for a few fleeting moments. I aimlessly walked around the field of battle, witnessing the carnage unfold. It was as if I had been thrust into a silent movie, and the soundtrack was turned off. Confused, bewildered, and not "all there," I walked around without any sense of direction. My comrades were either fighting any bird or beast that was aiming towards them or squirming in pain from being hit by a bullet or stray object. From their mouths they screamed at the top of their lungs, but I couldn't hear a single word. I looked to my right to see a human soldier with his stomach torn open by a pair of talons. He was screaming in agony and begging for help. To my left, was a young AVIACHT soldier, beaten and minus nearly all its feathers, limping towards a rock to rest, knowing it would die. All around me was death. This truly was hell.

I looked into the distance to see William, who was laying by Andrew's side. He was gravely wounded, dying slowly, and clutching onto his brother's uniform. He coughed as drips of blood exited his mouth. He tried to say something to William. I couldn't make out what he was requesting, but it must've been something important. I turned slightly to see my canine commander yelling straight into my face. At first, I could only hear a mumbling sound as my hearing returned, and then…

"WE'VE GOT TO GET TO BACK TO OUR TRENCHES!" he shouted, as reality set in. "ROUND UP YOUR TROOPS AND DEFEND THAT BASE! GO! GO! GO!"

I snapped out of it as I searched for anyone on my team. I grabbed body armor and placed it on their backs, hoping we'd make it back to our starting point.

"AIM FOR THEIR HEADS!" shouted a female macaw from above, who was leading her own squadron of parrots.

"YES, KANA!" they shouted back, to which they started mercilessly bombarding their pellets onto our position.

"DUCK!" I shouted, and we placed the shields on top of skulls, averting another massacre.

"FIRE!" shouted a human soldier.

As we shot back and took down a handful of birds, I remember the name that was shouted among the flock-Kana. Could this have been the bird Uncle Epi had been talking about? The one he had so wanted to marry and have chicks with? I had no time to think of that now. Besides, a plan had emerged from my thoughts.

CHAPTER 51

The following text is based on testimonials from the last few months of Episko Doulus' life

I was perched on top of a nearby tree that seemed to bend slightly out of the jungle canopy. There, I could watch the whole battle commence. Every bone broken, every face bruised, every innocent life taken, was witnessed by my weary eyes. I would've given anything just to end this senseless battle here and then. But sadly, it had now meshed itself into something not even the most authoritarian of leaders could control alone. The only thing I could do was to watch helplessly, and wonder if anyone I knew was inside the battlefield.

My wings were all worn out from trying to find a place to hide. My talons had given into numbness from carrying my satchel across miles of terrain. My beak could only mumble a few words, as I had saved all my energy for breathing and panting. My eyes were the most functioning part of my body; I knew I had to see how this would all end.

Off in a corner of the battle, I could finally make out a familiar face. The young Trisco, along with other hapless chicks, was equipping himself with a steel-like suit no bullet or arrow could penetrate. With each pad of armor, I could see the innocent boys disappear into mindless killing machines. Then I looked the other way and saw a few human and dog soldiers prepping themselves with warrior paint before they leaped into combat. It was like they were peeling away what made them civilized and revealing the savage brutes they had become.

I was wondering if either side was even worth saving. For the record, it even crossed my mind if life, itself, was worth saving. I mean, our planet was peaceful and quiet before life spawned from its primordial pool, no conflict, no issues, no war. It was just a barren landscape of serenity and tranquility.

Just as I begun to turn around, I felt the texture of a pistol poking against my back.

"I finally found you," said a menacing voice.

One of Helios's most trained assassins had caught up with me after all these days. How I was able to avert him this long was anyone's guess.

"How does it feel to betray your own kind?" he asked.

"How does it feel to become the very thing you despised?" I replied.

"Don't toy with me, Episko! It's only a matter of time before true freedom dawns upon all of us."

"You say those things, but do you even practice what you preach?"

With that question, the assassin smacked me against the cheek and threw me down to a lower branch.

"What justice will your quest do, if it only leads to bloodshed?" I asked. "Have you ever thought of that?"

"Silence!" the assassin snapped back at me.

"Have you ever noticed how much similarity there is between the ideology of yours and your foe's?"

"I said, SILENCE TRAITOR!" he shouted again smacking to my face.

Now I knew I had to defend myself. I sharpened my talons and massaged my beak.

"So, you want to see what you've become?" I screamed in anger. "I'll show it to you!"

I planted my head right into his stomach and we fell backwards about twenty to thirty feet into the tree trunk. Now it was a full-on brawl between the assassin and me. I dug a fresh gash into his thigh. He then gave a nicely-dented wound to my wing. I dodged a blow from his talon and pushed him back a few feet. Then I tried to scratch out his beak, but he blocked it in the nick of time and threw me headfirst into the tree. I didn't know who was going to win this brawl, but only one of us could survive.

After a few minutes of unending conflict, the two of us took a moment to breathe. We looked at each other with great disdain. Both of us were at our wit's end. For a moment I knew what it was like to be an AVIACHT cadet in the midst of battle.

"You know....It's funny," I snicker under my breath. "I could've sworn I saw…or at least heard…of humans acting just like you…when they attacked the jungle…wild…angry…no sense of calm."

For a few seconds there was deafening silence between the two of us. Then, without warning, the assassin bit me right at the rib, nearly snapping a bone in two.

"Why did you choose to throw your life away?" asked the assassin, who was now triumphantly standing on top of me. "You would've made a most exceptional private."

"I vowed…to help those in need," I replied. "I hope I have, and I vowed that I would finish my mission. This time, I will stand by my word.

Just as he was about to land the final blow to my neck, a stray bullet shot right into his skull, plummeting him to the muddy earth below. I turned around and looked below to see Christine with a rifle in her arms.

"What are you doing here?" I asked weakly. "You should be protecting the children."

"Not without returning the favor," Christine replied as she climbed up to cradle me in her arms. "Let's get you out of here." We then scurried to shelter.

Chapter 52

We were outnumbered. Our defenses were beginning to be compromised by AVIACHT's incoming forces. Over and ahead, I could see trenches being breached by wolves and boars. Dog and human soldiers tried in vain to stop them by jumping onto their hides and bellies, using their own bodies as means to cause friction against the enemy. I can still hear, to this day, their bones being crushed by the weight.

As I turned my face to cringe, Andrew suddenly got on his feet. As he fastened his rifle to his back and loaded a fistful of bullets into the holster, his brother William looked at him in amazement.

"A… Andrew?" he asked with tears in his eyes. "What are you doing?"

"Helping our species out," William replied under an exhausted breath. "Besides, it's not like there's anything left to do."

Despite our protests, Andrew marched toward a ravenous, large wolf who was ripping soldiers to pieces. No matter, Andrew's face looked cool and collected. He lifted his rifle into the air and fired several warning shots to catch its attention. A lifeless body dropped out of the beast's bloodied mouth as the wolf growled in furious anger.

"Come at me," Andrew uttered. "I have something for you."

"Andrew!" I shouted. "Get back here."

For a moment, as the wolf charged, Andrew turned his head

towards us and gave a little weak smile. Then he saluted us as, a single tear rolled down his damaged cheek.

"Andrew!" William shouted. "Don't do this!"

"Take care of yourself, Wadja," Andrew spoke calmly. "You will make a great brother-in-law, and hopefully uncle."

Then, as he put a small photograph of his family into his brother's hand, he turned to me.

"Mageck," he continued. "You must reach higher ground. I know your plan will work. You and your family made it this far. Don't waste it now. I love you both."

He turned his back to us one last time, and marched toward his fate, as I dragged a weeping William into the barracks to helplessly watch. For a moment, he looked like some kind of invincible force that could penetrate anything, as he trudged through a small sleet of shelled bullets. The blood drooling beast was now inches in front of him, with steams of anger coming out of its nostrils. But Andrzej just smiled as if meeting an old friend. Then he closed his eyes and aimed his rifle at the beast's face, and without a second of pain, he was decapitated by a set of fangs.

"ANDRZEJ!" William shouted in a pool of tears. "ANDRZEJ!"

I let the two of us cry in peace for a few moments. Our bodies were shaking in both shock and grief. We didn't know whether we could risk anymore. Our sanity and will to carry on was hanging by a thread. As I dried my eyes, I looked over to a rock formation where there was a large empty gap just wide enough to bring groups of humans to safety and towards the boats.

"So?" A somber William asked. "What's the plan?"

After a moment's pause…

"Follow me," I said.

We clumsily climbed up a hilltop of mud and moss. If we could divert the human refugee line to that open space I saw, we just might be able to lead them into the boats, without any casualties. It was not going to be easy, but it was our best chance.

From there, we turned around and were able to see a full view of the carnage taking place. It was as if it were something out of a Renaissance painting depicting Judgement Day. The majority of trenches had been breached by wolf and elephant drones, saddled by macaws commanding their number of kills. They shoved and plowed through piles of dogs and cats that tried in vain to work as a living barrier, only to be stomped and torn apart by their adversaries. The result was a pool of blood and guts left in their wake. William and I tried not to vomit as we took in the scene.

On the front line, soldiers and volunteers were retreating from incoming Brazil nut bullets, triggered by swarms of AVIACHT soldiers coming up front. Among them was a young boy, about five to six years younger than me. He was slower than the others. After a few more yards, he was shot down mercilessly by Kana and her infantry. A couple of dog nurses ran over to help the poor boy, but were shot down as well. This was followed by a few younger cat and human casualties, who were also too slow to outrun the bullets. I could see the whole thing happening in slow motion, even to this day, as if the cameraman in my head slowed down the reel and showed it to me frame by frame.

William and I hid deep behind mounds of clay, camouflaging ourselves in the texture. Above us were Kana and her crew laughing maniacally at the fatalities they were causing.

"Yes! Yes! The screams of pain excite us!" Kana laughed maniacally. "Annihilate! Annihilate them all!"

Now it looked like open season for us and them. They fired

their guns at any human without hesitation. Soldiers fell like toy figurines on a soiled carpet, splatting face first in the mud. In addition, elephant and boar drones smashed themselves into a barrage of army tanks and shacks, knocking them over and trampling anyone inside. Anyone who dodged getting shot retreated to the boats, where human survivors were waiting for them. Though they knew the enemy forces would catch up with them, they still fired shots at the swarm ahead of them, knowing it was the right thing to do.

As the last infantry pulled back, AVIACHT forces cheered and chirped in victory. Some danced on the corpses of their victims, and others flew in the air in celebratory formation. We had felt defeated, as if this were the end of humans in South America and Europe. The land was theirs for the taking, and the bird would become the dominant species, just as their dinosaur ancestors did before them. We did not have time to mourn our loss, for we knew that the diversion I planned was still our best chance to get the remaining humans to safety.

William and I huddled together as I drew in the dirt our coordinates and methods of our plan. I pointed to the field and after a moment's thought William nodded in agreement. But just as we were about to head to our destination, Kana spotted us over the hillside. In an instant she pinned us down along with two other macaw chicks.

"So," Kana stated as she observed our name tags. "You must be Epi's friends."

"How do you know that?" asked William, for which he was slapped in the face by a pair of talons.

"My father gathered information regarding your escapes," she replied coldly while aiming a machete knife to our skulls. "And now I have finally met a few of you face to fac. This is for my family!”

But before any final blow could be made to our craniums, a huge explosion occurred from behind. The shock wave was so strong that it blew us all back and cleared about three to four acres of forest. Though Kana stood her ground with talons dug into the soil, a cat soldier rose from underneath and bit her on the neck, rendering her unconscious. It was then that this feline comrade gave out a large growl that echoed into the debris. As the dust cleared and the two of us got back on our feet, we saw Photios and Demeter along with hundreds of other dog, cat and rodent comrades, silhouetted on a hilltop against the bright clouds. We didn’t know how they got here, or how they rounded up so many other recruits, but with the enemy down, now was our chance to execute our plan.

Chapter 53

Demeter and I were standing on top of the hill. Behind us were the thousands of once captive soldiers who lived and endured the most unspeakable of conditions. Our nostrils picked up the scent of every corpse that was now lying on the field of battle as our heads bowed in respect for our fallen comrades. Then, our ears picked up the signal from our cat soldier who had dug a secret underground trench, giving us the cue to strike. At first, we may have been small in number compared to AVIACHT, but now we were enough to take down their stronghold. We even had a few lines of infantry on the left and right of field barrier, among them being the cat who had signaled the attack.

"For humans?" Demeter asked at my side.

"For Spartak," I replied humbly.

And with those words, the two of us led the charge onto the field. The sounds of each canine, feline and rodent running together was like a symphony of brotherhood. The ray of the sun beaming on our fur and our paws digging into the ground. This battle that would determine our fate And this shining moment felt like a force of "otherworldly" power. Nothing could stand in our way.

We lunged our bodies forward, left and right, and pounced on our opponents like prey. Though they seemed sharp and unflinching at first, the birds quickly turned into lifeless, vulnerable corpses the moment we sunk our teeth in their necks. But it was the feline comrades that somehow got the most fun out of this attack, probably because they endured the worst conditions among our non-human allies. Finally, it appeared that AVIACHT really was no match against us. Some of the enemy even took cyanide pills to avert the horror of being captured. We were now getting the upper paw. Victory was surely near, and the humans could retreat safely to the United States.

As I looked up among the victorious carnage, I could see two familiar faces hiding behind a large boulder. Mageck and Wadja were somehow able to be among the lucky few that averted death, prior to our rescue. They were now running towards what looked like bunkers that housed human refugees, ready to escort them to freedom. Upon closer inspection, there were two other friends at the bunker door. A wounded Epi was being tended to by Christine; his broken wing was slumped under a carefully knitted cast. Christine was feeding him what looked like a liquid muscle relaxant, easing any pain he had in his body. I showed this to Demeter, and the two of us grinned a sigh of relief knowing that at least there were more who made it, and our earlier rescues were not in vain. For a moment, we thought that perhaps we had averted the worst of catastrophes for both sides, as the birds retreated into the forest outnumbered and out of luck.

Our feeling of triumph was short-lived however. It appeared we were too busy trampling over our enemy that the whole virus bomb plot slipped our minds. Demeter and I could see that further away, a few AVIACHT soldiers were unleashing their deadly plan. A large silo off in the distance stored the bombs loaded with the deadly virus from before. As the last canisters were being maneuvered in the hollow tank by a flock of macaw cadets, a soldier activated what looked like a ticking time bomb. The flock lifted the silo off the ground and slowly flew it towards the unsuspecting human refugees, with the goal of killing them without them even knowing. How could we let this one slip by? It was then I saw a rather humble and unfazed look on Demeter's face.

"Demeter?" I asked, "What are you thinking of doing?"

Demeter did not answer as he dug his paws into the ground.

"Demeter, I do not know what you're planning but whatever it is, reconsider."

"I have considered many things my friend," he replied. "And this one I know is the right thing to do."

Without a moment's thought, he sprinted towards the silo that was now only a few feet off the ground.

"Demeter!" I yelled as I got in his way. "Are you insane? I order you not to go after them. We can handle this together..."

"If we wait any longer on the battlefield, the humans will be done for sure," Demeter explained. "This is what I must do."

"I've already lost many friends, Demeter. And I can't afford to lose you too."

I threw him down on the ground and the two of us wrestled for a few moments. Demeter got the upper paw in the end.

"I can't stand to lose all of you either," Demeter replied as he hopped back on his feet. "I'll say 'Hi' to Spartak for you. Farewell, friend."

Before I could do anything else, he ran to the floating canister, and toward his fate. As a rodent private called my name, I ran back to the current battle at paw, with tears streaming down my snout. Looking back, as I beat the living hell out of several macaw cadets with my paws, I didn't know whether I was doing it out of revenge, anger, defense, or pain. I had seen too much carnage and casualty in this war, enough to push me on the verge of compromising my sanity.

I do not know much about what occurred when Demeter sacrificed himself. I cannot precisely comprehend how it played out between him and the enemy. I'm not even sure how precisely he was able to avert those plague-ridden missiles from being distributed all over the world. All I know is what I heard from off in the distance and what I was told from several living AVIACHT soldiers, and I believe the conversation I heard between them that day. We dogs have an exceptionally grand gift of hearing.

From what they recalled, Demeter once again ran to Helios himself. As Demeter approached the missile site, he shouted the name of a familiar face watching the event unfold up in a canopy nearby. Helios, and with his closest of generals, were perched on an outstretched branch each sipping a cup of Brazil nut brandy and awaiting their glorious "piece de resistance" to come into effect.

"My," Helios said as he spotted Demeter. "Look who came back to join our cause. I suppose you want a high position in our rankings?"

Helios' generals laughed from their position.

"I'm not here for any games, Helios," Demeter said under his breath. "I'm here to do what I must, for the sake of my friends."

"Your friends?" Helios chuckled. "What kind of friends would leave you alone to fend for yourself? Face it. You turned down the opportunity of a lifetime just for a pestilence of a species."

"Humans are not a pestilence," Demeter replied. "You are going to pay for what you did to those men women and children, for what you did to my friends, and for what you did to Spartak."

"That was not of my doing. The loyal Gorchak, rest his soul, was just following orders, and noble orders they were. Besides, none of this would've happened to you if you just joined sides. Trust us, boy. We are the good guys in this war."

"There is no good or bad in this war, only victims and perpetrators. And if you don't end this now, you will be the biggest perpetrator on the planet. You will have caused nothing but destruction. You will become what you hate."

I heard the sound of Helios throwing his drink against a wooden wall and flying down to Demeter with the swiftest of ease. The sound of his talons walking against the floor was like nails scratching against a concrete chalkboard.

"Very well, PET!" Helios shouted. "Let's finish this the way you asked. With blood!"

A one-on-one fight ensued between the two adversaries. From what I heard, it was a skilled and epic one. Helios clawed Demeter's face. Demeter kicked against Helios's ribs. Helios pecked at his skull, Demeter bit at his wing, and so on and so forth, while everyone else looked on. Then there was a pause in the noise. The two had probably taken a moment to breathe.

"I told you once I would give you and your friends a seat next to the throne." Helios said. "My offer still stands, if you put your guard down now."

"And I'm telling you now, that I will finish my mission, even if it ends me," Demeter replied. "I never walk away from things half done."

"Pity," Helios replied, and the sounds of fighting erupted again.

Kicking, clawing and punching sounds echoed across the canopies. Though I couldn't see what was going on, I knew that Demeter was putting up a good fight. He was just that kind of dog.

With that in mind, my confidence built back up again, and I

continued to fend off the AVIACHT forces with my brethren.

"Sergeant!" I shouted to a canine commander.

"Yes, sir!" he replied.

"Look for any stray humans and lead them to the boats. Tell them not to be afraid any longer."

He gave the salute and ran to the battlefield. Meanwhile I went back to my business while still honing into what sounded like a vicious battle between my friend and our enemy. From what I had gathered from surviving witnesses, Demeter had been distracting Helios, biding enough time not only for the humans to evacuate, but to jump onto the top of the silo and diffuse the launch code, which was drawing nearer and nearer.

"Is it really worth all of this?" Helios asked. "Putting yourself on the front for a petty cause to fight for more enslavement of your kind And to once again find yourself fighting against the very thing we both crave? Seek into your feelings, Demeter, you must know what you want."

"I believe I'm about to find out," Demeter replied as he lunged forward and grabbed Helios by the wing with his jaws.

I looked up and saw silhouettes of the two dueling it out now atop the tilted silo. Demeter must've been heading up a path of roots and vines in order to reach the launch code. He really did know how to trick his adversaries by distracting them when they were at their most vulnerable.

Before Helios could figure out he was duped, Demeter must've also coaxed the enemy to follow him into the silo because I could now hear echos from inside the structure. I saw their shadows pause, with Helios looking at Demeter in disbelief.

"Well," Helios commented. "It's been a while since I had such a challenge. I'll have a 'go' at it."

Helios trounced on Demeter as their brawl turned more brutal. Both of them biting and clawing any patch of skin they could get their paws and talons on. Even though I could only see their shadows, the whole sight looked like something out of a Renaissance play. It was a good fight. Then, after a few minutes of exhausting conflict, the two held each other at neck point. Demeter's paw on Helios's throat and Helios's talon on Demeter's.

"Seems you are out of options," Helios challenged.

"So are you," Demeter challenged back. "What do you think happens now?"

"Well," Helios explained, "...we can continue holding each other like this until the timer stops ticking and the beat of life ceases to vibrate, or one of us surrenders, which certainly won't be me. Either way, AVIACHT has already won."

"Are you really sure of that?"

Helios took a moment to examine the situation, and noticed what looked like a pin, dropping to the floor. His beak dropped in what was obviously disbelief, as Demeter showed him an activated grenade in his paw. A tear streamed down my snout, as I knew what would happen next.

"Guess it was worth it," Demeter said. "This is for you, Photios!"

And with those words he leaned back, paws outstretched, his snout smiling upward with not a care in the world. Before Helios could even get a chance to fly away, the entire silo turned into a fireball of red and green, taking the ruthless king, a few of his close-by, high ranking officers, and the deadly poisonous disease with it. The sheer explosion made everyone, including myself, fly back a yard or two. Dust and debris covered our peripheral vision, throwing everything out of focus, even our sense of scent and sound.

A few dozen seconds passed before dust settled and we got back on our paws to access the damage. But somehow it felt like we were all stuck in time, as if our bodies had lived a thousand lifetimes. The war was finally over.

While everyone else gathered to regroup, I bowed my head and let out a good howl of loss. My claws dug into the ground and more tears dropped out of my sockets. Sure, we had visibly won the war, but I had lost another friend. One so close and so dear to my life, I would even classify him as a sibling. But even though my heart was aching in pain, I knew his sacrifice was for the sake of all of us, all humans, and all life on earth.

But what really is a war? We get involved, we fight, and many of us die. There's nothing beautiful about war. It cripples us, breaks us, and turns us into fragments of our former selves. Things would've been so much better if the other side just listened to us. It didn't have to end this way. Not one bit. And while there were cheers from dogs, cats, rodents and other humans, the casualties on both sides were horrendous. Bodies lay strewn on the muddy ground, blanketing the landscape with flesh and blood.

"Lieutenant!" A feline private said as she came to me and coughed up a few feathers. "We have cornered the rest of the AVIACHT forces. What should we do now?"

My mouth trembled, thinking of what to say next.

"Assess our losses," I replied. "There will be a great many families that will not be seeing their loved ones return home.

"Affirmative," she replied.

As everyone attended to recovery assignments, I took a weary walk across the battlefield. Every few feet was a dead body, whether it be human, ally or bird. So, I respectfully and carefully, pushed carcasses to the side so as not to step on them.

Many of them were still in their adolescent years. So many youthful souls with so much potential and promise, wasted on a senseless, and preventable war.

I came across a body that was still moving. It was a small avian chick, wounded, scared, confused, and shaking from the trauma of the situation. I tilted my head to view a little name tag attached to his wing. It read: TRISCO.

"H...help," The poor thing grunted. "He...help...pl...please help me."

Trisco knew I was hovering over him, but he didn't know I was the enemy. He had been temporarily blinded by the shock of the blast. And even if he could see, I don't think he would've cared. He just wanted a bit of comfort.

So, I looked around for anything to aid him. I knew he was of the enemy, but he was still only a chick, and too much life was ahead for him. I finally came across a piece of branch sturdy enough to hold him upright until help came from the medical team.

"You be a good boy," I whispered to him as I carefully propped him on top of the branch. "You fly gracefully when you recover."

Without delay, I walked away and continued my duties.

Chapter 54

At last, the hell that was war had come to an end. After so much death, so much carnage, so much loss, and so much despair, the human species could now rest easy knowing that our biggest threat had surrendered. Now it was time to start over with our lives, to begin anew, and hopefully piece together something along with our non-human brethren that would be stronger and better than before.

William and I remember the explosion prior to evacuation, It happened so quickly. One moment we were escorting the humans to boats and next thing we knew a giant, earth-shattering boom blasted across the terrain, knocking everyone, including us, on our backs. As the dust settled, and the smoke gave way to the sky, we saw what was the remains of a silom shredded into hundreds of pieces, and a series of capsules that were certainly meant to end our species. But now they were gone, obliterated into harmless particles of residue.

Upon realizing this, everyone cheered in joyous celebration, knowing their troubles were over. It was so surreal. We had gotten so used to running and hiding and fighting, that it had become almost second nature for us. I felt like I wanted to just fall over and lie onto a big, beautiful bed. From the look on William's face, I bet he thought the same.

"Comrades," said a gruff bloodhound who was passing by. "Round up whatever humans you can and escort them to the boats."

We gave him a salute and began the process of evacuation. As lines were formed and we checked their identities, everyone looked weary and tired, eyes sunken in, hands brittle and shaking, and bodies clearly underweight. There was an injured mother with her frightened toddler child hugging against her leg. The blast caused her to limp a little to the side. William looked at me and carried the child on his shoulder.

"It so hard to believe it's finally over," said a familiar voice behind me.

Christine was standing by the boat's edge along with a face I thought I'd never see again. Uncle Epi was perched weakly atop her shoulder wearing a cast on his broken wing. I approached them with a smile on my face and gently hugged the two of them.

"We finally did it," I said weakly. "It's all finished, Epi. We couldn't have done it without you."

"Yes," he replied solemnly. "But at what cost? At how many lives lost?"

It was then the three of us gazed at the landscape of dead bodies and tortured souls. So many people, so many birds, so many cats, dogs and rodents lost to the unforgivable barbarity that was war. If only there were other ways to end the conflict. If only both could've listened to each other to understand their plights. If only a peaceful and civilized talk convened between the two factions, then none of this savage genocide would've happened.

"Here," Uncle Epi said as he reached into his satchel. "I want you to have something I found."

"What is it?" I asked.

"Some letter that a human soldier wanted to send," he replied. "I haven't read it, so I don't know what it says, but I think it's important that the receiver gets it."

For a few moments, I stared at the letter. The envelope was flattened and crumpled up. On the front was written, "From Nathan," and the address was slightly faded, but it was enough for a postman to deliver it to its intended destination. I nodded slightly and placed the letter in my coat pocket.

As Christine and Episko fell to their knees in exhaustion, I went back to my duty of evacuating the rest of the human refugees. It took practically the rest of daylight to get everyone on the boat. I checked for any open gashes and Williams looked for any broken bones. Then while I looked for those who looked ill, and William scoured for others with serious injuries. Those we found, we would escort to the other end of the ship for treatment. It had been so long since they received adequate; care that we didn't know if they would all survive. Everyone looked frail and battered from the horror that had finally ended. Did they even remember what their old lives were like, or what they themselves looked like many long days before? Would they even recognize their faces upon first glance in the mirror, or would they only see a stranger?

On the other far end of the boat was a makeshift hospital ward for the wounded. Soldiers and citizens alike were being treated by dog doctors, cat therapists, and rodent nurses. Though tattered and rickety in its presentation, the tone of the staff was nonetheless heartwarming and filled with assurance. A smaller feline and a dog was bandaging up one covered in wounds and bruises. A mouse was checking the temperature of another who was shaking from a recovering fever. Patients who were shell-shocked had their bodies caressed by the welcoming paws of a canine or two. And a border collie and Tabby were feeding one patient, while practicing nerve reflexes on another at the same time. Soon, they dismantled the ward and escorted those humans onto another opening in the ship.

Now, as night had fallen, and a thick mist coated the shoreline, all the living humans were accounted for and ready to travel to the United States. My sister and mother had been placed in their own compartments. Meanwhile, William and I were sitting just outside the ship's exterior along with Christine and Epi, who had gained a bit more strength. To our right and left, several dog soldiers were conversing and sharing a joke or two. They deserved a break for what they had endured. We were blindly gazing into the foggy abyss, where the brutal landscape was densely coated with a natural mist coming from the ocean. It was as if the forces of nature were washing away the horrors of war, ready to start again and revitalize the fragile earth. It was then we saw a limping figure coming from out of the distance. The voice sounded like a poorly-tuned wailing song, mixed with screaming.

"K… Kana?" Uncle Epi had uttered. "Is that you?"

Epi's former love was now a withered mess, a shell of a living being. Absent were nearly all the feathers from her skin. I later learned that as punishment for their genocide, a majority of high-ranking AVIACHT officials were plucked of every feather an allied force could lay their paws on. In addition, they were later paraded through the streets of Paris, Prague, Hamburg, Vienna and other towns AVIACHT laid waste to in the early years. As unforgivable as their actions were, I knew the enemy soldiers didn't deserve to be stripped of their dignity. After all, they had endured just as much loss and suffering. Streams of tears fell down Kana's cheeks and beaks, stemming from both sadness and anger.

Despite her frail walk and lack of feathers, her appearance still seemed to be menacing and threatening, like a creature that had been bred by war. Her body looked well-built and finely-cut from years of training. Her beak was sharp and shimmering in the moonlight. Her talons, finely-tuned would easily be able to slash open skin. Though hard to recognize at first glance, she was mostly everything Uncle Epi had described. Slinging on her back was a worn rifle with empty cartridges, only good enough to lay a few blows on anyone who would dare challenge her in a fight. But even now, there was no point in using it. So, with agony, she threw her useless weapon to our feet. Then, suddenly, her grief turned into rage.

"You…human," she muttered at me under a menacing breath. "You killed our leader. YOU KILL HIM WITH THOSE FILTHY HANDS OF YOURS!"

She lunged her naked body forward, running like a mad vicious being towards me. Her talons whacked across my face and pushed me to the ground. I tried to run, but she grabbed me by her beak and threatened to crack open my skull.

"Hey!" shouted the dog soldiers as they took out their firearms. "Stop right there! Drop the human now!"

"Kana!" Epi shouted. "Please don't do this."

"YOU STAY OUT OF THIS, TRAITOR!" Kana snarled back.

It was then that Christine smacked her across the face, to which she was answered by a slash of talons. So, my unwanted fight with Epi's former girlfriend continued.

"WHY COULD'NT YOU JUST GO EXTINCT LIKE WE WANTED YOU TO BE!" Kana shouted as she laid another blow on me. "IT WAS SO EASY FOR YOU TO DIE! BUT NO!"

She threw my body across the dirty terrain, somersaulting me down a steep hill where I landed headfirst on the ground. Kana walked over to me. I wearily tried to prop myself up as I looked directly at her face, her eyes burning red with anger. Steam came out of her nostrils whilst breathing heavily, and her talons massaged each other, but I just looked at her serenely and bravely. I was just too tired to hate anyone now.

"If you kill me, will it go away?" I asked her.

"What?" she asked.

"If you kill me," I explained. "will all your hate go away? Will it bring back Helios?"

"DON'T YOU DARE UTTER HIS NAME!" she screamed back at me with another blow. I was helpless. She was beating me up with every move she had, and I was just a worthless punching bag to her.

By about now, several more dog and cat soldiers arrived at the hill's edge. They shuffled down the steep hillside and ran towards the fighting.

"You there!" shouted a female dog. "Stop this at once!"

"Step away from the human!" shouted another.

"GET BACK, YOU PETS!" Kana screamed back.

She clasped her talons around my neck and pinned my head down in the mud. Meanwhile, the dog soldiers drew out their weapons once more and aimed to fire at her skull.

"Die," she muttered insanely. "Die, you sape."

Knowing it was she or me, I raised my weak fist up in the air, and with every ounce of strength, smacked at her skull. She flew back a few feet and landed in the mud. But she got up as if it were nothing and rammed head-first into my chest. The soldiers took a few warning shots, then grabbed her by her wingless arms and forced her into a headlock. She howled at the sky like a rabid animal and her eyes streamed with tears. Her beak gnashed in the air in a futile attempt to set herself free.

Meanwhile, I clumsily got back up on my feet and dug my hand into the pocket where I stuffed that letter. I would later learn that Kana had killed the human who wrote it.

For a moment, I stared at the envelope knowing the soldier's love was waiting back in the states to read what it said. I saw, off to the hill-side, Epi, who gave a nod of approval.

"These…" I spoke, "are the words…of…a human."

I tore open the envelope flap and unfolded the wording inside.

"*My dear love...*" I stated as I began to read. "*Believe me, I have only one regret, that I wasn't able to see you just one last time. So much we couldn't talk about, or get around to doing...*"

"Lies," Kana replied while heavily breathing.

"*Until now, I didn't know what war truly was. What you hear about back in the states about us is with all the grime, with all the dirt, with all the hate and fear taken out...*"

"You lie!"

"*Much as I hate being here, this is something I know I must do. It is not just for you, not just for our country, and certainly not just for humans. This is for the sake and sanity of all living things...*"

"NO, YOU LIE!"

"*When this is over, when or however this mess ends. I only hope to come back to a better world – a world where all beings great and small can live together in harmony, especially with you in it. I want that more than anything in the whole world. Miss you so much, and lots of love as always, Nathan.*"

As I refolded the letter and placed it back in the envelope, Christine came over and had me rest on her shoulder. To this day, I don't know why Epi wanted me to read that letter to Kana. It wasn't like it would change her mind or anything. Maybe he just still had a little love for her he couldn't shake off. Or maybe it was just the instinct of empathy that nearly every animal has. Either way, Kana broke down in tears, wailing like a newborn infant. The soldiers took her away to a detention center where she would spend a good number of years.

After I was attended to by the nearest medical aid, we boarded the boat and sailed off to the United States along with the other human refugees. Upon taking solace in our sleeping quarters, I had overheard from someone that AVIACHT had agreed to surrender unconditionally, requiring only that the human diplomats appeared fully naked during the treaty signing, as a final act of humiliation. Such was a justified act to equalize each side's suffering.

At last, we were able to rest without any worry of the future. We were all happy as a species; we were not happy about who won or who lost, but happy that all the carnage, all the bloodshed and all the destruction was finally over. There was no need to run in fear from anything, no need to constantly seek refuge, and no need to wonder whether we would live to see tomorrow.

I carefully laid back in my sweet, soft bed, caressing myself in its linen-coated texture, but making sure that the bandages would not get caught. It was a luxury I had not felt since the day before the invasion of our village. My eyes closed as I listened to the sounds of cheering and laughter, not just from humans, but from dogs, cats, rodents, and all the other animals that joined in the cause to save our species. Then I stared at the ceiling as the boat rocked back and forth across the sea. I had wondered who had truly won the war, whether there really was a winning and losing side. We had both suffered so much. Each victory came with a price, and each loss came with a lesson learned. Looking back, there really was no winner or loser in that hell that was war, only fools with mad irrational decisions, and victims who fell in the mess. I was just glad it was all over.

"Mageck?" asked a familiar voice by the doorway.

"Ch…Christine," I replied weakly.

She laid next to me as we kissed and caressed on the long but welcoming journey to our new, and hopefully beautiful home.

Chapter 55

The home we are visiting is standard for Brazilian trees. It is long, sturdy, and well rooted in the rich earth below. Its trunk is coated with an average amount of foliage, vines, and flowers in full blossom, panning in the direction of the sun's rays.

Father and I gently land our pod on a thickly-supported branch in the canopy. It is the first time in forty years that the Whitestone family has set foot in the Amazon jungle. Much has changed. Buildings, houses and man-made structures are scattered in various parts of this habitat, implementing a near-perfectly functioning foressity. In addition, the human residents are now awarded full-time employment thanks to grants from the local government. More importantly, relationships have also strengthened in both the land and tree dwellers.

We climb out of our pod with the greatest of ease. I support Dad with my arms as we approach the door located in the center of the tree's flora Dad lightly taps on the door with his shaking hand. Moments later, it opens. Surprisingly, it is a human who answers it. A caretaker sponsored by an outsourced medical organization.

"May I help you?" asks the caretaker.

"I would like to see, Kana" Dad replies.

"What business do you have with her?"

"She might not remember due to aging, but I was one of her….Prisoners."

The eyes of the caretaker open wide, first in confusion, but then in familiarity, like bumping into an old friend.

"Right this way, gentlemen." She nods. And with that we are escorted into a former mercenary's abode.

The place, with a hybrid of natural and artificial components is adequate for bird residents. The source of light either comes from the sun or an occasional lightbulb placed in the middle of the ceiling. The furniture, decor, appliances and knick knacks are made from the finest material the Amazon has to offer: all polished, all neatly displayed, all biodegradable.

To our left is a set of books and papers all on the subjects of conservation, the beauty of the habitats, and strangely. . .world peace. The books are all bunched up and dusty. Kana has clearly not read them in years. To the right, we see a case of AVIACHT memorabilia, proudly placed on each shelf, with every row different. The bottom is a collection of items and relics from the resident's childhood. The middle is a vast array of trophies and awards from her glory days, and the very top is a set of photos and reels, documenting all the times she had with her friends, family and boyfriend, Epi.

"Are you sure of this, Dad?" Alan asks.

"It is the best way after all these years I can make peace with my demons," Dad replies.

"Mrs. Metuke?" the caretaker calls from behind a curtain. "A visitor is here to see you."

"Who is it?" asks a weary voice.

"It is a pair of humans."

A moment of pure silence envelops the room. And then…

"Send them in."

The caretaker emerges from the curtain and gives the two of us the 'come in' sign.

Slowly but surely, we walk behind the curtain. It is a

darkened bedroom, only complimented by the slivers of light from outside. Silhouetted against this limited source is a dresser, a bookcase, a lamp, several more knick-knacks and of course, a bed which, as one would expect, is shaped like a nest.

The caretaker walks toward a smaller lamp on the dresser and switches it on. An elderly Kana is found half-awake in her bed. Health has not been so kind to her in recent years. With the look of her ruffled feathers and tattered wingspan, it is clear her flying days came to an end long ago. The last time she flew was on the day AVIACHT and its enemy had ended the war. Her eyes are sunken in, her beak is rusted, and her talons have been weakened to a point where so much as a scratch would break them off.

Kana tilts her head up and stares a long gaze into her guests. The caretaker grabs a glass of filtered milk, puts a straw in it and carefully levels it to Kana's beak. She tilts her head back a little further, allowing the liquid to slither down her throat. Her cheek is dabbed of any missed residue from the milk, as she wipes any morsels with her crusty feathers.

"I suppose you've come to show me how happy you are," Kana says scoffingly.

"Well, I…it's not that... it…" Father tries to think of the right words to say. All that comes out is "I'd just like to know how you feel."

"How I feel?" Kana asks. "What kind of a question is that?"

She starts coughing, to which the caretaker responds by patting her on the back.

"As you can see, I've been better," Kana comments with a chuckle.

"Well, I'm just glad to see you're still in one piece."

Kana eyes make a confused look, as if she were listening to

another language. She would expect someone of the species she imprisoned and tortured to just slap her in the face, or at the very least, spit in her direction. But complimenting on the state of her well-being would seem like the last thing on this human's mind. Then again, his senility might be getting the best of him. But what did she know?

"Thank you," she replies solemnly. "My closest of friends have been keeping a watchful eye out for me, making sure I don't drift in and out of my episodes. Speaking of which, how are you?"

"Like everyone." Dad replies. "There are days of joy and days of sorrow, nothing no other senior citizen hasn't experienced."

"Mom, I'm back from my errands!" Says a voice from outside.

It is at that moment another macaw, her adopted son, flies by, perching onto the windowsill, with a bag of crushed orchids in his left claw. Trisco is of adequate shape for those his age. His experiences have made him a strong bird, capable of fending for himself.

"What's going on here? Do we have a…"

Trisco's beak drops in shock whilst he lays eyes on Dad's arm and the words etched on his skin. It had been so long since he had met with a Holocaust survivor. The presence is nearly overwhelming. Yet, he knows he has a task at hand. So, he calms himself and flutters to his adopted parent.

"What's he doing here?" he asks bluntly while feeding Kana.

"It's all right son," Kana replies with a swallow. "I'm just having a visit from…an old friend. There's nothing to worry about."

The young bird flies towards us for closer examination.

There is some sort of familiarity in the older one's face. After a moment's gaze, the realization comes into fruition. At first, his face slowly tilts on the verge of anger.

"Is this one of your prisoners?" Trisco asks Kana. "The one who became friends with…"

"I believe so, Son," she replies calmly. "And I thank him for his companionship with Episko. For the record I can honestly say, he's like family for a Human."

The verge of anger on Trisco's face turns to one of sympathy and welcoming spirit, as if he were bumping into an old friend. He clears his throat and extends his talon, offering us a claw shake, to which we graciously accept.

"So, what have you been up to?" Trisco asks Dad. "I suppose you've kept yourself busy."

"Oh, the usual," Dad replies wearily. "My son's been dealing with more personal problems than I have: family, job, the old existential crisis."

"I never really got to know your kind," Trisco replies. "At least not enough. My species though, is trying to grasp the idea of you very enigmatic humans."

"I know," I add with a chuckle. "One moment we are gentle and vulnerable. Next thing you know, chaos becomes our philosophy…"

"Please, there's no need for such complicated thoughts." Kana interrupts. "For the record, I don't even know who was more chaotic. Maybe it's nature. Maybe it's choice. I don't know. It's a messy subject to grasp."

"Point taken," Dad adds. "There are too many subjects and themes to understand these days."

"I have enough trouble understanding my underwater wetsuit," I joke.

Everyone in the room bursts into laughter. Even Kana chuckles, but not without a sharp cough.

"Do sit down," the caretaker adds. "I've just batched up a warm cup of tea."

The four of us are escorted to the outside balcony overlooking the glory that is the Amazon. The air is warm and the breeze is just right. Waiting for us, as expected, is a quartet of cups filled with the finest herbal ginseng. With no hesitation, three of us sit down in easy chairs and pick up our refreshments. Kana follows suit with the assistance of her caretaker.

"I struggle with an apology," Kana sighed.

"No," Dad replies. "I think it is I who should be sorry. After all, my species was the cause of your anger and misfortune."

"That seems funny now," Kana chuckles. "I mean, back then, we really weren't on the same playing field of who suffered the most. Now by today's standards, we can be considered even, but I caused your suffering without a doubt Mageck."

"You had every reason to be angry, Kana," Dad comments. "You had a place to save and a race to protect. For the record, I don't even know which one of us was the bad guy. And to this day, I still wonder if…"

"I'm sorry," Kana said quietly.

The words spill out of her mouth without even thinking.

"What was that, Mother?" Trisco asks.

"You heard me," she replies, as if trying to be nonchalant. "I am sorry. I am sorry for what I did to you and your species."

A look of shock falls on everyone's faces. It is the first time this macaw has ever expressed a sliver of remorse and regret in her silly, stupid life. How she waited this long is anyone's guess.

"Well, I do not know what to say. I'm…glad…to hear that. Both of us are."

Kana nods as she takes a sip of her tea, and suddenly, her frown becomes a smile. One smile becomes two, then three, then four. All four stare into the balcony's open view of trees, buildings, flowers and gadgets. This is complemented by the sounds, chirps and mutters echoing around them. It is another peaceful, average afternoon on this side of the great, spinning blue ball.

Printed in the USA
CPSIA information can be obtained
at www.ICGtesting.com
LVHW050729091123
763265LV00063B/1634

9 781804 391419